Outstanding Praise for

JANE AND HIS LORDSHIP'S LEGACY

"Exquisitely leisurely, with time for whist, tea, strolls across the lawn, church homilies, digressions on those 'too high in the instep,' and plenty for Jane's banker brother and treasure-hunting mother to do, leaving her to savor her lover's papers." —*Kirkus Reviews*

"Readers who hope to recapture, if only briefly, the pleasure of reading Jane Austen for the first time will welcome Barron's eighth Jane Austen mystery. . . . The author expertly weaves the tale's disparate elements, sympathetically sketching in such secondary characters as Jane's mother and brother Henry, on both of whom she casts an ironic eye. As usual, Barron has masterfully imitated Austen's voice." —*Publishers Weekly*

"Barron continues to write a good, quick-moving plot with plenty of period details . . . [that] combines truth and fiction successfully." —*Drood Review of Mystery*

"Barron's latest, featuring plenty of drawing-room intrigue and long-buried family secrets, will continue to please both historical-mystery readers and the ever-growing Austen fan club." —*Booklist*

JANE AND THE GHOSTS OF NETLEY

"Barron's cause is aided by her deft marshaling of historical detail—the textiles alone (Sprigged muslin! Bombazine!) are worth the price of admission—and, of course, a dash of genuine erotic friction between Jane and the roguish Lord Harold." —*Time* magazine

"The latest installment in Stephanie's Barron's charming series . . . [is] a first-rate historical mystery. Barron writes a lively adventure that puts warm flesh on historical bones. The nice thing is she does so in a literary style that would not put Jane Austen's nose out of joint." —*New York Times Book Review*

"The books are well-written and well-crafted. Jane is an endearing character. And *Jane and the Ghosts of Netley* is the best of the lot—and its ending is the most memorable." —*Denver Post*

"Intrigue, treachery, and murder. . . . [with a] rousing conclusion." —*Booklist*

"Series and historical fans are in for a treat!" —*Library Journal*

"A wonderfully intricate plot full of espionage and intrigue . . . The Austen voice, both humorous and fanciful, with shades of *Northanger Abbey*, rings true as always. Once again Barron shows why she leads the pack of neo–Jane Austens." —*Publishers Weekly* (starred review)

"If you enjoy suspense novels with rich historical backgrounds and beguiling characters, Stephanie Barron won't disappoint you." —*Monterey County Post*

"With elements of an espionage thriller and a Regency romance, [this] is a book Barron fans have been awaiting. The suspense is superb. . . . Barron brings historical mysteries to a new level."
—*Romantic Times BOOKclub Magazine*

"Barron remains true to Austen's real character . . . [and] is equally skillful in depicting the daily life of impoverished gentility during the Regency era. . . . Well worth reading." —*Deadly Pleasures*

"Stephanie Barron's series wittily blends Austen's life and her novels into satisfying mysteries and what could have been. . . . Settle in for a long session of pleasurable reading." —*Mystery News*

JANE AND THE PRISONER OF WOOL HOUSE

"Jane Austen aficionados once again have cause to rejoice, as Barron maintains her usual high standards in this latest literary historical." —*Publishers Weekly*

"An ideal vehicle for the classic cozy murder mystery."
—*New York Times Book Review*

"If you appreciate the literary acumen of Jane Austen the author, you might be surprised to discover you are even more entranced by Jane Austen the detective!"
—*Aptos (CA) Times*

"The mores and manners of Jane Austen's 19th-century world are brought skillfully to life. . . . A skillfully told tale with a surprise ending."
—*Romantic Times BOOKclub Magazine*

JANE AND THE STILLROOM MAID

JANE AND THE GENIUS OF THE PLACE

"Barron artfully replicates Austen's voice, sketches several delightful portraits . . . and dazzles her audience with period details." —*Publishers Weekly*

"Barron has succeeded in emulating the writing style of Austen's period without mocking it."
—*Indianapolis Star*

"A gem of a novel."
—*Romantic Times BOOKclub Magazine*

"Barron tells the tale in Jane's leisurely voice, skillfully re-creating the tone and temper of the time without a hint of an anachronism."
—*Cleveland Plain Dealer*

"Cleverly blends scholarship with mystery and wit, weaving Jane Austen's correspondence and works of literature into a tale of death and deceit."
—*Rocky Mountain News*

JANE AND THE WANDERING EYE

"Barron seamlessly weaves . . . a delightful and lively tale. . . . Period details bring immediacy to a neatly choreographed dance through Bath society."
—*Publishers Weekly*

"Barron's high level of invention testifies to an easy acquaintance with upper-class life and culture in Regency England and a fine grasp of Jane Austen's own literary style—not to mention a mischievous sense of fun." —*New York Times Book Review*

"No betrayal of our interest here: *Jane and the Wandering Eye* is an erudite diversion."
—*Drood Review of Mystery*

"Delightful . . . captures the style and wit of Austen."
—*San Francisco Examiner*

JANE AND THE UNPLEASANTNESS AT SCARGRAVE MANOR

"Splendid fun!" —*Minneapolis Star Tribune*

"Happily succeeds on all levels: a robust tale of manners and mayhem that faithfully reproduces the Austen style—and engrosses to the finish."
—*Kirkus Reviews*

"Jane is unmistakably here with us through the work of Stephanie Barron—sleuthing, entertaining, and making us want to devour the next Austen adventure as soon as possible!" —Diane Mott Davidson

"People who lament Jane Austen's minimal lifetime output . . . now have cause to rejoice."
—*Drood Review of Mystery*

"A light-hearted mystery . . . The most fun is that 'Jane Austen' is in the middle of it, witty and logical, a foil to some of the ladies who primp, faint and swoon."
—*Denver Post*

"A fascinating ride through the England of the hackney carriage . . . a definite occasion for pride rather than prejudice." —Edward Marston

"A thoroughly enjoyable tale. Fans of the much darker Anne Perry . . . should relish this somewhat lighter look at the society of fifty years earlier." —*Mostly Murder*

Also by Stephanie Barron

Jane and the Unpleasantness at Scargrave Manor

Jane and the Man of the Cloth

Jane and the Wandering Eye

Jane and the Genius of the Place

Jane and the Stillroom Maid

Jane and the Prisoner of Wool House

Jane and the Ghosts of Netley

AND COMING IN HARDCOVER
FROM BANTAM BOOKS

Jane and the Barque of Frailty

Jane and His Lordship's Legacy

~ Being a Jane Austen Mystery ~

by Stephanie Barron

BANTAM BOOKS
NEW YORK • TORONTO • LONDON • SYDNEY • AUCKLAND

JANE AND HIS LORDSHIP'S LEGACY
A Bantam Book

PUBLISHING HISTORY
Bantam hardcover edition published March 2005
Bantam mass market edition / October 2005

Published by
Bantam Dell
A Division of Random House, Inc.
New York, New York

This is a work of fiction. Names, characters, places, and incidents either are the product of the author's imagination or are used fictitiously. Any resemblance to actual persons, living or dead, events, or locales is entirely coincidental.

Library of Congress Catalog Card Number: 2004048796

Bantam Books and the rooster colophon are registered trademarks of Random House, Inc.

ISBN-13: 978-0-553-58407-3

ISBN-10: 0-553-58407-3

Printed in the United States of America
Published simultaneously in Canada

www.bantamdell.com

OPM 10 9 8 7 6 5 4 3 2 1

Dedicated to the members of the
Jane Austen Society of North America,
who support and encourage my work
with such enthusiasm

All reference contained herein to the British Museums's holdings of the Wilborough Papers, Austen bequest, are entirely the mendacious product of the author's mind.

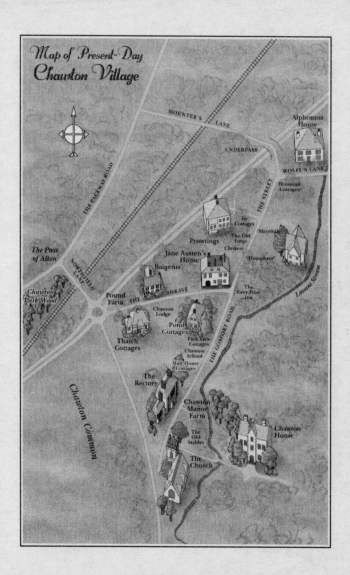

Chapter 1

All We Have

Tuesday, 4 July 1809
Chawton, Hampshire

~

I CAME INTO MY KINGDOM TODAY AT HALF-PAST two—or so much of one as shall ever be granted me on this earth. Four square brick walls, half a dozen chimneys, a simple doorway fronting on the London to Gosport road, and a clutch of outbuildings behind: such is our cottage in Chawton.

"Lord, Jane," my mother breathed as she surveyed the unadorned façade of her future abode from the vantage of our hired pony trap, "I should not call it *charming*, to be sure—but beggars cannot be choosers, you know, and we must admit ourselves infinitely obliged to your excellent brother. Observe, a new cesspit has been dug, and the privy painted! I declare, is nothing forgot that might contribute to our comfort?"

I did not reply, for tho' the raw mud near the new plumbing works looked dismal enough, my mother could not hesitate to approve the generosity Edward has shown. A man of considerable property, as the heir of our distant cousins the Knights, my brother chuses to reside at his principal estate of Godmersham, in Kent—but has given us the use of his late bailiff's cottage here in Hampshire. If a former alehouse, fronting the juncture of two highways overrun by coaching traffic, with rough-hewn beams, low-ceilinged rooms, and cramped stairs, may be considered a luxury, then we are bound to be grateful to Edward; he has saved four women the expence of lodgings, and for a household of strict economy and perpetual dependence, that cost must be a saving indeed.

There are some among our acquaintance who would hint that, in possessing the freehold of every house in Chawton village, my brother might have done more for his widowed mother, and done it years since; but I will not join my strictures to theirs.[1] My heart rises to smell the good earth again, and rejoices to think that my mornings will never more be shattered by the bustle of a town, and all the noise of commerce crying at

[1] The manor of Chawton, which included the Great House and the whole of the village, was deeded to Jane's third brother, Edward, in 1797 as part of his inheritance from distant cousins, Mr. and Mrs. Thomas Knight of Kent, a childless couple who adopted Edward as their heir. Edward enjoyed the freehold of more than thirty cottages and gardens in Chawton, as well as the Great House, farm, and Chawton Park. The entire estate, including the village holdings, was gradually sold off in the twentieth century by Knight family heirs.—*Editor's note.*

the gate! There is nothing, when one is broken-hearted, like the healing balm of the country!

"I shall plant potatoes," my mother declared briskly, "and if we are fortunate, we shall gather them by late September. The cottage's aspect might be softened, Jane. It requires only a flowering vine, I think, to grow romantickly across the door."

"—And to complete the picturesque, it ought to be sagging in its casements. It is too much to hope for a shattered roof or a tower crumbling into ruin; we must contrive to be satisfied with a building that is only ample, sturdy, and in good repair, Mamma."

The house's position at the fork of Chawton's two principal roads *must* be adjudged an evil—but out-weighing this are the broad meadows to north and east, the stout wood fence and hornbeam hedge enclosing the grounds, and the delightful promise of birdsong from the thriving fields. Mr. Seward, the late bailiff, maintained a shrubbery and an orchard, but Mrs. Seward cannot have loved her flowers; the borders must and shall be worked. Syringas, and peonies, and the simpler blooms of mignonette—all these we shall have, and Sweet William too.

While the carter jumped down to secure his horse, I studied the distant view of the privy and banished the idea of a water closet, soon to be installed in brother Henry's London house; such ostentation has no place in a country village. It is not for *Jane* to repine. I had found no love or joy in the habitation of cities—I had rather witnessed, in first Bath and then Southampton, the gradual erosion of nearly every cherished dream I held in life. It was time I made a trial of rural delights; it was they that had formed my earliest vision of happiness.

"The man will want something for his pains," my mother urged in an audible hiss as the driver helped her to descend. "See that he shifts the baggage before he deserts us entirely. And do not go spoiling him with Edward's coin! I am gone to inspect the privy."

She moved with determination in the direction of my brother's improvements, her gait marked by the stiffness of rheumatism. I stepped down to the rutted surface of the road and prepared to be—if not happy, then content.

WE HAD SET OUT FROM CASTLE SQUARE IN LATE April, bidding farewell forever to the glare and stink of a town. We made for Godmersham, where we tarried six weeks in the pleasant Kentish spring, tho' the place and all who live in it are remarkably changed from what they once were. My brother Edward's wife Elizabeth is dead now nearly a year and my sister Cassandra resident in the household, supplying the want of a mother; she is careworn but steady in her attachment to the little children, and a prop to Fanny, who at sixteen must now fill Elizabeth's place. Tho' the chuckling of the Stour was as sweet as I remembered, and the temple on the hill beckoned with serenity, I could not stomach the climb to its heights, nor rest an interval between its columns. In happier times I had sat in that very place with Elizabeth beside me—and once, looked up from my pen to find the tall figure of a silver-haired man climbing the grassy slope—

Edward has not yet learned to endure his Lizzy's passing. Indeed, he has come to see in it a deliberate blow of Divine Judgement: that having loved his wife too well, and delighting in the gift of every luxury and indulgence her fair form desired, he incurred the wrath of Providence—Who despised Edward's attachment to things of this world so much, that He tore from my brother's bosom the one creature he cherished most.

"Were it not for the children," Neddie observed bitterly as we sat together before the bare grate in the stillness of Elizabeth's drawing-room, "I should have gone into the grave with her, Jane. I should not have hesitated at self-murder."

"—Tho' the very act should damn you to Hell?"

"It is Hell I endure at present."

I could not assure my brother that I understood too well his sentiments; could not add my misery to his own, as he sat glaring at the waste of all that constituted his happiness. Edward knew nothing of the Gentleman Rogue, beyond a passing acquaintance with one who had called briefly at Godmersham several years before, and had long since been forgot. I could not explain that I, too, must submit to all the agony of bereavement—with the added burden of suffering in silence. Never having been Lord Harold Trowbridge's acknowledged love, I must be mute in misery before the world he deserted so abruptly last November.

As I studied my brother's countenance—grave, where it had once been gay; worn, where it had formerly appeared the portrait of inveterate youth—I concluded that there was at least this relief in publick grief: one was not forced to shield the feelings of others. The Bereaved might be all that is selfish in their parade of unhappiness. Whereas I was continually chafing under the daily proofs of inconsideration, imperviousness, high animal spirits, and insensibility that surrounded me, when every hope of happiness for myself was at an end.

When the Rogue expired of a knife wound on the fifth of November, some ten months ago, it was as though a black pit yawned at my feet and I trembled on the brink of it for days together without being conscious of what I said or did. I know from others that his body was fetched back to London in the Duke of Wilborough's carriage; that Wilborough House, so lately draped in black for the passing of the Rogue's mother, remained in crepe for this second son; that nearly five hundred men followed the cortège first to the Abbey church at Westminster and then, on horseback, to the interment in the Wilborough tomb. It was said that no less than seven ladies of Fashion fainted dead away at the awful news of his demise, and three fell into a decline. All this my mother read aloud from the London papers, offering comment and opinion of her own.

Murdered by his manservant, so they say, Jane, a foreigner his lordship took up with on the Peninsula. I'll wager that fellow knew a thing or two of Lord Harold's unsavoury affairs! It is a nasty end, Jane, but no more than he deserved. I always said he was a most unsuitable tendre *for a young lady such as yourself, and quite elderly into the bargain; but nobody listens to me, I am always overruled. Still, it is a pity you did not get him when you could—you might have been the Relict of a lord! And now all his riches will go to Wilborough's son—who will find no very good use for them, I'll wager. The Marquis is a rakehell and a gamester, so they say. Kinsfell has taken a page from his uncle's book, and will undoubtedly prove as disreputable a character. We must impute it to the Dowager Duchess's French blood, and habits of parading onstage. . . .*

Four days after the murder I took up my pen to compose a few paragraphs of explanation and regret that ought to have been despatched without delay to his lordship's niece, Desdemona, Countess of Swithin. That lady, despite her lofty position in Society and the cares attendant upon her duties as a mother, has been narrowly concerned—as much as a woman could be—in Lord Harold's affairs, and loved him more dearly, I suspect, than she did her own father. It seemed imperative to me that the Countess be in full possession of the facts of his lordship's death—of the bravery with which he embraced it, and his determination not to submit to a form of treachery that might imperil His Majesty's government—so that no scandalous falsehood put about by his enemies among the *ton* should shake her faith in his worth. From what I knew of Desdemona, I doubted that anything could.

Her answer was brief, correct, and exceedingly cold. I knew not whether she regarded my letter of commiseration in the light of an impertinence; or whether she charged me with having precipitated her uncle's death. Perhaps she merely judged his attentions to a woman so clearly beneath his touch as deplorable. I cannot say. But her ladyship's brevity cut me to the quick. I have had nothing from her since.

Only Martha Lloyd, who in Cassandra's absence has become as dear as a sister to me, understood a little of the pain I suffered. Tho' Martha referred to my grief as a chronic indisposition, she was quick to order me to bed, and leave me in silence with a pot of tea during the long grey winter afternoons. My brother Frank, who had witnessed the Rogue's death in company with myself, was a considerable comfort. Tho' he no longer shared our lodgings, his occasional visits afforded the opportunity to unbend—to speak openly of what we both knew and mourned in his lordship's passing. Even in Frank's silence I felt sympathy, and in his accounts of his naval activities—he oversaw the landing in January of the remnant of General Sir John Moore's Peninsular army, a tattered band of harried soldiers deprived too soon of the leadership of that excellent man—I felt some connexion to the greater world Lord Harold had known and ruled. We are forced to go on living, however little we relish the interminable days.

In April, Frank quitted home waters for the China Station and we devoted ourselves to the activity of household removal. My mother's querulous demands and persistent anxieties regarding the packing provided diversion enough; so, too, did the necessary farewells to naval acquaintance, the last visits to the little theatre in French Street, and a final Assembly endured at the Dolphin Inn. I even danced on that occasion with a black-eyed foreign gentleman too shy to enquire my name. But I had no joy in any of these things. The coming of spring mocked me with a promise of life I no longer shared. At the moment of our descent upon Edward's house in Kent, I had determined I should never feel hopeful again.

There is no remedy for the loss inflicted by death except remembrance. And so I tried to recollect what his lordship's dying words had been.

Promise me . . . you will write . . .

What is writing compared to life, my lord?

All we have . . . Jane.

He was wont to speak the truth, no matter how harsh its effect. It was one of the qualities for which I esteemed him: his unblinking gaze at the brutality of existence.

But I could not keep my promise. What are words and paragraphs in comparison of what might have been? A cold solace when love is forever denied. I had written nothing in the long months that followed Lord Harold's headlong flight from this world but stilted letters to Cassandra, remarkable for their brittleness of tone and the forced lightness of their jokes.

Before quitting Castle Square, however, I had gone so far as to enquire of Messrs. Crosby and Co., of Stationers Hall Court, London, whether they ever intended to publish the manuscript entitled *Susan*, which I had sold to them for the sum of ten pounds six years previous; but their answer was not encouraging. I was impudently informed by Mr. Crosby himself that he did not chuse to publish my work; that if I attempted to place it elsewhere, he should most vigourously prevent its appearance; and in conclusion, that I might have the manuscript returned for the same figure he had laid out for it. Being hard pressed to command so considerable a sum as ten pounds, I was forced to let the matter drop; and was dissatisfied enough with the scant consideration offered prospective Authoresses, as to ignore the burden of Lord Harold's dying breath.

Now, as I stood in the dusky heat of a Hampshire July, lark song rising about me, I felt the first faint stirrings of life. Feeble, yes—and a hairsbreadth from guttering out; but stirrings all the same. I unknotted my bonnet strings and bared my head to the sun. Lord Harold's gaze—that earnest, steadfast look—wavered before my mind's eye; I blinked it away. *Perhaps here,* I thought, as I opened the door of the cottage and stepped inside its whitewashed walls, *perhaps here I might begin again.*

Chapter 2

An Indifferent Welcome

4 July 1809, cont.

~

IT WAS AIRLESS AND DIM INSIDE THE COTTAGE, AS though the windows had been too long shut up, and I recollected that although the workmen had been busy about the house some weeks, Mrs. Seward had quitted the place full four months previous. I hesitated in the entry hall, my gaze taking in the uneven floorboards, and was reminded inevitably of my childhood home at Steventon Parsonage, where my brother James now lived. Just so had the spare rooms been whitewashed, the low ceilings crossed with beams.

The passageway divided on the right hand at the dining parlour and on the left at the sitting room. In the latter, Edward had caused the broad front window—so necessary to a publican's commerce, but injurious to our privacy—to be bricked up, and had ordered a bow thrown out overlooking the garden. This was all the main floor of the house for domestic use; an ell at the rear housed the kitchen; and a staircase from the entry led upwards to six bedchambers, none of them large. My mother was to have one, Martha Lloyd another, and I must share a third with Cassandra in a few days' time when Edward escorted her from Kent in his carriage. A fourth was set aside for Edward's use, should he care to visit—Chawton Great House, my brother's Tudor pile at the opposite end of the village, being let at present to a gentleman by the name of Middleton.

One glimpse of these modest arrangements, however, and I suspected that Edward should repair for comfort to the George Inn at Alton, where my mother and I had lately been staying. Alton is the principal market town in this part of Hampshire, and Edward the absentee owner of the George; Mr. Barlow, his publican, has been our especial servant in all the bustle of this removal. It was Barlow's man, Joseph, who drove us to Chawton today in the George's pony trap, and we have tarried under Mr. Barlow's roof on several occasions during the past twelvemonth— probably, in the poor man's estimation, frequently outstaying our welcome.

The remaining bedchambers were already apportioned to those as yet unknown servants we intended to employ: a maid, a cook, and a man to do the heavy labour about the place. Martha and I have settled it that the manservant—who naturally shall be named

William or John—is to marry the cook and seduce the maidservant, thus providing endless matter for conversation among ourselves.

I moved from dining parlour to sitting room and back again, drawing off my bonnet as I did so. Most of our furnishings from Castle Square had long since arrived by dray from the south, and been placed at random by the carter in various rooms. With a good airing and brisk activity we might contrive to make the cottage feel a home. From the side window I could just glimpse Chawton Pond, as I believed it was called: a shallow but broad expanse of muddy water across the lane, useful for the watering of cattle and the amusement of small boys given to skipping stones. From the rear I might observe a parade of riches: the well, with the pump newly-primed; the bake house that Martha will love to command with her cherished receipts; a granary just large enough to house a donkey and cart; and a henhouse. It is hardly the abode of people of Fashion, but for a party of women long since on the shelf, should do well enough.

We had each of us carried modest hopes to this place: Cassandra wished to procure a dog and raise some poultry; my mother yearned to grow vegetables again, while I was determined to purchase a pianoforte, the best that could be got for thirty guineas. I could scarcely believe that such a sum was now in my possession, or that I contemplated squandering it entirely for my own use.

Edward pressed the coins into my hand four nights ago as I prepared to quit Godmersham. When I protested that he had already done far too much, he curled my fingers over the leather pouch.

"It is nothing," he told me firmly, "or rather—it is a something in remembrance of one whose ears are forever stopped with earth. You know how much Lizzy admired your playing, Jane. It distressed her exceedingly that you were denied an instrument on which to practise. Pray play a song for her—now and again. . . ."

I could say little as he turned away, my throat constricted by tears; he has buried the carefree gentleman of Fashion, and we shall not see that ghost again.

A rough young voice disturbed my reverie.

"Are you the Squire's lady?"

I peered through the open doorway into the sunlit afternoon and espied a boy, of perhaps thirteen years, standing at the pony's head. He was sharp-eyed, brown as a guinea hen, and wiry of limb. Tho' his nankeen trousers were worn, they had been neatly patched. I judged him to hail from the yeoman class of Edward's tenants.

"I am Miss Austen," I supplied, "and the Squire is my brother. My mother and I are come to take up residence in this house. What is your name, young sir?"

"Toby Baigent," he returned promptly, "from Symond's Farm." One careless hand gestured somewhere west, beyond my ken; I had not yet acquired the necessary knowledge of Chawton village to be able to reply with authority. "We heard you were expected, from Dyer's folk. They've been working hard days a fortnight or more, now."

These words I interpreted as a reference to Mr.

John Dyer, of Ivy House in Alton, a builder whose men were responsible for the blocked window and new privy so admired by my mother. "And we are very grateful for their labour," I said.

Toby Baigent spat indecorously in the dust. "Labour wasted, so my pa says. You'll be leaving soon enough."

"I beg your pardon?"

"Reckon you'll be cursed, in a house not rightfully your own."

"That's enough, young Baigent," said Joseph, our driver, with a lowering expression on his brow. "Be off with ye, before I find a better use for my whip, and tan your hide."

The boy smoothed the pony's nose, his eyes fixed on the mane between the beast's ears, then lounged his way down the street without a word.

"Don't you pay no heed to that young chuff," Joseph advised me, his gaze following the boy's thin form as he ambled towards his home, big with news. "He's got more mouth than mind, as they say."

"What did he mean when he said this house was not rightfully ours?"

"Speaking where he ought not, mum," the driver replied; but he did not meet my gaze as he reached for my mother's heavy trunk, and hoisted it with a grunt to his back. "Every folk knows as how the houses hereabouts, aye, and much of the land, too, belong to Mr. Austen. Where would you see the trunk stowed, then?"

"The bedchamber at the head of the stairs." I stepped aside to allow him passage. "The boy suggested we should be *cursed*. Decidedly strong language, Joseph. Particularly for a child of his years."

"P'raps he's had it from the father."

"Is Farmer Baigent disposed to contest our right to the cottage?"

The man persisted in studying his boots. "There's been a bit o' feeling, like, about Widow Seward."

"—who quitted her home to make way for us. But surely she was accommodated elsewhere in the village?"

"Mrs. Seward's gone to live with her daughter, Mrs. Baverstock, in Alton." Another vague gesture, this time to the east. "It were a sad day when Mr. Seward died, mum. This house to be given up, and the tenancy of Pound Farm—which the Sewards've held for donkey's years—made over to that new man, Mr. Wickham. The Baigents in particular don't hold with Mr. Wickham, mum. They'd thought to lease Pound Farm themselves. Adjoins their property, like, at Symond's Farm."

"I see. But my brother settled his affairs in favour of Mr. Wickham, no doubt for excellent reasons of his own. And is the animosity towards ourselves quite general throughout the village?"

"I'm an Alton man," Joseph returned with some asperity, "and can't speak for those as live in Chawton. I did ought to be getting back to Mr. Barlow, if you take my meaning, once these bits of baggage are stowed."

I took his meaning; he did not wish to stand gossiping in the street with a relative stranger, under the scrutiny of his intimates and neighbours. It would require more than a protracted stay at the George to command Joseph's loyalty.

"The second trunk, and the two brown band-boxes belonging to myself, are to be placed in the room down the hallway on the left."

"Very good, mum." He bent slightly under the strain of my mother's things, and made his strenuous way into the house.

I CONFESS I DID NOT WASTE A GREAT DEAL OF TIME in revolving the grievances of the local folk during the ensuing hour, as I dusted china and aired linens. There were beds to be made up, foodstuffs to be stored, the Pembroke table to be positioned in a number of places, none of which pleased my mother; and our small treasure of books to be unpacked and placed upon the shelf. I may perhaps have considered with exasperation that security in his own position, in the essential rightness of his ideas, that had preserved my brother's complacency on the subject of his tenants, and prevented him from imparting a warning as to the sort of reception we might expect here; but I thought it very likely Neddie had been too distracted by private concerns—by the well of grief into which he continually dipped—to spare any thought for the villagers. Not arrogance, but absence of mind, was surely accountable for my brother's lapse.

"Well, Jane," said my mother as she entered the front passage, "here is our neighbour, Mr. Prowting, come to offer his services; but I have assured him there is not the slightest need to put himself out—Jane will have everything in hand, I told him, being a clever girl and decidedly capable when she sets her mind to it, though not so efficient in the domestic line as her elder sister, being no hand at all in the still-room. Make your courtesy to Mr. Prowting, my dear. My younger daughter—Miss Jane Austen."

Mr. Prowting was a man of some means—one of Chawton's dignitaries, in the commission of the peace of the county as well as its Deputy Lieutenant.[1] He was a grey-haired, portly, and rather carelessly-dressed gentleman of middle age, beaming all his benevolence.

I dropped a curtsey and said, "I have heard much of you, Mr. Prowting, from my brother Mr. Austen. You are our nearest neighbour, I collect."

"Indeed, indeed—our home is but a stone's toss from your doorstep, my dear Miss Austen, and easily accessible by a stile in the adjoining meadow."

I could not have avoided a glimpse of Prowtings, as the house was called, had I wished it; the place was a fine, modern building of substantial size on the same side of the Gosport road as our own, but happier in its situation, being set back a good distance from the carriage-way. *Their* beds should not be shaken in the dead of night by the passage of the London coach-and-six, as I imagined our own should be.

---

[1] To be in the commission of the peace for the county, as Jane phrases it, was to be appointed a justice of the peace, or magistrate. Deputy lieutenant was a post appointed at the pleasure of the lord lieutenant of the county, usually the county's ranking peer, and carried with it certain administrative duties.—*Editor's note.*

"Mrs. Prowting and my daughters, Catherine-Ann and Ann-Mary, would, I am sure, have joined me in this brief visit of welcome," he said, "but that the latter is practising upon the pianoforte, and the former is lying down with the head-ache. The heat of July, you know, is quite a trial to young ladies prone to the head-ache."

"So I understand. Tho' increasing age, I might add, is no preservative against the malady." I was too well acquainted with my mother's imagined sufferings whenever heat, or cold, or too much of both, should disoblige her expectations and send her reeling to her bed.

"Mrs. Prowting wished me to convey her compliments," he said with a bow, "and desires me to press you most earnestly to join us for dinner this evening at Prowtings. You need not make yourselves anxious on the subject of dress; we are all easy in Chawton, Mrs. Austen, with no unbecoming formality."

"Thank you most kindly," my mother replied. "We should be very happy to accept your invitation."

I was about to add my thanks to hers when the sound of an equipage drawing up in the street outside our door claimed all our notice. Mr. Prowting turned, as though in expectation of espying a neighbour come upon a similar errand of civility; but I understood instantly from his expression that the person now alighting from the chaise-and-four was a stranger even to him. A spare, stooped, ancient man, dressed all in black and grim of expression, hobbled forward as though a martyr to dyspepsia. The newcomer wore

.

a tricorn hat and supported his infirmities with a beautifully-carved walking-stick of ebony and gold, which stabbed at the pavings of our walkway with such vehemence that I almost expected sparks to fly from its tip.

He was followed by two lackeys in a livery of primrose and black, bearing between them a massive wooden chest bound with silver hasps. The chest's aspect was arresting: it was carved and painted with curious figures that were hardly native to England. It was clear that the party's object was our cottage, but what their purpose might be in seeking it, I had not the least idea.

"Good day to you, sir," Mr. Prowting said in the peremptory tone of one who has served as magistrate.

The gentleman in the tricorn lifted up his gaze, a withering look of contempt on his countenance. He did not deign to return Mr. Prowting's salutation, nor did he waste another instant in surveying his figure. He merely turned his eyes upon my mother and myself, came to a halt at our doorstep, and lifted his hat with extreme care from the exquisitely-powdered wig that adorned his head.

"Have I the honour of addressing the Austen household?"

"You do, sir," said my mother doubtfully. "I am Mrs. George Austen."

"My compliments, ma'am," he replied, "but I need not disturb you further. It is Miss Jane Austen I seek. Is she at leisure to receive me?"

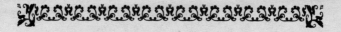

Chapter 3

A Contested Provision

4 July 1809, cont.

~

"I AM MISS AUSTEN," I ANSWERED, IN SOME BEWILderment.

"Bartholomew Chizzlewit, of Lincoln's Inn, at your service, ma'am."[1] The elderly gentleman bowed low. "I must beg the indulgence of perhaps half an hour of your time, on a pressing matter of business that has already been delayed some months."

"A matter of business, sir?" I repeated. I could claim no business in the world, save the arrangement

---

[1] Lincoln's Inn is one of the four Inns of Court, formed in the Middle Ages to provide lodgings for young men studying law. It sits roughly half a mile from Covent Garden in the center of London, and in Jane Austen's day was a common locus of solicitors' and barristers' chambers, as it remains today.—*Editor's note.*

of domestic affairs too inconsequential to be of concern to such a man.

"Indeed. A matter of so delicate a nature, ma'am, that I must demand complete and uninterrupted privacy"—at this, his gaze shifted narrowly to my mother's countenance—"for the discharging of my trust."

An instant of silence followed this declaration, as my mother attempted to make sense of it and I considered the disorder of unpacking that was everywhere evident within the cottage. How was I to even attempt a *tête-à-tête*?

"I am putting up at the Swan in Alton," the attorney added firmly, consulting a pocket watch, "and have ordered my dinner for precisely six o'clock. If you find you are unable to accommodate me today, Miss Austen, I must beg you to wait upon me in Alton tomorrow morning, well in advance of my intended departure for London, which I anticipate occurring at ten o'clock. I may add that I am unaccustomed to brooking delay."

"Extraordinary behaviour!" Mr. Prowting exclaimed. "You can have not the slightest pretension to these ladies' consideration, sirrah, much less the freedom to demand the terms of your admittance to their household."

"Sir," Chizzlewit declared in a voice rich with contempt, "I neither know nor care whom you might be, but I must emphatically state that a man of your obviously rustic experience and modest station can claim no influence with the representative of the noble and most puissant house of His Grace the Duke of Wilbor-ough, whose forebears and heirs I have had the hon-our to serve as solicitor these sixty years and more."

"*Wilborough?*" my mother cried in startled accents. "Good Lord, Jane—has the Rogue left you something after all? I should not have believed it possible! That a gentleman—even one of Lord Harold's unsavoury reputation—should offer the insult of monetary con-sideration to one whose reputation he has already sul-lied beyond repair—"

"Mamma," I said firmly, "I believe I should receive Mr. Chizzlewit and learn the burden of his news. I shall require the use of the dining parlour for an in-terval. You might walk in the direction of the Great House before dinner—and observe whether the ten-ant, Mr. Middleton, is entirely worthy of my brother's trust."

"But my dear Miss Austen—" Mr. Prowting protested. "A young lady of your sensibility—"

"I am nearly four-and-thirty years of age, good sir, and feel not the slightest anxiety at receiving so re-spectable a person as Mr. Chizzlewit. Would you be very good—and attend my mother on her walk?"

IF THE SERVANT OF THE NOBLE AND MOST PUIS-sant house of Wilborough was dismayed by the sur-roundings in which he presently found himself, he did not betray his discomfiture. I seated myself on one of my mother's straight-backed chairs and waited while Mr. Chizzlewit disposed himself in another. With a wordless gesture of his right hand, he had ordered his minions to follow him; they set the curiously-carved chest on the dining-parlour floor and then retreated impassively to await their master's pleasure.

"I have it on the very best authority, Miss Austen, that your understanding is excellent," he began, "and therefore I shall not sport with your patience. Under the terms of the late Lord Harold Trowbridge's Last Will and Testament, written by his lordship on the third of November last and witnessed by one Jeb Hawkins, Able Seaman, and one Josiah Fortescue, publican"—Chizzlewit's distaste for such witnesses was evident—"you have been named as the legatee of a rather extraordinary bequest."

I felt my countenance change, my visage flush. I knew all the circumstances under which that testament had been written: the third of November, 1808, the very day before Lord Harold's aborted duel with a young American by the name of James Ord. The former had opened his box of matched pistols—made to his specifications by no less a master than Manton in London—and affected to practise with wafers and playing cards in the courtyard of the Dolphin Inn. His aspect had been brutal that morning, and it had not changed when I pled for the young man's life. It was Lord Harold's I secretly hoped to save; but he had ridiculed me—and put one of the pistols into my hands. He would have challenged my shrinking, and sought to determine whether I could stomach his way of life. Had he drawn up his Will before that hour, or much later? Impossible to say.

"What can his lordship have wished to bequeath to me?" I enquired in a subdued tone. "I am wholly unconnected with his family."

"—As has been vociferously pointed out by His Grace the Duke of Wilborough, Her Grace the Duchess, the Marquis of Kinsfell, and indeed, Desdemona, Countess of Swithin, all of whom seem convinced that Lord Harold's wits were sadly deranged when he penned the document." Chizzlewit studied me with a shrewd expression, his ancient lips pursed. "I may frankly assure you, Miss Austen, that his lordship has been frequently drawing up his Will, as necessity and the perils to which he was exposed demanded it. That this document supersedes and governs any previous form is indisputable, as I repeatedly assured His Grace. My commission as solicitor and executor of his lordship's estate should have been long since carried out, to the satisfaction of all parties, had not the Wilborough family protested this legacy."

Another lady might have been humbled by a sense of shame and mortification; I confess I felt only indignant. "And what is his lordship's family, pray, that I should consider their opinion in a matter so sacred as a gentleman's dying wish?"

"Nothing," the solicitor returned with surprising mildness. "It is for me, as their man of business, to dispose of disappointment and outrage. I have been doing so, for all the Wilborough clan, for some six decades. I was but eighteen and a clerk in my father's chambers when the Fifth Duke proposed to marry a chit from the Parisian stage; and the furor over the marriage articles *then* may fairly be described as incredible. Instability and caprice have characterised all the family's habits, against which Lord Harold's lamented passing and general way of life may almost be called respectable. It has always been for the firm of Chizzlewit and Pauver to support the family and maintain a proper appearance of decorum before the *ton;* there our influence—and indeed, I may add our interest—ends, Miss Austen."

"What is the nature of the legacy?" I demanded.

"It is this." The solicitor drew a piece of paper—ordinary white foolscap, such as might be found in the public writing desk of an inn—from his leather pouch. Was it possible that this was Lord Harold's Will, penned in his own hand? I felt my heartbeat quicken, from an intense desire to glimpse that beloved script—but the solicitor did not offer the paper to me. Instead, he took a pair of spectacles from his pocket and set them carefully on his nose. With a dry rasp of the throat, he began to read.

"To my dear friend, Miss Jane Austen of Castle Square, Southampton, I leave a lifetime of incident, intrigue, and conspiracy; of adventure and scandal; of wagers lost and won. To wit: all my letters, diaries, account books, and memoranda, that she might order their contents and draw from them a fair account of my life for the edification of posterity. There is no one in whose understanding or safekeeping I place a higher trust; no one whose pen is so well-suited to the instruction of an admiring multitude. With such matter at hand, not even Jane may fail to write. I should like her to entitle the work 'Memoirs of a Gentleman Rogue.' Miss Austen

is to be the sole beneficiary of all proceeds from the publication and sale of the aforementioned work, to which my surviving family may have no claim. Neither are they to attempt to prevent its publication, upon pain of pursuit by my solicitors in a court of law."

Mr. Chizzlewit raised his eyes from the paper and studied me drily.

At such a moment, in contemplation of his own death, much might have been said. But it was like Lord Harold to utter not a syllable of assurance or endearment; not for him the maudlin turn upon Death's stage. He had probably believed this testament would never be read—but in the event it was, had been all business as he wrote: brisk, ironic, cynical to the end.

"Once the protests and objections of the family were laid aside—once all talk of contesting the Will's provisions in court was at an end—I attempted first to fulfill the bequest in Southampton," Mr. Chizzlewit said, "but learned that you had already quitted that city. It has been some weeks since I was able to trace you through your brother, Mr. Henry Austen of the London banking concern, and fixed the very hour you would be arriving in Chawton."

"Good God," I murmured blankly. "Is this a joke?"

"I fear not."

I rose from my seat and took a turn about the room, agitation animating my form. "All his papers—! His most intimate accounts—! He must have been quite mad!"

"So His Grace conjectured. The Sixth Duke

should rather have burnt the lot, than seen such a legacy pass into the hands of a stranger. Blackmail is the least of the ills Wilborough forebodes."

"Well may I believe it." At the thought of the outraged peer and his anxieties, I could not suppress a smile. "How is it that so much as a fragment of Lord Harold's papers has survived His Grace's wrath?"

"Lord Harold, being of a peripatetic habit, formerly made the chambers of Chizzlewit and Pauver the repository of his documents," the solicitor answered primly. "It has been a heavy charge. Our premises have been violated no less than four times in the past decade, as we believe with the specific object of robbing Lord Harold of his papers, requiring us to stoop to an almost criminal ingenuity: to greater measures and vigilance—as well as the addition of a variety of locks. I must warn you, Miss Austen, that there are many who would not hesitate to incur bodily injury in order to secure a glimpse of these papers, or to excise their own names from mention within them. It is a powder keg you observe before you, ma'am, in the form of a Bengal chest. I do not envy you the responsibility of shepherding his lordship's legacy."

"May I refuse it?"

Mr. Chizzlewit scrutinised me in silence.

How could I refuse it?

All the mishaps and alliances, the seductions and great passions—the acts of heroism or cowardice that might be contained within that Bengal chest! —Written, without flinching, in Lord Harold's own hand. It was possible he had even set down something of his sentiments towards *me*.

Of a sudden I was tempted to fall on my knees before the iron hasps and force them with my fingernails.

"I am empowered in the present instance only to discharge my duty," Mr. Chizzlewit rejoined. "What you do with the papers is your own affair. Read them— burn them—despatch them by the London stage to His Grace the Duke of Wilborough. *I* do not care."

But Lord Harold had cared very much indeed. *With such matter at hand, not even Jane may fail to write.* Lord Harold had been determined to influence my future, however little of it he might hope to share.

The elderly solicitor reached for his walking-stick and, with one hand braced on my mother's table, thrust himself to his feet. I was struck of a sudden by the devotion that had kept him sedulously in pursuit of his duty, when another man of his advanced years should have been already nodding by the fire.

"Mr. Chizzlewit, you have my deepest gratitude," I said soberly.

"No thanks are necessary." He stared at me as though I had uttered an impertinence. "I was honoured by his lordship's confidence. We are all of us diminished by his foul murder."

And pressing a heavy lead key into my palm, he wordlessly bowed.

The interview, I perceived, was at an end.

Chapter 4

Of Knights and Villains

~

"LETTERS!" MY MOTHER EXCLAIMED IN HORROR upon her return, unmindful of Mr. Prowting at her elbow. "What kind of a man leaves his paramour *letters*? A cottage perhaps, in a good situation—an annuity of a thousand pounds for the remainder of your days— but a bundle of papers not worth the ink smeared over them? Was the Rogue *mad*, Jane?"

"Never more so," I replied. "Have you enjoyed your walk, Mamma?"

"Fiddle my walk!" She rounded on Mr. Prowting. "You will have heard, I am sure, of Lord Harold Trowbridge—a Whig and an adventurer, for all he was the son of a duke; not content with having his fingers in every Government pie, and spoiling them all, but he must break my poor girl's heart! I can only say, Mr. Prowting, that murder is too good for him. He was born to be hanged!"

"So I apprehend, ma'am, from the London papers," the magistrate said stiffly. "I had not understood that you were on terms of acquaintance with the gentleman— For so we must call him, in deference to his birth. That *at least* remains unimpeachable."

"And a good deal of money the old Duke must have laid down to make it so," my mother retorted shrewdly.

I chose to ignore this impertinence, in deference to the heaviness of her disappointment, and turned instead to the magistrate. "His lordship's Bengal chest is of considerable size, Mr. Prowting. Would you be so kind as to assist me in securing it?"

Mr. Chizzlewit's warning had not been lost upon me. Lord Harold's enemies were numerous and determined; death alone should not quiet their fears. I had weighed the merits of henhouse and privy as unlikely objects of a thief's interest, but settled instead upon the depths of the cottage as being more convenient to hand. Our present abode having once served as an alehouse, it must be assumed that the cellars were commodious and in good repair. A double-doored hatch protruded from nether region to yard, undoubtedly for the purpose of rolling barrels of ale within; but this could be secured from below by a stout bar. I might sit upon Lord Harold's papers like a hen upon an egg, a priest upon a crypt, alive to every threat of violation.

"I am entirely at your service," Mr. Prowting said with a bow.

A foetid air rose from the damp and musty space as I descended the narrow stairs, a tallow candle held aloft.

"You will require a manservant," the magistrate declared. He was puffing from exertion, the wooden casket clutched precariously in his arms. "I shall take upon myself the task of securing a likely fellow from Alton."

"He must be called William or John, mind. I depend upon that." A scuttling of feet greeted my flame, and for an instant I hesitated on the bottom step. "Does the history of our former alehouse encompass smuggling, Mr. Prowting?"

"Every alehouse in the country must. Your brandy will not serve, unless it comes by stealth from France. But that is no Gentleman of the Night, Miss Austen. You will also be wanting a dog, I think—a stout little terrier to clear your cupboards for you."

In the glow of the tallow I observed several dark and stealthy forms stealing from a heap of sacking that filled one corner of the cellar. *Rats*. Decidedly rats. I repressed a shudder and quitted the final step, the fitful play of my candle throwing grotesque shadows about the stone walls.

"Pah—we must open the hatch." Mr. Prowting set the chest heavily on the sandy floor, and heedless of the dust and cobwebs that must adorn it, reached for the wooden bar that secured the double doors set into the cellar's ceiling. In an instant they were thrust wide, and light and air streamed down from the pleasant summer afternoon above like a benediction of Providence.

"*Ah,*" the magistrate breathed with satisfaction. "That shall soon mend matters. The atmosphere was better suited to a tomb—"

He broke off, mouth sadly agape, eyes fixed on the cellar corner. I turned my head to follow his gaze, and to my shame let out a cry. The bars of sunlight shafting through the open hatch revealed the pile of sacking to be something more: the figure of a man, laid out in all the rigour of death.

"Good God!" Mr. Prowting moved with surprising swiftness to the corpse.

The unfortunate wretch was clothed as a labourer—from village or field—and from the strength of his form, had been in the prime of life. His arms were slack by his sides and one leg sprawled akimbo, as tho' he had dropped off to sleep of an afternoon; but his countenance was unrecognisable.

The rats, I judged, had been feeding upon it some time.

"Quite dead," Mr. Prowting murmured.

"But how did he come here?" I exclaimed. "The house was shut up!"

The magistrate's looks were blank. "Mr. Dyer of Alton will have possessed a key."

Of course. The builder and his improvements. "Do you know this poor man at all? Is he one of Dyer's men?"

"With such a visage, who can say? How is his own

mother to know him?" Prowting stared down at the ravaged figure. "A dreadful business. And on the very day of your arrival—for the Squire's sister to make such a discovery—"

"It is a pity Mr. Chizzlewit is already gone," I observed. "We might otherwise have sent word to the George and summoned a carter. The body should be removed to the inn in expectation of the coroner. I am sure my brother would wish it."

My neighbour appeared to return to his senses from a great way off. He studied me strangely. "You are not overpowered by the sight, Miss Austen?"

"I am sadly lacking in delicate sensibility, Mr. Prowting. I have lived too long in the world."

His gaze sharpened and he drew me towards the stairs. "There is likely to be some unpleasantness these few hours. You will wish to retire, I think; and will be very welcome in Mrs. Prowting's drawing-room."

"But, sir— How did the unfortunate die?"

"A fit, perhaps."

"What sort of fit strikes down a healthy man?"

"There is a strong stench of spirits about the corpse," Mr. Prowting said abruptly. "I think it very likely he died of excessive drink, Miss Austen. And now, if you would be so good—"

I bowed my head, and went to break the news to my mother.

"YOU ARE NO STRANGER TO HAMPSHIRE, I collect, Mrs. Austen?" enquired the magistrate's wife as she served herself from a dish of chicken and peas. Dinner at Prowtings had been delayed until the fashionable hour of seven o'clock, from all the necessity of a corpse's removal. Mr. Prowting had found occasion to stand for two hours in the street, while a crowd of gawking village folk materialised to observe the proceedings. Word of the gruesome tragedy had spread like wildfire through every tenant's cot, but no one appeared in the guise of anxious mourner—no woman stood with wringing hands and suckling babe to claim the Dead as her own. I observed this, and drew the obvious conclusion: the corpse did not belong to Chawton. We should have to look farther afield for the dead man's name.

Poor Joseph, our driver of the morning, had returned from Mr. Barlow's establishment in Alton with a heavy dray, and an ominous object swathed in old linen was swung upwards from the cellar hatch. At the departure of the corpse, a few boys made to follow it into Alton; but the majority of our neighbours dispersed, hastened on their way by the magistrate's abjurations.

My mother, after an appropriate shriek and fainting fit, had suffered herself to be supported the length of the Prowtings' long gravel sweep under the eyes of the entire village—and hugely enjoyed her role as tragic heroine. There could be nothing like the Austens' descent upon their new home, I thought with some exasperation. First, a delegation of solicitors bearing mysterious chests; and then a dead man in the cellar—all in the space of a single afternoon!

We should provide the village with matter for conjecture sufficient to endure a twelvemonth, and feed young Baigent's claims that our household was indeed cursed.

Mrs. Prowting made my mother comfortable for an hour in a spare bedchamber; calmly bade her daughters leave off staring out the front windows; and observed that there was nothing like a body to drive folk from their work. She was a lady of significant proportions, her countenance placid; a woman whom even Death could not disturb. I observed, however, that she clutched a black-bordered square of lawn firmly in one hand throughout dinner—in expectation, perhaps, of being momentarily overcome by the Awfulness of the Event.

"I have lived in this country nearly all my life, Mrs. Prowting, with the exception of an interval in Bath," my mother declared in answer to her polite enquiry. "I do not count my childhood in Oxford—for that was decidedly long ago—and though Southampton is quite southwards, it is nonetheless Hampshire."

It had required several lessons in geography to impart this certainty to my mother's mind; I thanked Providence the point no longer admitted of doubt.

"And you are soon to be joined here in Chawton by two other ladies?"

"My elder daughter is, as we believe, already on her road from Kent; and our dear friend Miss Lloyd—who has formed a part of our household since the not entirely unexpected death of her mother a few years since—is presently visiting her sister at Kintbury. We look for both ladies every day—and Mr. Edward Austen as well."

"Mr. Austen is expected in Chawton!" ejaculated Mr. Prowting. "That is news indeed! We shall have to organise a party of welcome for the Squire. We shall indeed, my dear."

"Mr. Austen is always welcome in this house," rejoined his wife comfortably. "He is often in the country, as you must know, Mrs. Austen, for the settling of his tenant accounts. He is wont to engage a room at the George for that express purpose each quarter, and all his folk come and go to pay their respects—and their rents."

"We are quite the family party in this corner of the world," my mother sighed, as though rents and their accounting were all the joy she asked of life. "My eldest son, Mr. James Austen, is rector at Steventon, but a dozen miles distant; my fourth son, Henry, maintains a branch of his London bank—Austen, Gray & Vincent, perhaps you know it?—so near as Alton; and the wife of my fifth son, Captain Francis Austen, has lately taken a house in the same town."

"So many sons," observed Mrs. Prowting. "And which Alton house does the Captain's wife rent, ma'am?"

"Rose Cottage, in Lenton Street."

"I know it well! That is excellent news; you shall have a daughter within walking distance."

"I had almost considered removing to Mrs. Frank," my mother faltered, "on the strength of this dreadful business—I know I shall not sleep a wink in *such* a house—a house of *death* . . . but Mrs. Frank is indisposed at present, and I cannot presume upon the kindness of one in her condition. Her first child nearly killed her, you know."

"You are most welcome to remain with us, ma'am," Mrs. Prowting said warmly. "I should not *think* of sending you back to the cottage this evening."

My mother looked as though she might accept with gratitude—but I considered of Lord Harold's papers, lodged for the nonce in the henhouse, and interposed a negative.

"You are very good, Mrs. Prowting, but we are perfectly content in the cottage. A clergyman's family, as you know, is accustomed to the Dead."

A pompous speech enough; but Mrs. Prowting looked as though she admired it. My mother was nettled, and kicked my shin quite savagely beneath the table. She had the grace, however, not to engage in public argument.

"I think you said that Captain Austen is serving on the China Station?" Mr. Prowting enquired. "Excellent! Excellent! We hope to welcome another member of the Navy into the bosom of our family before very long; a young man we greatly esteem—"

"Papa! I beg you will not run on in that unbecoming way! I am sure I shall die of consciousness! The Austens can have no interest in Benjamin Clement—and to be sure, he is grown so odd of late—so inconstant in his attentions—that I protest I have *no* interest in him either!"

This impassioned cry fell from the lips of the youngest Miss Prowting, a girl I should judge to be at least twenty. She was fair-haired, blue-eyed, and full-figured; her white muslin gown was bestowed from neck to hem with fluttering primrose ribbons. It was clear she was accounted a Great Beauty, but I could not join in the general acclaim. Tho' Ann's complexion was good, it bore an expression of peevishness, and she had not the slightest pretension to either wit or conversation.

"Eh, do not be pouting at me, miss!" her father returned fondly, chucking her under the chin. "Young Benjamin is always the most constant of your beaux, no matter how little you are inclined to notice! Quite the belle of the village, our little Ann!"

It was as well, I thought, that my mother and Ann Prowting had divided the dinner table between them; for I had rarely been so ill-disposed to the rigours of Society, nor been so woefully unable to concentrate my energies. My mind was full of Lord Harold's bequest and the puzzle of the corpse in our cellar. I could not be attending to the insipidities of a country neighbourhood, however congenial the party.

"The Squire was well, I hope, when you quitted Kent?" Mrs. Prowting enquired. A brief silence ensued; her gaze, I saw too late and with sudden horror, was fixed upon *me*.

"My brother was very well, I thank you, Mrs. Prowting," I returned in a rush.

"It's a sad business, a gentleman of Mr. Austen's circumstances being left with all those children on his hands." Mrs. Prowting continued to study me, as though attempting to discern some likeness in my features—but it is Henry whom I resemble, not Edward. "A sad business, indeed; but Man proposes and the Lord disposes, as we have good reason to know. Does Mr. Austen think of giving up the Kentish place, and settling here in Chawton, with so many of his family fixed in the neighbourhood?"

"I do not think my brother has any idea of quitting Kent," I replied. "All his affections and interest are bound up in the environs of Canterbury."

"I should adore to go into Kent!" Ann Prowting sighed. "Hampshire beaux are nothing to those of Canterbury, I am sure! All the smart *ton* fellows descend upon the place for the races in August, Mamma!"

Mamma did not appear inclined to notice this effusion; and it was the elder daughter, Catherine, who turned the conversation. She was dark where her sister was fair, and retiring in her disposition. We had not yet had five words together from her lips.

"We were very sorry to hear of Mrs. Edward Austen's passing," she managed. "That lady only came to Chawton once within memory, but she left an impression of goodness as well as of fashion, and appears to have been everything that is amiable."

"Thank you," I said. "We have all felt my sister's loss most keenly; and as Mrs. Prowting observes, my brother's children above all. There are no less than eleven little Austens, and the youngest has not yet attained a year of age."[1]

---

[1] It was customary, in Jane Austen's day, to refer to the spouse of a sibling as one's sister or brother. The term *in-law* often referred to step-relations.—*Editor's note.*

Mrs. Prowting lifted up her eyes to Heaven, and then retreated for a moment behind her square of linen.

"Mamma is thinking of William again," Ann observed in a bored tone, "or perhaps of John. They were both of them odious little boys; I am sure I cannot count the times they teazed me unmercifully, and pulled my hair."

"*Ann*," Catherine whispered fiercely. "*Consider where you are.*"

But her sister continued insensible of danger.

"Perhaps your brother will chuse a second wife, Miss Austen," Ann suggested brightly, "should he ever return to Chawton. He will not find the ladies so high in the instep as in Kent! We are all easy here! I should set my cap at him myself—but as he is so *old*, I do not think there could be any fun in it. He shall do very well for Catherine."

"Minx," Mr. Prowting said fondly. "She is a sad baggage, Miss Austen."

"Catherine cares nothing for flirtation or good jokes," Ann added with a curl of her lip, "and would not object to so many children, provided she were left in peace with her harp. Lord, Mamma! Only conceive of the look on Jane Hinton's face, when Catherine was presented as the Squire's wife! How you should love to parade it over the Hintons, with their endless preaching about *entailments* and *usurpers*."

An appalled silence greeted this sally, but as Ann was engaged in adjusting her bodice lace, she failed to notice. Mrs. Prowting had flushed rosily, and her elder daughter could not lift up her eyes. It required only this united weakness, I supposed, for Ann's impudence to rule the Prowting household.

"The Hintons?" my mother innocently enquired. "I do not recollect the name. Are they also our neighbours?"

"Mr. John-Knight Hinton is the son of our late rector, who was a most excellent man," Prowting said with an appearance of discomfiture. "I wish that I could say the same of his son. But Jack Hinton is an indolent fellow, dissatisfied with his station in life, and unequal to improving it by either wit or exertion."

"You are too unkind, Papa." Catherine's countenance was suffused with a blush. "Mr. Hinton's character is good, and his understanding—tho' perhaps not brilliant—"

"—is as high as you may safely look for a beau," her sister observed waspishly.

"*Ann,*" Mrs. Prowting protested.

"The Church would not do for him," continued the magistrate with impatience, "—nor yet the Army; and as he is the youngest child and only son, Mrs. Austen, he has been much spoilt. Tho' now fully five-and-thirty years of age if he is a day, Jack lives in idleness with his elder sister at Chawton Lodge, directly opposite the Great House."

My mother glanced from one Prowting to another in considerable puzzlement. "The Lodge did not pass to the new incumbent, I collect?"

"Dear Mr. Papillon—such a kind gentleman, and so eloquent on the subject of forgiveness—rebuilt the old Rectory when Mrs. Knight gave him the Chawton living several years since," Mrs. Prowting supplied. "But the Lodge was not in that lady's gift; it was formerly the Dower House, and has passed through the female line to the Hinton family."

My mother frowned. "Then I must have seen the place not an hour ago, when you were so kind as to escort me to the Great House gates, Mr. Prowting. I wonder you did not mention it. And Mr. Hinton's Christian name is John-Knight, you say? And he lives in the former Dower House? Are the family at all related to the Kentish Knights?"

It was the Knight family that had adopted my brother Edward as their heir, and the Knight family that had inherited the manors of Chawton, Steventon, and Godmersham that Neddie now enjoyed. There had once been Knights in Hampshire, but they were all died out; and their Kentish cousins had come into these distant properties as a matter of course. My mother's questions were posed in all innocence, but their effect was galvanic.

"Lord!" cried Ann Prowting. "Do you mean to say you are ignorant of what everybody hereabouts knows—that the Hintons and all their relations are the last true descendants of the Hampshire Knights?"

"*Ann,*" her mother attempted once more. "I do not think it is for us—"

"But, Mamma," she retorted impatiently, "it is beyond everything great! Here Jack Hinton has been saying for an *age* that he ought to be Squire of Chawton—and the Squire's mamma don't even know it!"

Chapter 5

Chapters in a Life

Wednesday, 5 July 1809

~

A FLOOD OF BIRDSONG ROUSED ME AT HALF PAST six this morning. I opened my eyes to find the sunlight full in my face; the bedchamber looks south and the window is still undraped. *Strange,* I thought, *to hear no sound of the sea.* The relentless murmur of wave upon shingle was one aspect of Southampton life I should regret.

With consciousness came the memory of the dead man in the cellar; there might be intelligence today of both his name and the nature of his end. I reached for my dressing gown and crept quietly out of the room, determined not to wake my mother—but I need have had no fears for her slumber; the shock and exertion of yesterday, coupled with Mr. Prowting's excellent claret, ensured that she should lie slumbering yet a while.

The peace of this country morning was indescribable, a balm for jangled nerves. I stood in the silent kitchen, and listened to the rustling of some small creature against the exterior boards, the lowing of cattle in the distance, and the crowing of a cock—then threw open the back door and stepped out into the yard. A tin pail hung on a hook nailed to the lintel; I took it up, and moved to the well to draw some water. This, I decided, as the pump moved easily on its oiled hinge and the clear water began to flow, should be the work I would claim within our new household: the drawing of water and the preparation of fires in the early morning, the making of a simple breakfast, when everyone else lay abed. The freedom and quiet of an undisturbed hour should be a luxury beyond everything; indeed, it was all the luxury I desired.

Having escorted us from his dining parlour the previous evening, Mr. Prowting had helped us to lay a simple bed of coals in the kitchen hearth before departing for his own bed. The fire, properly banked, would serve to boil our tea this morning. The cottage boasted no ingenious modern stove, nothing but a spit and a quantity of iron hooks for the arrangement of kettles, and even Martha might find the conditions less than desirable; but Mr. Prowting had pledged himself to the task of securing a few servants among that class of village folk as were accustomed to labour in genteel houses—had several prospects already in mind—should be happy to interview them so early as today, etc., etc.—and should send the likeliest recruits to my mother for final approval. I foresaw little difficulty, delay, or exertion for myself in the business, and was content this morning to set my mother's kettle on the fire.

The task done, I hesitated briefly in the small kitchen. Ought I to dress and walk out into the street, in search of the woman Mrs. Prowting assured me was the best baker of fresh bread in the village? Or could I trust to Providence and my mother's slumber a little longer, and steal a glimpse at the contents of Lord Harold's trunk?

After yesterday's discovery of the corpse, Mr. Prowting had carried my bequest to the henhouse for safekeeping, as I did not think it kind to require the gentleman to enter a stranger's bedchamber. The Rogue's lead key hung heavily in my dressing-gown pocket. I curled my fingers around its length and walked swiftly back out into the yard, in the direction of the outbuildings.

It is in the nature of treasure chests to yield their contents unwillingly. I expected a lengthy engagement with the lock that dangled from the hasp; expected to be reduced to stratagems and tears, blood flowing from my ravaged fingers—but in the event, the key turned in a well-behaved fashion and released the heavy iron pad easily from its bolt.

Barely breathing, I lifted the trunk lid with care.

From Lord Harold's last testament—his wish that I might bring order to his correspondence and somehow construct a narrative from a chaos of events—I had anticipated much confusion of parchment. But it seemed that this morning all my cherished notions were to be o'erthrown. Before my eyes was a compartmented cabinet, as neatly arranged as a solicitor's desk, and filled with all manner of letters bound up tidily in varicolored ribbons. In one area of the cabinet was a place reserved for leather-bound copybooks; in another was a grouping of ledgers. Several rolled documents, when unfolded, were revealed as ships' charts and battlefield maps—at a glance, I could discern the entrepôts of the Indian Ocean, and a plan of the city of Paris.

One last despairing hope was finally laid to rest. I had not allowed myself to form an idea of a single piece of paper, hastily scrawled with the word *Jane* and sealed in black wax. But the idea had formed itself even so. I longed for a parting gesture from the man—a bit of foolscap I might carry in my reticule like a relic of the True Cross. But there was nothing. How could there be? Lord Harold had written his will in anticipation of that duel; but never had he truly believed he would die.

I reached for a packet of letters at random and slid the first from beneath its bonds of faded blue silk.

It was dated January, 1770, Eton College—and bore the direction of Eugenie, Duchess of Wilborough.

My dearest Mamma—
    I must thank you for the box of comfits you sent down with Attenborough, for they have made me the toast of the form, as you might expect. My

*brother would have denied me the whole, but that I
hid the parcel amidst the soiled linen until he was
safely away in his own house, and brought out the
feast last evening with a stub of candle that I had
secured in my gown. I received twelve lashes across
the buttocks this morning when the Crime was
discovered, but care nothing for that; my
alienation from the Realm of College at present
merely affords me the occasion to compose a proper
letter of thanks to my most Beloved Mother . . .*

Such assurance! In 1770, he had been all of ten
years old—and I was not yet born. I held the childish
scrawl between my fingers and tried to imagine him:
thin, lanky, with a shock of blond Trowbridge hair. He
had cultivated even then the talents of a spy.

I ran my fingers swiftly through the packet: there
were more than twenty letters preserved from Eton
days. Had the blue satin ribbon been Eugenie's? I
folded the missive carefully and returned it to its
place, selecting as I did so another quantity of en-
velopes.

*Calcutta
17 August 1784*

*My dear Fox—
I received your last, written nearly six months
ago, only yesterday; and must assume that the news
of Whig politics it contains is now irrelevant. I
cannot read your strictures on my respected employer,
however, without offering this response. You speak of*

crimes—of offences that stink in the eyes of the
Nation—with all the fervour of one unduly
influenced by Edmund Burke. And yet, of what can
you honestly accuse him? Mr. Hastings has engaged
in all manner of peccadilloes: a devious military
campaign against the Afghans; a bit of extortion in
the matter of Benares; an injudicious killing of a
native ruler; a duel in which he failed to despatch
his principal enemy and thus ensured the man
would poison his Company's councils ever after. But
against this accounting is all the glory of Mr.
Hastings himself: a cultivated mind that has
mastered both Urdu and Bengali; a commanding
knowledge of the historical, geographic, and
commercial truths of the Subcontinent; a subtlety of
manner and appreciation for the customs of the
region that have won him numerous friends, vital to
our interest. Should this bill of Pitt's succeed in
wresting the Company's power to the side of
Government, it will ensure Mr. Hastings's quitting
his post—a loss not only for the East India
Company, but for the Crown. I must urge you to
transcend the petty divisions of party and class. Far
more is at stake than a toss of the dice at Brooks's.

You will be happy to learn that I have succeeded
in winning to my side the Princess of Mysore, who
proclaims herself to have abandoned everything for
love of me; or love of my pocketbook, as the case
may prove. I anticipate a scented paradise in her
tent these next three months as she follows me to
Madras.

*Do not die of apoplexy, old fellow, before I
glimpse the cliffs of Dover again. My exile shall
conclude in another year, at which point I intend
to cut up my father's peace most dreadfully—*

I reread this letter twice in some puzzlement. I
knew Lord Harold to have been an intimate of the late
Whig leader, Charles James Fox; yet never had he mentioned a period of employment with Warren Hastings,
the former Governor-General of Bengal. Indeed, I had
not understood the Rogue to have lived in India at all.
Mr. Hastings, on the other hand, was remotely con-
nected with my family, as the putative father of my
cousin, Eliza de Feuillide; he was a man whose reputation we had been taught to both revere and suspect.
And what was the exile to which Lord Harold referred?
Had he fallen out with his father at the tender age of
four-and-twenty? I could well believe it possible. A
duel—an elopement—a significant loss at cards . . . or
simply the defection of his interest from the Tory party
to the Whigs, might have achieved it.

Another letter, this time from 1788:

*His Majesty's bilious attacks continue apace,
with the novel variation of insanity: this morning
he cawed like a crow and defecated in his bed,
called the Queen a whore and a poxmonger, while
Her Majesty cried out and could not be comforted,
tho' her Ladies attempted to restrain her. His
madness certainly increases, and the moment for
the Prince to seize power is nearly ripe . . .*

And this, from a year earlier:

> *Mrs. Fitzherbert is brought to bed of a son, and how we shall prevent a revolution when the truth is out, I know not—*

The henhouse was growing hot. I was aware that a considerable interval had passed, and that my mother would soon be rising. I surveyed the wealth of packets with dismay. There was too much to be read, too much to digest in an ordered fashion, beginning with the earliest dates, to achieve much. I should have to devise a more orderly method—and I must secure a place of safety and solitude in which to work.

I replaced the correspondence and was about to close the chest's heavy lid, when of a sudden I reached for one of the leather-bound copybooks. Perhaps, in his journal, he might once have made mention of me . . .

> *Paris*
> *8 September 1793*
>
> *I walked out into the Rue de Sévigné this morning convinced that I should be seized and thrown into the tumbrel myself as a renegade and an Englishman, and caring little for the outcome. If my head were to fall to the blade, what would it matter, in the end? There are corpses piled beneath the trees of the Luxembourg and the stink is unimaginable. What we require is a cleansing fire—a fire that might rage like a storm about the limestone walls of this city and burn its evils to*

ash, as the souls of the dead in India are sent up in smoke on the holy river of Benares. This is Liberty, then, that Burke was wont to prattle of: The freedom to exact revenge for the inequities of life; to tear down and trample beneath one's feet all that is beautiful and forever denied; to cut and maim as one has been maimed. Last night, as I stood beneath the vaulted walk of the Palais de Justice, I saw the tumbrel go by: and in it a young girl with her hair shorn for the blade, her face as white as her cotton shift: Jouvel's daughter, with whom I danced the quadrille two summers ago at the château near Cluny. Her brother stood beside her: face stark and shadowed, an expression of rage about the lips—quite useless. A smear of shit on his brow where someone had insulted him. He was perhaps fifteen. At that age I thought of nothing but riding to hounds. They are both dead this morning—they were dead even as I watched them roll past, and stepped backwards against the archway's wall that they might not recognise me— might not hope for a fleeting second in their own salvation. The long brown hair is tossed like offal into the basket, her terrified gaze fixed on God or Hell—one and the same, for those who ride in the tumbrel. I could kill myself for failing to save them. I could place a pistol against my head and pull the trigger. All that stops me is my duty to the boy—

I slowly closed the book, my hands no longer steady.

He had given me much in this cavalier bequest: the key to a lifetime of agonies and dreams. I had believed that I understood his character—I had even thought that I loved him. But it was clear to me now that I had tasted only a draught of the deep waters that o'erwhelmed Lord Harold's life.

"Jane? Jane!"

My fingers clutched around the copybook, I gazed quickly through the henhouse door.

"Henry!" I cried. "Good God—where did you spring from?"

"Alton," my brother replied carelessly. "I keep a bank there, you know. What do you mean by sitting in the middle of a poultry yard in your dressing gown at eight o'clock in the morning?"

Chapter 6

Coincidence, or Pattern?

~

IT IS IMPOSSIBLE TO DESCRIBE MY ASTONISHMENT at this sudden apparition of my brother, in a place that—although not wholly alien to him—was nonetheless the very last in which I expected to find him. I had understood our Henry to be fixed with his wife, the aforementioned Eliza de Feuillide, at Godmersham with all our Kentish party; and failing Kent, I should have expected to learn that he and Eliza were returned to London, where they intended a removal to a new home in Sloane Street. Henry's banking concerns had fared so well of late, and his affluence was so obvious, that the affairs of the Alton branch of Austen, Gray & Vincent might suitably have been left in the hands of his partners for the duration of the summer months;

and yet, here was Henry: large as life and impatient for his breakfast.

As I rose from the henhouse floor, he sauntered towards the chest. "Good Lord! Is this the Rogue's Treasure?"

"What do you know of it?" I demanded indignantly.

"Half of Alton is talking about this article, my dear; besides, Mamma told me the whole the moment I walked in the door."

"She is already awake?" I peered out at the sun. "I had no notion the morning was so advanced."

"The cask is undoubtedly from the Subcontinent, and must have been carved a hundred years ago at a pasha's orders," Henry murmured, ignoring me entirely. "Observe the figures cut into the teak!"

"They are most indecent," I said primly, "and I beg you will not draw them to Mamma's notice."

"I suppose his lordship must once have visited Bengal."

"I believe, Henry, that he lived there some years—and was in a position of some trust to your wife's benefactor, Mr. Hastings."

"Lord Harold knew old Warren?" Henry's startled expression was comical, as tho' Mr. Hastings was the preserve of the Austens alone, instead of a man who had encountered half the world and commanded the rest. "I shall have to tax him with the acquaintance when next we meet. He is getting on in years, Jane—must be five-and-seventy if he is a day—but he would remember such a figure as the Rogue. Should you like me to lock this in the Alton bank?"

"Certainly not! The chest shall ascend to my bedroom, if you please. You may carry it there immediately, like the good brother you are."

"Be so good as to hold my coat." He drew off the elegant article and bent to lift the chest.

"Heavy enough to be filled with gold," he gasped. "Is that what he left you?"

"No questions, Henry."

"Very well. But you might reward me for my labour."

"Only when you explain your presence in Hampshire!"

"I left Eliza with young Fanny," he managed as I led him, staggering with the chest's weight, into the cottage, "and set out with Neddie and Cass from Kent two days ago. Neddie's chaise broke an axle not far from Brompton, and he has put up at the Bell until the equipage is repaired. I rode on with the intention of making your minds easy. I reached the George late last night—and learned you were already established in Chawton."

"My sister was not hurt, I hope, by the accident to the chaise?"

Cassandra had suffered greatly during an unfortunate overturning we experienced near Lyme, some years before, and I did not like to think of her cast down with the head-ache in a strange inn.

"Not a whit—so do not be exciting Mamma with your talk of injury," Henry admonished me. "This seems a comfortable little place," he added doubtfully, as he set down the chest on the kitchen floor and peered through the doorway to the sparsely-furnished rooms. "Could do with a bit of paint. Something bright and cheerful, in the yellow line."

"Thank you," I returned with heavy sarcasm. "Perhaps you could find us a painter among your Alton acquaintance? And a manservant? Or possibly a cook?"

"I cannot spare above a few days in the neighbourhood, Jane," he assured me hastily. "I suggest you consult Mr. Prowting. He dearly loves to dispose of other people's lives. Have you any coffee?"

"You shall have to be content with tea." I glanced at the kettle; my supply of water had entirely boiled away while I sat in the henhouse. "The well is in the yard. After you have seen Lord Harold's legacy safely beneath my bed, you may employ your talents with bucket and pump while I repair upstairs to dress."

"IT IS THE ODDEST THING," HENRY OBSERVED AN hour later as we walked out into the Street—as the London to Gosport road is termed where it winds through Chawton village. We were gone on the errand of discovering the local bread baker—my mother had sorely missed her customary toast. "*You* enter the cottage for the first time, only to discover a dead man; while I am greeted at my Alton branch with news of a mysterious burglary. I must consider my decision to descend into Hampshire this week as a matter of Providence."

"Burglary," I repeated in a lowered tone, and glanced about me at the sparse population of local folk: two children and their mother, a market basket over her arm, who drove a flock of geese before them in the direction of Alton; and a labourer engaged in shifting a quantity of grain from his dray into his cottage yard. None of these persons so much as offered us a *good morning,* or pulled a forelock; the children, at least, stared openly at the strange lady who had found a corpse in her cellar.

"I was met with the tale upon my arrival at the George," Henry continued. "The publican—Burbridge? Berlin?"

"Barlow," I supplied.

"—thought that I had been summoned to the place. *'Ah, Mr. Austen,'* he said, with obvious relief. *'You've come, then, about the bank.'*"

"What about the bank?" I demanded, frowning.

"Naturally I enquired. It seems that poor Gray"—by this he meant Mr. Edward-William Gray, his partner in Alton—"had been suffering every kind of anxiety that morning. The windows of Number Ten High Street were forced, if you will credit it—glass lying about the carpet, chairs overturned, and all our papers in a considerable disorder. Gray had spent much of yesterday attempting to determine what, if anything, had been stolen."

"And?"

"He cannot make head or tail of the business. Neither our post bills nor our banknotes were touched."[1]

---

[1] At this time, country branches of London banks were authorized to print notes backed by currency held in their London branches. For a full description of Henry Austen's banking activities, see "Jane Austen's Banker Brother: Henry Thomas Austen of Austen & Co., 1801–1816," by Dr. Clive Caplan; *Persuasions* (Jane Austen Society of North America), No. 20, 1998, pp. 69–90.—*Editor's note.*

My brother Henry has made a considerable fortune in recent years as a payroll agent for several valuable regiments around the country, including some in Hampshire, Kent, and Derbyshire. He serves, in essence, as go-between for the disbursement of salaries to officers and enlisted men, which sums are sent out by the Paymaster General in London to regimental representatives such as Henry. The role of agent is a coveted one, held in the gift of each regiment's Colonel; and that Henry has secured so valuable a living, may be attributed to his polished manners, his knack for cultivating The Great, his former commission in the Oxfordshire Militia, and the connexions of his wife—who is everywhere received in Society, and does not hesitate to turn her acquaintance to advantage. Henry's prosperity has induced my brother Frank to become another partner of the London concern, bringing naval patronage within Henry's orbit; and if I suspected that Henry occasionally turned a profit on the negotiated sale of commissions in prized regiments, which we are taught to consider beyond the pale of the law, I have never taxed him with the subject.

"What, then, can have been the burglars' object?" I enquired.

"I have not the smallest notion." He hesitated. "And that is not the only oddity. Leaving that Bengal chest aside—Mamma tells me you have had an interview with Lord Harold Trowbridge's solicitor."

"Mr. Chizzlewit. Yes—he came to me yesterday

before dinner. It was in the act of securing the chest belowstairs that we discovered the corpse."

"Your solicitor paid a call on Gray in all his state not two days ago—lackeys and trunks behind—enquiring your direction in Chawton. Curious gentleman, by all accounts."

"But perfectly respectable," I returned.

"All the same—he *did* draw notice, Jane. The better part of Alton was positively agog at his errand. I heard talk of pirates' treasure and a king's ransom of jewels—not to mention the name of *Austen*—everywhere. Do you think it possible that this burglary of my branch was an attempt to secure whatever Chizzlewit carried in that heavy great chest of yours?"

For all his style and badinage, Henry is possessed of considerable understanding, and not above speaking plainly when necessity absolutely requires it.

"I think it very likely," I replied. "No doubt your burglar believed a bank the properest place for safekeeping such a bequest. I am sorry for your trouble, Henry, but indeed I had no notion of causing it."

My brother cast me a sidelong glance. He would not attempt to force my communication; but having been a little acquainted with the Trowbridge clan in London, he was naturally curious. "If you should ever wish—if there is a matter of a legacy involved, and you require advice as to the terms of investment—in short, dear Jane, I should be happy to serve you in any way I can. As banker or brother."

"Thank you. His lordship was far too discreet to ruin me with gold, however. Lord Harold offered me *carte blanche* neither in death nor in life. The solicitor delivered a quantity of papers only."

"So Mamma said. But I made certain you were giving her a Banbury tale. Why should anyone attempt to steal old letters?"

"Perhaps with the object of turning them to good use. All of London and half the Continent appear in his lordship's communications."

Henry stopped short in the middle of Chawton, his gaze suddenly intent. "You never mean *blackmail*, Jane?"

"Why not?"

He whistled softly. "This places a different complexion entirely on that wretched fellow you found in the cellar, my dear girl. If the dead man was intent upon the same errand—and came to his end in an ugly fashion—"

"By my own reckoning, the man had been dead some time," I said gently. "Days before the existence of the chest was even known in the neighbourhood. I cannot believe the poor man's demise had anything to do with Lord Harold's papers. I *will* not believe it."

Henry's eyebrows rose. "Very well. Believe what you like. Have you another explanation?"

"Did you not know that our house is cursed?" I demanded lightly. "—Or perhaps it is more properly the entire Austen family that labours under ill-fortune. I was told as much by young Toby Baigent, of Symond's Farm, upon my arrival."

"Village nonsense!"

"All the same—I fear that Neddie has managed his

tenants ill, or at the very least with a want of proper attention. He has excited considerable feeling among the yeoman class with his disposition of houses and farmland. Moreover, his ownership of the Great House—indeed, his right to all his Hampshire estates—is apparently contested by an upstart clergyman's son, resident in the Lodge, and claiming to be the last true heir to the Hampshire Knights."

"Not Jack Hinton?" Henry exclaimed.

I turned to stare at him. "You are acquainted with the gentleman's name?"

"With his name and his entire history."

"I suppose Mr. Hinton thought that as Edward was no more than a jumped-up clergyman's son himself, he might as well make the attempt. We were treated to the entire history last evening."

"The fellow is a complete flat, Jane! And a dead bore into the bargain! He is forever writing tedious letters under the advisement of his solicitors, and delivering them to Neddie at Accounting Day. Lord!"

"You might have told me, Henry," I returned in exasperation. "Has a protracted residence in London completely deprived you of that knowledge of a country village in which you were reared? The Hintons appear to be related to half the families in the surrounding parts; Mrs. Prowting related the whole to us only last evening. The indignation of all Chawton is allied against the Austens. We are seen as yet another example of Neddie's abuse of privilege: the indigent females of the family, thrust upon the bosom of the village to the detriment of the true heirs of the Great House."

"Is it as bad as all that?"

"I should not be surprised if it were. When Edward *does* descend upon Chawton in a few days' time, I intend to wring his neck!"

"He has been sadly distracted of late," my brother admitted soberly. "Grief will work a wondrous change in the most frivolous of men. I was forced to read *sermons* after dinner in the drawing-room at Godmersham, Jane, instead of the plays we formerly chose to amuse ourselves. If you could have observed little Marianne yawning over her prayer book of an evening—!"

We had strolled nearly to the end of the Street, observed only by a number of children too young to be helping with the hay-making and three elderly persons who preserved a cautionary silence. The village was pretty and unspoilt enough, with hops growing verdantly on the left hand and a line of cottages on the right. There were no shops or tradesmen in Chawton—commerce being the purview of Alton, a mile distant—but at the approach to one thatched house, we observed an inviting basket with a dozen loaves of bread wrapped in white cloth.

"The baker," Henry murmured.

We halted and my brother drew out his purse. The woman who lived in the place—Mrs. Cuttle, as she informed us—appeared in the doorway, wiping floured hands on her smudged apron. Henry bought two loaves—one for my mother and a second he intended to consume on our walk. "Do you supply much of the bread to households hereabouts?" he enquired easily of Mrs. Cuttle.

"That I do, sir. Are you staying at the Great House, with the rest of Mr. Middleton's guests?"

"Sadly not. I am merely taking in Chawton on my road to London. But my sister, Miss Austen, is lately come to the late bailiff's cottage."

Mrs. Cuttle's eyes widened and without a word, she dropped a swift curtsey.

"Would you be so good as to deliver a loaf of your excellent bread each day to my mother and sisters?" Henry suggested. "We should be infinitely obliged."

The woman's gaze fell. "Take the loaves ye have, and welcome, sir," she said, and without another word, she turned back inside her cottage and firmly latched the door.

"Well," I said into the silence. "I must be glad that Martha Lloyd's culinary accomplishments include baking."

"There, Libby," interjected a breathless accent, "I've misplaced my key *again,* and what Old Philmore will have to say to me if it is not found, I do not like to think!"

A lady of middle age and neat tho' shabby appearance was exiting the cottage adjacent to Mrs. Cuttle's. She patted her shawl and reticule with one gloved hand as she spoke, as if much distracted; in her other hand was clutched a posy of flowers; a pair of spectacles perched on her sharp nose, and what was visible of her hair was quite gray.

"*Three shillings* he demanded for the copy last time, and *where* such a sum is to be found I'm sure I *cannot* say. Is it possible, my dear, that one of your *delightful* children has made away with it as a prank?"

She surveyed us without recognition, somewhat surprised to find that Mrs. Cuttle—for so I assumed *Libby* to be—was nowhere in sight.

"May I be of assistance, ma'am?" Henry cried, approaching the distracted lady with a satiric light in his eye I knew too well. "Perhaps you set down your key when you took up your flowers."

"My flowers?" she enquired, blinking about her doubtfully. "So very *kind* . . . but I do not think we are acquainted . . . or perhaps I am being *foolish* again . . . is it Mr. Thrace?"

"Mr. Henry Austen at your service." He raised his hat obligingly.

"Austen?" she repeated, and peered from Henry to me. "Did you say *Austen?*"

"I did, ma'am. And you are . . . ?"

"Miss Benn." Her faded blue eyes travelled the length of my brother's form with that same expression of doubt.[2]

"May I beg leave to present my sister?" Henry's glance was eloquent of mischief. "Miss Jane Austen, lately arrived at the former bailiff's cottage."

"Bailiff's cottage?" Miss Benn echoed vaguely. "I do not think . . ." Comprehension broke upon the

---

[2] Miss Benn is held to be the original from which the character of Miss Bates was drawn in *Emma.—Editor's note.*

lady's countenance. "The corpse! So very silly of me, and the whole village talking of nothing else. Then you will be the *Squire's* family! The ones who have come into a quantity of jewels! I *had heard* something to the effect that you would be arriving this summer— I am not sure—from Mrs. Prowting, perhaps, or Mr. Baigent?—"

"Shall I hold your flowers while you search for that key?" Henry enquired.

"My flowers . . . ? I only intended to step across to the church—dear St. Nicholas's, but of course you will *know* that is the church's name, if you are indeed a member of the Austen family—I often do the flowers of a morning, I think it makes such a *difference* to the air of a church, do not you?—My brother, Mr. John Benn, Rector of Farringdon, has often wished he could summon *my* posies to his vestry—so of course I don't really *require* the door to be locked, as I am sure Mrs. Cuttle will kindly keep an eye on the cottage for me; tho' Old Philmore is *terribly* particular, quite the *ogre,* Mr. Austen, if you understand my meaning, and much given to *threats* if he believes his property is liable to come to harm—tho' how such a disreputable and *sad* little place could possibly deteriorate further, is quite difficult to say . . ."

She plucked at her shawl as she spoke, as though conscious of a draught despite the July heat, her near-sighted gaze roaming distractedly from myself to the half-open door to the basket of loaves before Mrs. Cuttle's door; and of a sudden, I pitied her.

"We are walking that way ourselves," I said, "and should be glad to accompany you into the church."

"That is excessively kind of you, Miss Austen! Let me just leave the door off the latch—and if perhaps Libby would not *mind* casting her eye over the place now and again while I am away—and perhaps *fibbing* on my behalf if Old Philmore should materialise . . ."

The steady clip-clop of a pair of horses put paid to this speech, and a beatific smile suffused Miss Benn's withered features. "And there is Mr. Middleton! Such an *excellent* man," she informed us, "and so exceptionally considerate, despite the *numerous* cares of the children. The Squire is indeed fortunate in the *character* of his tenant."

Two gentlemen were approaching from the direction of the Great House, their horses—a young chestnut, and a strengthy grey—progressing at a walk. One I judged to be in his middle fifties: stout, ruddy of feature, and a model of deportment in the saddle. The other was a gentleman of perhaps half his companion's age. Beautifully arrayed in the best Bond Street fashion, he possessed the easy seat and careless grace of a punishing rider to hounds. This must be Mr. Middleton and his son; I had understood from Neddie that there were several children, left motherless some years before.

Beside me, Henry let slip a low and speculative whistle.

"Devil take it!" he muttered. "What has Julian Thrace to do in Chawton, of all places?"

**Letter from Lord Harold Trowbridge to Eugenie,
Duchess of Wilborough, dated Eton College, 23 January
1767; three leaves quarto, wove; no watermark.**
(British Museum, Wilborough Papers, Austen bequest)

My dear Mamma——

*Benning will say that I ott not to adress you in so
Informal a Way, you being amung the Grate of the
Land; but he is a Prig and a Swot and I do not care for
his vews on what is owd to a Duchess, tho I must serve
him as Fag. I shall give one of the soverains you left me
to Wilkins at the Gate, and he will post this letter
without Benning having to know.*

*I miss you eckseedingly, after all the happy times of
the holydays, and I cannot help crying at night in my cot
when the others have gone to sleep. I recall the noise of
the streets around home, and the fires in the Park, and
the smell of rosting chestnuts, and the good steemy smell
of Poll my pony when we have had a run in Rotten
Row, and I feel such a desire to leave this place and be
back with you and Nanny that I have three times tryed
to run away. My efferts have not been graced with
success. After the last, I could not sit down for two
days, Mr. Pilfer being librul with his switch and
Benning having topped the whole with a slipper aplyed
to my backside. I hate Benning but my brother says he is
a Great Gun and I must do as he says. I hope he gets the
Pox as some of the older boys have got it and two have
died. Perhaps if you are fearful of the Pox you will send
for me? Pilfer says he shall write to Papa if I run away
a forth time, so I shall not.*

It seems an age until the end of term. You will not forget me?

When I am grown I shall take you back to live in Paris and you will never cry in the evenings when Papa is away again, and I shall never cry for missing you.

Your loving son,
Harry

Chapter 7

The Bond Street Beau

MR. JULIAN THRACE, AS HENRY LATER INFORMED me, is the latest sensation of the *ton:* a gentleman who appears to have sprung from exactly nowhere as recently as January, breaking upon Fashionable London with all the force of a thunderclap: his looks, his air, his manners, and his social graces being of the finest. For a young man of two-and-twenty, who possesses neither title nor fortune, to gain the kind of introductions Mr. Thrace everywhere obtained, was no less extraordinary than it was wondered at; he was carried into Carlton House on the arm of the Earl of Holbrook; was proposed for membership at White's by as many as half a dozen of its standing members; was admitted to the most exclusive assemblies without hesitation; and was no more suspected of seduction by the careful mammas parading their daughters in the Green Park of an afternoon, than was the local man of the cloth.

"But who *is* he, Henry?" I demanded, as my brother regaled me with the tale during our return to the cottage.

"An orphan, reared for some years abroad," my brother replied. "His history is a delicate one—and thus discourages the impertinent from delving too far into Mr. Thrace's business. It is said that he is the illegitimate son of a peer, and will shortly be proclaimed that gentleman's heir, as the nobleman in question has no legitimate male issue; and on the basis of rumour and his expectations alone, Thrace has been living on tick for the past six months.[1] I admire the fellow's audacity; but I wonder at his prospects. Those of us in the banking profession—and any number have been applied to, Jane, for the support of Mr. Thrace's debts—have taken to calling him the South Sea Bubble, from a belief that he is just such an object of speculation, and likely to leave any number of his current backers awash in future."

Mr. Middleton had reined in his horse, and deigned to recognise the brother of his landlord in a very abrupt but kindhearted fashion; had suffered an introduction to myself, and welcomed me stoutly to Chawton; had offered up his young friend Thrace to the notice of the Austen party; and avowed that he

[1] To "live on tick" was to live on credit.—*Editor's note.*

intended that very morning to call upon my mother and offer his deepest congratulations on her present fortunate state, in possessing the cottage.

"—Tho' I cannot admire the manner of your welcome," he observed with a sober look. "My deepest sympathies, Miss Austen, on the distress of your discovery in the cellar. A most unfortunate business—quite unaccountable."

"And certain to be much talked of," Miss Benn added in a sprightly fashion.

"We must suppose, however, that the affair will be concluded with despatch. Mr. Prowting is a commendable magistrate when necessity affords him occasion to act; he will already have communicated with the coroner, whom I believe must be summoned from Basingstoke." The invocation of so august a town conferred a certain weight to Mr. Middleton's words, and we all fell silent in contemplation of Death and its exigencies. Mr. Thrace, I observed, looked suitably grave; but as he uttered not a syllable, I had no opportunity to judge of his sense.

The gentlemen of the Great House went on their way, being bound for Alton and some trifling errands among the tradesmen, but not before Mr. Middleton recollected to issue a general invitation to dine with his party the following evening. As the gratifying notice included Henry and the simpering Miss Benn, we parted in the middle of the Street with satisfaction on all sides.

"I am determined to return to the George with all possible haste," Henry breathed, "so as to be certain that my partner, Mr. Gray, refuses Julian Thrace's depredations on the Alton branch. Burglary and corpses are as nothing, I assure you, Jane, when compared to the demands of a Bond Street Beau."

"You are too cruel, Henry. I suppose many a warm man must be similarly stingy."

"I am sure I do not wish penury on any of my fellows," my brother protested as we parted before the cottage door, "but I should feel more sanguine regarding the monies disbursed to Mr. Thrace's account, did I have an inkling of *which* peer he purports to belong to."

"Surely the rumour-mills have supplied a name."

"They have supplied two, Jane," Henry returned. "—The Earl of Holbrook, who carried Thrace into Carlton House; and the Viscount St. Eustace, who is so ill and bedridden he is said to rarely quit Eustace House in Berkshire. Both men have sired only daughters, and both are as rich as Croesus. Rather than pass their titles and wealth to distant cousins, they think to legitimate babes born on the wrong side of the blanket."

"Thrace himself lays claim to no one?"

"What would be the sport in it, if he did? The betting-book at Tattersall's is offering odds of seven-to-one for the Viscount; but at Brooks's Club they will have it all for the Earl."

It was extraordinary, I thought as Henry rode off in the direction of Alton, what men could adopt as the point of a wager. Lord Harold's visage rose suddenly before my eyes—an intimate of Brooks's Club these thirty years, perhaps. I missed him then sharply and inconsolably; for the Rogue would have taken Mr. Thrace's measure in an instant.

THE DAY PASSED SWIFTLY IN ALL THE BUSINESS OF unpacking, my sole relief from the incessant chatter of my mother having come in the form of a visit from Mr. Prowting and his eldest daughter. He came to be important and grave; Catherine brought a gift of eggs and cheese and a palpable desire for conversation.

"I bear sad tidings, Mrs. Austen," the magistrate pronounced. "Mr. Munro—Coroner of Basingstoke, and no mere surgeon, but a most accomplished physician in his way, and a creditable player at whist—has arrived in Alton not half an hour ago. He is even now engaged in an examination of the unfortunate person discovered by myself and Miss Austen"—this, with a bow for me—"in your cellar."

"And has he decided who the poor fellow is, Mr. Prowting?" my mother enquired with an expression of interest.

"One Shafto French, as I understand—a nephew of Old Philmore, who is a tenant of Mr. Edward Austen and the freeholder of several cottages in the neighbourhood."

"Are the Frenches a respectable family?"

"They are certainly a prodigious one. You cannot spit anywhere on the ground between here and Alton—begging your pardon, ma'am—without striking a French, or a Philmore, come to that. Good Hampshire stock, all of them, and long-established in the neighbourhood; but Shafto was given to drink and indigence. It is not to be wondered at, after all, that he should end as he did. Still, he leaves a hopeful family behind—and this death will go hard on his wife, Jemima."

"Can Mr. Munro say at all how French died?" I asked.

"Not as yet."

"—Nor how he came to be in our cellar?" my mother interposed.

"Such questions, dear lady, may be answered in good time," the magistrate replied. "Due to the sad state of the corpse, Mr. Munro gives it as his opinion that the inquest into French's demise should brook no delay. As magistrate, I should have liked to await the arrival in Chawton of Mr. Edward Austen, whom you have given me to understand is even now on his road from Kent; but in matters of physick I have no authority. I must give way. The inquest is to be held at two o'clock."

"Today?" I enquired.

"Indeed. In less than three hours' time, in the private parlour at the George. Naturally, I shall be present."

"I should like to attend," I said firmly.

Mr. Prowting's eyes bulged from his head, and I am convinced he choked a little as he formed his reply. "My dear Miss Austen, there is not the slightest need. Not the slightest need. Naturally you feel some interest in the man's history, having found him as you did—"

"—And some responsibility, as well, to inform the coroner's panel of what I observed," I rejoined calmly.

"You cannot dissuade me, Mr. Prowting—I am determined to go. I should be very much obliged, however, if you would convey me to Alton in company with yourself."

"My daughter, as you see, is a veritable ghoul when it comes to inquests and murder, Mr. Prowting," my mother observed. "I cannot count the number of panels Jane has attended; and given evidence, too."

Catherine Prowting, who overlistened the whole, gave an audible gasp.

"Many are the hours I have spent in enlarging upon the subject," my mother continued, "but Jane will not see that no respectable man will take up with a lady who is so mad for blood. It is unnatural in a woman. But she will not understand me. She will not listen to reason. I am sure, Mr. Prowting, that you suffer similar trials yourself—being the father of daughters."

"An *inquest* cannot be the proper place for a lady," Mr. Prowting said doubtfully.

"In the present case, sir," I replied with dignity, "I believe attendance to be my duty. The man was found in this house; and surely we must learn the truth, at all costs, of how he came here."

The magistrate looked for aid to his daughter; but such a recourse must be useless. Catherine Prowting was pale as death, her hand gripping the back of my mother's chair; and in an instant she had slipped to the floor insensible.

. . . .

WE PREVAILED UPON MR. PROWTING TO LEAVE HIS daughter a little while in our care, and Catherine appeared—when consciousness was regained—not averse to the suggestion. We laid her upon the sopha in the sitting room, and my mother went in search of vinegar-water, while the magistrate patted her hand in loving awkwardness.

"You will never be as strong as your sisters," he told her fondly. "It is the head-ache, I suppose?"

"Yes, Papa," she said tearfully.

"Well, well—rest a little in Miss Austen's care, and then return to your mother. But do not be alarming her with talk of an *indisposition*. You know what her nerves are."

"Yes, Papa."

I saw the magistrate to the door and closed it quietly, so as not to disturb my suffering neighbour; and indeed, tho' returned to her senses, Catherine looked very ill. Had it been the talk of blood and corpses that had unnerved her so?

"I understand you will be dining at the Great House tomorrow," she managed as I dipped a cloth into the vinegar-water my mother had provided, and prepared to bathe her temples. "We are all to go as well, and my sister is devoting the better part of the morning to new-dressing her hair."

"At your sister's age—a period of high spirits, charm, and natural bloom—one's appearance is of consuming interest," I observed.

"Perhaps. There are four years' difference in age between myself and Ann—she is but two-and-twenty;

but I confess I have never wasted a tenth part of the hours that Ann believes necessary to the perfection of her toilette. Of course, I have not her beauty; but is it not remarkable, Miss Austen, that the more beauty one possesses, the more one is required to nurture and support it?"

"A tedious business," I agreed with a laugh, "that must make the disappearance of all bloom a blessing rather than a pity!—As I have reason to know."

"But you are charming," Catherine protested.

"I am in my thirty-fourth year, my dear, and must put charm aside at last."

"I have lived the better part of my life with Ann's beauty and foibles as though they were quite another member of the family. There is more than enough of *them* to supply two women, I assure you—and when such a prospect as dinner at the Great House is in view, and in the company of a Bond Street Beau, there is hardly room for us both at Prowtings!"

This was bitterness, indeed, let slip so readily to a virtual stranger; but not all sisters are happy in possessing that perfect understanding and cordiality that have always obtained between Cassandra and me. I gazed at Catherine—at the sweetness of expression in her mild dark eyes, and the nut-brown indifference of her hair; and understood that a lifetime of denial and self-effacement had been hers: supported almost unconsciously by the fond indulgence of parents whose collusion in their youngest daughter's vanity, though perhaps at first unwitting, was now become the sole method of managing her.

"That is enough vinegar," Catherine said abruptly. "I am very well now, I thank you—indeed, I cannot understand how I should have come to be overpowered in the first place. It is so very silly—"

"We were too frank in our conversation. We should have considered that you were not equal to it."

"I ought to have been, Miss Austen. I ought to be equal to . . . many things." She turned towards the window and stretched out her arms, as though she would fly from its casement to a wider world. I had been that way myself, once, in a small vicarage in Hampshire; I had dreamt of crossing the seas—of being an Irishman's wife—had exulted in hope of adventure and limitless skies, and chafed against the boundaries of glebe and turnpike. A surge of fellow-feeling from my breast to Catherine's, then; a recognition of hopes blighted and dreams put away.

"Is Ann your only sister?" I enquired.

"Elizabeth, my elder, is long since married," Catherine replied. "We were all so unfortunate as to lose my two brothers to illness and accident; William being carried off while at school in Winchester; and John but a year later at home."

I had carelessly used the very same names in my request for a manservant; how Mr. Prowting must have felt it, and misunderstood my levity's cause! I felt a surge of colour to my cheeks. "You have all my sympathy. Were they very young?"

"William was fifteen, and John but nine."

"How dreadful!" I thought of Mrs. Prowting—of the black-edged handkerchief that appeared to be wedded to her palm—with a deeper comprehension. Despair and grief may appear to greater advantage when writ on an elegant form; but Mrs. Prowting's large, comfortable bulk, though better suited to laughter, held as much right to suffering as my own.[2]

I saw Catherine over the stile in the meadow, with profuse thanks for the gift of eggs and cheese; and as she walked slowly into her house—into that orgy of preparation and exhilarated transport in which she was expected to take no part—I went back to the cottage.

If I hurried, I might just have time to read another of Lord Harold's papers before I journeyed to Alton, and met the coroner.

---

[2] Jane makes a similar observation of her character Mrs. Musgrove, in *Persuasion*, who has lost a troublesome son in the navy.—*Editor's note.*

Excerpt from the diaries of Lord Harold Trowbridge, dated 12 December 1782, on board the Indiaman *Delos*, bound for Bombay.

... it is no bad thing to be a young man of two-and-twenty, with the Paradise of the Subcontinent looming off the bow, and all the riches of a sultan's court waiting to be plucked. There are the women lodged in all the acceptable quarters—no longer young, or lacking in fortune and looks, and in short the very dross of English gentility, sent out as brides to men they have never met and a life in a climate likely to kill them before very long. They are desperate for sport and fun before the voyage should be over—knowing, from the most ignorant of presentiments, that marriage to a stranger cannot be very agreeable, and seduction from a shipmate must provide present excitement and the comfort of stories for telling hereafter. I have lifted five skirts to date in the languid forenoon of a becalmed passage, and Freddy Vansittart is no less lucky—with his dark looks and his roguish smile, he can win any number of hearts. Stella from Yorkshire will have him, and he does not take care.

We have sunk to betting on the women as we do at cards, the boredom of this voyage being almost insufferable; and on occasion, when I am feeling low, I am thankful to God for Freddy Vansittart—his wild laughter and neck-or-nothing heart are all that stand between me and a pistol ball in the head. Like me, Freddy is a scoundrel and a second son; and if we do not hang together we shall most assuredly hang separately.

I believe I have borrowed that last sentiment from another, but cannot recollect whom.

I am not often so low. In truth, I cannot regret the chain of events that have sent me here—the violence of that meeting at dawn; the cut on Benning's face that will scar it like my signature forever after; the loss of my father's good opinion or the anger I met on every side; my mother's tears or the sober interview with the solicitors. It is not as tho' Benning died; but his father believed he would, the fever from the wounds having put him on a kind of death-bed; and when one report of the heir's passing was put out, damnably unproved, the Viscount St. Eustace suffered a fit. In short, the old man was carried off in a matter of hours—and Benning is now Viscount, and must be called by his title, the prospect of which he used to dangle sneeringly before me, all those years ago in school, when he called me a commoner and a spy who should end in the gutter. I hated him then and I hated him that morning when we met in the duelling ground at Hampstead Heath. I wish that I had killed him; his brother is a better man, and like all second sons, I wish him greater justice.

No—if I regret anything at all, it is the stupidity and the waste of those London days. The harlots lounging in the arches of Covent Garden, the befuddlement of drink, the desperate crying of a heart that loved only Horatia, and knew her to be pledged to another. She will be a Viscountess these five months or more, and great with child—tho' it shall not be Benning's. I have that satisfaction at least.

And so to exile. Mr. Hastings awaits. "He shall be

your envoy to a better life," His Grace the Duke told me sternly; "pray that you do not return having disgraced him." The burden is more likely to be reversed. I have heard a little of Mr. Hastings: how he fathered a girl by one partner, and wrested his wife from another; how his slow ascent above his fellows has been managed with cunning and industry. Hastings is a man after my own stamp—a self-made creature, who owes his reputation and fearsome respect to no title or gift of birth. I shall profit by Mr. Hastings; I feel it in my blood.

And we shall both return to England invincible.

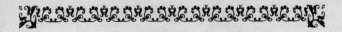

Chapter 8

The Man Who
Drank Deep

5 July 1809, cont.

~

THE GEORGE INN SITS IN THE VERY MIDST OF Alton's High Street, not far from its rival, The Swan, where Mr. Chizzlewit had undertaken to lodge. I had quitted Mr. Barlow's house only yesterday morning in Joseph's pony trap; but a revolution of thought and feeling had occurred in the interval that far outstripped a single turn of the globe. I left the George an impoverished and dependant relation; I returned but four-and-twenty hours later an Heiress who had excited the Notice of the Great. Moreover, I had discovered a body—one mysteriously dead; and this must always lend a lady distinction. Mr. Barlow himself handed me down from Mr. Prowting's gig, and bowed over my hand to the admiration of a group of tradesmen gathered especially for the coroner's panel. The escort of a local magistrate could only add to my consequence.

"I've put the crowner in the back parlour as Mr. Austen always uses come Quarter Day," Mr. Barlow confided to me in an undertone. "I hope as it will suit. I do not know what Mr. Munro may be accustomed to, in Basingstoke."

This being a market town where any number of London parties were used to change their post horses, at a quantity of inns bearing the names of Wheatsheaf, Angel, Maidenhead, and Crown, I did not wonder at Mr. Barlow's quailing before so awful a figure as a Basingstoke man; but I bestowed upon the publican a smile and said, "Any room my brother elects as adequate for his business cannot possibly disappoint."

We were ushered within, and conducted through the public room to a chamber at the rear of the building, where Mr. Barlow had set a scrubbed oak table and an arrangement of chairs. Always a hospitable man, he had placed a jug of ale on a serving tray and provided a baker's dozen of glasses for Mr. Munro's Chosen. These individuals were standing about uneasily near the plank table, waiting for the coroner to appear—and uncertain whether it was permissible to drink the ale until he did. Half the chairs provided for those of us who came to gawk were already filled with people of the town. There was a little bustle of expectation when we entered the room—a glancing at Mr. Prowting and myself, and a muttered communication behind gloved hands—and then the noise died away, and I was conveyed to a seat conveniently near what I judged to be Munro's chair.

Only one other woman was present in the room: perhaps four-and-twenty years of age, with reddish-blond hair tied in a knot on her head, a worn gown that might once have been red, and a black shawl about her shoulders. From the look of her face, she had been weeping; some relative of the dead man's, then—his widow perhaps. She was quite alone, and the townsfolk preserved a cordon of distance around her, tho' seating was scarce.

In the opposite row, not five feet from where I was placed, sat Mr. Middleton and his young friend Julian Thrace. Both rose at my appearance and bowed politely. A third gentleman, unknown to me, made another of their party. A slight figure of unremarkable aspect, he was the sort of man who should rarely excite a lady's interest; and yet a slow flush suffused his countenance as he met my gaze. A poet, perhaps, ill-suited to the public eye—but my study of the gentleman was curtailed by the approach of Mr. Middleton.

"I am surprised but gratified to find you here, Miss Austen," he said heartily. "You are come as your brother's proxy, no doubt. Such attention does you credit; we must hope the exertion is not overpowering."

"I attempted to dissuade the lady," Mr. Prowting assured him, "but Miss Austen is firm where she sees her duty."

"And why not? It is her home that has been violated, after all."

"Indeed, sir—I believe it is poor Shafto French we must regard as the injured party." I offered Middleton my hand, and he bent over it with swift gallantry. As when I had first encountered him on horseback a few hours before, I was struck by his vigour—remarkable in a gentleman of advancing years. He must be of an age with the magistrate, but from his general air of health, might have been Mr. Prowting's son.

"You will observe Jack Hinton behind me," Middleton confided. "Thrace and I fell in with him here in town, and carried him along from a scandalous desire for gossip. I shall make him acquainted with Miss Austen, eh? We shall all meet tomorrow evening in any case, at the Great House. I have asked Hinton and his sister to dine."

Mr. Prowting glanced at me doubtfully.

"I should like to meet . . . a man of whom I have heard so much," I said evenly.

But Mr. Hinton was studiously engrossed in conversation with Julian Thrace, and avoiding all our gaze. His intent was to offer the cut indirect—a glancing insult, and one that might be ascribed simply to diffidence or poor manners. I, however, saw a purpose in his actions: Hinton meant to publish his petty wars against the Austens before all of Alton.

Mr. Middleton frowned and looked perplexed.

"There will be time enough tomorrow for introductions," I suggested. "The coroner's panel looks to be upon the point of convention."

It had been impossible for the proceedings to begin without Mr. Prowting's presence, but the coroner had awaited only the magistrate's arrival to make his entrance. A door in the far wall, communicating to a lesser room beyond our own, was opened discreetly and quietly and the man himself strode towards the chair. I liked his looks immediately: he was neatly and elegantly dressed in black superfine and pantaloons; his face was clean-shaven; his gaze direct and uncritical as it roamed the room. I detected intelligence in his wide brow, and an eloquence in the fingers that bespoke the natural philosopher. I was pleasantly surprised. Mr. Munro was something above my usual experience of coroners.

He inclined his head to the assembly, glanced towards the men lounging about the perimeter of the room, and said without preamble: "Have you a foreman?"

"Ellis Watson, sir," returned a grey-haired fellow as he stepped forward, cap in hand.

"Very well, Mr. Watson, you may urge your panel to take their places. As coroner for Basingstoke, Steventon, and Alton, I call this inquest to order. We are convened to discover the manner of death of one Shafto French, labourer and free man of Alton, and you are each of you charged with the most solemn duty of judging whether Deceased met his end by misadventure, malice aforethought, or his own hand. Mr. Watson, will you come and be sworn?"

Beside me Mr. Prowting sighed heavily, but not with boredom; rather, it was a settling into the familiar and the comforting, a small animal noise akin to a horse in its stable. The magistrate's gaze was fixed on his colleague, but no hint of his thoughts could be read on his visage. I wondered, fleetingly, if I had taken the full measure of Mr. Prowting. It was possible a brain of some subtlety worked behind his country façade.

The members of the panel, having placed their hands on Mr. Munro's Bible, were led in single file to the adjacent room from which the coroner had entered. Here, no doubt, the mortal remains of Shafto French reposed, and must be viewed by those charged with determining how the poor man had died. I should have liked to ask Mr. Prowting whether the physician had troubled to anatomise the body, or whether consideration for the feelings of the man's wife had prevented this excursion into Science—but I was confident the magistrate would regard such a question as grossly unsuited to the experience and sensibility of a lady.[1] I must trust to the proceedings to unfold what intelligence they would.

An interval of perhaps ten minutes elapsed; the men returned, singly and in groups, with one poor fellow dashing out of the chamber entirely, to be sick as I supposed in Mr. Barlow's stable yard. The coroner took no notice of this, save to await the man's return before proceeding. When all were reassembled, Mr. Munro glanced up from his foolscap and pen, eyes roving about the room until they fell upon Mr. Prowting.

---

[1] Anatomization, or the dissection of a corpse, was a fate usually reserved for hanged felons. Autopsy was regarded in Austen's time as a violation of a God-given body, abhorred and reviled by all but those familiar with medical interests.—*Editor's note.*

"I should like to call Mr. William Prowting of Chawton, who holds the commission of the peace for this county, to be sworn before God and this panel."

Mr. Prowting rose to his feet, and made his ponderous way towards the enclosure reserved for witnesses at Munro's right hand. He made his oath, and composed himself with an air of gravity; told the coroner and the townsfolk of Alton how he had assisted his neighbours with the disposal of some heavy articles in the cellar at approximately four o'clock the previous afternoon, and therewith, in all innocence, discovered Shafto French's remains.

"There was no possible entry to the cellar except through the rooms of the cottage itself?"

Mr. Prowting affirmed that this was so—"despite the hatchway set into the cellar ceiling, a remnant of the place's former usage as a public house."

"The hatch was closed at the time of the body's discovery?"

"Closed and barred from within. I opened the hatch myself, as I just described to you, and may attest that the dust had not been disturbed."

I wondered at that statement; in the dim light of my tallow candle, little could have been observed of either wooden bar or the dust that coated it. But it was not for me to say what Mr. Prowting had seen; it was not my hand that had lifted the hatch's bar.

"And the new tenants of Chawton Cottage opened the house only yesterday?"

"Mrs. Austen and her daughter arrived before the

gate at half past two o'clock, as I observed from my parlour window directly opposite."

"You paid a call upon the household soon thereafter?"

It was a point of conjecture whether Mr. Prowting would now condescend to mention the appearance of so extraordinary a visitor as Mr. Chizzlewit, with liveried lackeys behind; but the former was a magistrate of long standing, and had been trained to observe the brevities of a public proceeding. Mr. Chizzlewit did not pertain to Shafto French; furthermore, Mr. Chizzlewit had treated him, William Prowting, with the grossest condescension. Mr. Chizzlewit might hang in obscurity for the nonce.

"I wished to afford the ladies an interval to investigate the cottage in privacy," the magistrate told the room, "and thus paid my call of welcome perhaps half an hour after they arrived."

"Very well. Did you observe any sort of disturbance, Mr. Prowting, to the cellar floor where Deceased lay?"

"I did not. The place was as quiet as a tomb," the magistrate observed; and considered too late of his choice of words. "From the closed air of the room, I should have thought the place shut up a decade or more. I was astonished to discover the remains."

"You did not notice a shifting of the dust," Munro persisted, "on the surface of the floor, as might have been occasioned by the passage of feet?"

Mr. Prowting replied in the negative.

"Nor yet any stain, as of water spilled and later dried?"

At this last question, I straightened in my chair with interest. To what end did the coroner's questions lead?

Mr. Prowting had seen no stain of dried water. "The floor being unpaved, and the dirt of a sandy composition, any moisture might probably have drained away. The body, after all, had been lying where it was some days."

Mr. Munro might have protested this statement, or wondered how Prowting could be so sure of the date of death; but it was common knowledge by now that French's face had been entirely et away—and nobody would dispute the conclusions to be drawn from the activity of the rats.

The magistrate stood down.

I awaited with interest the summoning of the next witness; and it was, indeed, myself—who after being sworn, attested simply that I had never set foot in my present abode before yesterday afternoon; that I had not been in Chawton, indeed, except for a fleeting visit to the Great House two years before; that I had received the keys to the cottage from Mr. Barlow, the George's publican, who at my brother the Squire's instruction had held them in safekeeping ever since the departure of the previous tenant, Widow Seward, four months earlier; and finally, that I had ventured to the cellar only after Mr. Prowting appeared to assist me in the conveyance of some heavy articles requiring storage.

It was probable, I thought as I made my way back

to my chair, that the entire town of Alton had now concluded that a hoard of jewels—a king's ransom, Henry had called it—was locked in my cellar. I had been wise to shift Lord Harold's papers to my bedchamber.

"The coroner summons Jemima French."

The woman I had observed at the front of the room rose before Mr. Munro, and was apparently stricken instantly with paralysis.

"You may take this chair, Mrs. French," he said with blunt kindness, "and make your oath, if you please."

She moved waveringly towards the proffered seat, and I saw with pity that she was increasing. *A hopeful family*, Mr. Prowting had said. How many children did Shafto French leave behind? And how ill-provided for?

"You are Jemima French, wife of Deceased?"

"I am, sir," she answered faintly.

"I will not trouble you long. When did you last see your husband in life, Mrs. French?"

She made as if to speak, and then her features crumpled with misery and she buried her face in her hands. "Saturday," she managed, "as he was leaving for the Crown."

"The Crown is a publick house?"

"Yessir. Shafto liked it better'n the others."

"I'm that sorry, then, that he has to lie in the George," cried Mr. Barlow, considerably put out.

Mr. Munro ignored the publican. "Your husband did not come home that night?"

Mrs. French shook her head.

"Nor yet the next day?"

"No, sir. I did not lay eyes on him again until yesterday, when Mr. Curtis's boy brought word."

The unfortunate woman wiped her eyes with her apron.

"Was your husband in the habit of disappearing for several days together?"

"Shafto, he sometimes went a good distance in search of work."

"Had he been employed of late?"

"Yes, sir, it being summer and the season good for building. Mr. Dyer often found a use for Shafto, shifting stone and such-like."

"I see. In your husband's sudden absence, did you think to enquire of Mr. Dyer whether he had hired Mr. French?"

Jemima shook her head once more.

"Glad to be shut of 'im," a rude voice called out from the back of the room, "and no wonder! Shut of 'im for good you are, now, Jemima!"

The grieving widow half-rose from her witness seat, face flushed. "Who *said* that? What heart of stone would speak ill of my Shafto? Three little 'uns he's left, and the good Lord alone knows how I'll feed 'em. Vipers, all of ye, to spit upon a man's name, and him lying yonder with his eyes closed on this world."

There was a silence, and the turning away of heads; for my own part, I could have applauded the woman's speech. Fighting words had afforded Jemima French the strength at least to leave off weeping.

"Mrs. French, you have our deepest sympathy," Mr. Munro assured her. "You may stand down. If any man has the desire to be heard in this proceeding, he may come forward and be sworn. Otherwise, I must beg you to preserve a respectful silence. Recollect that we are all of us in the presence of the Departed."

A chair scraped the floor some distance behind me, as though in protest, but no further gibes were uttered.

"At this juncture," the coroner declared, "it is perhaps best that I state for the understanding of one and all my conclusions as a physician regarding Shafto French's death.

"Mr. Prowting summoned me by express last evening to preside over this panel. In the interval between last night and this morning's proceeding, Deceased was attended by Mr. Curtis, a surgeon who resides at No. 4, High Street, and declared to be Shafto French. French's wife was summoned, and having viewed the body, named her husband conclusively. Mr. Curtis further gave his opinion that Deceased departed this life several days before the discovery of the corpse.

"I examined Deceased only a few hours ago, and found a man in his late twenties or early thirties, to judge by his teeth and the general character of his limbs; a man fairly well-nourished and in tolerable health. No wound is observable in the body that might account for Deceased's passing; no blow to skull or limbs could I find. Neither was there any evidence of sickness—no voiding of the stomach or bowels that should suggest the work of poison. I may add that had Deceased suffered apoplexy or some other convulsive fit, we might expect to discover blood at the mouth and nostrils. This I did not find. There was, however, a strong smell of spirits about the corpse—and it has been suggested to me that French may have met his end from excessive drink."

The coroner paused, his gaze fixed now upon the men of the panel, some of whom were shifting in their seats. It was likely any number had been acquainted with Shafto French from birth; and from the knowing glances being thrown about the room, the man was no stranger to a publick house.

"Deceased's clothes were doused with a quantity of gin," Mr. Munro continued in his clear and imperturbable fashion, "and inebriation may have contributed to the clouding of senses that led to his death. But it is my duty to inform this panel that however deeply Shafto French may have drunk before his demise, it was not of alcohol alone. I discovered Deceased's lungs to be filled with water—a discovery with which the surgeon Mr. Curtis agrees. Deceased met his death by drowning."

In my mind's eye I saw with clarity the muddy surface of Chawton Pond, so close to the house in which I had spent the night—its smooth, dark waters not very deep, perhaps, but sufficient to kill a man. Involuntarily, I shuddered.

"How French came to be found in the cellar of a stranger's house is indeed a mystery," the coroner continued serenely, "but we must conclude he did not arrive there under his own power."

A murmur of excited interest surged through the

room. Beside me, Mr. Prowting uttered a short bark of dismay and sat up the straighter in his seat. "But that is utter nonsense!" he protested. "Why should someone carry Shafto French to the cottage cellar? Why not leave him in the road for all to see, if he had gone and drowned himself?"

"Is it not obvious, sir?" I enquired gently. "Because someone killed him."

Letter from Lord Harold Trowbridge to Eugenie, Duchess of Wilborough, dated 2 November 1783; one leaf quarto, laid; watermark device coronet over escutcheon containing post-horn (see Heawood Nos. 2752–62); marked Calcutta to Southampton, by Grace of the Royal Navy.

(British Museum, Wilborough Papers, Austen bequest)

My dear Mamma—

You will be pleased to learn that I received your last bundle of letters—spanning full six months, I perceive, of industrious quill-mending on your part—in one fell swoop, all of them having arrived by various routes about the globe in the hull of the same ship, which put in to Calcutta and disgorged its burdens of Staffordshire dishes, Lancaster woollens, China tea, and good English salt beef to the admiring multitude. The letters found their way to me only after a plodding journey of several weeks, the Governor having trundled us all off to Madras to deal with one Lord George McCartney, a man whose head is as thick as a spotted dog pudding. He stiles himself President of Madras, and has the support of our good Company; but his idiocy in the handling of his subordinates and the native Nawabs alike surpasses all belief. Lord George is everywhere known in London and everywhere liked; but his knowledge of India could not be fitted into my little fingernail, despite which fact he has presumed to interfere in the Governor's negotiations with the Marathas, in the conduct of the Mysore War, and in the dismissal of General Stuart for systematic disobedience.

*McCartney went so far as to have the good General
bodily removed from his quarters and bundled upon a
ship bound for London, complete with his cork leg and
some fifty packages. As the General holds his
commission at the will of the King, not the Company,
Lord George is regarded as having dangerously
overreached himself; and the officers under Stuart's
command have threatened to mutiny. Naturally, the
Governor was at his most subtle in defusing the
situation; but I daresay he shall have to send his
lordship packing before too long—or sail for London
himself.*

*I tell you of these trivial matters, by the by—which
cannot amuse you a ha'porth, who will be thinking
instead of the latest* ton on-dits *and scandal among your
friends—because in truth my heart is breaking. And
only you must know that, Mother dear, and repeat the
fact to no one. You alone have my counsel, and must
forget everything I tell you as soon as the words are
read.*

*While travelling in the Governor's train I chanced
upon Freddy Vansittart, en route from a trading
expedition in Madras; he looked as well as ever, and is
groaning with wealth, as should be natural for one of
his wit and luck. He tells me of news from London—in
truth, that Horatia is dead in childbed, and the babe
with her. I can see it all: St. Eustace grinning like the
Devil's own dog as the screams of labour were torn from
her, convinced he had found his revenge at last. O,
God—that I had never seen her face! Or touched a hair
of her head. I have been the ruin of several lives,*

Mamma, as I own to my sorrow; my soul is black. Horatia died in torment, and I had no knowledge of it for months after—I sat in the sun while she died, and gazed at the women of Pondicherry.

And still I cannot leave off hating him. It was he who kissed her cold cheek when she breathed her last; and it is in his tomb she will lie forever. She cannot have achieved her twenty-first birthday.

Freddy could tell me nothing of the babe—whether it was boy or girl. Write what you can, when you can—and believe me ever your loving son,

Harry

Chapter 9

What the Cellar Told

~

"AND SO," MY BROTHER CONCLUDED, "A VERDICT was returned of death at the hands of a person or persons unknown?"

"It was—with Mr. Munro adjourning the proceeding, and placing matters in abeyance until Mr. Prowting should inform him otherwise."

"It is a curious business." Henry drained his dish of tea and pushed back from the breakfast table. He had appeared at the cottage early this morning agog with the news of yesterday's inquest, which had spread rapidly throughout the town and was subject to every kind of exaggeration. Henry had been unable to attend the proceeding himself, detained by that bank business which had occasioned his descent on Hampshire; but knowing *Jane* far better than Mr. Prowting, he was confident I should acquaint him with the particulars.

"Drowning and murder might arise in a country village from any number of causes," he mused, "—jealousy, petty hatreds, a dispute of long-standing between two parties. A woman might come into it—or several women, if you like. But why not leave the body with a great stone tied to its neck, sunken in the pond, to be discovered a twelvemonth hence? Why stow the poor fellow in our cellar, deserted as it may have seemed, to be found the very moment the new tenants turned the key in their door?"

"In order to give as much trouble as possible," my mother replied with indignation. "I am quite sure there was some deliberate design in the business. The mortification is all ours; I do not regard even the unfortunate wife as having any claim to greater misery. It was we who had the trouble of finding the corpse, and suffering the agonies of carters and magistrates and public notice; the widow is merely called upon to bury it."

"Mamma!" Henry cried in mock terror. "You cannot be so heartless!"

"But design, Henry, there certainly was," I insisted. "Whether to bring shame and suspicion upon the name of Austen—as we may believe *some* in Chawton village should like to do—or merely to employ the most convenient method of hiding an unwanted corpse, there was a good deal of thought in the business. Recollect the matter of the keys."

The final witnesses Mr. Munro called the previous afternoon, to conclude his panel's education, were illuminating—and must give rise to further comment and rumour in the neighbourhood. Kit Duff, publican of the Crown, stated simply that Shafto French had drunk deep of his house's best ale Saturday night on the strength of a week's pay, had kept entirely to himself, and appeared disinclined for sociable conversation. Some small dispute had arisen between French and his fellow labourer Bertie Philmore— "what is Shafto French's cousin on his mother's side"—and the two men's argument had stilled most of the public room, with Philmore accusing French of an unpaid debt, and French asserting that he should be a warm man before very long, and would settle all his debts with enough left over to rule them all, besides. The two had quitted the inn just before midnight, when the Crown closed in deference to the advent of the Sabbath.

Bertie Philmore was next called—and admitted in a surly fashion that Shafto did owe him near to five pound, unpaid this year or more. He insisted that the two had parted at his door, with Bertie bound for his wife and bed, and Shafto saying as he had a man to meet—"tho' who should be abroad at such an hour but thieves and footpads, I dare not think." Mr. Munro attempted to divide Bertie Philmore from his assertions—to intimate, indeed, that the two men had carried their dispute so far as Chawton Pond a mile distant, and that death by drowning had occurred as a natural result of a drunken mill—but Philmore was not to be led. He offered his virtuous helpmate as sworn witness to his boots having crossed the threshold at the stroke of twelve, and could not be swerved from his purpose.

Mr. Dyer the builder proved most edifying in his communications. He was a square-bodied, powerful individual with a lean and weathered face. He commanded instant respect before Mr. Munro's panel, as a tradesman with the livelihood of half Alton's labourers in his pocket. He was little inclined to talk, and answered the questions put to him with a brevity that bordered on the pugnacious. He had indeed used Shafto French in various odd jobs of work that required brute strength but little sense; he could not rely upon the man's appearance from one day to the next; he had thought nothing of a failure to report for work on the Monday, as no doubt French had been drunk of a Sunday. In these opinions, Mr. Dyer seemed to speak for the entire town.

At Mr. Munro's further questioning, however, matter of a more serious import was gleaned. Shafto French had been set to work at Chawton Cottage the week immediately preceding our arrival, in digging the new cesspit. Three other labourers, including Bertie Philmore, were engaged, under the direction of Mr. Dyer's son, William, in blocking up the unfortunate front parlour window and throwing out the new bow overlooking the garden. The keys to Chawton Cottage had thus been in Mr. Dyer's possession—which the builder purported to have returned to Mr. Barlow at the George, according to previous arrangement with my brother, at the conclusion of his firm's work.

"And the work was complete on what day?" Mr. Munro then demanded.

Mr. Dyer looked all his discomfort. He had intended the repairs to Chawton Cottage to be finished on Saturday, as his men were expected in Sherborne St. John on Monday; but work on the cesspit, or French himself, had given some trouble. Rains and indolence delayed the business's conclusion. When Shafto French did not appear as expected Monday morning, Mr. Dyer's son painted the privy himself and set all in order before handing over the keys to the publican Mr. Barlow's safekeeping—much relieved to learn that we had arrived at the inn from Kent only that day.

"Your son noticed nothing untoward as he was locking up the house?—A suggestion, as it were, that someone had entered the premises prior to himself?"

"Bill had no cause to go down cellar, nor any of my men neither, being that no repairs were to be done in that part of the cottage," Mr. Dyer said sharply. "Don't you be accusing my boy of murder, Mr. Crowner, when all he's done is another man's honest day of work."

Mr. Munro had soothed the builder's injured feelings, and reverted instead to the matter of the keys. Had Mr. Dyer been assured of their possession throughout the interval between Shafto French's disappearance on Saturday, and the conclusion of work on Monday?

Mr. Dyer thought that he had. An impression of reserve was given; and at Mr. Munro's persistence, the builder confessed that it was his son, Bill, who'd been the keeper of the keys—and that Bill was at work to-day in the aforementioned parish of Sherborne St. John, and must answer later for himself.

"Bertie Philmore or young William Dyer killed the man and hid his body in the cellar," Henry told me thoughtfully, "or someone unknown to us obtained the builder's keys through stealth with the intention of committing, and hiding, murder. We can be certain, however, that the deed was done between midnight on Saturday and Monday morning, when the keys were apparently once more in the publican's possession."

"If," I rejoined to Henry's chagrin, "there is only one set of keys."

WHEN HE HAD BREAKFASTED, I PREVAILED UPON my brother to descend the cellar stairs and study the floor there, with a lanthorn held high against whatever spectres might haunt a place of violent death.

"Not a happy part of the house," Henry observed feelingly as the dank coldness of the air hit our faces, despite the warmth of the summer morning above. "It wants a number of casks and wooden crates of smuggled claret—sawdust on the floors to take off the damp—and a spot of whitewash on the stone walls."

"If you know of a single man in Alton or Chawton courageous enough to undertake the labour of painting this death-room, I beg you will send him to us directly," I retorted. "Not even Mr. Prowting can discover a person of the serving class willing to enter the cottage. Like all ill-gotten gains, it is tacitly understood to be cursed."

"I shall have to speak to young Baigent's father. The boy ought to be horse-whipped."

"So ought Neddie. I shall whip him myself, for having ignored the claims of Widow Seward and Jack Hinton alike."

The lanthorn, swinging in Henry's hand, threw wild shadows against the ceiling and walls; I tried not to find in the flickering shapes the humped menace of rats.

"Munro was interested, you say, in any disturbance—or the stain of dried water?" Henry asked.

"—Tho' Mr. Prowting insisted he saw neither."

"Then he did not observe the ground closely," my brother objected. He held the lanthorn perhaps a foot above the dirt floor and moved it in an arcing sweep over the surface. "Look, Jane. Faint footprints, and a poor effort at scrubbing them out."

He was correct, as Henry must always be: in the stronger light of the burning oil, I could discern what a candle flame had not revealed: The impressions of a boot in the dirt, near the corner of the room where Shafto French had lain. They were partial and indistinct, and ought to have been obliterated by the careless feet of Mr. Prowting and myself, not to mention those who had removed Shafto French's body. I gathered my skirt in both hands and crouched down, the better to observe them. The mark of a right heel, broad and flat; and two impressions of a boot toe.

"Henry," I murmured as I studied them, "do these appear to be the marks of a labourer's shoe?"

"They do not," he replied grimly, "tho' I should certainly believe them a man's. There are no impressions of hobnails, as one would expect from a heavy working boot, and look, Jane—the leather sole was so fine as to leave an imprint in one place of the fellow's left toe. I should judge these marks to have been left by a good pair of leather boots such as . . ."

". . . a gentleman should wear."

We looked at each other, both of us frowning.

"Could they be Prowting's?" Henry demanded.

"Perhaps. But I imagine Mr. Prowting's impression might be found here, at the foot of the stairs"—I motioned for my brother's lanthorn—"where he stood an instant with the full weight of the chest in his arms. Observe how distinctly the marks are left, Henry."

"And of an entirely different size," he added. "There is another set of those marks beneath the hatch, where Prowting stood to unbar the doors."

"We must invite our neighbour the magistrate to test his footwear in this room, and I myself shall sketch the remaining impressions," I said soberly. "We ought not to delay. Mr. Prowting may have an idea of Shafto French's enemies among the gentry of Chawton."

"Then why did he not offer them at the inquest, Jane?"

A slight sound from the cellar stairs drew my head around, and forestalled my answer.

"Mamma? Is that you?" I called upwards.

A woman's face swam in the darkness at the head

of the stairs: white, frightened, with large clear eyes and a trembling lip. A knot of red-gold hair crowned the whole.

"It is Mrs. French, is it not?" I said in surprise. "How may I help you, my dear?"

SHE STOOD IN SILENCE AT THE FOOT OF THE STAIRS, glancing about the ugly stone walls and the scuffed dirt of the floor. Henry had bowed to the woman and murmured a word of sympathy; but he did not tarry in his errand to Prowtings. I could hear his heavy tread even now above our heads, making for the front door.

"The lady said as I might come down," Jemima French muttered, "and should be in no one's way. I had to see this place, if you understand me, ma'am. I had to see where my Shafto died."

I might have told her he could have met his end in any horse trough between the Crown Inn and Chawton; but I did not like to seem so unfeeling. I considered of this girl—for, indeed, she was little older than Ann or Catherine Prowting—lying alone in her bed with the little ones breathing softly beside her, and seeing in memory again and again the ravaged face of her husband. They had asked her to view the body and name it for Shafto French. Had she gone alone to that interview with the surgeon, Mr. Curtis?

"It *is* dark down here, in'it?" she murmured, tho'

Henry had left us the lanthorn. "You will tell me where he lay?"

I nodded assent, and pointed towards the corner of the room. "Just there. I must ask you not to touch the place. There are marks we should like the magistrate to observe."

Her eyes were once again wide with horror, as though she imagined the trail of a convulsive fit, or perhaps the traffic of a legion of rodents emanating from the walls. "What marks?"

Caution, and a knowledge of the habits of country folk—of the impossibility of any fact remaining private—made me deliberately chary. "The marks of your husband's form, of course. Shall I carry you upstairs, my dear, and fix you a cup of tea?"

"I should've known," she said dully, "when he didn't come back. A bit o' light-skirt, I thought it was—Shafto always having been a man for a doxy. It was pride, ma'am, as prevented me speaking; but *pride goeth before destruction, and an haughty spirit before a fall*, as my mother used to say, being a great one for quoting Proverbs."

"Had you any reason to think your husband at risk of injury, Mrs. French?"

She stared at me fixedly; but it was not a look of incomprehension—of indecision, rather, as tho' she could not determine to trust me.

"Had he an enemy?" I persisted. "Some person you knew of, who wished him ill—or who might perhaps profit from his death?"

A slow flush o'erspread her features, and her gaze fell. "No, ma'am. Nobody could want my man dead."

"But someone clearly did. The coroner is convinced your husband did not meet his death by chance."

She turned her head restlessly. "He'd been talking wild for days, about the blunt he was going to have off some'un as was plump in the pocket; blood money, he called it, as'd set us up forever. *Silk gowns, Jemima my girl,* he said, *and no worrying about wood for the fire when the cold winds blow.*"

"Was he often given to publishing hopes of that kind, when he had lately been paid for work?" I enquired with an unstudied air.

She shook her head. "It was a rare struggle for us to make one end meet the other, ma'am, and how I am to manage now I cannot think."

"Have you any family?"

"A brother, with a good number of his own to feed. But I can ply a needle, ma'am, and may find piecework at the linendraper's. I have worked all my life, and am not afraid of it."

I preserved a tactful silence. Between the demands of war and the limits to commerce we suffer at the hands of Napoleon, times are very hard in this country. I myself have felt the pinch of articles too dear for my purse, and I had not Mrs. French's encumbrances.

"You have no further expectation of these funds your husband spoke of?—He gave you no hint of the person from whom he expected his money?"

"Not a word, ma'am. And who should it be, when all is said? I've known Shafto's mates since we were all little 'uns together, running through Robin Hood Butts of a spring morn.[1] None of our kind of folk would come into a treasure; and none owed him money. 'Twas too often t'other way round. My man had no head for business, ma'am."

"And yet—Bertie Philmore asserted that when he parted from your husband, Mr. French was intending to meet with a man. You have no notion of who this man might be?"

"His murderer," she rejoined in a voice creased with misery. "Shafto thought to make his fortune, and met his end! Blood money! I'll give 'im blood money!"

"It *is* a curious phrase," I observed, "potent with violence."

"He always was a fool, my Shafto—but that kindhearted. He'd never raise his hand to me or the little 'uns," she said hastily.

"That is not what I meant. I meant that the words *blood money* suggest payment for a killing—or, perhaps, for your husband's silence regarding one. He expected to gain from guilty knowledge, that much seems certain. —Tho' the guilt may not have been his own."

This time her confusion was evident.

"Did he say anything else that might help us, Mrs. French?"

"Only that it was the air as would pay."

[1] Robin Hood Butts was an area of open land between Chawton and Alton that served as the site of Alton's April Fair.—*Editor's note.*

"The air?" I repeated blankly.

"Yes, ma'am. Someone as stood to inherit a good deal, and could afford to buy Shafto's silence."

The heir as would pay.

I had heard two men described in such terms in as many days—Julian Thrace and Jack Hinton. Both had witnessed the inquest. I felt a sudden longing to seize the gentlemen's boots and make a trial of both pairs on the cellar floor.

"Was your husband well known in these parts?"

"He'd lived here all 'is life."

"So he would be quite familiar to any number of people in both Chawton and Alton—the Prowtings, perhaps, or the Middletons; even the Hintons, I suppose."

Her reaction to this gentle query was swift as a viper's. "Why should the Hintons care? Who's been talking about Shafto and Mr. Jack?"

"Nobody," I replied, bewildered. "Has there been talk before?"

"Among his mates, there was always a kind word for Shafto," she retorted defiantly, "whatever that Bertie Philmore will say."

"And Mr. Hinton? Did he also think well of your husband?"

"Mr. Hinton be blowed!" She buried her face in her hands and sobbed pitifully. "Oh, God, Shafto, me lad—I should've known when you did not come back! I should have looked for you myself!"

"You could have done no good, had you roused the entire country," I told her gently, and placed my hand on her shoulders. "A thousand men in search of your husband could not have saved him. If he *was* killed by the man he went to meet at midnight on Saturday, he found his end before you even understood he was missing. And no one but a tenant of this house could have discovered the body."

She lifted her visage, blue eyes all but drowned. "A proper wife would've known he was gone."

"Indeed, you take too much upon yourself." I grasped the lanthorn in one hand and put the other carefully on the young woman's shoulder, drawing her towards the stairs. "Your duty now is to preserve your children from exposure to the malice of your neighbours, and to fix in their memories a picture of their father in life, such as shall comfort and support them the rest of their days. Have you both boys and girls?"

And in speaking of her children, Jemima French discovered some fleeting comfort; enough to carry her into my kitchen, and sustain her for the length of time required to drink my tea.

Excerpt from the diaries of Lord Harold Trowbridge, dated 26 February 1785, on board the Indiaman *Punjab*, bound for Portsmouth out of Bombay.

. . . I walked about the quarterdeck this morning at Captain Dundage's invitation, glad for the freedom it afforded from the seamen holystoning the decks and the constant activity of the Indiaman. It is as nothing, of course, to the relentless toil of His Majesty's Navy—two such ships of the line hovering in escort just off our port and starboard bows; but such a knot of bodies is constantly passing to and fro amidships that I should be hard pressed to achieve any sort of exercise without the Captain's kind intervention. There is very little society, either. Freddy Vansittart has made a friend of the First Lieutenant, Mr. Harlow, and spends his hours in firing a gun off the stern rail at any creature that moves; tho' well enough to look at without his powdered wig, and possessed of high courage that makes him a fine fellow in a fight, Freddy was never one for discussing philosophy, and is certain to prove tedious company in a voyage so long as this. My esteemed employer, Governor-General Hastings, being a prey to seasickness and in no mood for conversation—the politics of my friend Fox having succeeded in cutting up his peace and requiring his resignation from a post the Governor prized above all others in life—I am left to my own devices more often than not. I find I can bear the solitude quite cheerfully. It affords me the opportunity to consider of my future.

In four months' time I shall be five-and-twenty.

Which is to say that, despite my father the Duke's concerted effort to thwart every impulse of my existence, I must come into my late uncle's fortune under the stipulations of his Will. With sudden wealth, any number of avenues are opened to me: I might establish a high-flyer in Mayfair and offer her carte-blanche; I might squander my yearly income in a fortnight at picquet, as Fox himself has done; or I might spurn the obligations of a Man of Fashion and Birth, and throw the lot into the India trade. The Governor himself has told me the recent India Act is designed to clip the wings of the Honourable Company, as its profits are too great and its threat of dominion over the Subcontinent, with Mr. Hastings as its king, all too feared. Hence his departure in high dudgeon for the English coast. I see in my employer's present fall an opportunity: I shall take my money and become part-owner in a ship—an opium trader bound for China. Like any gaming hell, the China trade has all the appeal of high risk and rich return, with the added attraction of being deeply offensive to His Grace the Duke of Wilborough. But as his lordship the Viscount St. Eustace once observed, I was born a commoner and a commoner I shall always be.[2]

I have profited from my turns about the quarterdeck in conversing on certain points with Captain Dundage, who is a veteran of these seas for the past decade. What

---

[2] According to the practice of primogeniture, only the first-born son and heir of a peer was considered ennobled at birth; the rest of the Duke of Wilborough's children, like Lord Harold, were considered commoners, and accorded courtesy titles of lord or lady only during their lifetimes. Their children, in turn, were plain Mr. or Miss.—*Editor's note.*

he does not know of Indiamen and tea and the fortune to be made in poppies is not worth asking. And there is an added incentive in this: the Captain has in his safekeeping a young lady of retiring habits and infinite charm—a virtuous and well-born French girl of eighteen, reared in Madras and bound for a betrothal in England with my very enemy the Viscount St. Eustace—a man she has never met.

How has it come about, this bizarre and distant proposal from a stranger nearly twice her age? She cannot have an idea of his lordship's depravities—of the Beauty he has already crushed beneath his fist. She cannot know his dangerous proclivities, his desire for mastery, his miserly clutch on the riches he claims, his delight in other people's misery; she cannot understand the Hell her life is to become. I must know more of this girl and her history.

I confess on this page that the temptation to ruin St. Eustace's hopes is fierce upon me like a fever. But the Captain is scrupulous in shielding his charge from all eyes, and when Mam'selle takes the quarterdeck air, I am not permitted to ascend.

There are months yet to surge through the southern seas, in fair weather and foul, and months may work a wondrous change. In the meanwhile I strive to impress old Dundage with my air of industry, my keen questions regarding triangular trade, my well-bred manners and unimpeachable connexions.

We shall see how long is required for the French citadel to fall.

Chapter 10

The Joiner's Tale

~

"IT IS DECIDEDLY A GENTLEMAN'S BOOT," MR. Prowting agreed as he peered at the footprints in the cellar's dirt, "and most decidedly not mine. I wonder, sir, if we might compare your apparel to these?"

Henry obediently held out his shoe for the magistrate's observation. Mr. Prowting placed a pair of tongs from heel to toe, and then applied the span to the mark in the dirt. Henry's foot was a full inch longer and perhaps a quarter-inch wider.

"It will not do," our neighbour decreed sadly. "Clearly there has been a third set of well-made boots in this place that cannot be accounted for. I do not regard the marks of the labourers who removed French's body—they are all about, but clearly distinguishable in their heavy soles and hobnails from *this*. It is as Mr. Munro observed—tho' I did not like to credit it at the time. Shafto French was brought here already dead, and hidden of a purpose. And by a *gentleman*! It does not bear thinking of, Miss Austen. I had made certain the drowning was an accident—a terrible mishap born in the heat of fisticuffs between French and one of his fellows."

"—Bertie Philmore, perhaps?"

"—Tho' his wife was prepared to lie about the business. I made certain we should have the truth from Philmore in time. But it will not do."

I almost pitied Mr. Prowting as he crouched with his tongs in his hands, ample stomach uncomfortably swelling over the band of his breeches; he had certainly comprehended the trouble that the marks presaged. Only a handful of persons in the neighbourhood of Chawton and Alton could be described as gentlemen—and most of these should have known of the cottage's desertion. The magistrate was faced with the unhappy duty of suspecting some one of his neighbours—or subjecting all of them to an examination of their footwear.

"Mr. Prowting, are you aware of any dispute that may have existed between French and some one of the gentlemen hereabouts? A small thing, perhaps, that grew to ugliness over time?" I enquired.

The magistrate preserved a thoughtful silence, his fingers loosely grasping his tongs. "I should have thought nobody in these parts could have put a name to the fellow's face! French was a common labourer, merely, and much of a piece with all the rest—shift-less, drunken, of no particular account. I confess, Miss Austen, that I am at a loss to explain the entire episode."

"And yet: he must have held enormous signifi-cance to one of our neighbours," I persisted gently. "Shafto French was fearsome enough to be lured to the pond, and violently killed there."

"What I do not understand," Henry said, "is why the fellow was put in the cellar at all! Why not leave him, as Mr. Prowting has suggested, exactly where he lay? It is probable French was drowned after mid-night, and that no one was abroad to observe the deed. Why not allow the body to be discovered in the morning?"

"Perhaps," I said thoughtfully, "because the mur-derer required time."

Mr. Prowting looked at me with a frown. "What do you mean to say, Miss Austen?"

"Perhaps the murderer wished French's body to be discovered several days after death, to confuse the public knowledge of exactly *when* murder occurred. Perhaps he was safely distant from Chawton for most of the period in question—the period of French's dis-appearance—and by hiding the body, wished to delay discovery and thus divert our attention from the Sat-urday night in question. It is unfortunate for our mur-derer, then, that the last sighting of French at the Crown Inn should have been so exact, and his ab-sence throughout the Sunday and Monday noted. Our murderer cannot have anticipated this."

•

Mr. Prowting was staring at me in an incredulous fashion. "Miss Austen," he said accusingly, "I do believe you are a *bluestocking*!"

"Certainly not, sir!" I protested in an outraged accent.

"But her understanding is regrettably excellent," my brother added with a sigh. "It is to this we may attribute her refusal to enter the married state, despite the many opportunities that have offered."

I chose to ignore his impudence. "Mr. Prowting, you have long been a neighbour of Mrs. Seward's. Can you tell me whether she entrusted a spare set of keys to this cottage, to you or any other friend in the village?"

"Good Lord," he muttered. "Worse and worse. You cannot even allow it to be Dyer's fault!"

"In the interest of furthering the truth," I admitted delicately, "I cannot. You will admit the appearance of the body in this place becomes more explicable if someone other than simply Mr. Dyer was in possession of a set of keys."

"The Sewards did not honour me with their confidence. Being your brother's steward and a close man by nature, Bridger Seward was jealous of his trust. But his widow may have given the means of entry into other hands, after her husband's death, and forgotten to retrieve them once she quitted the cottage."

"Then I suppose I must speak to Mrs. Seward. I do not like to think of a set of keys to this house continuing to wander about the countryside. I should sleep far better if they all came home to roost."

Henry's eyes met mine over Mr. Prowting's head with a sombre expression. Both of us were thinking of the same thing: Lord Harold's Bengal chest, now hidden beneath my bedstead.

"Pray tell me, sir— Where does Mrs. Seward now reside?"

"In Alton, with her daughter Mrs. Baverstock. The Baverstocks have long been brewers, and their establishment sits on the High, just opposite the Duke's Head." The magistrate rose, dusting off his hands. "I cannot say that this is a happy discovery, Miss Austen. I should rather these marks to have remained obscured. The suspicion of a neighbour in so grave an affair as murder must be a most distasteful business."

"But justice, my dear sir, is owed to the lowly as well as the great."

From his looks as he parted from my door, I doubted that Mr. Prowting agreed with me.

AFTER A BRIEF NUNCHEON, HENRY INFORMED ME that he was required in Alton that day, and had already tarried too long.

"Would you allow me to ride pillion, Henry? I feel it incumbent upon me to pay a call of mourning."

"But you've already seen the widow, Jane!"

"And had Shafto French no friends to grieve at his sudden passing?" I demanded indignantly.

"More likely creditors filing to the door in search of payment. No wonder his unfortate wife fled to Chawton this morning as soon as may be."

"Very well—if you are so unfeeling and so selfish, I will *walk* to Alton."

"Of course you may ride pillion," he retorted impatiently. "Only do not be clutching at the poor horse's neck in that odious way. You look such a flat when you do."

"I have never been a horsewoman," I admitted despairingly.

"Have you a riding habit?"

I shook my head. A made-over gown of Lizzy's had served to carry me through Canterbury Race Week four years before, but that was long since consigned to the scrap basket, and should probably form a part of my mother's scheme for a pieced coverlet before long.

"I daresay you are going to force an acquaintance on the Widow Seward, as well. You mean to pursue this murder," Henry said, his gaze narrowed. "You *will not* let matters rest. I blame Lord Harold, Jane—he has had a most unfortunate influence on your headstrong nature."

"Bertie Philmore knows more than he admitted."

"Undoubtedly. But must you be the one to tell him so? Why cannot you allow our neighbour Mr. Prowting to do his duty?"

"Because he shall undoubtedly do it so *badly*, Henry! Jemima French deserves some justice, does she not? Consider all she has lost!"

"A lout of a husband who drank, and boasted, and owed the world his living before it reached his pocket." My brother looked away, a muscle in his jaw working. "There has never been any justice for people of French's class. You know that, Jane."

"But I cannot stand idly by, and watch a wrong go unrighted. Recollect, Henry—*I saw the dead man's face. Or what remained of it.*"

"Should you be surprised to learn that Bertie Philmore is, at this very moment, engaged in mending the window frame of Austen, Gray & Vincent? Philmore, as it happens, is a most accomplished joiner. He reposes somewhat higher in Mr. Dyer's trust than his late colleague French."

"Henry!" I cried. "You are *heartless*. How long did you intend to keep this from me?"

"I had no notion it was a secret." He smiled ruefully. "You had better change your dress. The dust on the road is fearful in this season. And do not tell Mamma what you are about—she will have endless commissions among the tradesmen; and I must accomplish *some* of my business before returning to London, or Gray will be finding a new partner."

HENRY SET ME DOWN IN ALTON'S HIGH STREET and led his horse to the hackney stables behind Mr. Barlow's George. I passed an enjoyable interval in strolling towards No. 10 past the various houses and shops, and took the opportunity of purchasing some bread and a couple of chickens newly dressed from the poulterer. Tho' the town cannot match Canterbury's ancient charm or rival Southampton's gentility, it offers a stout and occasionally elegant little clutch of modern buildings. I could not despise it, and felt sure that our proximity to Alton—neither so close as to oppress, nor so far as to inconvenience—was a blessing.

I found the place known as Baverstocks' without difficulty: the family has long been in the business of brewing in Alton, and a brief enquiry at the premises as to the location of the Widow Seward soon directed my footsteps towards a side lane known as Church Street. Here the younger Mr. Baverstock, one James, was established with his even younger wife and a baby, while his mother-in-law did the mending in a chair by the door.

She was a woman no older than Mrs. Prowting, tho' of less ample proportions: a frail, angular woman with a greying head and a pinched expression about the mouth. Her dark eyes swept my length as I stood in her doorway, and for an instant after I spoke my name, I was doubtful of admittance. But then she stepped backwards, with a wooden expression on her countenance, and said, "Come in, miss, and very welcome."

The hall was narrow and low-ceilinged, giving a clear view of the kitchen at the building's rear; there was a sitting room at the front, a dining parlour behind, and an abrupt staircase leading from the hall to presumably two cramped rooms above. This Widow Seward had won as her due after years of inhabiting Chawton Cottage—and I cannot say the exchange was a fair one. Had my brother Edward known to what a hovel he was sending his faithful bailiff's relict, when he disposed of her cottage elsewhere?

The babe wailed from the direction of the stairs, but Widow Seward affected not to notice. She gestured towards a free chair. "Pray sit down, miss."

I did so.

"I must thank you for the excellent condition in which we found the cottage," I said. "Everything was in order—the premises most clean and in good repair. It is a delightful place, and we are most happy to be there."

"I had heard as you were come to Chawton."

"I think the whole of Hampshire is now acquainted with the circumstances of our arrival."

She inclined her head, but did not deign to comment.

"I wonder, Mrs. Seward, whether you can tell me if there is more than one set of keys to the cottage? We collected those left in Mr. Barlow's keeping, but should like to be assured that *all* the keys are accounted for. As a matter of housekeeping. I am sure you will understand."

Her eyelids flickered and her entire spare body seemed to stiffen. "I shall have to think."

"Of course. I do understand. In a matter of keys, so much is attributable to chance. Some may be lost, others simply mislaid in a chest of drawers; or some lent to friends and relations who neglect to return them. I should assume, for example, that your daughter and son-in-law were in possession of a set—merely to accommodate you during periods of absence from the house."

"I was never absent," she said drily. "Chawton has been my home all my life. I was a Gibb before I became Seward, you know—and like the Philmores and Frenches, the Gibbs are everywhere found in this part of Hampshire. It is a very settled place. We do not often have people like yourself, from other parts of the world."

"I was born but twelve miles from Chawton," I observed, "tho' I suppose to some people, that would seem another country. When you have thought about those keys, Mrs. Seward, I should be greatly obliged if you would see that they find their way to the cottage. Otherwise we shall be put to the trouble of changing all the locks."

"You must do as you see fit, I am sure," she said austerely, and rose to indicate my interview was over.

I could not congratulate myself that it had been conducted with any success; and I felt certain that one set of keys, at least, was still sitting in this very place— in the keeping of the Baverstocks. As I exited the wretched place, I encountered a young man on the doorstep, and hesitated while he raised his hat in greeting.

"This is Miss Austen, James," the Widow Seward said in that same colourless tone. "She has just come from Chawton to visit me. Is not that a very great condescension, from the Squire's family? My son-in-law, Miss Austen—Mr. James Baverstock."

The young man bowed, with a degree of civility I

had not expected in a brewer's son. "I have already heard much of your party, ma'am, from my uncle."

"Indeed?" I said. "And have I the pleasure of acquaintance with that gentleman?"

"I fancy only by reputation," he replied. "He is Mr. John-Knight Hinton, of Chawton. My mother was his elder half-sister. If you have not yet been introduced to him, you cannot long escape the acquaintance. Good day."

BY THE TIME I ARRIVED AT THE DOOR OF HENRY'S establishment, and had been ushered within by Mr. Gray, my brother was some minutes ahead of me and happily immersed in his accounts.

"Ah, there you are, Gray—and I observe you succeeded in having the burglar's depredations attended to," Henry said carelessly as his partner entered the room. "You remember my sister, Miss Austen?"

"Indeed I do." Mr. Gray bowed deeply, welcome on every feature of his face. He was a short, rotund, and beaming man with high colour in his cheeks; his aspect suggested domestic felicity and an unhappy inclination towards gluttony. The two clerks under his management were similarly bobbing their respect in my direction, and appeared so desperate to return to their work that I felt a surge of pity for so much masculine distraction trapped in a single room. Of Bertie Philmore there was no sign; I must assume he was occupied with a window in another part of the bank.

"We are most happy to have an addition to the

Austen party in Alton," Gray assured my brother. "*Most* happy."

"Is that fellow nearly done?" Henry demanded, as tho' much harassed. "—One of Dyer's men, is he not?"

"I believe there has been some difficulty with the glazier," his partner returned. "Jorrocks has too many claims upon his talents at present to attend to our little room."

"Nothing the price of a tankard of ale won't answer. I shall speak to the joiner about it. Come along, Jane." And with breezy assurance, my brother led me into the bank's inner office—a spare, whitewashed chamber furnished with a desk, several chairs, and a quantity of ledgers.

Bertie Philmore stood by the window that gave onto the building's side aspect, grimacing with concentration. At his feet were several splintered lengths of wood, and I understood of a sudden how Henry's privacy had been forced. Not the glass alone, but the entire windowsill had been torn out of its place by the intruder's violence. Had the Rogue's legacy done all this?

"Ah, Philmore," Henry said as he closed the inner door. "What's this I hear about trouble with a glazier?"

"Jorrocks is that busy, sir, as he don't rightly think he can get here today."

"I cannot run a bank with the windows insecure to the world, Philmore. Is Jorrocks prepared to stand guard on my premises throughout the night, and discourage thieves with the menace of his gun?"

"I don't know as he 'as a gun, sir, 'cept what might be used for rabbit-hunting."

"All the same—you take my point."

The joiner gazed through the bare window, as tho' in expectation of seeing the glazier on the paving beyond; but as he turned back in evident confusion, his eyes fell upon my face. His own was instantly suffused with red.

"Why, it is the man who gave testimony at the inquest," I said with spurious surprise. "You were a friend of the Deceased, I believe. Are you happy with the coroner's result?"

"It's not for me to say, ma'am."

Henry made for the door. "I must just speak to Gray on a matter of business, Jane. I shall not be a moment."

He left me in possession of the room. Bertie Philmore looked as tho' he should like to follow my brother, but I motioned to him vaguely and murmured, "Pray go on with your work. I should not like to delay you further; my brother is a most awful object when thwarted in his expectations. You were a friend of Shafto French's from childhood, I believe? His poor widow is very sadly left."

"As are all those what gave him blunt, ma'am, and shall never see it again," Philmore said bitterly as he took up his tools once more.

"You do not credit his tale of future riches, then?"

Philmore glanced at me sidelong.

"Mrs. French came to me this morning, to gaze upon the place where her man died. It is clear that she believes the poor fellow was likely to come into funds—and went to his death in the deluded hope of finding them."

I drew off my gloves with a thoughtful air. "It does seem hard that such a young woman should be left without support of any kind. Unfortunate, too, that you have no chance to retrieve your debt, Philmore. If French's murderer were to be found, however . . . if one could but put a name to the man he intended to meet . . . it is possible affairs might be settled more equitably."

"You mean to say I might get my own back?" Philmore demanded, his plane dropping to his side.

"It is, of course, possible. But so long as the person who killed French remains obscured—so long as justice is *not* done—there can be no hope of amendment."

Philmore considered this, his rough hands flexing with his thoughts. "I'm a man of heart, ma'am. I've no grudge 'gainst Jemima French, what I've known since we was both little 'uns."

". . . Running through the fair at Robin Hood Butts," I murmured distantly. "It *is* sad that she should be left in such distress of circumstances."

"You're a relation of the Squire's, aren't ye?" he observed. "Be it likely he'll have heard of this business?"

"We expect Mr. Austen in Chawton every hour. I only hope he arrives in time to prevent Mr. Prowting from moving under his own authority. The magistrate has not so deep an understanding as my brother; he is likely to act in haste, and commit a regrettable error. He seems convinced French was killed in a matter of fisticuffs. *A row between two mates,* the magistrate said, *will likely account for the business.*"

Philmore visibly blenched. "I never did it! I left him at my door, same as my wife Rosie'll tell you."

"I am sure you did, Philmore—but I cannot vouch for Mr. Prowting's good will. He is a magistrate, and magistrates *must* charge somebody."

The joiner stepped towards me, wavering as tho' ill. "You'll speak for me, ma'am? You'll speak to your brother the Squire? You'll tell him as how I couldn't have done it, being shut of Shafto before ever he left Alton?"

"But I cannot know that," I said gently, "having been miles from Alton at the time."

He swallowed hard, and appeared to come to a decision.

"I don't rightly know what French's business were, ma'am. He were too far gone in drink to tell me much that night, and cagey with it. But I guessed it had to do with a job of work old Dyer put us onto up Sherborne St. John way. French knew summat as had to do with Stonings—and he was that puffed up about hisself, like a cock o' the walk come egg-laying day. Blood money, he called it."

There it was again—that chilling phrase, so suggestive of both blackmail and murder. Whose blood, after all, had been lost but French's own?

"Sherborne St. John," I mused, familiar with the name of the village from my girlhood, tho' I had not visited it this age. "Mr. Dyer told the coroner his men were wanted there on the Monday. But French, you say, had been at work about the place already some time?"

"Digging trenches fer walls, Shafto were. Stonings is a grand old pile, but falling to rack and ruin, ma'am. There's a deal of work to be done—should keep old Dyer in fine feather a year or more."

"Stonings? That is the name of the estate in Sherborne St. John? I do not know it. Who might the master of Stonings be?"

Philmore shrugged. "A military man just back from Spain, and limping with it. Spence is his name. It's not for me nor Shafto to deal with the likes of *they;* we take our orders from Dyer. How the poor fool thought to turn a shilling by his knowledge of Stonings, I know not. Maybe the Squire can tell. He's a rare man for sense, Mr. Austen is."

"Thank you, Philmore," I said as Henry reappeared in the doorway. I drew a few shillings from my reticule and dropped them into the joiner's hand. "It is not five pounds—but may start you a little on the way to recovering them."

"ARE YOU AT ALL FAMILIAR WITH A PLACE CALLED Stonings, Henry?" I enquired as my brother escorted me to the street.

"It is the Earl of Holbrook's seat in Sherborne St. John," Henry replied, "tho' I do not think his lordship has lived there in years—he prefers his London house, or the shooting box in Leicestershire, I believe. Why do you ask?"

"Is the Earl's family name Spence? Is he an officer who nurses a limp recently earned in the Peninsula?"

Henry stared. "Not at all! Holbrook never stirs from Carlton House if he can help it. I told you, Jane—he's the man believed to have sired Julian Thrace. Tho' there are as many who would insist it was not Holbrook at all, but the Viscount St. Eustace."

"Henry—Shafto French was put to work at Stonings with Dyer's men a few weeks ago. And now we find Julian Thrace is descended upon Hampshire. Is it not a strange coincidence?"

"Strange—but no less happenstance," he retorted impatiently. "You might mention it to Thrace when we dine at the Great House tonight. I intend to learn as much as may be about our interesting friends the Middletons and their even more curious guest this evening; the engagement forms one of the chief objects of my Hampshire interest."

"You should never have remained in Alton so long, in fact, with only your sister to entertain you."

"Indeed I should not. The country is a dead bore, Jane, without violent death to lend it spice." He bowed me satirically on my way.

As I QUITTED THE TOWN ONCE MORE IN THE DI-rection of Chawton, I was surprised to notice my informant of the morning, Bertie Philmore, on the point of entering the Swan Inn. He was probably intending to spend the shillings I had just given him on a draught of ale—but his path was blocked by a most surprising interrogator: slight of figure, elegant of appearance and sharp in his grasp of Philmore's sleeve. The Romantick Poet of yesterday's inquest was unmistakable. But what could Mr. Jack Hinton have to say to Bertie Philmore, that must animate his countenance with distinct anxiety?

Excerpt from the diary of Lord Harold Trowbridge, dated 17 April 1785, on board the Indiaman *Punjab* out of Calcutta, bound for Portsmouth.

Her name is Hélène, third and most lovely daughter of the Comte de Pont-Ravel, of an obscure and little-travelled family locked in the Jura. Her father fled the boyhood domains at a tender age, having a lust for adventure not shared by his fellows; and but for the untimely death of the eldest and heir, might have remained forever in Madras and made a fortune for the Compagnie des Indes. Sadly, the Comte was recalled last year to take up his estates, and show a proper face to the local gentry, and Hélène remained behind. In a convent school run by the nuns of Sacré-Coeur, who rely upon the good will of the French officers brought in to defend the French traders from the rapine of the British— except that the British have slowly and surely become the masters of the French on the Subcontinent, and the convent school is closing, and Hélène is bound in all irony for England itself, aboard an English ship.

And how, I asked her lightly, did this betrothal come about?

She lifted her pretty shoulders, and twirled her parasol. Papa has known the English Viscount's family for many years; there was a time when they were united by blood; and Papa has found his circumstances much embarrassed since his return to the Jura. The estates are not in good repair, the harvests are bad, the wine-making imbecilic; in short, all Papa's Madras gold is unequal to the necessities of his domain, and he has sold his youngest daughter to the highest bidder.

This much I learned from his daughter's piquant mouth as we strolled about the quarterdeck in the cooling world of the southern hemisphere autumn, while the passage of the Horn and its terrors loomed still ahead of us. I have so far advanced the trust of Captain Dundage that he sees no harm in these young British noblemen entertaining the young lady, as assuredly she must improve her English; and it required only the knowledge of my acquaintance with her espoused husband, tactfully dropped in Dundage's ear by Freddy Vansittart, to win the right to place the lady's arm through mine and lead her about the stern.

Freddy makes a third in these jaunterings, and unlike myself is fairly well lost to the charms of Hélène. I observe her parted lips—how they swell childishly in the sea air—observe her hair, whipped free of her bonnet by the compelling wind and shining gold in the sunlight; I hear her melodious voice, like lark song in the morning; and I am unmoved. She is but a child, and I no longer find children enchanting. Hélène, be she ever so fair, is doomed like the victim of tubercular fever, like the prisoner of a castle already under siege. I was foolish enough once to believe love could change the terms of one's very existence, if only one loved hard enough; I was ready to kill or be killed for love's sake; and I have since learned that the murder of the innocent is the true end of passion. I would not win this chit's heart now, if I could; I am certain that in working my revenge upon St. Eustace I should only succeed in destroying Hélène's *peace—and should never land a blow upon the Viscount's impassive façade.*

If I am weak, so be it. I have the satisfaction of knowing that I am not yet beyond the reach of all human feeling.

Freddy, having a more carnal object in view, is no such respecter of the fair Hélène's predestination. "Bollocks," he said, when I would have pled St. Eustace's case. "Don't tell me you don't hate the man. I know that you do. He's a Viscount; well, by God, I'm an Earl now, Harry—and I claim my droit de seigneur." I must hope that if Bertie is thrown from his horse one day, and leaves me in possession of the strawberry leaves and Wilborough House, that I do not commit the same follies of arrogance that Freddy has come to, since the receipt of that letter from Hampshire.[1] Droit de seigneur. And so, regardless of whom she may love, Hélène de Pont-Ravel is forever a chattel, the property of one man or another who proposes to claim her. No wonder Mamma saw fit to run off to the Parisian stage. Freedom is worth any amount of scandal.

I should not be a woman for anything in this world.

---

[1] We are to assume from Lord Harold's oblique reference that Frederick Vansittart acceded to his elder brother's earldom sometime in 1785, and that for this reason he returned to England aboard the *Punjab* with the governor-general's party.—*Editor's note.*

Chapter 11

The Steward

6 July 1809, cont.

~

CHAWTON GREAT HOUSE, CONSTRUCTED OF FLINT in the Tudor style, sits at the southern end of the village on a gentle rise above the church of St. Nicholas. It is a noble and somewhat eccentric old gentleman's house, with wings facing awkwardly to west and north, and any number of curious, ill-considered passages running through its interior. I spent more than a week as an intimate of the place two years ago, while Edward made some repairs to the property prior to Mr. Middleton's taking up his lease, and was thus prepared for the archaic splendours within.

Tho' the light of a summer's evening was still strong as the Austen party approached the entrance porch for our appointed dinner, Mr. Middleton had caused flaming torches to be set into brackets near the door.

"Quite a feudal note, Jane," Henry observed; "I wonder whether we shall be compelled to share our joint with the hounds?"

As a sportsman, Mr. Middleton might be expected to keep a pack of hunting dogs, or at the very least a family of spaniels; and the galleries running off the top of the main staircase *do* possess a Dog Gate, designed to prevent the beasts from invading the upper storeys. There is a Great Hall within, accessible through a gap in an ancient oak screen; a draughty, inhospitable space, such as may serve for the reception of tenants on Publick Days, but cannot hope to cheer a family party even in July. Oak panelling rises on every wall, much of it carved, and a massive fireplace struggles in winter to heat the room—notable for its fireback, which is engraved with the name John Knight, and the date 1588—the year of the Hall's completion as well as the Spanish Armada. In addition to all these, the house boasts a dining parlour; a stone-flagged kitchen; a buttery; a drawing-room where the chief treasure of Chawton—the Lewkenor Carpet[1]—is hung; and a much-neglected garden.

The Knight family line failed in 1679, when Sir Richard Knight—whose imposing effigy is carved in stone on his tomb in St. Nicholas Church—died childless, and all the subsequent owners of Chawton

---

[1] The Lewkenor Carpet is a tapestry roughly sixteen feet by seven feet, executed in the mid-sixteenth century in France and now in the possession of the Metropolitan Museum of Art, New York.—*Editor's note.*

have been obliged under his will to take the name of Knight in order to succeed to his riches. In death Sir Richard exerted a powerful influence over as-yet-unborn kin: the Martins and Broadnaxes, and now the Austens. It was inevitable, I supposed, that my brother Edward and all his progeny would one day exchange their name for Sir Richard's—and I should have done the same to possess even *one* such house.

Mr. Middleton had caused a fire to be lit in the massive Hall grate; and around this cheerful if superfluous blaze several persons were gathered. I recognised Miss Benn, looking self-consciously fine in a gown of black sarcenet; all the Prowtings; Mr. Julian Thrace, whose attention was claimed by Miss Ann Prowting; and standing a little apart from them, another gentleman perhaps five years Thrace's senior, in close conversation with a handsome young woman whose dress and air proclaimed her an established member of the *ton*.

Mr. Middleton, who was listening to Miss Benn's effusions regarding his kindness, patted that lady's gloved hand gently and broke away long enough to pay his respects to the Austen party. A sharp-featured and brilliant-eyed lady was before him, however, her hand imperiously extended.

"My brother should have brought me to your door already, Mrs. Austen, but that he is too intent upon showing his guests the country; I hope you will forgive our appalling manners."

"My sister, Miss Maria Beckford," interposed Mr.

Middleton hastily. "She is so kind as to do the duties of the Great House."

From the difference in the lady's name, I must assume she was actually the sister of Mr. Middleton's deceased *wife*, and had established herself in the household to oversee the education of his five children. However long ago Mr. Middleton's lady had departed this world, he had not learned to love her sister instead; but Miss Maria Beckford appeared entirely in command of the situation, in her richly-trimmed silk gown and her dignified posture. I should not have judged her to be much beyond the middle thirties, an age I am myself approaching; her hair, though pulled back severely from her forehead under a lace cap, was still a rich reddish-brown, and an expression of intelligence and good humour lit her dark eyes. This was no female dependant or shrinking drudge sacrificed to her family's service, but a lady who could command all the glories of Mr. Middleton's income and establishment—without the bother of being his wife. I thought her rather to be congratulated than pitied.

"You are Miss Austen?" she demanded.

"Miss *Jane* Austen. My elder sister is as yet on her road from Kent."

Miss Beckford surveyed me from head to foot; lingered an instant in contemplation of my own unwavering gaze; and then nodded slightly as though in approval.

"And are you fond of books and reading?"

"I am, ma'am."

"Do you sketch or paint in watercolours?"

"Unhappily I lack that talent."

"A pity. The beauties of Hampshire afford innumerable subjects for contemplation. But perhaps you play or sing?"

"I am a devotee of the pianoforte—although my own instrument . . . is not yet arrived."

"That is very well. You may delight us with a performance this evening. We are happy to welcome you to Chawton, Miss Austen. The accomplishments of ladies in these parts are most unfortunately limited. But for Miss Hinton and the Prowtings we should have *no* society worth the name. —But I see that the Hintons are arrived. If you will excuse me—"

She brushed past, intent upon the couple who now stood in the doorway; and as I had no desire to hasten my meeting with the avowed enemies of the Squire, I stepped forward to claim the notice of the rest of the party, to whom my brother Henry was already speaking. He intended, I knew, to make the most of his proximity to such exalted circles, and dine out on the strength of his intelligence regarding Julian Thrace for the next twelvemonth.

"Mr. Thrace and Miss Benn you know," Mr. Middleton was saying, "but I do not think you are as yet acquainted with Lady Imogen Vansittart."

The handsome young woman inclined her head with a regal air, but uttered not a syllable. She was tall, slender, dark-eyed, and eloquent of feature; her gown was white muslin; she wore a circlet of emeralds in her dark hair. Tho' I should judge her to be several years younger than Miss Catherine Prowting, who stood a little distance apart from the elegant Lady Imogen, she was so far beyond Catherine in countenance and assurance that *she* seemed the woman, and Catherine the girl.

"And Major Charles Spence," my host continued, "who comes to us, in company with Mr. Thrace and Lady Imogen, from Stonings—the Earl of Holbrook's seat near Sherborne St. John."

If my own heart quickened at the name of that man and that estate, Henry was before me. My brother's keen grey gaze was immediately fixed upon Major Spence.

"Sherborne St. John!" he cried, with unforced delight. "But then you must be acquainted with the Chute family, our friends these two decades at least. As a boy, my brother James and I hunted with the Vyne."[2]

"—As it was my privilege to do only last winter," Major Spence returned amiably. "Mr. Chute is a very respectable, gentleman-like man, and a most welcome neighbour."

"I cannot perfectly recall Stonings, however."

"My father caused it to be let to a family from the North for much of the past two decades," Lady Imogen supplied. "But the Rices have lately given the

---

[2] The Vyne, or Vine—ancestral home of the Chute family at Sherborne St. John a few miles beyond Basingstoke just north of Chawton—was the site of one of the more famous hunting groups in southern England. William Chute (1757–1824), the patriarch in Jane Austen's time, was both Master of the Vyne Hunt and a Member of Parliament for his borough.—*Editor's note.*

house up—and I took a fancy to see it. It is possible the estate may fall to my lot in time—and I have never been the sort of woman to buy a mount without first having a look at its teeth."

She threw a look of challenge at Julian Thrace. There were several meanings implicit in such a speech, and I thought I had missed none of them. Lady Imogen was the Earl of Holbrook's daughter—the legitimate issue about to be supplanted in the bulk of her inheritance by a man sprung from exactly nowhere. Her looks said plainly that she was fiercely determined to rout her rival, and expose him to the world's censure as an imposter; but she should never fail in politeness while she did so. I guessed her to have courage and wit enough to meet any trick the Bond Street Beau might serve her.

Henry smiled at the lady, his face alight with all the interest of the party before him. There was a fortune to be made among the betting books of the St. James clubs, and if truth was to be drawn from present company, my brother was poised to reap the whirlwind. The Viscount St. Eustace was as naught; the wise money should be entirely on the Earl of Holbrook. I wondered Henry did not post immediately to London.

"I should not wish you to put the horse through its paces at present," Charles Spence observed. "Stonings has been sadly in want of refurbishment for many years. I am presently employed by the Earl of Holbrook as his steward, Mr. Austen—and am charged with the duty of bringing order where neglect has been the rule."

"The place is in such a degree of decay," Mr. Middleton added, "that I pressed Spence most earnestly to make a stay of some duration here at the Great House. It cannot be a pleasant thing, to sleep amidst dust and plaster, with the sound of Dyer's joiners toiling away in the lower parts of the house; but our Stonings party comes to us for this evening only, and will depart on the morrow—depriving Chawton of its most lovely flower."

He bowed in Lady Imogen's direction.

Dyer's joiners, I thought. Had any of the present labourers discovered Shafto French's secret? And did the handsome party assembled before me share his guilty knowledge—or that of his sad end?

As Mr. Middleton quitted us to greet another of his guests, Major Spence said, "Am I to understand, Miss Austen, that you are but two days arrived in Chawton?"

"That is true, sir. We are hardly strangers to Hampshire, however, having lived in this county the better part of our lives. My father was once rector of Steventon, where presently my brother James is incumbent."

"A clergyman's daughter," he observed with a smile, "and I am a clergyman's son."

"Are you, indeed? From what part of the country do you hail?"

"The North. I was raised in Yorkshire. Do you know that part of the world, ma'am?"

"I regret to say that I do not. But how are you

come to be in this part of the world? It is a great change of scene, surely?"

"It does not follow that such a change must be unwelcome. Unlike your brother, I had no inclination for the Church, Miss Austen, and broke my father's heart at the age of seventeen by running away to the Army. I am recently sold out from the Eighteenth Light Dragoons, having suffered a trifling wound at Vimeiro."

A military man just back from Spain, and limping with it. I had not yet observed the game leg in action—but should have dearly liked to examine the Major's footwear more closely. The notion of this particular gentleman riding some twelve miles at night in order to drown a man and hide his body in my cellar seemed, however, fantastic. "You were with Sir Arthur Wellesley, then, last September?"

"I was—altho' the injury to my leg required me to be taken off the coast of Maceira immediately following our engagement with the French. I was not required to endure the privations later visited upon my fellows during Sir John Moore's catastrophic retreat—to my enduring shame."

"My brother, Captain Frank Austen of the *Canopus*, carried away the remnant of Sir John's men this past January," I said in a subdued accent. "From his account I must suppose the losses to have been frightful."

"But no worse than we shall serve Buonaparte in future," Spence replied stoutly.

We were both silent an instant, our thoughts far removed from the frivolity of a summer evening;

mine were travelling in memory to Southampton the previous autumn, and the low-voiced communication of a government spy in the hold of a Navy ship. Where Major Spence's thoughts might be wandering, I could not hazard a guess; but from his expression, it was no Elysian Field.

"And so I threw myself upon the mercy of my relations," he resumed with forced lightness, "and accepted employment as the Earl of Holbrook's steward. I may say that I am entirely unfitted to the task—being a soldier is no recommendation for business—but his lordship was prevailed upon to accept me. I am a second cousin to the Earl, once removed, on the distaff side."

"I am sure he has every reason to be grateful for your stewardship of Stonings," I observed. "Mr. Dyer's men have been very busy about the place, I collect?"

"It is a noble estate," he said thoughtfully. "But the degree of neglect is much to be deplored. The Earl, being an intimate of the Carlton House Set, formed the early habit of repairing to Brighton in the summer months. He spends the winters at his hunting box in Leicestershire. The remainder of the year is passed in Town. I do not think the Earl has descended into Hampshire above three times since his accession to the title." He glanced about the panelled hall, gaze roving among the leaded windows. "Your brother, I believe, is the owner of this house! It is a very fine old place—Elizabethan, I should judge?"

"Exactly so. But like your Earl, my brother does not deign to live in Hampshire."

"Middleton informed me that he is an excellent landlord; so very liberal, in fact, that Middleton cannot keep away from Chawton. He has leased this estate twice in recent years."

"And is a most agreeable tenant in every respect. Are you very much acquainted with Mr. Middleton?"

"A sporting acquaintance, one might call it," Spence said diffidently, "formed on the hunting field. He is all affability, however, and does not disgrace your brother's good opinion. I hope to see more of him."

"And was it you who introduced Mr. Thrace to Mr. Middleton's acquaintance?"

"Not at all. Thrace fell in with the Middleton family while travelling on the Continent, I believe. But Thrace will have to tell you how it was himself; I am not perfectly in command of the history."

Henry had referred to Thrace's past as being obscured by war and curious incident—a childhood in France, or a French mother, perhaps. It was impossible not to speculate at what point he had first sought the Earl of Holbrook's notice, and claimed the relation of son to father—impossible not to wonder how the Earl had received this news. Or broken it to Lady Imogen.

I found my eyes lingering on the Beau's face, attempting to trace some likeness between himself and Lady Imogen; but I confess I could find none. One so dark, the other so light, they appeared to excellent effect—but hardly as brother and sister. But then I recollected: they were related in half-blood only. Much might be attributed to the influence of different mothers.

Thrace, I noticed, was exerting himself to engage Catherine Prowting in conversation—despite the jealous attempts of her sister to divert the gentleman's attention. Catherine's colour was high, her eyes brilliant; and tho' she remained the picture of elegant self-possession, I thought she did not meet Mr. Thrace's attentions with indifference.

"I hope I do not intrude—but I could not forbear to offer my sympathy for the trials you have so lately undergone," Major Spence continued in a lower tone. "Thrace told me of the shocking affair only this morning, as I was arrived with Lady Imogen from Sherborne St. John. I trust you have suffered no ill-effects from the anxiety?"

"None at all, I assure you."

"And your home . . . it was not unduly disturbed? There were no losses of a personal nature?"

His concern was so earnest, his expression so truly amiable, that I could not be unmoved. "You are very good, sir—but the losses were not ours to tally. That has been poor Mrs. French's office."

"You will wish to take greater care in future, I am sure, Miss Austen, to secure your valuables against a similar invasion. The coroner, I understand, could arrive at no solution to the mystery of the labourer's death? —Or at least, how he came to be in your cellar?"

"You must question Mr. Prowting on that score. He is our magistrate, and must be in command of more particulars than I." With more courage than tact

I added, "The poor man was often at Stonings, I understand, in recent weeks. Did you never notice him there?"

An instant's confusion clouded the Major's countenance, but any reply he might have made was forestalled by the approach of Miss Maria Beckford.

"Miss Austen," she said in her brisk, decisive way, as tho' commanding a parade ground, "allow me to introduce Miss Jane Hinton to your acquaintance."

Major Spence stepped aside, and bowed; I curtseyed to the woman at Miss Beckford's right hand, and regarded with amusement this new trial.

Jane Hinton was some years older than her brother—a woman nearly forty whose bloom had long since gone off. She appeared correct and unremarkable in a prim white cap and a pair of spectacles, behind which her flat brown eyes were intently appraising. Her dress was of a most unbecoming yellow hue, her skin coarse; and when she spoke, it was with a pronounced lisp that made her speech singularly unpleasing.

"I have heard your name everywhere, Mith Authten," she said without warmth. "You are quite the talk of the village—indeed, of every habitation for mileth around. We are not accuthtomed, in our retired country way, to ladieth condethending to vithit a coroner'th inquetht; but I thuppothe, when the lady in quethtion hath actually thtumbled over the body, that we mutht be prepared for anything."

"My brother *did say* that he met with you in Alton yesterday," Miss Beckford observed, "and I thought it most courageous of you to attend, my dear. The notice of a member of the Squire's family must be a great comfort in a death of this kind, and shall be felt as it ought, among the lower orders. May I present Mr. John-Knight Hinton, also of Chawton Lodge?"

My slight poet of the cut indirect was arrayed this evening in primrose knee breeches, a white satin waistcoat, and a black evening coat with stiffly-padded shoulders. His snowy cravat was of so intricate a construction that it bewildered the eye, and a quizzing glass dangled from a fine gold chain about his neck. Mr. Hinton clearly prided himself on his ability to ape the most current London fashion, and his magnificence might have turned the head of many a green girl; but to my more practised gaze, Julian Thrace's neat elegance—or even Major Spence's quiet rectitude—more clearly proclaimed the gentleman.

He raised his quizzing glass, surveyed me impudently, and scraped a bow.

"I have already had a glimpse of Mr. Hinton," I told Miss Beckford with a smile, "at yesterday's inquest, and again today in Alton. What was your opinion of the tragic business, sir?"

"I thought it very singular that such grievous trouble should arise in so peaceful and respectable a place," Mr. Hinton returned. "Indeed, I may say that I was *ashamed* the shades of Chawton must be so polluted."

"And yet you could not keep away from the coroner's panel," Miss Beckford observed astringently. "I suppose it is of a piece with your usual sporting amusements. Mr. Hinton is quite a slave to the Corinthian Set, Miss Austen. There is not a prize-fight or a cock pit within thirty miles that is unknown to him."[3]

"Indeed?" I murmured with an air of surprise. "From your appearance, Mr. Hinton—so much the Sprig of Fashion!—I should have thought you aspired to the Dandy Set."

The gentleman dropped his quizzing glass as tho' struck to the quick.

"I observe Mr. Papillon is arrived," Miss Beckford supplied quickly. "If you will excuse me—"

She moved off, with a nod for Mr. Hinton that flavoured strongly of contempt; but the gentleman did not seize the opportunity to follow her, as I might have expected. Miss Beckford was as a fly he swept aside with a careless hand.

"Violence is quite foreign to those who truly love this country, Miss Austen; and certain it is that a corpse should never have been discovered in *Widow Seward's* cottage," Mr. Hinton observed. "But she was most truly the lady in all respects. I need hardly add that the presence of Dyer's labourers would not have been necessary prior to her forcible eviction. *She* saw no reason to complain of the cottage's arrangements."

His implication was clear: we Austens had brought this trouble upon the village ourselves, and we Austens alone must bear the burden of its

[3] The term *Corinthian* is derived from Shakespeare's *Henry IV, Part I:* "a Corinthian, a lad of mettle . . ." and connoted a gentleman practiced in such manly sports as boxing, fencing, cocking, horse-racing, gambling, hunting, and carriage-driving.—*Editor's note.*

disgrace. I flushed in the sudden heat of anger—
which discomposure was undoubtedly Mr. Hinton's
object—but any words I might have uttered were
overborne. The bell was rung, the ladies' hands disposed among the gentlemen—and we were all sent
in to dinner.

Letter from Lord Harold Trowbridge to Charles, Earl Grey, dated 2 June 1791, one leaf quarto, laid; no watermark; signed *Trowbridge* under a black wax seal bearing imprint of Wilborough arms; marked, *Personelle, Par Chassure Exprès*, in red ink. (British Museum, Wilborough Papers, Austen bequest)

Rue de Varennes, Paris

My dear Charles—

I thank you for your last, and am most happy to know that you perceive a change in the political fortunes of our party in coming months. If the Duke of Devonshire will lend his weight where weight is necessary, anything may happen; and your good angel, my beloved Georgiana, may yet effect the necessary push. Canis will not act, as we know to our misfortune, and the Duchess does not will it; but her affection for yourself and her high courage shall see us all through.

I dined with Jouvel in the country near Versailles last evening, and he begs to be remembered to you. He has a very pretty daughter of but fifteen, and were I in the habit of carrying off girls half my age, I should be sorely tempted; but as it is, I must direct my energies elsewhere. I am charged with no less, and the stakes— as we used to say at Brooks's—are murderously high.

You will be pleased to know that the difficulties attendant upon Revolutionary fervour that you and I foresaw, in Cornwall this spring, are already anticipated among our friends on this side of the Channel. I stand ready to ship any number of "wine casks" and "horses of racing blood" in the small vessels you have promised to have ready off Marseille, and have found a likely lad to help me in the transport. His name is Geoffrey Sidmouth, and he is tied by blood to any number of people we esteem and value; he is a handy fellow with the management of ships, and is in good heart. I will send word when the need arises; I hope it may not for some time, but I fear that my hope is false.

I remain, my dear Charles—

Trowbridge

Chapter 12

The Devil in the Cards

~

AS EVENING PARTIES GO, OURS WAS MORE GENER-
ally unequal in its composition than most. We were
treated to Miss Benn's simplicities and vague utterances, which had the appalling habit of falling directly
into such lapses in the conversation as must make
them the most apparent. Lady Imogen Vansittart, on
the other hand, deigned to speak to no one not of her
intimate party and at her end of the table—that is to
say, no one other than Major Spence or Mr. Thrace;
while Henry, who was positioned at the table's centre,
spent the better part of the evening attempting to
catch the conversation proceeding above him, while
evading the notice of those conversing below.

The Prowtings were divided between volubility

and silence, with Catherine—who was placed next to Mr. Hinton—staring painfully and self-consciously at her plate. I several times observed Mr. Hinton to speak to her in a low and urgent tone, but she repulsed the gentleman's attempts at conversation. Her earnest gaze was more often fixed upon Julian Thrace, but what attention he could spare from Lady Imogen was entirely claimed by Ann Prowting, who had been placed at the Beau's left hand.

Ann's devoted efforts at new-dressing her hair had certainly achieved a degree of novelty: the girl's golden curls were gathered in a rakish knot over one ear, with a few tender wisps straggling to her nape. A quantity of white shoulder was exposed, as was an ample décolleté; and I might almost have suspected Ann of dampening her shift beneath the white muslin gown, in order that the thin fabric should cling to her limbs. She sat opposite to Henry, but succeeded in ignoring my brother completely. With a Julian Thrace at hand, who could spare a thought for an aging banker?

The young man who aspired to an earldom was the picture of easiness. Thrace could flirt with Ann Prowting, reduce a quail to bones with graceful fingers, listen to Lady Imogen with every appearance of interest, and address an amusing story to his host. Had I yearned to converse with him, I was placed at a disadvantage. My seat was towards the lower end of the table, next to Mr. Prowting; but I was able to observe the Beau's artful swoops from one conversational plane to another, and decided that it was all very well done.

He had claimed my attention first by declaring, with affecting candour, that he had never before found an occasion to witness a coroner's inquest—and had discovered the experience to be infinitely diverting.

"As a man raised for much of my life on the Continent," Thrace explained to the table in general, "I am not so familiar as I should like with the conventions of English justice. To observe your yeoman class, displayed on a hard wooden bench and endeavouring to do their utmost in consideration of the Departed, was as instructive as a treatise on philosophy should be. I admired the succinctness and learning of Mr. Munro, the subtlety with which he asked his questions, and the respect with which he treated high and low alike."

"I wonder," the exquisite Mr. Hinton replied with a curl of his lip, "that you can reap so much benefit from so vulgar an episode. I could only endure the two hours I spent in the George, by resolving never to be found there again!"

Mr. Thrace smiled at the gentleman. "But perhaps, sir, you had not the peculiar interest I felt in the man's demise. When I consider that had I left Middleton but five minutes earlier that evening, I might have saved the labourer's life—or, heaven forbid!—met a similar fate at the hands of his murderer, I could not be otherwise than compelled by the coroner's proceeding."

A storm of questions greeted this pronouncement, with Mr. Thrace throwing up his hands in protest as the ladies all demanded that he explain himself.

"There is no mystery," cried he. "I dined alone on Saturday with our excellent Middleton, Spence being absent from Sherborne St. John on a matter of business in Basingstoke, and Lady Imogen being as yet in London."

"We sat in conversation so long," Mr. Middleton added, "that it cannot have been earlier than midnight when you quitted the house, tho' I pressed you most earnestly to remain, and should have summoned the housemaid to make up your room, had you allowed it. But you would not put me to the trouble, and rode out directly, the moon being nearly at the full, and the road well-illumined."

"You noticed nothing untoward, sir, in your way back to Sherborne St. John?" Mr. Prowting asked keenly. "No *mill* in the roadway, as I believe these affairs are called among the sporting set?"

"My road did not lie in the direction of the pond, if indeed the poor man met his death in that place," Thrace explained. "I set off at a canter in the direction of Alton, and thence towards Basingstoke, and achieved Stonings by three o'clock in the morning— my hunter, Rob Roy, being a devil to go, begging the ladies' pardon."

Ann Prowting here exclaimed at the beauty of Mr. Thrace's horse, and the conversation turned more generally to the hunting field, and Mr. Chute's mastery of the Vyne, and the particularities of certain hounds the gentlemen had known; and my attention might have wandered, but for Mr. Thrace's enjoyment of general conversation, and his tendency to bring the attention of the whole table back to himself. Had I not observed the easiness of his manners, and the general air of modesty that attended his speech, I might have adjudged him a coxcomb, and despised him at my leisure. As it was, I merely wondered at his reverting so often to the unfortunate end of Shafto French. It is quite rare in my experience for a gentleman to concern himself with the murder of a labourer—unless, of course, he harbours some sort of guilty knowledge, or hopes to expose the same in another. I determined to make a study of Mr. Thrace, and refused a third glass of claret that my mind might be clear.

Over the second course, a pleasurable affair of some twelve dishes, the Bond Street Beau related a roguish tale, full of incident and melodrama, concerning a necklace of rubies stolen by a British officer at the Battle of Chandernagar; a necklace of such fabled import, that it was said to have once graced the neck of Madame de Pompadour, and to be worth all of two hundred thousand pounds.[1]

"I am certain the stolen jewels are to blame for that unfortunate man's death in your cottage, Miss Austen," affirmed he with a gleam in his eye. "I might

[1] The Battle of Chandernagar refers to the English East India Company's assault, under the direction of Robert Clive, of the French Compagnie des Indes Fort d'Orléans in Chandernagar, India, in 1757. At the cost of significant casualties among Royal Navy troops brought in to fight against the French, the British decisively established control of Bengal for commercial trading.—*Editor's note.*

have offered the story to the coroner yesterday morning, but from a fear of putting myself forward in such a delicate proceeding."

These words could not fail to alert Mr. Prowting's attention; the magistrate was suddenly all interest. "Say your piece, man," he instructed from his position opposite Henry. "If you know something that bears on the murder, you must disclose it to the Law!"

"Well—" Aware that the notice of the entire table was united in his person, Mr. Thrace inclined his head towards Lady Imogen. "I had the tale from your father, the Earl—who spent some years out in India as a young man, and heard the story at its source. It seems that a fabulous necklace was stolen at sabre point from one of the gallant French defenders so routed by Clive in that illustrious battle, which occurred in the last century, I believe."

"Clive took Chandernagar from the French in 1757," Major Spence supplied. "The battle secured Bengal for the English."

"Exactly so," Thrace returned. "The story, as the Earl told it to me, is that an English Lieutenant seized the fabled gems from a French defender at the fort's capitulation, and brought them to England after much intrigue and bloodshed. They were later lost on the road—somewhere near Chawton, if you will credit it."

Mrs. Prowting emitted a faint scream, one plump hand over her mouth, the other clutching her handkerchief.

"It is said," Thrace further observed, "that, hounded across land and sea unceasingly by Indian pursuers of a most deadly and subtle kind, the Lieutenant landed in Southampton and made his way by feverish degrees towards London. Coming to St. Nicholas's Church"—this, with a bow for Mr. Papillon, Chawton's clergyman, who was seated at the bottom of the table—"he sought refuge in the sanctuary, where the Hindu fakirs, being unmoved by Christian belief, wounded him severely. In Chawton the trail of the purloined rubies comes to an abrupt end."

"Are you thuggethting, thir, that thith thimple village ith in the unwitting potethion of the Thpoilth of War?" enquired Miss Hinton. It was the first remark I had heard her to address to the upper end of the table; and I applauded its natural sense. *She* was not to be taken in by a spurious fribble, a Pink of the *Ton;* *hers* was a sober countenance, suggestive of a lady much given to reading sermons, and making Utheful Extracth.

Mr. Thrace, his eyes on Catherine Prowting's glowing countenance, slowly crumbled a piece of bread between his fingers. "The necklace was believed to be cursed—not simply from the manner of its possession, but from a flaw inherent in the stones themselves. Rubies, so like to blood, must draw blood to them; and so it proved in this case. The Rubies of Chandernagar destroyed each of their successive masters."

"For what doth it profit a man, if he gain the whole world, and loothe hith Immortal Thoul?" observed Miss Hinton with complacency.

"I had not heard this story of my father," Lady

Imogen imposed, "tho' I know him to have moved in a very rakehell set while in India. Chandernagar, however, was some thirty years before his time on the Subcontinent."

"I believe the story has achieved a permanent place in the Indian firmament," Thrace said, "due to its bloodthirstiness. No doubt your respected father learned it of an eyewitness."

"But surely the marauding Lieutenant was a man of parts?" Lady Imogen objected. "What are a whole company of Hindu against one hardened English soldier? Major Spence, for example, should never be parted from his treasure so easily!"

Her liquid eyes were dark with excitement, her voice throbbing and low. I observed that while her gaze was fixed on Julian Thrace, Major Spence was observing *her;* as he did so, an expression of pain crossed his countenance.

"The Lieutenant who seized them, to the ruin of their French owner, had his throat cut while he lay in that very inn which you, ma'am"—this, with a gracious acknowledgement of my mother—"have now the happy fortune to inhabit," Thrace continued. "The wounded man dragged himself to the publick house, wounded and bleeding, seeking refuge from his pursuers. His body was discovered on the morning following—but of the rubies no trace was ever found."

"Perhaps this is the root of the cottage's illfortune," Mr. Hinton observed languidly. "If your story is true, Thrace, the digger of the cesspit was not the first corpse to lie there. I daresay it was the necklace that good-for-nothing ruffian French was searching for, in the depths of Mrs. Austen's cellar."

"But it will not do, man!" Mr. Prowting exclaimed, and threw down his napkin. "Shafto French was *drowned,* as the coroner has said. He cannot both have been treasure-hunting in the cottage cellar, and breathing his last in Chawton Pond!"

A slightly shocked silence followed this outburst; one which the clergyman Mr. Papillon had the grace to end.

"But in the case of the Earl's Indian story," he observed with a correct smile, as though improving an archbishop's views on Ordination, "nothing is clearer. Naturally the rubies were not to be discovered. The thieving Lieutenant gave up his booty with his life, and his murderer lived ever after on the proceeds."

"One should suppose no such thing," Mr. Thrace retorted, "it being attested by those who study these matters, that the stones never afterwards came onto the market. What sort of thief makes away with a considerable prize, and does not attempt to profit by it? No, no, my dear sir—the Rubies of Chandernagar are in one of two places: either hidden beneath the stones of your own St. Nicholas's crypt, where the errant Lieutenant—already fearing for his life—placed them before receiving his deadly wound; or concealed still about the grounds of the late inn."

My mother's looks were eloquent: a mixture of rapacity and uneasiness.

"And does our home accommodate the murdered soldier as well?" I demanded lightly, "—his ghost creaking of nights upon the stairs of the cottage, crying out for vengeance?"

"You may inform us whether it is so in the morning, Miss Austen."

Amidst general laughter, Lady Imogen protested, "For my part, I think it imperative that a search party be formed after dinner, as a kind of amusement, so that we might fan out across the countryside with lanthorns and dogs and discover the treasure. We might call the entertainment 'Hunt the Necklace,' and begin in St. Nicholas's vestry!"

"Under the very flags of the church," murmured Mr. Papillon distractedly, "or perhaps in the crypt! I cannot believe it possible—for there are several of the Deceased newly-laid in that part of the building, you know, and I cannot recollect any irregularities about the interments."

"It is all a piece of horrid nonsense!" cried Ann Prowting with an arch look for Mr. Thrace, "but I am sure I shall not sleep a wink tonight, for gazing out my window at the cottage in my nightdress, in an effort to glimpse your ghost!"

"Let us hope, Miss Prowting," murmured Mr. Hinton acidly, "you do not encounter Shafto French—or his murderers—instead."

WHEN THE LADIES RETIRED FROM THE DINING parlour, it was a most ill-suited party that collected around the tea table in the Great House drawing-room. Lady Imogen took herself off to the instrument

standing near the tall windows giving out onto the
lawn, there to turn over the leaves of music with a
deeply preoccupied air; she showed no inclination to
revive the sport of Hunt the Necklace. Ann Prowting
threw herself into a chair and yawned prodigiously,
her conversation confined to such peevish utterances
as, "Cannot we get up a dance this evening? I declare
I am *pining* for a ball!" Her mother contented herself
with arranging the stiff black folds of her dress and
conversing most animatedly to Maria Beckford of the
merits of Benjamin Clement, RN, who was perhaps
not unknown to that lady; Miss Beckford listened in
any case with the attitude of a sparrow trained upon a
worm. Miss Benn had seated herself on the opposite
side of Mrs. Prowting and was industriously knitting;
while Jane Hinton drew forth a volume of sermons
from her reticule and commenced reading, lips visibly lisping over the inaudible words.

This left me a choice of companions until the appearance of the gentlemen should restore Henry to
me: Miss Elizabeth Papillon, sister to the rector of St.
Nicholas's and his spinster housekeeper, with whom I
thus far had exchanged only curtseys; and Catherine
Prowting. Naturally, I chose to approach the latter.

She was a solitary figure positioned near the
hearth, in which no blaze burned; her eyes were fixed
upon the empty firedogs, and so painful an expression of unhappiness was in all her bearing that I
would have turned away without speaking to her, but
for the sudden swift glance she gave me, and the lift-
ing of her right hand as tho' in supplication.

"Are you unwell, Catherine?" I asked without preamble.

"Only this wretched head-ache," she replied in a suffocated voice. "I suppose I must ascribe it to the heat; but indeed I cannot bear it, and as soon as my father returns, I shall beg him to escort all our party home."

"Are you displeased with the party? Is the Bond Street Beau not to your liking?"

She flushed. "Mr. Thrace is a most gentleman-like man in every respect. I own I am pleasantly surprised. If only the rest of the company were so well chosen!"

"Should you not lie down? I might enquire of Miss Beckford whether there is vinegar-water, for bathing your temples—"

She shook her head fiercely, which I should have thought would increase her pain; but if so, she was determined not to regard it. "Miss Austen—you have lived in the world more than I, and know far more of . . . gentlemen, and such things. . . ."

"A little, perhaps," I returned guardedly; but my heart sank. Was I about to receive an unlooked-for confidence, and be burdened hereafter with an intimacy I had not sought?

"If only I knew what I *ought* to *do*," Catherine whispered, her fingers on her temples and her eyes closing in pain. "If only I understood my *duty*."

"Duty is the clearest path we know," I told her. "It is the path of the *heart* that descends into obscurity."

These words seemed to arrest her thoughts. The

fluttering hands fell to her sides, and her mouth opened in a soundless O.

At that instant, the drawing-room door opened and the gentlemen returned—faces flushed, heads thrown back in laughter at some jest of my brother's—all except one. Mr. Hinton alone was morose and solitary. His sneering gaze fell upon Catherine where she stood at my side, and I observed her to stiffen, her lips compressed. Then, with an attitude of resolution, she approached her father and spoke low in his ear.

"All in good time, my dear," he said heartily. "All in good time. The night is young, you know—and the card tables about to be brought out!"

She looked despairing; but her mother and sister were insensible to her pleas of ill health, and determined to remain as long as possible in such interesting company; and so Catherine retired to the far end of the room, intending to form no part of the groupings around the tables.

In a few moments I observed Julian Thrace to join her there. He seemed to enquire after her health, and unlike Mr. Hinton, I thought he should not be repulsed.

"Jane," my mother said indignantly as she approached the fireplace, "*wait* until you hear what that woman has been saying to me. I *will* not call her a lady; I will not *condescend* to offer her that distinction."

"Which woman, Mamma?"

"The Hinton creature. In her lisping, oily way she has desired me to understand that his lordship's treasure chest is everywhere known to be residing in our cottage, and that speculation is rife as to the morals of my younger daughter. That *intimathy on both thideth undoubtedly exithted,* Miss Hinton would have me know, *without the benefit of the marriage vow,* is firmly established; and the horror of the ladies in the surrounding country, at being forced to acknowledge a hardened bit of muslin such as yourself—if only to remain on good terms with the Squire, whom she also suggested is of the lowest depravity imaginable, as evidenced by his heartless actions towards his tenants—is an insult from which the best local families are unlikely to recover. As though you were a Cyprian of the most dashing kind! It is too bad, Jane, when all he left you was a quantity of paper! I could *cry* with vexation!"

"Miss Hinton said all this?" I demanded with amusement. "I am astonished at her powers of articulation."

"I do not mean to say she spoke it out plain," my mother retorted impatiently, "but I am not so green that I cannot divine the meaning of a pack of lies. It is insupportable, Jane, that the Rogue should see fit to sink your character from his very grave! And you not a penny the richer!"

"Lord Harold's notice remains one of the chief delights of my existence, Mamma," I answered quietly, "and I shall never learn to despise it. If I care nothing for the malice of a Jane Hinton, why should you listen to her words? It is all envy, ignorance, and pride; and we need consider none of them."

My mother being very soon thereafter claimed for

a table of whist, I was relieved of the necessity of calming her further, but longed to share Miss Hinton's absurdity with Henry—who should value it as he ought. That the spite of the lady sprang in part from the ill-will of the brother, I had little doubt; and wondered whether Jack Hinton was determined to part Catherine Prowting from my dangerous company. The girl's indecision might account for the troubled looks, and pleas of a head-ache.

One fact alone in my mother's recital gave rise to apprehension: that so many of the inhabitants of Chawton and Alton purported to know of my affairs, and were conversing freely about Lord Harold's chest. I had not yet accustomed myself to the littlenesses of a country village; and tho' I had perused some part of the chest's contents, I was not yet mistress of the whole. I resolved to spend the better part of the morning in achieving a thorough understanding of Lord Harold's early life.

The resolution was strengthened by a chance comment from a surprising quarter: Lady Imogen Vansittart, who passed so near to me in her progress towards the gaming tables that she *must* speak, or appear insufferable.

"I find, Miss Austen, that we have an acquaintance in common," she said with her bewitching smile. "The Countess of Swithin is my intimate friend. I believe you were acquainted with her uncle, the late lamented Lord Harold Trowbridge?"

"I have had that honour—yes," I replied.

"Poor Desdemona is very low. She practically lived

in Lord Harold's pocket, from what I understand. And who can blame her, with *such* a father? Bertie is the meanest stick in the world—I should not be saddled with him for a parent for all the Wilborough fortune! Marriage was the wisest choice Mona ever made. It freed her from one form of imprisonment—tho' we must hope it did not throw her into another."

I was at a loss for a proper response to this observation, and so managed only to say, "I cannot wonder that the Countess should mourn her uncle. They were very good friends as well as relations."

"I understand Mona nearly rode out from London in search of you herself," Lady Imogen observed. "She was quite wild with fury that his lordship had left you all his papers. *Careless,* she called it."

A thrill of apprehension coursed through my body, setting it to tingling as tho' Lord Harold's hand had caressed my skin. "Papers? What papers?"

"Those in the Bengal chest, of course. The diaries and correspondence his lordship guarded with such vigour in life." Lady Imogen tossed me an arch look. "Do not play the village idiot with *me*, Miss Austen. The Great World has long been agog to know what was recorded of its vicious propensities in Lord Harold's inscrutable hand. My own father—who has been intimate with his lordship these thirty years—would part with half my inheritance to know in what manner he himself figures in those pages, and which secrets have been let slip like the veriest cat out of the bag."

"Lady Imogen," said a gentle voice at my shoulder, "I believe you are wanted at the faro table. Mr. Thrace is attending you."

"Good God, Charles, do you wish to see me ruined?" Lady Imogen reached her hand to Major Spence's cheek, where he stood correctly awaiting her with no quarter offered his weak leg. "You know my luck is damnably out. There will be a line of duns a mile long awaiting us at Stonings, and you do not prevent me from wagering everything I have!"

Major Spence's sombre gaze shifted a fraction to meet my own, and I thought I read in its depths a kind of apology, and a plea for discretion. But then the steward's grey eyes returned to the bright image before him, and he lifted her hand from his cheek. "Julian will not be happy unless you play. Therefore I charge you only to *play well*, my lady."

"Such a steward!" Lady Imogen observed mistily; "so caring and thoughtful in every respect, that I might run roughshod over your heart and mind both, and you will not presume to manage me. Take care, Charles," she threw over her shoulder as she left him, "or I shall accept that proposal of marriage you offered me. It would ruin us both, I assure you."

Major Spence did not allow his expression to change as his eyes followed Lady Imogen to the faro table; and in that perfect reserve and preservation of countenance I read the strength of the man. Perhaps I alone would name such a look as passion—but I, too, had loved a wild thing once to my loss. A simpleton could perceive that the steward was languishing for the Earl's daughter.

Spence bowed correctly in my direction, enquired if there was anything I wanted—if I was amply supplied with muffin and tea—and then took up his place beside my mother at the whist table.

I am no card player. The elder Prowtings and the Papillons made up one party of whist; Mr. Middleton, Miss Beckford, my mother, and Major Spence another; while Lady Imogen was claimed by Julian Thrace.

"She is said to be a gamester of the most hardened kind," Henry murmured in my ear, "tho' she is but two-and-twenty. It is not to be wondered at, with the Earl for a father. The gaming trait is fatal in the Vansittart blood. It is said to rival even that of the Spencers."

"Did you know, Henry, that the Earl was a friend of Lord Harold's?"

"I did not. But they were both of a Whiggish persuasion; and I confess I cannot be surprised. The Earl's society is rackety enough, Jane—his lordship being cheek by jowl with the Carlton House Set; and Lady Imogen's mother, you know, ran away with a colonel of the Horse Guards when her daughter was only three."

"How diverting is your knowledge of the Great, Henry!" I sighed. "The appearance of Mr. Thrace— the prospect of losing so considerable an inheritance as Stonings—must make her ladyship quite blue-devilled."

"I should think the earldom would be entailed on the male line," Henry said doubtfully. "Absent the upstart Beau, the title will pass to a cousin of some kind.

But it is certainly true that Stonings at present forms a significant part of Lady Imogen's jointure. At her marriage or her father's death, the estate should come to her; but his lordship *now* appears inclined to allow Thrace to live in it. Spence told me as much himself."

"So it is for *Thrace* that Major Spence is undertaking repairs?" I enquired in astonishment. "That cannot be an easy circumstance—when the Major has so clearly lost his heart to Lady Imogen."

"Do you believe it? Perhaps he means to rescue her ladyship from an unendurable future. Julian Thrace will be three-and-twenty in three weeks' time, and on that date the Earl will throw a ball and invite the entire county. His lordship intends, so Spence assures me, to appoint Thrace his heir—to Lady Imogen's loss. She must either marry, or in some other wise put an end to the Bond Street Beau's pretensions."

"—By discovering, perhaps, that Thrace is not at all what he claims," I said slowly. Three weeks was little enough time to secure a fortune. Who would know the truth about Thrace? An acute observer—a man of the world—a self-trained spy with his finger in every *tonnish* plot. Lord Harold might know, and guard the facts in his subtle papers. Did Lady Imogen comprehend as much? Was direst need the spur to her playful conversation?

My own father . . . would part with half my inheritance to know in what manner he himself figures in those pages, and which secrets have been let slip like the veriest cat out of the bag.

"Is Lady Imogen expensive?" I asked Henry.

"Ruinously so. It is said that young Ambrose, the Viscount Gravetye's heir, cried off from an engagement when acquainted with her true circumstances, and that only old Coutts stands between her and disaster.[2] Observe: Lady Imogen will end the evening by wagering that emerald circlet with young Thrace—for she cannot abide to lose."

"Particularly to *him*."

They were a compelling pair: the Beau with his guinea-gold hair in fashionable disorder and his coat of the most elegant cut gracing a sportsman's form; the easy humour of his smile; the warmth in the lazy blue eyes. And Lady Imogen: dark, hectic, her lips parted with excitement at the turning of every card, her alabaster throat a lily rising from the vessel of her gown. They reminded me of two others who had once played at faro—Lord Harold, and the woman he believed a spy, long since fled from England in the arms of her betrothed. But Lord Harold had always been in command of himself as well as the cards; I doubted Julian Thrace was so masterful.

"The lady looks to win," Henry said admiringly.

It is a curious game, faro—played upon a little baize table set between the two players. One must deal the cards, and the other guess as to their face value be-

---

[2] Thomas Coutts (1735–1822), a cautious Scot who became the chief banker and financial support of the most fashionable people in London during the late Georgian period, was known for having privately floated the Prince of Wales, Charles James Fox, and Georgiana, Duchess of Devonshire, whose fatal habit was gambling away a fortune.—*Editor's note.*

fore each is overturned; a talent for tallying sums, and holding a keen memory of all the cards played, will serve the gambler well. The tension in Lady Imogen's body suggested that a good deal rode on the outcome of this hand; she was half-risen from her seat, her cheeks flushed and her dark eyes sparkling.

"And so to the final card," she said in that low and throbbing voice, "and so to the final card! Turn it over, Thrace! Show its face! My luck cannot desert me now!"

He smiled, and with long fingers turned the card to the fore; she sprang from her chair, face exultant and fierce as a huntress's, oblivious of those who watched her from the flanks of the room.

"The Devil!" she cried out, impassioned. "The Devil is in these cards, and by God, *the Devil is with me*! I shall outrun you yet, Thrace—you and all the petty duns of England who would see me ruined!"

In the heavy silence that followed this extraordinary outburst, the doors of the sitting room were thrust open to reveal a manservant bearing a note on a silver tray. The assembled guests stared at him in fascination as he moved towards the magistrate, Mr. Prowting.

The gentleman took up the note, perused it swiftly, and then raised his head to stare accusingly at *me*.

"Is anything amiss, sir?" I enquired.

"Gentlemen and their boots be demmed! Footprints in the cellar, likewise! It is as I expected. Bertie Philmore has returned to the scene of the crime—and has been caught stealing into your cottage, Miss Austen!"

Letter from Lord Harold Trowbridge to Mr. Henry Fox, later 3rd Lord Holland, dated 13 December 1791; one leaf quarto, laid; watermark fragmentary ELGAR; signed *Trowbridge* under black wax seal bearing arms of Wilborough House; *Personelle, Par ChasseurExprès*, in red ink.
(British Museum, Wilborough Papers, Austen bequest)

My dear Henry—

You ask if I am well; and I suppose that I am in health enough. The trifling mark of a foil on my left shoulder is healing nicely, and gives no trouble, save to impair my aim with a pistol in that hand—but as it is not the one I write with, I may give you a letter long enough to satisfy the main points of your last.

Many of our old friends are gathered here at Aix and elsewhere in the province, laying in provisions and bartering for places in the boats putting off at Marseille. There is a rumour abroad that a party of considerable size is lost and wandering in the Pyrénées, giving the Comte much cause for uneasiness; the snows are already deep at the pass's height, and his daughter has not appeared although she is daily expected. I hope to meet you soon, with a group of thirteen, and drink a bumper of wine to your health; but if the Comte pleads his cause well enough I may be forced to return and form a search party for Hélène—even if only to retrieve the frozen end of a father's hopes. It is said that the Committee intends to seize all émigré goods before long; let us trust we shall be paid before they do.

My most cordial regards, dear Fox—and God keep you—

Trowbridge

Chapter 13

That Perfect Understanding Between Sisters

Friday, 7 July 1809

~

"I MUST SAY, JANE, THAT YOU HAVE ENDEAVOURED to distinguish yourself and the name of Austen as much as possible, in as little time as possible—an exertion I should have expected to be beyond even *your* spirit and understanding," my sister Cassandra observed.

She was sitting in the single hard-backed chair I had placed near the window of the bedroom we were to share, her bonnet lying on the little dressing table and her hair still disordered from the effects of too many days' travel in an open carriage. Her face was somewhat tanned, but shadows lingered in the hollows of her eyes and her hair has turned quite grey; at six-and-thirty, she begins to look the middle-aged woman. A young dog was asprawl in her lap—a gift from Neddie towards the formation of our new household. I was pleased to note that it was neither a bird-dog nor a hound, but a useful little terrier of cunning aspect. The rats, I felt sure, were already disposed of.

"I have determined to call him Link," Cassandra confided, "after the link-boys of Bath; for he is always dashing ahead, to lead the way!"

I smiled at her as she crooned over the pup like a new mother with a long-awaited child; but the vision was not one of unalloyed happiness. I see in my sister the mirror of myself—a lady with hardened hands and correct posture, a gown done up to her neck, and a suggestion of strain about the mouth; and I remember her fleetingly as she was at nineteen, in all the flush of youth and a strong first attachment, when she accepted Tom Fowle's proposals. We both meant to marry Toms, Cassandra and I—and all our happy plans went awry, the men we had chosen being disposed of, in their fates, by other persons more powerful than ourselves: Tom Fowle despatched to the Indies and his death at the whim of Lord Craven; and Tom Lefroy packed off to the law courts of Ireland, and the safety of the heiress he eventually married. I never think of him now, except when my mind reverts to those silly, happy days my sister and I passed so unconsciously at Steventon Parsonage; he is no doubt a father these many years, and balding in his pate, and gouty in his foot, while I have long since given my heart and soul to another.

"I am sorry, Cass, if my publick exposure has occasioned any difficulties for you or Neddie," I returned, with what I considered admirable control of my temper; "but I could not consider your descent upon Chawton, in all the style of a Kentish lady, when I confronted a corpse in our cellar."

"It is not of *that* I would speak. It is a most disturbing affair, to be sure, and not at all what one would like in the Squire's circle—but as the poor wretch came there well before you and my mother appeared in the village, the business cannot be helped. No, Jane—it is your continued association with his lordship that I must deplore. I need not elaborate."

She proceeded to do so.

"When I learned, from the safety of Godmersham, that you had continued to court Lord Harold's notice—that you had so far forgot what was due to your family, as to involve my dear brother Francis in the unseemly circumstances of his lordship's murder!—when I understood, from a chance remark in one of Martha Lloyd's letters, that your intimacy had given rise to the general expectation of an *union* between yourself and the gentleman—for so I am forced to call him—I confess I believed you had taken leave of your senses."

"No doubt I had."

"And now I am not a quarter-hour arrived in Hampshire," my sister added, drawing off her gloves with a complacency that must cause me to grit my teeth, "before I learn that Lord Harold had the presumption to notice you in his Will. It is as Mamma observes: even from the grave the Rogue would destroy your reputation."

"I must beg you, Cass, not to speak of what you cannot understand," I said stiffly.

"Jane, your intimacy is everywhere talked of. I heard it mentioned on a stranger's lips while Edward halted at the George, and must have blushed for the exposure of a most beloved sister. And our house broken into!" She lifted up her hands in amazement. "Would that the chest is never found! Then perhaps we may be rid of the odour of scandal his lordship has brought upon us."

At the thought of the stolen chest, I felt a tide of misery rise up within me. We had hastened from the Great House last evening, Henry and Mamma and I, in the company of Mr. Prowting and Mr. Middleton both. We had not tarried to take proper leave of the Stonings party, nor yet of Mr. Prowting's family, who remained in the drawing-room with the delightful prospect of canvassing our private affairs behind our backs. I read triumph in Jack Hinton's looks as I bade him farewell, and knew that he regarded me with derision and contempt. But it made no matter: my thoughts were all for Lord Harold's legacy. Wretched, wretched woman that I am, not to have detected in our convenient absence from the cottage, while dining at the Great House, an opportunity for plunder!

We found the new bow window torn from its frame, glass panes smashed, with a small knot of folk collected in the garden. I recognised the baker woman, and Toby Baigent standing by the side of a burly man who must be his father; the others I could not name. And there was Bertie Philmore, his back thrust up against a tree that shaded the Street, his arms securely gripped by a pair of strangers and a surly expression upon his face.

"Well, then, Morris," Mr. Prowting called out to one of Bertie's captors as we approached, "what have you found?"

"This lad a-climbing out of the cottage's bow window, Mr. Prowting, sir," Morris replied.

"That is my groom," the magistrate told Henry, "and a likely fellow if ever I knew one. I thought it probable that Philmore would return to the cottage once your mother deserted it, and so I set Morris to watch upon the place, and inform me when the ruffian appeared."

I had wondered if Mr. Prowting's powers of intellect were stouter than they had at first seemed, and was amply satisfied with this answer. "But why should Philmore return, sir—if indeed he was ever within the cottage before?" I enquired reasonably.

Mr. Prowting wheeled upon me with a look like thunder. "Is it not obvious, Miss Austen? Because he is drawn to the place where he murdered his friend, Shafto French—because his guilty conscience compels him to return to the gruesome pit in which he left the body!"

Henry's eyebrows rose. "I agree that the cellar is malodorous and damp, but to call it a—"

"I never killed Shafto!" Philmore burst out. "I

were at home in bed when he died, same as my Rosie'll tell you!"

"Was anything found on this man's person?" I demanded.

Mr. Prowting glared at Morris. "Well, sirrah? Did the ruffian make off with the Austens' property?"

"No, sir. It were just him, sir, jumping down from the windowsill."

"You see, Miss Austen? A guilty conscience will prove the answer!"

I studied Philmore's countenance as he strained against Morris's grip. Far from appearing terrified at the tendency of the magistrate's accusations, there was a suspicion of smugness in his looks, an air of having bested all comers. My heart desponding, I took the key to the door from my mother's hand and made my way past the knot of gawkers. Henry followed.

My brother emitted a low whistle as he stepped over the threshold.

The contents of the trunks and wooden boxes we had meant to unpack during the course of the week were everywhere scattered about the room: a few earthenware plates smashed and ground to dust, linens strewn in disorder, books tumbled from the shelves. A quantity of paper had been trampled underfoot, and a bottle of ink spilled over all. A trail of ruin led from kitchen to dining parlour and up the main stairs, and I knew before I reached my bedroom what I should find.

The drawers of my dressing table were emptied,

the mattress torn from the bedstead, and my clothes thrown in a heap on the floor.

I dashed to the empty bed frame and felt beneath the tumbled coverlet.

The Bengal chest was gone.

"But who can have taken it, Henry?" I demanded for the tenth time as we endeavoured, late that night, to restore order from chaos. "Philmore is mute on the subject and Morris is adamant that Philmore had nothing in his hands when he stepped through the window. We have searched house and garden alike."

"Then we must assume Morris was too late, Jane," my brother patiently replied, "and that Philmore gave the chest to a confederate before quitting the house himself."

"One man alone cannot have accomplished all this," my mother agreed, from her position of collapse on the sitting-room sopha. She was lying at her ease with a vinaigrette and hartshorn, the better to observe our labours. "I should think a party of ten much more likely."

"One such another as Philmore is sufficient," I retorted, "to make off with my chest and destroy it forever. I could throttle the man from sheer vexation!"

"Tho' strangulation is unlikely to encourage him to speak," Henry supplied.

Philmore's story was that he happened to be passing the cottage when he noticed a light and observed the shattered window. Approaching with the intention of offering his services to Mrs. Austen, as he said, he swiftly ascertained that none of the family was within—and plunged with no other weapon than his fists into a battle of the most fearsome kind. Philmore had fought a man—a man he could not describe—and tho' he emerged without a scratch upon his person, had been so soundly beaten as to lose his senses, and awoke some time later to find the miscreant gone. He had met with Mr. Prowting's man Morris upon exiting the window, and had been most cruelly set upon, tho' he endeavoured to explain the virtuousness of his actions.

Mr. Prowting declared this a Banbury tale, and insisted that Philmore's soul was black with guilt.

When taxed with the disappearance of the chest, the joiner had preserved an awful silence. Neither threat of hanging nor the prospect of a protracted lodging in the Alton gaol could move Philmore to a confession, save to utter the obvious: he had no trunk in his possession at present, and could not be proved to have made off with it. This was a sticking point in Mr. Prowting's deliberations—and Philmore clearly believed it should secure him from guilt in the eyes of the Law.

The magistrate muttered darkly about charges and the Assizes, but Philmore only stared at his boots with that expression of satisfaction I had previously observed so strongly writ on his countenance.

"He is hardly the disinterested hero," I mused, "and believes himself in possession of a fortune,

Henry. He will not split on his confederate, however, for fear of losing the same. He intends to profit from his appearance of innocence—and guard the truth of the chest's whereabouts like a bulldog. We shall have to use other means to discover the name of his accomplice. I mean to have my papers returned."

My brother paused in collecting the scraps of fabric my mother intended for a pieced quilt. Any number were ruined with ink.

"What exactly does the joiner believe he has stolen, Jane? A King's Ransom in jewels, as is popularly believed—or an unknown object of great worth to *another party*?"

I stared at him. "You would suggest that Bertie Philmore took the chest without knowing what it contained?—That he was *set* to steal it, by his confederate or . . . or another person?"

"Perhaps he was offered a considerable reward," Henry said mildly. "By someone who had reason to know that our entire party would be from home this evening."

"One of Mr. Middleton's guests?"

"Any number of our fellow diners would give a good deal to know what Lord Harold has written about them, by your account."

"That is true," I said blankly, a scrap of fabric in my hands. A parade of faces revolved in my mind: Jack Hinton, whom I had observed in urgent converse with Philmore only the previous day—and might easily secure a key to the cottage from his nephew, James Baverstock; Julian Thrace, who might find in Lord

Harold's papers an end to all his ambitions; and Lady Imogen, who should regard the chest as her chief weapon in a ruthless struggle to preserve her inheritance.

"So you see—it is possible the chest has not been destroyed after all," Henry concluded. "Nor may it be so very far away. It is something, is it not, to consider our genteel neighbours in the light of thieves?"

I confess I did not sleep at all well last night.

I LEFT CASSANDRA TO UNPACK HER THINGS IN PEACE this morning, and descended to the sitting room, where my brother Edward was arranged in a chair with his elegant hat balanced upon one beautifully-tailored knee. He looked every inch the Squire of Chawton, and an established man of property—save for the expression of deadness in his eyes I understood too well.

"My dear Neddie," I said as he rose to greet me, "how very good of you to bring my sister all this way from Kent!"

"I could wish that I had come sooner," he observed, "when I hear what has been happening in my absence. The corpse in the cellar and the invasion of the cottage are bad enough—but Mamma would have me to understand that you have been greeted with a degree of coldness from the local people that I must find offensive, Jane!"

"Mamma refines too much upon a trifle," I replied easily. "The Prowtings and the Middletons have been kindness itself."

"Jack and Jane Hinton are hardly trifles," my brother retorted. "They are mushrooms of the very worst order, for all that their father was a clergyman. Shall I remove your party to the George until these distressing matters are settled?"

"And what then? Are we to live in an inn all our lives? Or quit Hampshire in defeat, and know ourselves to be the laughingstock of the entire county? No, no, Neddie—allow us to fight our battles on our own ground, if you please. You must consider your dignity as Squire. Your claim to Chawton and all its goods is under the most subtle of attack in the court of publick opinion. It will not do for your tenants to believe you shaken."

He studied my countenance an instant before his own gaze dropped to the floor. "I have been idle too long. My cares and my grief—my privileged misery— have occasioned neglect."

"I fear that is true—however much my knowledge of your excellent propensities would excuse it. Your tenants, Neddie, hesitate to give you a good name. There is much resentment among the common folk: over the eviction of Mrs. Seward, who must leave her home of many years and give way to us; and a dozen other paltry matters that loom unfortunately large in Chawton minds. You would do well not to leave the neighbourhood without a thorough audience with all the outraged parties. You could do much to win back good will, Neddie, did you only exert yourself."

His eyes came up to my own. "And the happiness

of those I leave behind me, you would suggest, depends upon that exertion?"

"It does. We can endure all manner of slight and injury at present, provided we have reason to believe in future good. We have this consolation at least: our standing in the village can only rise."

"I believe," Edward said with careful consideration, "that I shall make it known among the tenants that I will hold Quarter Day at the George tomorrow. And I shall make every effort, Jane, to hear their grievances to the last detail. Even if I must remain a fortnight to do it."

"That is excellent news. We should dearly love to keep you in Hampshire so long."

"But first, I must pay my respects to Mr. Middleton. Do I ask too much—or will you walk with me to the Great House?"

WE ENCOUNTERED ALL THE STONINGS PARTY AS we achieved the entrance to the sweep: Julian Thrace and Charles Spence astride a pair of high-blooded horses, walking mettlesomely at either side of Lady Imogen's carriage. The gentlemen reined in, while the lady put down her window and extended her gloved hand to me and my brother. He stared at her an instant too long, as tho' entranced and horrified at one and the same moment—and too late, I saw the danger. Lady Imogen, in all the freshness of two-and-twenty, could boast a dark beauty reminiscent of his dead Lizzy's own.

"I trust your cottage was not *too much* disturbed by that miscreant last evening," she said with solicitude as Edward released her hand. "My poor Miss Austen! What shocking ill-treatment you have received, I declare, since your arrival in Hampshire! You must believe us a pack of brigands!"

I should have liked to order her out of the carriage and search the baggage strapped within and behind, but such a course must be impossible; and so I murmured a polite nothing, and allowed the gentlemen to bid me *adieux*.

"It is a pleasure to meet at last the owner of the Great House," Major Spence said in his quiet, well-bred way. "We have heard much of you, Mr. Austen—and all of it praise."

"I thank you, sir. It is good news indeed to learn that Stonings is under repair. We have need of steady families in the neighbourhood—tho' I say it as should not, who persist in living such a great way off."

"You must all come to Stonings tomorrow," Mr. Thrace remarked gaily, "for we mean to have a sort of picnic on the grounds, and show our Chawton friends over the house. The weather could not be finer for such a scheme; and tho' the strawberries are done, the peaches are sure to be ripe. Middleton is charged with seconding my invitation—he intends to bring all the children, and Miss Beckford, and Miss Benn as well, in every open conveyance he can borrow or steal; and shall call upon you at the cottage directly to explain the whole!"

Major Spence looked as tho' he should have liked to curb his friend's speech, of the word *steal* at the very least; but he added his pressing assurance of our welcome to Mr. Thrace's, and closed with the words, "Pray bring all your family, Miss Austen—your other brother not excepted. I should like his advice on the best way to go about the Vyne hunt, well before next season."

And so we parted with satisfaction, and some little interest, on all sides.

**Excerpt from the diary of Lord Harold Trowbridge,
dated Paris, 3 January 1792.**

. . . *My memory of these past few weeks is of one
long and barely endurable privation, first on the passage
between Marseille and the Spanish coast, where the
jagged reefs and the monumental seas at our point of
landing would have driven us on the rocks, and we were
forced to wear and wear back out to sea, almost to the
point of achieving the Dorset coast, and might have put
in there but for the Comte's protests. The women, all
sick belowdecks and too weak even to tend to their
children, one of whom was nearly lost overboard when
the ship was swamped under a wall of water; and all
the while, Geoffrey Sidmouth shouting like a madman,
half in French, half in English. I like Sidmouth's looks,
and love his courage; I shall want a good deal of both if
Grey's plans for the French are to achieve fruition.*

*And then the return to Aix, and the intelligence that
Hélène was not to be found—the party lost in the
Pyrénées having emerged from the snows of the pass at
last, and without her. Freddy Vansittart, his noble
reputation forgot, tearing at my sleeve in frantic
supplication. Promising me money, promising me
support, promising me a lifetime of servitude if only I
will undertake this journey— Too afraid to venture
himself, but too overwrought to sit in idleness, never
knowing—and so I am gone again on horseback,
working my way north by slow degrees and worse roads,
the people everywhere about in the most wretched
condition, and blood running in the streets.*

I fear she has remained in Paris when all counsel would have had her flee to the south. Perhaps it was the child—a sudden chill or fever, and the desire to remain where food and shelter were at least certain. But for how long? How long before the tumbrel arrives for the Comte's fair daughter? I must find out where she is hidden. I must see Hélène safe, and the boy with her. Not for Freddy or the Comte or the discomfiture of St. Eustace—but for Horatia, my poor lost girl lying cold in the Viscount's tomb. I must save Hélène and her boy for the sake of those whom long ago I sent to their ruin.

Chapter 14

Catherine's Confession

~

NEDDIE THOUGHT IT ONLY PROPER TO CONTINUE on to the Great House, and pay his respects to his tenant Mr. Middleton, and listen with becoming gravity to all the discussion of roof-slates, stable accommodation, and patches of damp, while I made my thanks to Miss Beckford for the previous evening's entertainment.

"My brother tells me that you have suffered a loss, Miss Austen, as well as a second violation of your privacy," she said soberly. "A very valuable chest, I believe, that had only lately come into your possession."

"That is true. And the man Mr. Prowting has detained cannot tell us what has happened to it."

"Bertie Philmore," she said succinctly. "The

Philmores are an odious lot. Bertie's uncle, Old Philmore, is the owner of that group of hovels known as Thatch Cottages, where poor Miss Benn resides. Old Philmore drives a very hard bargain in rents, I believe, and does absolutely nothing towards the maintenance of his property. We really must endeavour to find Miss Benn more adequate accommodation before the winter; for the place is barely fit for stabling cattle, when the storms of January set in."

"Miss Benn is awkwardly left, I take it?"

"Very sadly so. Her father was once rector of Chawton, before old Mr. Hinton's time; and her brother, while possessing a fair living in Farringdon, is so beset with children himself that he cannot provide much towards his sister's support. For a gentlewoman of good breeding and nice habits to be reduced to Miss Benn's present degree of poverty is lowering in the extreme. We do what we can for her, of course, by including her in some of our amusements; and she is very grateful, poor soul, for any attention."

But for the generosity of my brother Neddie, and the steady contributions of my other brothers towards the maintenance of our household, Cassandra and I might have been left in similar poverty at the demise of our clergyman father. I had viewed Miss Benn with easy contempt for her silly manners and vague understanding, for the spinster effusions to which she was too much given; but my conscience smote me at Miss Beckford's communication. My contempt for Miss Benn was too much like self-hatred at the aging woman I was myself become.

Miss Beckford led me to the wilderness that comprised the back garden, and here, for the first time in my acquaintance with the household, I observed no less than five children—four well-grown girls and a little boy of perhaps six—at play in the grass under the watchful eye of a maidservant.

"What fine, stout creatures they are," I observed with a smile. "And how lovely to think of this house populated with young people! My brother, I am sure, is happy to find it so!"

"The eldest, John, has been at sea from the age of ten," Miss Beckford told me, "and at fifteen, is now become a Midshipman. I wish that my sister could have known of his success; she died the year before he went away, in 1803—after little Frederick was born."

The small boy was laughing as he tumbled down the gentle slope behind the Great House, and I thought of dear Elizabeth, and the babe she had left behind, with a pang. Someday her eleventh child would play even so with his sisters, forever ignorant of the lovely woman who had given him birth and marred his father's life with her passing. The impermanence of existence—the cruel lot of women in childbed—impressed me with a weight of sadness that was become too familiar. As the years advance, we find more cause for sorrow, and less occasion for laughing in the grass.

"Mr. Middleton has had much to do with so many children to rear," I observed. "He is indeed fortunate in possessing an aide as admirable as yourself, Miss Beckford."

"I am happy to do it," she answered simply. "In truth, having no penchant for matrimony, I might otherwise have ended my days a governess. Here I may instruct and educate in the guise of a beloved aunt, without the discomfort of being forced to earn my living; and in the two eldest girls, I might imagine my sister revived again. To live in their presence, and watch them grow, is to fight a little against the awfulness of Death."

"And you have been travelling *en famille*, I understand, some months on the Continent."

"Yes—we spent the better part of last summer in Italy and the mountains of Switzerland."

"What courage! But I must suppose that Buonaparte's attention was happily fixed elsewhere."

"On Spain—that is very true. I should have regarded the adventure with trepidation, I confess, but for the steady influence of my brother, Mr. Middleton; and of course, we were accompanied from Rome to Spa by Mr. Thrace."

She had reverted in all tranquillity to a subject I was longing to introduce, but had known not how to do, without arousing a suspicion of inquisitiveness.

"He seems a very gentleman-like man," I said cautiously. "Was he, too, a traveller like yourselves?"

"Mr. Thrace is an orphan—raised in the household of an English couple resident some years in Rome, I believe; the gentleman who oversaw his early education is Mr. Henry Fox, nephew to the late Whig leader, and now elevated to the title of Lord Holland. His lordship has spent much of his life abroad—

owing to the extraordinary circumstances surrounding his marriage. His wife, Lady Holland, was once married to another, and eloped with his lordship."

"I see." The perfect household for the bastard son of a peer.

"John—Mr. Middleton, I should say—was acquainted with Henry Fox at school, and naturally called upon him during our travels. He suggested that Mr. Thrace might serve as tutor to young Frederick for the remainder of our trip, and then return to England in our train—Mr. Thrace having intended to visit London in any case. We were most happy in the arrangement, and must look upon Mr. Thrace as quite an intimate friend. But tell me, Miss Austen," she said decisively, "before I bore you too much with our family histories—is the damage to your house very great?"

"One window only; but we are less than fortunate in having the local joiner locked in Alton gaol. The likelihood of repairing the casement is thus put off."

"I am glad to see you retain your sense of humour," she retorted drily. "Another woman would have quitted the house entirely under such provocations, and sought lodgings elsewhere."

"But then we should be satisfying the dearest wish of our enemies, Miss Beckford," I replied tranquilly, "and *that* I mean never to do."

She studied me with her sharp, intelligent eyes. "I have often thought that the evils of a Town existence—the constant dangers and ill-health to which one is exposed—are as nothing compared to the quiet malice of a country village. The people look too much inward, and nurse their grievances in solitude."

"We have received nothing but kindness from the Prowtings and yourselves."

"But the Baigents would have it your house is cursed; Libby Cuttle refuses to sell you bread; and that impudent scamp, James Baverstock of Alton, offers you insolence in his own house. I know it all, Miss Austen. I have heard from Mrs. Prowting what the Hintons are saying—and it is my opinion they should both be horsewhipped through the village. Such conduct, before the dear Squire and his family! Had I known of their behaviour before, I should never have asked them to dine with us last evening, I assure you."

"We have no wish to make of Chawton a divided camp," I protested.

"And no more you shall. By the serenity of your response to every adversity, Miss Austen, you show the Hintons their proper place. I am not the sort of woman to indulge in idle gossip—but I cannot like Jack Hinton. For all his fine manners, he has a taste for low company—for idleness and the kinds of vulgar pursuits that cannot become a gentleman—and I fear his morals are very bad."

Here was a source from whom I might profit. "You mentioned his fondness for *mills,* as I believe they are called—but with every Corinthian in the country an enthusiast, it is not to be wondered that Mr. Hinton is no less immune."

"A prize-fight or two should be nothing," she returned dismissively. "Even dear Mr. Middleton has been known to indulge the taste. But I cannot disguise, Miss Austen, that there have been other habits which every person of sense and feeling must deplore. I will not offend you with particulars; I will say only that two housemaids at least have quit Mr. Hinton's employ, and complained of ill-usage—of *improprieties*—at his hands. Neither girl was friendless, and Mr. Hinton has inspired a degree of dislike in the surrounding countryside that is not to be wondered at."

"I see. Miss Beckford—I wonder—"

She stared at me enquiringly.

"Was either housemaid any relation at all to Shafto French?"

Her expression altered. "I cannot undertake to say. I am not in possession of the girls' names—my intelligence derives from local gossip only, not personal experience. Tho' Mr. Middleton leased the Great House once before, my sister was alive then, and my place was elsewhere. He has only been returned to Chawton under the present lease for a twelvemonth."

"I understand. My thought was a passing one only. I did not mean to suggest—"

"Naturally not." She drew her light shawl about her shoulders as tho' suddenly chilled. "I hope that you will join us for the picnic at Stonings on the morrow, Miss Austen. The Hintons are *not* to be of that party."

"I look forward to the day with every possible hope of enjoyment," I told her; and after a quiet interval of examining the flower beds, and discussing my intentions for the cottage garden, I bid Miss Beckford *adieu*.

THE MORNING WAS A FINE ONE, AS ALL HAMPSHIRE mornings in July must be; and as I exited the gates and made my way along the Street past the Rectory, I observed Mr. Papillon hard at work among the herbaceous beds, with a straw hat on his head and his shirtsleeves encased in paper cuffs against the dirt. John-Rawston Papillon is a diminutive, apple-cheeked man with luxuriant silver hair and the correct, if fussy, conversation of a determined bachelor. His sister Elizabeth, whom I had glimpsed the previous evening, keeps his household, and both appear so comfortably situated in life—so decidedly happy with the lot they have chosen—as to never wish for amendment. Having attained the age of six-and-forty without encumbering himself with a wife, Mr. Papillon might have been supposed safe from the speculation and notice of the impertinent; but my mother is no respecter of single men's peace. My brother Edward's patroness, elderly Mrs. Knight of Kent, having once voiced the thought that Mr. Papillon should be the very husband for her own dear *Jane,* my mother has been insufferable in her impatience to meet with the gentleman. Despite the dazzling alternative offered by Julian Thrace last evening, Mamma had not been disappointed. She had no notion I was as little likely to win the heart of an aging clergyman as an Earl's putative son nearly ten years my junior.

"So very amiable!" she had exclaimed in a barely contained whisper when first Mr. Papillon was introduced to our notice. "So clearly the gentleman in looks and address! I declare I am quite overpowered, Jane! You could do far worse than to set your cap at him!"

The rector of St. Nicholas's straightened as I neared his garden, his hands full of lilies, and smiled at me benignly. "Ah, Miss Austen, is it not? I must offer my sympathy this morning. Your cottage was violated, I understand, and a valuable article stolen."

"Thank you, Mr. Papillon," I replied with a curtsey. "I am sure my mother would join me in thanks, did she know of your concern."

"—And stolen, it seems, by poor Bertie Philmore! It is a dreadful business, when one of our fellow creatures falls in the way of temptation. We must certainly pray for him."

"Are you at all acquainted with the Philmores? I had understood them to be Alton people."

"And so they are, in the main—but Old Philmore, Bertie's uncle, is quite the Chawton institution. He is landlord to Miss Benn, you know, and a rare old character. I wonder that he did not appear in front of your home last evening, to intercede for his nephew. It is not like Old Philmore to preserve a respectful silence, when one of his own is in danger of hanging for murder!"

"Perhaps he is from home at present."

"Then it will be the first time he has shaken off our dust in the eight years I have lived here," Mr. Papillon observed. "I must send Elizabeth to Old Philmore's cottage, and make certain he is not unwell. It would be a dreadful thing, if he were lying alone on his cot, suffering from some disorder, while Bertie is in want of a steady hand and counsel!"

"Are the two men very attached?"

"Old Philmore has served Bertie in place of a father these many years. Indeed, they are most devoted—in the rough, unschooled fashion of their kind. I could wish for the younger man a *kinder* example, perhaps—Old Philmore is very close with his money, quite the miser of Chawton, as Miss Benn has found!—but in truth, there is no real harm in either of them."

"I see." It was possible I saw a great deal more, in fact, than the rector. Old Philmore had been absent from the scene of Bertie's arrest. What better confederate for the younger man than the trusted figure of the uncle? Complicity within the family would surely ensure Bertie's silence in the hands of the Law; and if Mr. Papillon's opinion of their bond was to be believed, Bertie was unlikely to incriminate Old Philmore.

"It is decidedly odd," Mr. Papillon mused, "that we have heard nothing of Old Philmore this morning. I should have expected him to have paid me a visit, with the earnest desire that I should bring the air of Christian charity to his nephew's gaol cell, as indeed I shall before the day is out."

The old scoundrel, I thought with sudden heat, was probably miles from Chawton even now, and my chest with him.

I left the rector pulling off his paper cuffs, and

finished my walk in pensive silence. I could not reconcile myself to the loss of Lord Harold's papers; it was too much like losing the man himself, all over again.

AT MY RETURN TO THE COTTAGE I WAS SURPRISED to discover Catherine Prowting waiting upon the doorstep with a cheerful, plain-faced young woman of perhaps twenty by her side.

"Good morning, Miss Austen," Catherine said. "My father has charged me with bringing Sally Mitchell to you, and offering you her services as maid of all work. She is a good girl, reared in the village; her mother is our cook."

Sally Mitchell bobbed a curtsey. Tho' young, her hands were roughened and red from hard labour, and her general appearance was of tidy cleanliness—positive signs in a domestic servant. Her dress had been neatly mended, and her half-boots were in good repair.

"I should have first consulted Mrs. Austen," Catherine said apologetically, "but that I knew her to be steadily at work in the garden, and did not wish to intrude."

I stood on tiptoe to overlook the hornbeam hedge, and observed my mother busily digging in the field beyond the privy. She wore an old green sack gown and a battered straw hat, and tho' all of seventy, was turning the earth with a vigour that belied her years. She might have been taken, in fact, for one of her son's tenants. Could the prospect of planting potatoes have excited such ardent activity? Of Cassandra there was no sign; she was probably lying down in the bedroom with the shades drawn, after the exhausting journey by post-chaise from Kent. I must therefore interview the girl alone.

"Good day to you, Sally," I said. "Have you heard that this house is cursed?"

A startled look passed over her features, and then she opened her mouth wide and laughed. "Many's the time I've sat in Widow Seward's kitchen, and had a biscuit of her Nancy, begging your pardon, ma'am," she said. "This here house is no more cursed nor what I am. I daresay it could do with a good scrubbing, however."

"Do you wish to live in, or out, Sally?"

"In," she said succinctly, "if it's all the same to you, ma'am."

"Better and better! We have two bedrooms over the kitchen reserved for the purpose. You have heard, I suppose, that our parlour window was broken and some articles taken from the house last night?"

"Bertie Philmore," she returned acidly, "what has a great lump for a brain. But he's got what's coming to 'im, so I've heard."

"It would greatly relieve our minds to have you living above the kitchen, all the same. I shall consult my mother as to your wages; you shall receive your board as well—and probably be cooking it. We expect another lady to join us next month, a Miss Lloyd; and as she is a great one for meddling with pots and fires, I hope you shall not mind another pair of hands in your domain."

"It's not my place to mind."

"We intend, moreover, to hire a manservant, if one can be found who shares your spirit of defiance. It is probable that he will be living *out*."

Her eyelids crinkled merrily. "That will suit me very well, ma'am."

"You'll do."

Sally grinned at me again; and the thought occurred that I should often find the freedom of her good humour a welcome relief from the moods and oppressions of a household full of women.

"Pray go through the yard to the pump," I told her. "You will see the kitchen door on your right. We should be greatly obliged if you would undertake a thorough cleansing of the scullery area, Sally—and then proceed to dusting the parlour."

When she had bobbed in my direction once more, and made her way through the outbuildings towards the rear of the house, I turned to Catherine Prowting with a smile. "You are very good to think of us, my dear. I hope you will convey our deepest thanks to your excellent father."

"I shall certainly do so," she returned, in a voice of some trouble; "when next I see him. Father went very early to Alton, on this dreadful business of Bertie Philmore. Papa *will not* consider that the man may be innocent of murder."

"A predisposition towards guilt is a definite flaw in a magistrate," I observed.

"I own that I am of your opinion." Catherine lifted her hands to her temples, as tho' yet plagued by the head-ache. "Is it true that we are all invited to visit Stonings tomorrow, Miss Austen?"

"So Major Spence and Mr. Thrace informed me, when I encountered them this morning."

"Mr. Thrace . . . ? I had not the pleasure of seeing the Great House party." She lowered her head. "Do you know whether . . . whether Mr. Hinton is also invited to Stonings?"

"I do not," I replied, "although from something Miss Beckford said, I believe he is otherwise engaged."

"That is a relief, indeed!" she burst out. "I may now look forward to all the charms of a great estate, without the oppression of spirits under which I have laboured these several days!"

I frowned at her. "Catherine, has Mr. Hinton given you cause for uneasiness?"

She glanced at me, on the brink of confidence. "I hardly know what I should say. I fear my duty is to my father, first. But perhaps, Miss Austen—if you are free—we might walk in the direction of Alton together? I should like to unburden myself. I should feel clearer in my mind."

"Of course," I murmured. "Do but wait, while I fetch my bonnet."

"Well, Jane," my mother said as I nearly collided with her in the back passage, her face dewy with exertion and the hem of her old green gown six inches deep in mud, "I have made a fair start on the excavations. I cannot report that I have encountered success, however. It will require some days, perhaps."

"You are planting potatoes, Mamma?"

"Potatoes?" She stared at me incredulously. "What do I care for *potatoes,* you silly girl, when there is a priceless necklace of rubies to be found? Mr. Thrace was most adamant. The booty of Chandernagar is ours for the taking, Jane! You might assist me, if you can but find another shovel—"

"Pray enlist Cassandra, Mamma," I said firmly. "I am engaged to walk with Miss Prowting. Her father has hired a maidservant for us—one Sally, who is even now established in the kitchen."

"That is excellent news!" she cried, brightening. "You might inform her, Jane, that I prefer a simple nuncheon of bread and cheese at eleven o'clock. She may bring it out to the field, so as not to interrupt the excavations. And if she has any ability with a trowel or hoe—"

I delivered the first part of this message to the scullery, my bonnet dangling from my hand.

"Sally," I said as almost an afterthought, "you are acquainted with Bertie Philmore, I collect?"

"All my life, ma'am."

"And also his wife—one Rosie Philmore?"

"Rosie's sister to my elder brother's Nell."

"Where in Alton does she reside?"

"The Philmores live in Normandy Street. Rosie takes in washing—you can't miss the linen and small clothes hanging in the yard."

"Thank you, Sally." The girl, I reflected, had already earned her day's wages.

CATHERINE WAITED UNTIL WE HAD PASSED THROUGH the village and put the Great House Lodge behind us—the Lodge, where even now Jack Hinton might be gazing out his sitting-room window, and observing our progress—before she undertook to speak.

"You said last evening that the path of duty must always be clear, Miss Austen. And that it is the path of the *heart* that descends into obscurity."

"So I have found it."

"I lay awake some hours in my bed, considering of your advice."

"It was not intended as such. I could not undertake to advise you, knowing you so little. I merely made an observation, based upon my own experience of life."

"But that has been considerably greater than my own," she returned in a low voice, "and as such must command my respect. I have known for some time where my duty lay. It was the urgings of my heart that counselled otherwise."

"Can you perhaps explain the circumstances?" I suggested. "I have no right to force a confidence, of course; and if you believe the particulars are better left unsaid, I will certainly understand."

"No, no—" she cried. "It was to make a full confession that I begged you to accompany me. I feel, Miss

Austen, that I have been a reluctant party to a very great injury that has been done to you and your family!"

I had expected some flutterings of the heart over Mr. Hinton; had expected to be consulted in a painful affair of unrequited passion for Julian Thrace; but never had I considered myself as the *object* of Catherine's avowal.

"In what manner?" I enquired cautiously.

"As regards the corpse of that poor man discovered in your home." She came to a halt in the middle of the Alton road, the wide expanse of Robin Hood Butts stretching beyond her. "You see, Miss Austen—I know who placed him there."

Chapter 15

Damning Evidence

"I SHOULD EXPLAIN, MISS AUSTEN, THAT I HAVE found it difficult to sleep of nights for some weeks past. The heat, perhaps, of July—"

Catherine broke off, and began to walk slowly once more in the direction of Alton. I studied her averted countenance, and recognised the marks of trouble; the girl had not been easy in her mind, I should judge, for too many days together. I had an image of her lying alone in her bedchamber, a picture of stillness beneath a white linen sheet, while a furious tide of thoughts swelled and resurged within her brain.

Resolutely, Catherine began again. "On the evening of Saturday last, I went to my room at ten o'clock, as is my habit. I was not conscious of the passage of the hours as I lay wakeful in my bed, the usual sounds of a summer night drifting through the open window; but I recollect with the sharpest clarity the tolling of the St. Nicholas church bell at midnight. I sat up, and counted the strokes, and told myself that this wretched want of peace must end, or utterly destroy my pleasure in life. I lit my candle and took up the book that sits always near my pillow, and read for a little; and when the heaviness of my eyes suggested I might at last find rest, I first got up, and fetched a drink of water from the washstand. I was returning to the tumbled bedclothes once more—when I heard the most dreadful noises arising from the darkness."

She glanced at me appealingly, as tho' wishing to be spared the next few words. "It was the sound of men fighting. I went to the window and lifted the sash so widely that I might lean out into the summer's night. The moon was almost at the full, and the scene below was as clear to me as daylight. In the distance, well beyond the reach of our sweep and the angle of your cottage, two men were locked in a furious embrace, grappling."[1]

"Could you distinguish their faces?"

She shook her head in the negative. "I could not. The distance at which they moved prevented me from recognising their features."

"But I thought you said . . ."

"Pray hear me out, Miss Austen," she demanded. "This is difficult enough."

---

[1] The *sweep*, in Austen's day, was the term for a driveway.—*Editor's note.*

I inclined my head, and so she continued.

"They were emitting the most horrid noises imaginable. Or I should say: *one* of the men was doing so. Grunts, hoarse cries, squeals of pain. The other—the taller of the two—preserved an awful silence, as tho' so intent upon his object, that he could not spare a thought for his injuries. As I watched, he o'erwhelmed his adversary and drove the man down towards the earth. I heard nothing more. I believe, now, that he had succeeded in thrusting Shafto French's head—for so I guess the lesser man to have been—beneath the waters of Chawton Pond. After an interval, all grappling ceased; and the victor rose."

"Good God," I said. "Why did you not scream? Why did you not sound the alarum, and rouse your father?"

"I was paralysed by the violence and horror I had witnessed," she returned quietly. "Fear pressed so heavily upon my breast that I do not believe I could have spoken, had I tried; and my trembling arms could barely support my frame as I leaned without the window. It is fortunate I did not swoon entirely away. And there was also this, Miss Austen: the quality of the scene, in its flood of moonlight, was so spectral as to convince me I had witnessed nothing but a dream, a nightmare of my own mind's fabrication. Altho' terrified, I could not be convinced in that moment that what I saw was *real*."

I could, in truth, comprehend the disorder of her wits, and the cruel doubt of her mind. "And the rest of the household heard nothing?"

"My sister Ann is a sound sleeper, and her room—like my parents'—is at the rear. We are all so accustomed to the noise of coaches passing along the Winchester Road of nights, that little can disturb our slumbers. I believe I overheard the scene by the pond solely because I was already awake."

"I understand. And what did you then?"

She shook her head furiously, as if she might shake off the hideous memory. "I could not move. I remained by the window, staring out in an agony of indecision and disbelief. The man rose—the man whom I now comprehend was French's murderer—and moved into the shadows of the trees bordering the pond. He must have untethered a horse at that point, for the only sound I subsequently heard was that of hoofbeats, as his mount made its way down the road."

"Did he ride south, in the direction of Winchester—or north, past your sweep, towards Alton?"

"South," she replied. "He did not pass within my sight at that time."

I was silent an instant, revolving the intelligence. Julian Thrace had admitted to riding out of the Great House a little after midnight, but would claim that he had gone north in the direction of Alton. Had he indeed murdered Shafto French, this declaration was no more than wisdom. Thrace must assume that Mr. Middleton would freely disclose his presence in Chawton on the night of the murder and his departure at very nearly the hour of French's death. Had Thrace quitted the Great

House by previous arrangement with his victim? Was Thrace the *heir as would pay,* in Shafto French's words?

"It was as I stood there, drawing shuddering breaths and attempting to calm my disordered wits," Catherine persisted, "that the sound of hoofbeats returned."

"Returned?"

"Even so. The horse drew up near the pond, and after an interval of silence—which might have encompassed a minute or an hour, Miss Austen, I scarcely know—I observed a figure to dismount, and bend over a dark object lying like a felled tree in the grass. Next I knew, the living man was struggling across the Winchester Road with the ankles of the other in his grasp, dragging that mortal weight in the direction of your cottage. I stared through the darkness, my heart in my mouth, for I knew the place to be deserted. I lost sight of them both at the hedge enclosing your property."

I gazed at Catherine Prowting, aghast at such a want of resolution: "And even then, you did not go to your father with a cry of *murder?*"

"I did not yet know that French—for it must have been he—was indeed *dead,* Miss Austen. He might only have been insensible, from the effects of his beating or the drink that might have inspired it. How could I *know?* I merely stood, in the most dreadful suspense imaginable, by the open window. And presently, the second man returned."

She paused at this point, as tho' summoning strength for what she must now say.

"He approached his horse and mounted; and this time he rode in the opposite direction—towards the Great House, and Alton beyond. As he passed by the end of our sweep, I discerned his profile clearly in the moonlight, and knew in an instant whose it was. No other gentleman's could be so immediately recognisable."

The path of duty, versus the urgings of the heart.

"You *saw* Julian Thrace?" I whispered.

"Mr. *Thrace*?" She blushed with a swift and painful intensity. "No, no, Miss Austen—it was Mr. *Jack Hinton* I observed in the Street that night."

I COULD NOT CONTAIN MY ASTONISHMENT AT THIS revelation, and must be thrice assured of its veracity before I could take it in. Mr. Hinton! Mr. Hinton, who had professed disdain for the coroner's proceeding, tho' sitting pale and silent through the whole; Mr. Hinton, who had affected to abhor violence and the pollution of Chawton's shades. Mr. Hinton, who called himself the *heir* of the Hampshire Knights, and who thus might reasonably be styled the object of Shafto French's greed, did the blackmailing labourer know somewhat to the gentleman's discredit. And there was the fact of Hinton's blood tie to James Baverstock, who might have provided a key to our cottage. But Mr. Hinton—the indolent poet of my imagining—seemed the unlikeliest candidate for murder in all the countryside. What could be the meaning of it?

"Why should Jack Hinton kill Shafto French?" I demanded of Catherine.

"I do not know. Perhaps it was . . . a mistake of some kind."

"You did not describe a mistake, but an episode of deadly intent. What you witnessed from your window that night was a deliberate act of murder."

"I know! I cannot account for it! Do you not apprehend that the scene has arisen in my mind hour after hour until I thought I must go mad? Why does one man ever take the life of another?"

"—From jealousy. From greed. From hatred or fear. But Shafto French? Can you think of any reason why Jack Hinton the gentleman should hate or fear the labouring man?"

She was silent, lips compressed. "Only what may be found in the idle talk of any tavern in Alton," she said at last. "The whole countryside would have it that the child Jemima French now bears is in fact Jack Hinton's."

"Good God!" I cried. "*There* is a motive for murder if ever I heard one. The dead man a cuckold—and no one sees fit to mention it to the coroner?"

She turned scandalised eyes upon me. *Cuckold,* I must suppose, was the sort of word that should *never* be mentioned around the dining table at Prowtings.

"I do not credit the story," she rejoined firmly, "and no more does any sensible person in Alton or Chawton. Jemima was once in service at the Lodge, and was dismissed over some disagreement with Miss Hinton. But rumour has followed her, as it will any pretty girl; and French did nothing by his manners or treatment of his wife to discourage it."

I have worked all my life, Mrs. French had told me, *and am not afraid of it.* Brave words for a woman with no more reputation to preserve. *Improprieties,* Miss Beckford had said, and *ill-usage.* And so the gossip had come round in a circle: from the Great House to Alton and back again to Prowtings, to form a noose for Jack Hinton's neck.

"You must assuredly speak to your father," I told Catherine, "and endeavour to explain why you have waited nearly a week to do so."

"I know that I am much to blame," she muttered brokenly, "but pray believe me, Miss Austen, when I declare that it was from no improper desire to shield Mr. Hinton from the full weight of the Law!"

Her accent in pronouncing this final word was so akin to the dignity of her father's, that I very nearly smiled. "I had thought it possible that you preserved a *tendre* for the gentleman."

"A *tendre*! Indeed, the esteem—the appearance of interest or affection—has been entirely on Mr. Hinton's side. I may like—I may have respected him once, before I knew— That is to say, any sentiment of regard has been thoroughly done away by Mr. Hinton's repulsion of my efforts to make all right."

"Your efforts—? My dear Miss Prowting, do not say that you have informed the gentleman that you *observed* him to drag a body towards my cottage!"

"But of course I have! I could not so expose him to the censure of his neighbours, or indeed the risk of his very life, without taxing him with all I had seen, and begging him most earnestly to make a clean breast of his guilt to my father in private!"

I stopped short on the very edge of Alton, my feelings almost incapable of expression. "Do you not realise, you silly girl, that where a man has murdered once, he may easily do so a second time, merely to save his own neck? Your life should not have five seconds' purchase in Mr. Hinton's company! I only pray God you have not encountered him alone!"

"No," she admitted, "I had not *that* courage. Indeed, I have loathed Mr. Hinton's very presence since the discovery of French's body in your cellar, and my comprehension of what it must mean. I have pled the head-ache, and taken to my room, excepting the necessity of social obligations that could not be overborne. I spoke to Mr. Hinton in the Great Hall at Chawton last night, and by way of reply, was given to understand that if I preserved any regard for his reputation, I must reveal nothing of what I had seen. He did not go so far as to *threaten* me—"

"Then he is not so stupid as I believed him."

"—but neither did he reassure my darkest fears with an explanation that could soften me. He intimated—if you will credit it!—that if I might offer this proof of loyalty and esteem—if I could go so far as to shield him with my silence—that I might reasonably expect to be mistress of the Lodge one day." She laughed abruptly; no fool Catherine. She should value such an offer as she ought, and know it for a bribe.

"When I understood, a few hours later, that my father meant to charge poor Bertie Philmore with French's murder, I knew that I was left no choice but to act, since Mr. Hinton refused to do so."

I placed my arm within Catherine Prowting's as we passed the first of Alton's shops and houses. "You are possessed of singular courage, my dear. I am determined all the same not to let you out of my sight until I have seen you safely into the care of Mr. Prowting. Let Jack Hinton do his worst—we shall be ready for him!"

WE DISCOVERED, THROUGH THE SIMPLE EXPEDIENT of vigourous interrogation at the George Inn, that Mr. Prowting had been observed to enter Mr. John Dyer's premises at Ivy House—a trim building not without charm, and the attraction of a series of Gothick arched casements. The magistrate was as yet engaged there. I accompanied Catherine to the builder's door, and tho' curious as to the nature of Mr. Prowting's business, declined to intrude. I had an idea of the conversation: the magistrate in his heavy, forthright way demanding to know whether Bertie Philmore could have stolen Dyer's keys to Chawton Cottage on the Saturday night of French's murder; and Mr. Dyer—in his succinct, pugnacious style—steadfastly refusing to allow it to be possible. Mr. Prowting was destined to suffer a revolution of opinion, and a disorder of all his ideas, when once his daughter's story was heard; but I did not like to witness his discomfiture.

Let him endure the severest pangs of regret beyond the reach of his neighbours, and collect his faculties during the brief walk home from Alton to Chawton. Prowting would require the full measure of his sense for the coming interview with Mr. John-Knight Hinton, Esquire.

The murder of Shafto French might well be explained by Catherine Prowting's confession, but the disappearance of Lord Harold's chest was not. I made my own way to Normandy Street, and kept a keen lookout for a yard full of laundry.

Halfway up the lane, on the opposite side of the paving, I detected a quantity of white lawn secured by wooden pegs to a line of rope. A tidy picket preserved the yard from the ravages of dogs and children, and a few flowers bloomed near its palings. No figure moved among the hanging linen, and the door of the nearby cottage was closed. I glanced upwards at the chimney, however, and observed a thin thread of smoke.

A girl of perhaps ten years answered my knock, and stared at me gravely from the threshold.

"Is your mother within?"

She nodded mutely.

"You may tell her that Miss Jane Austen is come to call."

"Bid the lady welcome, Mary," a voice commanded from the interior.

The child stepped back, pulling the door wide. I moved into the room, and saw that it was no foyer or front passage, but merely the cottage's place of all work, with a few benches drawn up to a scrubbed pine table, a hob with a great kettle boiling on the banked embers of the hearth, and several irons warming in the fire. A woman sat rocking an infant at her breast; she gazed at me with neither welcome nor trepidation on her features.

"Are you Rosie Philmore?"

"I am."

"Miss Jane Austen, at your service. It was at my home in Chawton, Mrs. Philmore, that your husband was . . ." I glanced at the silent little girl named Mary and hesitated. ". . . *found*, last evening."

"What of it?"

The child moved swiftly to her mother's side and stared at me with wide and frightened eyes.

"Would it be possible to talk a while," I attempted, "in private?"

"Do you go in search of your brothers, Mary," Mrs. Philmore said. "They'll be down near the Wey, I'll be bound, fishing with young Zakariah Gibbs. Tell them their dinner's waiting. Go on, now."

The girl fled out a rear door, two washtubs visible in the grass beyond it. I waited until the door creaked shut behind her before speaking again.

"Mrs. Philmore, I know that your husband is detained in Alton gaol at this moment. He may be guilty of entering my home—he may even have taken something of great value that belongs to me—but I do not believe he murdered Shafto French."

"He was home at midnight Saturday," she said stoutly, "like he said. I'll swear to that, to my dying day."

"I am sure you will. But Mr. Prowting thinks otherwise, and Mr. Prowting is magistrate for Alton, and determined to hang somebody for French's murder. I do not think it will concern him much if he hangs the wrong man."

In this, I may have done my neighbour an injustice; but my words had the effect I desired. Rosie Philmore closed her eyes, as if surrendering to a sudden shaft of pain, and drew a shuddering breath.

"It's all on account of those jewels," she said.

I frowned. Had Thrace's tale of the rubies of Chandernagar reached so far as Alton?

"—That chest of yours, what the great man from London brought special in his carriage. People will talk of anything, ma'am. You're a stranger in these parts, so you're not to know. Scandalous it was, how they talked—about the fortune you'd received from a dead lord, and what the man might have been paying for. I didn't listen no more than others—but Bert's ears grew so long with hanging on every word, I thought they'd scrape the floor by week's end. And then he told me, two nights past, the truth of the tale."

"The truth?"

She opened her eyes, still rocking the infant, and stared straight at me. "That 'tweren't jewels a'tall, nor gold neither, but a chest full of papers. Papers as somebody'd pay a good bit to see."

A thrill of apprehension coursed through me. "Your husband *knew* what the chest contained?"

"Of course. Heard it of his uncle, Old Philmore, he did."

"Old Philmore? But I am not even acquainted with the man."

"Old Philmore knew, all the same."

As had Lady Imogen. Was it she who set the joiner's family on to stealing Lord Harold's papers?

"Your husband was engaged by Mr. Dyer to work at my cottage. He was also employed, I understand, at Stonings in Sherborne St. John—the Earl of Holbrook's estate. Was Old Philmore ever working there?"

"Of course. It was from Old Philmore my Bert learned his trade. He's a rare joiner, Old Philmore."

"Has your husband's uncle been to see you? Has he called upon Bertie, in Alton gaol?"

She appeared to stiffen, like a woods animal grown suddenly wary of a trap.

"He'll be along, soon enough."

"You do not know where he is at present?"

"In Chawton. He lives there, same as yerself."

"Old Philmore has not been seen since your husband was taken up last night, Mrs. Philmore."

She leaned forward in her chair, the babe thrust into her lap. "What do you mean?" she demanded.

"Old Philmore appears to have fled. Is not that a singular coincidence? —That your husband should be sitting in gaol for a theft that cannot profit him, while his uncle is nowhere to be found?"

For an instant, I watched Rosie Philmore comprehend the import of my words. Then she laughed with a bitter harshness. "Not if you know Bert's family, ma'am. If there's a way to turn a penny from hardship, Old Philmore'll find it."

• • •

FROM NORMANDY STREET I MADE MY WAY TOWARDS
Austen, Gray & Vincent, feeling exposed to every eye
and the subject of every chance conversation. Far
more of my business was known than I had understood before, and the knowledge could not help but
make me uneasy. Lady Imogen had spoken of the existence of Lord Harold's papers with easy familiarity;
but this I had dismissed as the knowledge of a family
friend. I must now assume the contents of the chest
were also known to Major Spence and Mr. Thrace,
with whom her ladyship was intimate; as clearly they
were known to the Philmores and their circle. I could
no longer suppose the information to be privileged.

Last night I had presumed the chest was stolen because of the rumour of fabulous wealth attached to it.
I apprehended now that Lord Harold's legacy had
been seized for exactly the reason it has always been
so sedulously guarded by the solicitor Mr. Chizzlewit
and his confederates—because of the danger inherent in its communications. The theft had not been
made at random: deep in the chest lay a truth that
one person at least could not allow to be known. Was
he content in having stolen the trunk and the dangerous memories it held? Or did the threat still walk
abroad, with an intelligence that lived and breathed?

Was I even now in peril, by virtue of what I had already read?

I revolved what little of Lord Harold's history I had
perused. There were anecdotes of Warren Hastings; an
old scandal of early love and a hasty duel; the animus

between Lord Harold and one man—the Viscount St. Eustace—and his friendship for another, the Earl of Holbrook. A vague suggestion of activity on behalf of noble French émigrés during the Reign of Terror, and Lord Harold's dedication to the salvation of a few; and the mention of Geoffrey Sidmouth, whom I had known myself in Lyme Regis some years before, and remembered with poignant affection. And then there was the Frenchwoman named Hélène, whom the Rogue first met while en route from India to England in 1785. But I had found no firm indication as to the *father* of Hélène's child, to whom he later referred. It was possible, I supposed, that Julian Thrace might claim to be the woman's son. But as to his paternity? Had Thrace been sired by her affianced husband, the Viscount St. Eustace? Or by wild Freddy Vansittart, smitten on the *Punjab*? Or Lord Harold himself?

At that thought, I stopped dead in the middle of the High. And saw again in my mind's eye the lazy beauty of Thrace's face. It bore not the slightest resemblance to Lord Harold's sharp features; but neither did it resemble Lady Imogen Vansittart's. And the Rogue, I felt sure, was the sort of man who should always know his sons.

The truth was somewhere in Lord Harold's papers.

That the chest was seized on the very night I had dined with the intimates of Stonings, must cause me to believe that one of them—Lady Imogen, or Thrace himself—had long been aware of the danger Lord

Harold's writings posed. One of them had hired Old Philmore and his nephew.

"Jane," my brother Henry said with a frown as I entered his rooms at No. 10, "it has been as I predicted. Julian Thrace has had the poor taste to stop here on his way to Sherborne St. John, and require of me a *loan*."

"Lady Imogen's Devil in the cards?" I enquired. "How much is demanded for the preservation of the Beau's honour?"

"All of five hundred pounds! —To be issued in notes backed by gold in my London branch! The effrontery of the fellow, Jane, to presume on such a slight social acquaintance! But what else, after all, has Thrace ever done?"

"You *are* a banker, Henry—and I must suppose a gaming debt contracted in a gentleman's household is a pressing affair, that must be paid with despatch. Particularly when one is living cheek by jowl with the lady demanding payment."

"He might have offered her his vowels," Henry retorted crossly, "and applied to friends in London for the whole.[2] I cannot be easy in my mind regarding Thrace's security for any sum advanced to him, despite the Earl's apparent regard, and all the frenzy of activity in rebuilding Stonings."

"Perhaps you shall be easier once you have visited the place."

---

[2] A person's "vowels" were his or her I.O.U.—a signed note promising repayment of a debt of honor that could not be immediately settled.— *Editor's note.*

My brother merely stared.

"We are all invited to picnic there tomorrow—yourself expressly desired by Major Spence, who should like to interrogate you regarding the Vyne hunt, Henry."

"But I had meant to return to London in the morning!"

"Poor sport, Henry! Consider the heat and stink of Town in such a season; and then, you know, nobody worth your notice is likely to be there."

"No more they are," he replied thoughtfully, "but Eliza is sure to have my head if I desert her in all the packing. We intended our removal for the end of July, you know—in time to join our friends in Scotland for the shooting months."

"August is weeks away," I said equably, "and if you stay in Hampshire, you might assist me in the treasure hunt."

"Not the rubies, Jane?"

"Mamma will have discovered those before the month is out," I told him dismissively. "No, Henry—it is Lord Harold's papers I mean to find. I am convinced they are even now well hidden at Stonings."

Chapter 16

If the Boot Fits . . .

7 July 1809, cont.

~

IT WAS A PLEASANT THING INDEED TO FIND DINNER
on the table at my return—a roasted capon, a bit of
white fish Sally had got by proxy from Alton, and
beans from Libby Cuttle's garden—"her being that
ashamed of herself, ma'am, when I told her how respectable you all were, and how good to me." I
guessed that the inclusion in our household of a
Chawton girl born and bred, with all the hundred ties
of obligation and habit that knit her close to the surrounding country, must prove a decided advantage.
Sally Mitchell was worth ten times the notice of a Mr.
Middleton, in being related to the dairy man, the
sheep farmer on her mother's side, and the fellow
who mended tools from his cart each Wednesday; and

to crown all, we should not be reduced to stratagems and subterfuge in order to buy bread from the baker each morning. Even Cassandra had interrogated the new housemaid and was satisfied—"for she is not un-intelligent, and will prove a useful set of hands in the stillroom, Jane—which you must know I intend to establish as soon as Martha Lloyd is arrived from Kintbury. And I find Sally is not at all incommoded by dogs, which is an excellent thing, as Link means to learn all about the stillroom—don't you, you cunning scamp?"

The stillroom meant Cassandra's orange wine; I should have to profit from my association with the Great in the days remaining to me before Martha's return, and drink deep of the claret they offered.

Henry sat down with us in the dining parlour, and we had just enough chairs for four disposed around the table. Tonight was our first evening spent entirely *en famille* since our arrival, and the first in many days that Cassandra had enjoyed in her own abode. For ten months she had been resident at Godmersham—and I had almost despaired of my sister's ever returning, in the belief that Neddie must grow so dependant upon her as to regard her as another of his innumerable possessions. I had broached the subject only once in Kent, during my visit there the previous month; but Cassandra had averted her eyes, and after a little hesitation observed, "Dear Fanny is quite a woman, now. It cannot be a comfortable thing, to see her aunt sitting always in her mother's place, and taking precedence. I flatter myself I have been useful among the little children—but with the boys soon to be returned to Winchester, and Fanny grown so capable . . . I cannot feel I am needed, Jane."

That truth must be a sorrow to Cassandra, who has made a kind of life from devoting herself to her brothers, as tho' the selflessness of her quiet ways must in some wise justify her having remained single when Tom Fowle died. We must each of us in our own way earn the keep we require of our brothers' pockets.

"There is this comfort at least," she concluded now. "Frank's Mary must be confined at any moment—and I shall be much in demand at Rose Cottage in Lenton Street, once the second child is arrived. How fortunate that we are not above a mile from her door!"

My sister is exceptionally *good*, and accepts the cruel injustice of her lot without complaint or reversion to the hopes of former days; but with advancing age, I have observed Cassandra's tendency to take pride in her very sublimation to the uses of others. I cannot admire it; it is too much like martyrdom. For my part, I have never been one to submit readily to denial.

"I wish that Mr. Thrace had been more exact in his intelligence regarding the necklace," my mother mused pensively as she stabbed a chicken thigh with her fork. "I have devoted quite three hours to turning over the earth in the back garden, and have only blisters on my palms to show for it, Jane."

"We must beg some cuttings from Miss Beckford's

garden at the Great House, Mamma, and have you plant while you dig," I suggested. "Only this morning, she promised me a syringa and a plum sapling."

"As we are to meet with Mr. Thrace on the morrow, Jane, perhaps you could ascertain more narrowly where the rubies were hidden," Henry suggested with devilry in his eye. "I should not like all Mamma's work to be wasted; and, too, there is the trouble of thieves in the neighbourhood. What if they should come again by night, and profit from our labour?"

"Mamma may hit them stoutly over the head with her shovel, and so make an end to the business," I replied.

Scarcely had these words been spoken than we heard a knock upon the outer door, and having failed to discern the approach of a visitor over the clamour of our own conversation, were at a loss to name the caller. I waited for Sally to answer the summons, while Cassandra said with obvious satisfaction, "That will be Neddie perhaps. He was to dine in Alton with Mr. Middleton, I believe, and will have escorted his tenant home."

"Seems a foolish thing to do," Henry observed, "when he might be comfortable with the port to be found in Barlow's cellars."

Mr. Prowting appeared in the dining-parlour doorway.

Behind him, hat in hand, stood Mr. Jack Hinton.

"Good evening, Mrs. Austen. I must beg your sincere pardon for incommoding you at this hour," the magistrate said, "but I am come on a matter of some urgency. May I beg leave once again to enter your cellar?"

"Of course, my dear Mr. Prowting. Of course. You have a particular point to ascertain regarding that foul murder, I must suppose." My mother's countenance was alive with interest; but Mr. Prowting did not explicate his business, and never should she have conjectured the true object of his urgency. "What a delightful surprise to see you again, Mr. Hinton! Had I known we were to have such a party, I should have invited you all to take pot-luck with us!"

The clergyman's son stiffly bowed, and murmured some politeness. He should probably disdain to dine at so unfashionable an hour, and was as yet arrayed in his morning dress.

"I do not think you know my eldest daughter—" my mother began, when Mr. Prowting broke in abruptly.

"As I said, ma'am—it *is* a matter of some urgency."

"Very well. Henry shall be happy to accompany you below."

My brother had already laid down his napkin and made for the door.

At such a moment, I was not about to be confined abovestairs with the women, and silently went to request a candle of Sally. She stood by while the little troupe crossed her kitchen to the narrow stairs, her eyes round as buttons. Imagining, no doubt, that there was yet another corpse beneath her feet.

"A lanthorn, I think, Miss Austen—if you have not an oil lamp you may spare," the magistrate suggested.

I exchanged the candle for a lanthorn, at which Mr. Prowting gestured me politely down the stairs. With a stiff nod, he then herded Mr. Hinton before him. The gentleman was exceedingly pale, his eyes sparkling with an unnatural brilliancy, as tho' at any moment he might succumb to a fit. Henry brought up the rear, his gaze acutely trained on Mr. Hinton. I had not neglected to relate the whole of Catherine Prowting's story while my brother accompanied me home from Alton; and at the conclusion of it, Henry had declared that he would not be gone to London on the morrow for worlds.

Our ill-assorted pilgrimage came to a halt at the foot of the stairs.

"Mr. Austen," the magistrate said heavily, "I must apologise again for the intrusion. There is no help for it. I have heard today such an account of the night in question—Saturday last, when Shafto French undoubtedly met his death—as must give rise to the gravest concerns and trouble. It is a weight, Mr. Austen, upon me—a weight I alone must bear. Mr. Hinton now stands accused of French's murder."

"That is a lie," the gentleman retorted coldly, "as I have reiterated this half hour or more."

"I am afraid, sir, that in so serious an affair as murder, I must subject you to certain proofs."

"But I have told you I did not harm the man!" Hinton cried. "Does my word mean so little, Mr. Prowting?"

The magistrate stared at him from under lowering brows. "I must beg you to step over to the corner of the cellar. Mr. Austen, you are my witness as to what is about to pass."

Mr. Hinton swallowed convulsively, his right hand rising to the knot of his ornate cravat. Of a sudden, he appeared to me a small, ill-natured boy of a kind too often hounded in his lessons; the sort of raw cub who should mishandle his mounts and be thrown at every hedge. A coward, parading as a man of Fashion; a fool who should attempt to get by intrigue what he could not command from merit. A paltry, unfortunate, and ill-bred whelp, who should always labour under the severest conviction of ill-usage at the hands of his neighbours, resenting and envying the world by turns.

"Miss Austen, would you raise your lanthorn?"

At the arcing beam of light there was a scuttle of rats, grown by now to seem a commonplace. *Link,* I thought; but the terrier's work must be forestalled at least another hour, until Mr. Prowting had seen the marks on the floor undisturbed by ravaging paws. We moved carefully towards the corner, an executioner's lockstep honour guard, until the magistrate held up his hand.

"And now, sir—if you would be so good as to press your foot into the dust at exactly this place."

"What?" Hinton exclaimed. "Are you *mad*?"

"Pray do as I request, sir—or I shall have no alternative, I am afraid, but to abandon you to the Law."

"I shall do no such thing!" Hinton protested. "It is absurd! The affronteries to which I have been subjected this evening—"

"For God's sake, man, do as I say!" Mr. Prowting burst out.

The gentleman glanced at Henry, but found no support; and then, with an expression of grimmest necessity, lifted his boot and pressed it into the dirt.

I sank down with the lanthorn, so that the light illuminated the cellar floor distinctly; and discerned the outline of Mr. Hinton's boot fresh on the floor. The footprint my brother and I had detected previously could still be seen, a ghost of the present one. To the naked eye, it appeared that the boot prints matched in every particular.

"Mr. Hinton, pray explain your movements on the night of the first of July," Mr. Prowting demanded in a dreadful voice.

"I was from home and from Chawton," the clergyman's son returned defiantly, "having ridden out that morning to meet a party of friends near Box Hill, where a prize-fight was to be held. I did not return until quite late. Any of my friends will say the same."

"Do you have an idea of the time?"

"—The time I reached home?"

"Was it before or after midnight?"

Hinton's gaze wavered somewhat, as tho' he began to understand his danger. "I cannot undertake to say."

"Would it interest you to know that you were seen to dismount your horse near Chawton Pond at perhaps a quarter-hour or twenty minutes past midnight, early on Sunday morning last, and to take up the body of a man you found there—a man, I would put it to you, Mr. Hinton, whom you had *left there for dead some minutes before*—"

"Mr. Prowting!" the gentleman cried. "You forget yourself, sir! If you will credit the silly imaginings of a goosecap girl—"

"Sir," Mr. Prowting seethed, "it is *you* who forget yourself! Observe the footprints! Can you deny that it is your boot?"

"I do not deny it." Hinton's lip positively curled. "You made certain you were provided with witnesses. But any boot may be much like another. The similarity in these marks can mean nothing to a man of reason."

"Can it not?" The magistrate looked to be on the point of apoplexy. "Who is your bootmaker, sir?"

There was a pause before Hinton replied.

"I hardly know. As I said—one boot is much like another."

"But not yours," Henry interposed softly. He, too, was crouching now near the lanthorn's beam, his eyes trained upon Mr. Hinton's footwear. "These Hessians look to be of Hoby's make, I should say, and are quite dear.[1] From the wear that can be observed on toe and heel, I should judge that you ordered them fully a twelvemonth ago, and shall probably have them replaced during a visit to Town in the autumn or winter; indeed, such an economical practise may long have

---

[1] Hoby's establishment sat at the corner of St. James's and Piccadilly, and was considered the most elegant gentlemen's bootmaker of the period. Hessians were a style introduced in the early part of the nineteenth century, worn outside the trousers and curving under the knee, with a leather tassel dangling from the center front.—*Editor's note.*

been your habit. It is not every man who can afford to patronise Hoby—and only gentlemen possessed of the most exacting tastes. There cannot be another such pair of boots within twenty miles of Chawton, Mr. Hinton. I expect Hoby will have your measurements to account, and will be happy to provide them to the magistrate."

With a swift and vicious precision, the cornered man swung his foot full in my brother's face. Henry cried out and fell backwards, his hand clutching his nose.

I cast aside the lanthorn and went to him. Blood trickled between his fingers, but still he strained against me, as tho' he should have hurled himself at Hinton's throat.

"Take care, my dear," I muttered. "You cannot demand satisfaction of a murderer, Henry. He is beneath your notice."

"Mr. Hinton!" the magistrate said accusingly. "Must you be tried for assault as well as murder?"

"I did not kill Shafto French," he spat between his teeth, "and well you know it, Prowting. French may have found cause enough to kill *me;* but I regarded the man as little as I should regard a slug worming its way through my cabbages."

"So little, in fact, that you carried his body across the road and left it for the rats in this very cellar! Did you use your nephew Baverstock's key for the business? We are aware, Mr. Hinton, that he may possess one. You cannot deny, man, that you stood here. For the last time, Mr. Hinton: *What explanation will you offer for your actions?*"

Of a sudden, the fury seemed to drain from Hinton's countenance, to be replaced by the coldest contempt. "I should never feel myself called upon to offer an explanation to you or any of the present miserable company. I am the *last true heir* of the Knights of Chawton, Prowting—and must consider myself above your jiggery-pokery *Law.*"

"Very well," the magistrate replied. "Then John-Knight Hinton, it is my painful duty as magistrate to arrest you—for the murder of Shafto French."

Chapter 17

Too Long in the Back

~

"AS THE HOUSE WAS BUILT IN THE LATE SEVEN-teenth century," Lady Imogen observed as she led us into a long gallery at Stonings that was more lumber room than habitable space, "it remains firmly rooted in Palladio. The serene limestone façade, for example, is virtually free of adornment; no Jacobean chimneys or Tudor panelling are to be found, and as successive generations did not see fit to alter the original style, the house preserves a delightful unity—without the awkward shifting from epoch to epoch one so often observes in less modern creations."

"Lord!" Ann Prowting exclaimed. "I wonder you can find your way to breakfast of a morning! I should require signposts in each passage to direct me from place to place. It is a vast pile, is it not?"

"Nearly three hundred rooms. Mr. Wyatt, whom we consulted regarding the improvements, has widened the whole and brought reason to the arrangement of the principal apartments.[1] This is the saloon," Lady Imogen added, throwing open a set of lofty doors surmounted by a pediment, "—where we often play at cards of an evening. The music room, where my instrument is set out, is adjacent. The apartment is our chief delight at present, as Mr. Wyatt's work here is nearly complete."

Mr. Prowting, whose anxious bulk hovered at my right elbow, managed a phlegmatic "Magnificent!"

It was a bright and airy chamber, with ivory-coloured walls and mouldings picked out in gold leaf; a massive chimney piece of carved white stone, in the form of nymphs supporting a plinth, dominated each end. The chief virtue of the room, however, lay in its great windows, which gave onto a delightful prospect of lawns and trees sloping gently towards the lake. This was skirted and surmounted in its narrowest part by a great stone parapet, over which our carriages had clattered only a few moments before.

We had set out from Chawton at ten o'clock, taking in Henry on our way. It was a smaller party than originally planned, my brother Neddie having pledged himself to all the cares and irksomenesses of

---

[1] Lewis Wyatt was one of a family of architects who, collectively, were responsible for some of the most significant buildings of the late Georgian and Regency periods.—*Editor's note.*

Quarter Day, and being even now established in Mr. Barlow's back parlour awaiting the appearance of his numerous tenants. My mother could not be torn from the vigourous excavations undertaken in her back garden, of which she had unflagging hopes; and Mrs. Prowting was indisposed for a long carriage drive in the heat of summer, but thought it highly necessary that her husband accompany the two girls. We had therefore placed ourselves at Miss Maria Beckford's disposal, Cassandra and I taking two seats in the Middleton carriage. The three Prowtings and Miss Benn went in the magistrate's barouche; and the three eldest Middleton girls went in a hired equipage with their maid. Henry had made a dashing cicisbeo, trailing beside Miss Benn on his hired hack, and offering charming observations on the suitability of the party; and the weather had not seen fit to disappoint. We had achieved the intervening miles at an easy pace, and arrived in Sherborne St. John a few moments before noon.

We had been cordially met by Major Spence and Lady Imogen, who tarried only long enough to see our wraps bestowed on a housemaid, before conducting us through the marble-floored entry hall to the delights within.

"I am reminded," Cassandra said in a lowered tone, "of the Duke of Dorset's establishment at Knole, in Kent; but tho' easily as extensive as this, that is a house in an entirely different style."

Mr. Thrace, we were told, was still engaged in his morning's ride, but was every moment expected.

Lady Imogen looked as tho' she did not notice her rival's absence. She was in excellent spirits, her manner a mixture of the arch and the sweet that could not fail to please. She was clothed this morning in a light muslin gown of pale jonquil colour, with beribboned sandals on her feet, her countenance glowing with the animation of her speech. There was a kind of triumph in all her aspect that suggested a victory gained—and I felt a surge of anxious solicitude on the subject of my stolen chest. Such happiness could not be due merely to last evening's win at cards—she had a deeper game in train, and appeared confident of her luck. The admiration of every gentleman in the room was evident; the rest of the ladies must be cast in the shade; and it was as well for my brother Edward that he had stayed in Alton—this lady was far too bewitching for *his* fragile state to bear.

Major Spence did not need to proclaim his captivation: tho'. correct and more often silent than not, he frequently bent his dark eyes upon Lady Imogen's face or form, and she did not move to a door or a chair but he was before her instantly as guide. How difficult must be the trials of such a man, placed in a position of subservience to the object of his ardent love! To offer his heart, as he clearly had done, in the shattering knowledge that were she to accept him, the match should be called a misalliance by the Great. Had she ever attempted to use her power over him? —Attempted, perhaps, to employ his allegiance *against* Julian Thrace? I could hardly say. Lady Imogen showed Spence nothing more than easy affection, of a sort she might have reserved for a groom that had placed her, long ago, upon her first pony.

As I stood near Cassandra in the elegant saloon, and gazed out at the picturesque view offered through its windows, I considered of the beauties of the Earl's estate—and very nearly forgave the theft of Lord Harold's precious documents. To be mistress— or master—of Stonings was an ambition that might inspire any number of crimes!

"And to think that all this has been left slumbering for years!" Henry declared.

"Having never expected to inherit the title—he was a younger son, you know—my father was disinclined to live in the style befitting an Earl," Lady Imogen replied. "I do not think his lordship's memories of childhood in this place are entirely happy ones. And having been a single gentleman for much of his life, he naturally prefers to maintain an establishment in Town—near his clubs and cronies—or retire to his shooting box when a craving for the country seizes him. I cannot remember when we last visited Stonings together; when I was no more than three, I daresay."

The year the Countess of Holbrook ran away with a Colonel of the Horse Guards, I thought; and from Henry's looks, his mind was reverting to the same. But whatever the Earl's past feelings towards the house, he did not seem disposed to hold it in contempt *now.* So much sudden and expensive activity, on behalf of a putative heir—or an elegant daughter with habits of expence?

"Stonings frightened me when I was little," Lady

Imogen confided. "It was always cold and cheerless, and the servants were not the ones I knew. I used to lose my way in the upper storeys and be found crying behind some moth-eaten curtain, convinced I had been buried alive. But now I am grown, I see the place for what it is: an ancient and honourable seat that ought not to be allowed to fall into ruin."

"Mr. Dyer's folk have much to do, I presume?" Mr. Prowting enquired.

Charles Spence inclined his head. "They have been engaged on the repairs nearly three months, and are likely to continue their labour a year or more. The roof tiles had given way extensively in a number of places—the south end of the east wing, and the central hall—so that there is damp in nearly every ceiling and wall, and the plaster has required to be replaced throughout. Then there are the ravages to wainscoting and floors from a variety of feral creatures we are even still discovering in various corners, and the collapse of stone walls about the property. For you must understand, Mr. Prowting, that however grand the house itself, it is as nothing to the gardens, which were extensively improved in the last century by the present Earl's grandfather, with the assistance of Mr. Capability Brown."

"Major Spence is a fund of knowledge regarding Stonings," Lady Imogen observed, "and his work is tireless. I believe Charles loves this place better than all of us."

"When one has been far from home, and privileged to defend it," he replied, "one cannot help but hold English soil more precious than anything else in life."

"My father would not agree with you!" Imogen chortled. "If you could hear him deplore this rackety old barracks!"

"And yet he chose wisely, in placing the Major here," I observed. "Perhaps the Earl will descend upon Hampshire soon, and inspect the progress."

"The Earl will be arrived in less than three weeks' time," said a voice from the music room doorway, "and intends, so I believe, to give a ball. I will be three-and-twenty then, you know—and you must all drink to my health!"

It was Mr. Thrace, arrayed in his riding dress; he strode towards us, bowed, and was made known to Cassandra, who alone of the party was yet a stranger to him.

"A ball!" Ann Prowting cried. "I am longing for a ball!"

"Then you must certainly come," Mr. Thrace returned easily, as tho' the office of inviting guests to Stonings was already his, "and as the distance between our homes is so great . . ." his gaze moved with warmth to Catherine Prowting, ". . . you and *all your family* must certainly spend the night."

"Julian," Major Spence interposed gently, "we must leave the details of her party in Lady Imogen's capable hands."

"Does she plan to attend? I had not thought she would remain so long in the country." Mr. Thrace bowed, a satiric expression about his lips. He lacked her ladyship's high animal spirits this morning—the natural result, perhaps, of his losses at the faro table; but he appeared no less certain of himself than when I had first observed him. He was determined to display himself as the lord of Stonings. The battle, then, was well and truly joined.

But which of them—*which of them?*—had Lord Harold's proof ranged on their side?

It seemed unlikely that Lady Imogen should have hired Old Philmore or his nephew to steal the chest; she was too little known in the country, and too high in the instep to condescend in Normandy Street or at Thatch Cottages. But necessity might work the cruellest alteration in a person's habits, and necessity was Lady Imogen's goad. She was distressed in her circumstances, and on the brink of losing her fortune. In such a case, might she avail herself of those same bonds of obligation and custom I had remarked in our servant Sally Mitchell? Lady Imogen's *maid* might be familiar with every soul in Alton, and be despatched with certainty to the very man required to do the job.

In the case of Mr. Thrace, the matter was entirely easy. He came and went from Chawton and Alton as tho' Hampshire born and bred. He was in the habit of dining at the Middletons', and might have encountered Old Philmore any time these past several weeks; for a gentleman to engage the discreet services of a labourer was a simple matter of pounds and pence. And there was *this* that must arouse the deepest suspicion in my breast: Thrace had regaled our entire dinner party with the history of the Rubies of Chandernagar—a story which must be apocryphal, and employed for only one purpose: to explain the sudden appearance of strangers at Chawton Cottage, searching by stealth for a hidden treasure—or entering the house by force when its owners were absent.

"Pray come through to the terrace," Lady Imogen commanded. She did not rebuke the upstart Beau for his pretensions, or throw down her gauntlet in public; indeed, she looked blithely unconscious. "It is in a dubious state of repair, but will serve charmingly for a nuncheon. See, Charles, how I have ordered Rangle to scatter the little tables about, and arrange the pyramids of fruit so delightfully? This is the only sort of picnic I will bear: with firm stone underfoot, and ample accommodation for every guest, and no fears of dirt or damp to tarnish one's clothing."

"An excellent arrangement," he replied with playful courtesy, "but hardly so like a picnic."

"Bah! You cavalry officers are never content unless you may bivouac on the hard ground, with a fire at your feet and a Spanish maiden to boil your coffee. I know how it is! Don't attempt to beguile *me*, Charles—I know you for a blackguard of old!"

WHEN THE RASPBERRY CORDIAL AND THE MADEIRA wine had been drunk, and a quantity of cold meat and peaches eaten, there was nothing to do but watch the Middleton girls chase one another through the grass. Mr. Prowting, with all the beauty of the lake spread before him, expressed a regret that he had not thought to bring rods and tackle; and this began an exhaustive discussion of coarse fishing among the gentlemen, Mr. Thrace in particular being addicted to the sport. He and Mr. Prowting determined to walk down to the water itself, but could not tempt the ladies to join them. Mr. Middleton and Miss Beckford elected to rest in the shade before the arduous journey back to Alton; Cassandra was observing the little girls at play; Henry amused Lady Imogen with an anecdote regarding their mutual acquaintance in Town; Major Spence listened courteously to some effusion of Miss Benn's. I guarded my privacy jealously, and cast about for the most effective means of searching the vast property.

It seemed a ridiculous hope, this idea that I might discover a single chest amidst all the objects of a noble household amassed over more than a century, and that house presently under repair. Even to attempt such a search was folly, and dangerously offensive to my hosts. I suspected Mr. Thrace and Lady Imogen equally, but I could not bring myself to steal away from the company, and lose my way in the passages of Stonings, where I might encounter any number of servants duly engaged in their proper affairs. How was I to discern which bedroom belonged to the principal parties, and how to justify my presence in either of them?

"Do you hunt with your brother, Miss Austen?"

Lady Imogen stood before me, her arm through Henry's.

"As my brother will expose me to derision without remorse—I must confess I am a sad horsewoman."

"But how is this!" she exclaimed. "Your brothers all mad for sport—intimates of Mr. Chute at the Vyne—and you will not undertake to ride? I have just such a little hunter in my stables even now as should tempt you, Miss Austen. You must walk down with me to visit Nutmeg."

"With pleasure," I assented, "provided you do not compel me to mount. I will stand outside the box and admire your Nutmeg all you wish."

"That will do for a start. Take some of the sugar from the table—we must not arrive empty-handed."

The scheme of a walk being generally broached, and the Prowting girls—no riders themselves—being eager to admire the cunning little hunter, a rather larger party set out for the stables than originally planned. Lady Imogen monopolised Henry with her desire to be made known to the Master of the Vyne, and admitted to all the revels of the local hunt; from her playful words it seemed she intended to be established at Stonings by autumn.

"I have long been allowed to hunt with the Quorn," she informed Henry, "and must own that I prefer the Melton country; but what is that to the delights of one's neighbours, and the intimacy of a local pack? I shall not disdain it. Perhaps my father may go so far as to look in once or twice. He is a punishing rider to hounds!"

Mr. Thrace placed himself beside Catherine Prowting, and talked to her of the Prince Regent. "It is a fearful crush at Carlton House, but nothing compared to the present scene in Brighton, where the Prince is established for the summer months. And the Pavilion itself is so exquisitely curious—it is a treat akin to Astley's Amphitheatre, to be bidden in attendance!"

"I have never visited Astley's Amphitheatre," Catherine returned hesitantly, "and Papa is most adamant in his opposition to Brighton. Watering places he regards as insipid, and dens of vice."

"As a man of the world, he must fear the effect of your beauty on the town," Thrace observed with gallantry. "You should be carried off within a day of descending upon Brighton, Miss Prowting!"

There were half a dozen horses turned out in the loose boxes; among them I recognised the powerful grey Mr. Thrace had ridden in Chawton. Lady Imogen called for her groom—a spare figure with a weathered face and sharp eyes rather like a monkey's—and said, "Lead out Nutmeg, Robley; I will have my girl admired."

The groom entered the box, and led the mare into the stable yard, so that all the gentlemen might examine her lines and comment upon her excellence as a hunter.

"You paid all of six hundred guineas for her, Lady Imogen?" Mr. Thrace enquired with an air of surprise. "Very showy, I grant you—and yet she is too long in the back. You will gladly take five pence for her from anybody who will offer it, after your first hard outing, I'll be bound."

"Say that again if you dare!" the Earl's daughter flashed. "Say that again, Thrace—and I'll whip you myself! I was riding with the Quorn when you were still a raw schoolboy. She is as neat a filly to go as any you've seen! Admit it!"

"She is *too long in the back*," the gentleman repeated, and turned away.

Lady Imogen was white with fury. The insult to her horse—the insult to her own powers of judgement and her experience in the field—piqued her as Thrace's milder pretensions to mastery could not. Her hands clenched convulsively, her breast heaved with a powerful emotion—and I feared she might hurl herself on her putative half-brother if Major Spence's firm hand had not restrained her.

"Too long, perhaps, for a rider like yourself, Thrace," the steward said mildly, "and I should not like to test her either—but in Lady Imogen's hands, she will be the sweetest of goers."

Thrace smiled. His suggestion of contempt only enflamed Lady Imogen further.

"Fetch your grey!" she cried. "Fetch your grey, and let us see who is the better judge of horseflesh!"

"But you are not dressed to ride, my lady," the groom Robley protested.

"What is that to me? I am among friends, not parading in Hyde Park. Pray saddle Nutmeg."

"Hold the horse, Robley," Thrace said with sudden choler. "I will fetch the saddle."

He disappeared into the tack room, while the rest of us looked on in suspense. Henry sidled over to me.

"Her ladyship is in a rare temper," he said, "and for my part, I should say the right is all Thrace's. The mare is assuredly too long in the back."

"But he need not have thrown the fact in her face," I returned softly. "It is almost as tho' he would incite her to betray herself. He wished her to appear unbecoming before her guests."

"Even so—this will be a spectacle worth recounting at my club! The Earl of Holbrook's heirs disputing their rights over open ground!"

At that moment, Mr. Thrace reappeared with a small leather saddle in his hands. "Here, Robley— saddle the mare while I fetch Rob Roy."

He led out the grey, who looked fresh and handsome as ever; tossed his own saddle over the hunter's back with a practised hand, and placed his boot in the stirrup.

"Have a care, Julian," Spence muttered. "She will work herself into a passion."

"Let the course be set," Mr. Thrace declared, "as the span of sweep between the stable yard and the main gate, a distance of nearly a mile. Are we agreed?"

"Agreed," Lady Imogen declared. "But what will you wager, Thrace? What is the price of your honour? —The sum of your losses at faro? For I know you cannot settle that debt."

Her seat was graceful and easy, her gloved hands light on the reins. The dreadful pallor of anger had fled, to be replaced by the high colour of excitement.

"Are you so dubious of victory, Lady Imogen? Why not wager something we both hold dear? Let us say—"

Thrace hesitated, as tho' measuring his odds. "Let us compete for *Stonings*."

The look of elation drained from her ladyship's face. "That is not mine to stake, Thrace, as you very well know. Nor yours to demand."

"If you would already concede defeat—"

"Very well!" she cried. "Stonings it is! And may the best judge of horseflesh win!"

Chapter 18

Neck or Nothing

8 July 1809, cont.

~

"LADY IMOGEN—" CHARLES SPENCE RAISED HIS hand to her bridle. "I beg of you—"

"Let me go, Charles," she retorted cuttingly. "I am not a green girl to be led by your rein. Will you call the start?"

Nutmeg wheeled before he could answer. As Lady Imogen leaned forward and cantered towards the entrance to the yard in considerable style, I thought the little mare looked skittish—as tho' she might prove difficult to manage. The natural result, I must suppose, of a mount offered too little exercise in such a season.

Mr. Thrace was already waiting, his grey prancing beside the mare. Major Spence limped towards the mounted pair.

"Race if you must, but call off this foolish wager," he begged.

"I am determined, Charles," Lady Imogen replied.

His hand moved abruptly as tho' he might have forbidden all gallops this morning; but at Lady Imogen's impatient twitch of her mount's head, Spence stepped back from the contenders without another word. He raised his right arm, then let it fall. The two horses sprang forward in a cloud of dust.

"It's always neck or nothing with her ladyship," Robley observed cryptically to anyone who might listen. "It don't do to put a fence in her way—she'll throw her heart over, every time."

The Major was still standing at the entry to the yard, his attention fixed on the careening pair. I moved to join him, the others only a little behind me.

"Who is winning, Henry?" I demanded. My eyes have never been strong, and the horses had achieved such a distance that I could no longer discern which was forwarder.

"I believe it is Thrace. No—Lady Imogen has pulled to the fore!"

"We ought to have placed a man at the gate," Spence said tensely. "—To observe the outcome."

"But Thrace is a man of honour," my brother objected. "He shall certainly own the truth, once he knows it!"

"With such a prize as Stonings in view?" Spence demanded bitterly; and then he stepped forward, as tho' torn from his position.

"Good God!" he cried. "She is thrown!"

He began to run down the sweep with painful ineptitude on his injured leg, but Henry was the faster. He passed Major Spence while the rest of us were still collecting our faculties and exclaiming over the fate of Lady Imogen—and in a matter of moments, could be seen halfway down the sweep. He came to a halt by the crumpled figure; I discerned him to lift her in his arms.

Mr. Thrace had wheeled his tearing mount and galloped back towards the little mare. Nutmeg had skittered away from the sweep as tho' shying from the burden she left behind. As Henry staggered towards us, I was dimly aware of Mr. Thrace coursing alongside Lady Imogen's mount, and leaning forward to grasp the mare's bridle.

"Spence!" Henry shouted. "You must send for a doctor!"

"Is she gravely hurt?" the steward cried, and lurched forward to meet my brother. I was only seconds behind him, Catherine Prowting at my back.

Charles Spence bent over the face of his beloved, his own white with shock. His fingers fumbled at her pulse, felt for sense in her neck—and then abruptly he stepped backwards.

"The doctor," he said numbly. "What can a doctor hope to do here? She is already dead."

I DO NOT THINK, IN THOSE FIRST MOMENTS OF tragedy, that Charles Spence could trust himself to speak. He merely reached for the limp form of the

Earl's daughter, and my brother placed her gently in the steward's arms.

Ann Prowting took one look at Lady Imogen's insensible features—the brutal angle of the head where it rested on the Major, so suggestive of a broken neck—and gave way to a fit of strong hysterics. Thin, high-pitched screaming akin to the hiss of steam escaping a teakettle—until Catherine firmly slapped her sister's cheeks, and led the sobbing figure back towards the house.

"My lady!" cried the groom, Robley, his monkey eyes staring. "My lady *Imogen*! Enough of your pranks! Don't be giving an old man what's served you faithful a heart attack!"

"We must carry her into the house," Henry said, "and send for a doctor. She must be seen, Spence— tho' all hope is gone."

The steward nodded vaguely, as if unsure of his ground; and at that moment Mr. Thrace pulled up on his lathered grey, Nutmeg's rein in his left hand.

"Charles! What the *Devil*— Here, Robley, take this horse back to her stable." He dismounted, a look of wild dismay on his countenance. "She's not badly hurt, I hope?"

Spence turned on the Beau his same expression of vague uncertainty.

"She's dead!" Robley groaned. "The sweetest, most madcap minx what ever slipped her foot into a stirrup! Oh, my lady—I allus said as how your temper would plant you a facer one day, and now look! Dead, and how I am to meet the Earl—*Look after her, Robley,* he said afore we so much as left London—"

"Stable the horse," Thrace muttered viciously to the groom; and with tears streaming down his crabbed cheeks, Robley complied.

Charles Spence began to walk towards the terrace we had only lately quitted in such a spirit of enjoyment, but Lady Imogen was no feather weight in death, and his game leg was decidedly unsteady.

"Let me take her," Thrace said, "lest you fall."

"No!" Spence retorted savagely. "But for *you*—" Whatever reproach he might have uttered was allowed to die in silence. He trained his gaze on the house's distant portal, and staggered forward; and so fixed was his purpose that it achieved a kind of sacred beauty. We all of us fell back from respect, and followed in the soldier's train across the unmown lawns.

He laid her in the saloon, on a gold and white sopha only lately refurbished; and knelt at its head with her limp hand in his, a courtier at the bier of a sleeping princess. Thrace stood like a stone near one of the long windows, his face turned to the lake's prospect. The casement had been thrown open, and birdsong drifted on the air, impossibly sweet. Of all those assembled with heavy hearts in the silent room, Thrace must be the most severely tried by guilt and regret.

"Oh, God," Spence muttered brokenly from his bowed position on the floor—"when I think of her father!"

Henry stepped forward—alone among the gentlemen still cool and collected. "I shall ride into Sherborne St. John and summon the surgeon."

"His name is Althorp," Thrace said over his shoulder. "I will accompany you, Austen."

"Would that I could offer any assistance in such distress," John Middleton said heavily, "but I fear you have long been desiring our absence, Spence. We shall wait only for the doctor, and then depart for Chawton."

The steward raised his head, as tho' the words recalled him from a far country, and glanced towards the door. It had opened almost soundlessly on new-oiled hinges, and I saw that the groom, Robley, stood there. Beyond him in the main passage were assembled a hesitant group of domestics, their faces o'erspread with the most potent expressions of shock.

"Beggin' yer pardon, sir." Robley's voice rang with a power quite alien to his earlier tone of sorrow. "I reckoned you ought to see *this*."

He held his right hand aloft.

Spence scowled and rose to his full height. "What is it, Robley?"

"A thorn," the groom said, "near two inches long, and sharp as the dickens. I found it beneath the saddle when I put Nutmeg in her box. Cut the flesh so deep the mare was bleeding, she was."

"What is that to me, at such a moment?" the steward cried.

"It ought to be everything, sir," the groom retorted. "This here thorn's the reason yon mare tossed her rider, and it was put there a-purpose. *This thorn killed my lady Imogen.*"

Chapter 19

A Bolt into the Blue

THERE COULD BE NO TALK OF RETURNING TO CHAWton now.

Mr. Prowting stepped forward and grasped the great double doors, as tho' desirous of shutting out the crowd of domestics assembled in the passage. "You must come in, sirrah, and explain yourself."

The groom walked determinedly towards Charles Spence. "You're accustomed to cavalry, Major. You know what it should be like, with a great sharp thorn such as this beneath the saddle, as soon as her ladyship leaned into her race."

Spence reached out as if in a dream, and grasped the thorn between his fingers.

"Pressing down on it she was, without even knowing, and the thorn stabbing Nutmeg all the while. It's no wonder as the horse bolted and threw my lady; wanted to get the saddle off her back, she did."

"But how—"

"That thorn weren't there when I unsaddled the mare yestiddy," Robley persisted obstinately. "The mare was clean. A thorn like that don't just happen to find itself under a saddle. You take my meaning, sir?"

"You are saying that it must have been placed there," Mr. Prowting declared, as Charles Spence remained silent. The steward was turning the thorn between his thumb and forefinger, fascinated, but at the magistrate's words a terrible look of understanding burgeoned on his face.

"*You* saddled the mare, Robley."

"But I did not *fetch* the saddle for the race. It was Mr. Thrace as did that," the groom returned meaningfully. "—Mr. Thrace, who allus rides out alone of a morning, and is in and out of the stable yard at all hours, and dislikes my lady with a passion to equal her own. Thought to put a noose around my neck, he did. Me, what has served her ladyship near twenty year!"

As we stood in horrified silence, aware of what the groom's words must mean, Spence wheeled to stare at the Beau, who still stood by the great windows.

"*Julian,*" he whispered. "Can it be possible?"

Thrace did not reply. His handsome countenance had gone white—with fear or guilt, I know not—and all his easy manner was fled.

"Will you not speak, man? Defend yourself— explain yourself—but for God's sake, *speak!*"

Thrace's gaze moved from one of our faces to another. "I can no more say what has occurred than you, Charles."

I believe Spence might have thrown himself at the man in fury then had my brother not stepped forward, quick as a flash, and restrained him. Catherine Prowting cried out as the two struggled; but Henry's strength proved greater than Spence's weak leg. The steward gasped, then sank to the floor near Lady Imogen's still form.

"She was so joyous this morning—so proud of her home and her horse!" he muttered. "All of life, all happiness before her. A life snuffed out—"

It was then Julian Thrace made his mistake.

With a look of panic on his countenance, he dived without warning through the open window.

"Hi!" Henry shouted, and rushed to the casement. "He's making for the stables! He shall bolt, and we do not take care!"

Robley turned with the swiftness of the monkey he so resembled and cried to Charles Spence, "Your gun, sir, if you take my meaning. I'll fetch Rangle and the others and head 'im off at the gate!"

In an instant he was gone from the saloon.

Henry looked as tho' he might follow Thrace through the open window, but John Middleton was before him.

"It is for the magistrate to act now, I think, Mr. Austen. Else we shall have a second murder done."

Mr. Prowting was already standing before Charles Spence, his aspect the picture of painful dignity. "No gun, Major. No swift and untimely justice. The man shall be seized, and his guilt weighed in a court of Law."

Spence turned his head towards the yawning casement, listening for a sound perhaps only he expected; and at that moment, I heard it too. The rapid patter of the great grey hunter's hooves as they galloped, far beyond the reach of Robley and his baying pack, down the length of Stonings' sweep.

"AND SO THE GENTLEMEN COULD NOT CATCH UP with him," my mother said that night, "tho' they rode out directly in pursuit of the scoundrel?"

"Mr. Thrace's horse was too swift," Henry replied. "My hired hack was as nothing to his grey. Spence's mount—an old cavalry charger—might have done the trick, but for the man's delay in reaching the stables. Spence is a brave fellow, and I admire him exceedingly; but he could not at present be described as a *great walker*. I believe the Major would be as yet abroad in the countryside, combing hill and dale for Julian Thrace, had Mr. Prowting not recalled him to his duty."

"—Funeral rites for that unfortunate girl," my mother agreed mournfully. "And to think how we all admired her, only two nights since at the Great House! Such charm! So much conversation! Such an air of fashion! She cannot have been more than twenty!"

"She was two-and-twenty." As my mother had previously declared Lady Imogen to be a sad romp, with a deplorable want of conduct, I ought to have found this encomium amusing. But my spirits were decidedly oppressed. I could not throw off the memory of Catherine Prowting, standing by the window through which Julian Thrace had disappeared, with an expression of the acutest misery on her countenance. I had understood then why the magistrate's daughter had been sleepless of late, and why her contempt for her sister's artless flirtation with the Bond Street Beau was so pronounced. Her affections seemed to be entirely bound up with men who figured as murderers.

"What has Prowting caused to be done?" my brother Edward demanded as he paced our small sitting room with an air of irritation. He had been too much pent up in the heat of the day in the back parlour at the George, hearing every manner of complaint from the surrounding countryside. "Has he alerted all the toll keepers between here and London?"

Neddie is a magistrate in his own county, and as such is disposed to be officious in other people's.

"I believe so," Henry told him, "but as Thrace is on horseback, not in an equipage, it is probable he will spurn the travelled roads. Then, too, he may make for one of the Channel ports rather than London, and take ship for the Continent. It was Middleton who suggested we alert the dockmasters at Southampton and Deal—but you know the ports are never very secure against gentlemen with the means to buy passage at three times the usual sum."

"But does he possess such means?" I objected. "I had thought his pockets were entirely to let."

Henry had the grace to look conscious. "Not entirely, Jane. He may be carrying some five hundred pounds in notes issued against the reserves held by Austen, Gray & Vincent."

"Oh, *Henry*." I sighed.

Edward looked perplexed.

"I could not within reason deny him the loan!" my brother protested. "Thrace looked to be the heir to an earldom!"

"But of a certainty he was not," I mused, "else why undertake to murder Lady Imogen?"

"That is what I cannot make out at all," Cassandra said wearily from her corner. She had retreated to our bedchamber upon the return to Chawton, overcome by the apprehensions and terrors to which we had been exposed. "You say that he was her ladyship's rival to inherit Stonings—her rival, indeed, for the Earl's favour—but how should Thrace's chances be improved by killing Holbrook's daughter? It does not follow that his lordship must accept an imposter, simply because his daughter is dead!"

"Perhaps Thrace thought to buy a little time, and forestall disaster," I suggested.

"—By tying a noose around his own neck?"

"No, Cassandra. By preventing Lady Imogen from revealing the truth: that he was wholly unrelated to the Earl, which she must certainly have believed. I thought her looks this morning were not only easy— they were triumphant. She had learned somewhat to her advantage. She knew herself in the ascendant."

"From your papers, Jane?" Henry demanded.

"I must believe it to be so. Lady Imogen let slip her knowledge of the nature of Lord Harold's bequest while we dined together at the Great House. She went so far as to say that her own father the Earl would give a good deal to know their secrets. I believe it was she who arranged for the burglary at this cottage, and that it was to Stonings the documents were carried."

"—Dyer's men having worked at Stonings," Neddie said thoughtfully, "and thus being in a way to encounter her ladyship. We must tax Bertie Philmore at the Alton gaol with our supposition, now that his mistress is dead, and cannot be in a way to help his cause. But do you believe the papers are as yet at Stonings, Jane, along with their deadly knowledge? I do not like to think of such a burden left untended."

"Nor do I. A letter, I think, must be sent to Charles Spence—with a request for the privilege of searching her ladyship's effects. But how is such a note to be penned? To a man involved in such misery! It is a delicate business—accusing the Deceased of pilfering my belongings."

"Poor child," my mother murmured. "How that smiling beast could have coldly plotted her end—"

"Thrace acted as he did from the direst necessity," Henry threw in. "He deliberately goaded her ladyship into a display of temper over her horse, knowing that the fatal gaming habit in the Vansittart blood must encourage her to demand a contest—to submit to a wager. Then he relied upon our several witnesses to sustain the impression of a dreadful accident—a mishap beyond all our imaginings, or ability to control."

"And it might have worked," I agreed. "But for Robley, Thrace should be at Stonings even now, putting on black clothes for her ladyship—instead of racing over the countryside in a desperate bid for freedom."

"Prowting tells me there is to be no inquest, as he witnessed himself both the murder and the flight of the accused," Neddie supplied. "His chief concern now must be to spare the Earl any further exposure, and conclude the capture of Thrace as soon as possible."

"Poor Mr. Prowting is most distressed," Cassandra observed. "*In all my days as magistrate,* he told me, *I have never presided over a matter of murder; and yet, in the past week, I find two men of my acquaintance under the most severe suspicion of their lives. I cannot explain it, Miss Austen.*"

Edward laughed brusquely, and threw himself into a chair near Cassandra's. "The people of Alton and surrounding parts can account for the problem. I was forced to listen to the direst hints in the course of nearly every interview. *Want of a proper squire,* they said; and *misfortunes brought from afar.* You were correct, Jane, in your admonition to me—the tide of public sentiment has turned against the Kentish landlord. I must consider what it is best I should do. Perhaps I may find a place near Godmersham for all of you after all."

"What!" my mother exclaimed. "When there is a priceless *fortune* buried in the soil somewhere about this cottage? I would not be parted from it for any amount of gain, my dear Neddie; indeed I should *not.*"

He stared at her in surprise.

"I think a sudden removal of our household will hardly aid your cause," I agreed. "We must be seen as steadfast—and impervious to the weight of our neighbours' opinion. And we have this to look forward to: the fall of Mr. John-Knight Hinton's star. A thorough drubbing at the hands of the Law, as Mr. Prowting so proudly terms it, should do much for our standing in Chawton. Hinton is not universally liked."

"And his sister is a dreadful woman," my mother added. "No countenance, and most insipid in her manner. Having listened to her presumptions on the matter of the Rogue, I should dearly love to twit her on the rakehell nursed in the bosom of the parsonage."

"AND SO YOU RIDE TO BRIGHTON AT DAWN, HENRY?"

My brother was to take the sad news of Lady Imogen's death to the Earl of Holbrook. So much had been decided before we parted from Charles Spence; the steward's place must be at Stonings, where he should hold vigil over the body and do what he could to organise the hunt for Julian Thrace. It was unthinkable that a mere Express Messenger should carry such tidings to Brighton— Better a gentleman, even one as yet unknown to the Earl, who should break the news in person. On an errand of such delicacy, there was no one to be desired above Henry.

"I wish you will take care, Jane," my brother said as

he retired for the night. "In your brain and heart you hold the key to Julian Thrace's past—and we know him for a desperate character. His very flight confirms his guilt; and having lost an earldom, he must hold freedom cheap. Remember that the papers are still at large—and that even were they not, you already know too many of their secrets. I should not like to think of you as Thrace's next victim."

Chapter 20

The Effect of Blue Ruin

Sunday, 9 July 1809

~

"*To me, avarice seems not so much a vice, as a deplorable piece of madness.* So said one Thomas Browne, in his work of nearly two hundred years ago, the *Religio Medici*," observed Mr. Papillon from his pulpit; "and what may serve to describe the benighted followers of the Popish faith then, may also serve to instruct us in Chawton today."

He gazed out over his congregation: the gentlemen ranged in the box pews on the north side of the aisle, the ladies—including my mother and sister and myself—on the south side. Behind us in the galleries were assembled the common folk of Chawton, most of them Edward's tenants. I do not know whether the *Religio Medici* had ever come in their way before—it certainly had not come in mine, as I am no Latin scholar—but Mr. Papillon was swift to instruct.

"Who among us—what man or woman, whether born high or low—is a stranger to avarice? In its gentlest form we know it as thrift; in its worst, as miserliness; at its most evil, we recognise the kind of jealous hoarding that may inspire all manner of violence. It is avarice that walks among us now, the kind of madness that brings theft and injury and even death among men. I see all about me the desire for riches or honours not won by merit or birth—but taken at the sword's point, like the rapine of a pagan horde. This is the Devil's work, not the Lord's. I must urge all of you most earnestly to throw off the chains of sin, and turn your backs upon immodest desires; for assuredly the road to ruin lies in pursuing what does not come from the grace of God."

We bent our heads, and prayed most earnestly for the peace of acceptance—for the good will of others—for contentment with our lot. But I could not help glancing about me, to observe how the rest received the rector's admonition. The Prowting girls stood subdued and pale beside their mother. Jane Hinton was attired in black, her gloved hands clasped tightly on her prayer book, her thin lips moving as she prayed. Miss Benn smiled serenely at Mr. Papillon, with what was almost a transcendent look; *she* could not be pierced by his words, who had never regarded any soul in the world with the kind of envy that was native to the rest of us. Across the aisle, my brother Edward looked self-conscious, as tho' he felt the sermon might be offered in defence of his interests—and yet perhaps it was *he* the rector would warn off from rights and riches not rightly his. Poor Neddie should feel no anxiety, I thought; Mr. Papillon's loyalty was all for the Kentish Knights, and his distress at the crimes of the neighbourhood—calumny, burglary, murder—was perhaps the more acute, for having offended his belief in the natural order of things.

Mr. Papillon stood down, and led us in prayer; a hymn was sung, and the sacrament offered. Catherine Prowting, I noticed, did not take the Host—but remained in her pew, head bowed over folded hands. It is no very great thing to stay the sacrament—I have done so myself, when conscious of being in a state of Sin— but I must regard Catherine's attitude of penitence as singular. Was all this for Julian Thrace? I suspected she had lost her heart to the renegade Beau, and must repent of it bitterly—but was that, in truth, a *sin*?

Or did some other cause keep her rooted in the posture of prayer?

I could not interrogate her on so delicate a matter as the state of her own soul; but I resolved to watch Catherine closely in future. I did not like the look of her heavy eyes, or the pallor of her face. They were too suggestive of despair.

IT IS NOT OUR HABIT TO ENGAGE IN SUNDAY travel. A long, sober morning of contemplation and reflexion stretched before us; even my mother must forbear to excavate in her garden on such a day.

Edward seemed disposed to remain in Chawton rather than return to his lodgings in Alton, but a restlessness pervaded all his movements that could not be satisfied with opening a book, or strolling the length of the Street under the notice of all his people.

"When do you intend to desert us for Godmersham?" I enquired at last, after he had inspected several articles of china on my mother's mantelpiece without the appearance of enjoyment. "I am sure you feel some anxiety for the children in your absence."

"I am always concerned for the children," he replied, "but I know them to be well looked-after. Fanny is so capable—and then there is Caky. What would become of us without *her*—"[1]

"Yes," I agreed. "Caky is wonderfully suited to the comfort of little ones. But having settled your affairs at Quarter Day—I cannot wonder that you wish to be gone."

"I did not intend to stay in Alton above a few days. But matters are so miserably left at present—I cannot feel it wise to bolt to Kent, Jane, however much I should wish to do so. Thrace is still at large; Hinton sits in the Alton gaol, accused of murdering the man he cuckolded; and your papers have not been found. Have you written to Major Spence?"

"I am still composing the letter." I studied my brother from my seat at the Pembroke table. "I

---

[1] "Caky" was the Austen-Knight children's name for Susannah Sackree, nursemaid at Godmersham from 1793 to 1851.—*Editor's note.*

understand your discomfort, Neddie—but the unpleasantness of the past week is not only yours to resolve."

"No—because I have not chosen to make it so! But if I would call myself Squire, Jane—if I would assert my authority over Chawton's rents and freeholds—have not I an obligation to manage my tenants' affairs?"

"You cannot live their lives for them. You cannot serve as conscience to an entire village."

He sighed in exasperation. "Do you not see—that in my bereavement—my loss of my excellent wife—I have read a *warning*, Jane?"

"What kind of warning?"

"I have been shown, in the most dreadful manner possible, that life and its comforts are not a surety! One may be taken off at any moment. To live therefore in the frivolity of self-indulgence is to waste what must be precious. I want to be *doing something*, Jane, to win the respect of the people in my charge. I want to be the kind of landlord and master that is remembered when I am gone, for the soundness and worth of my actions."

I smiled at him faintly and set down my pen. "I am sure you will be, Edward. —In particular by those of us whose lives you have directly altered, through the generosity of your heart. But if you wish to impress your Chawton neighbours with your goodness, there is one gesture of benevolence you might immediately make. You might visit Mr. John-Knight Hinton at the Alton gaol."

My brother's colour changed. "That pup?"

"He is fully five-and-thirty years old. And he is at present embroiled in considerable difficulty. The appearance of magnanimity such a visit must offer the surrounding country should do you much good in publick opinion."

"I should not like to meddle in Prowting's province."

"You are Squire; Mr. Prowting is not. And it might behoove us to hear Hinton's version of the story. I have wondered, of late, if Catherine Prowting is entirely to be trusted."

"Good Lord, Jane—how can you talk so?" my brother returned impatiently. "Recollect the fact of the footprint—the boot mark in the cellar. Prowting told me of it himself!"

"True—but what if it was left there some time ago? I believe Catherine Prowting carries a *tendre* for Julian Thrace, and might do much to shield him. What if she did *not* in fact recognise the man near the pond that night to be Mr. Hinton—but his rival for her affections?"

Neddie whistled beneath his breath. "We ought to tax her for the truth."

"She is likely to plead the head-ache, and retire to her bedchamber in an attitude of misery. We shall get no more from Catherine, Neddie; we must try the man she has accused." I sealed my sheet of paper with wax and wrote *Major Charles Spence, Stonings, Sherborne St. John* on the reverse. "Should you like to walk with me into Alton? I might post my letter—and we might take in the gaol on your way to the George. The constable is likely to prove no more particular about the disruption of his Sunday than we."

My brother stared at me with narrowed eyes. "Do you know, Jane—I believe you possess more wit beneath that linen cap than any of the rest of us."

"*Avarice,* Neddie," I reminded him. "Do not be wishing for what is beyond your God-given merits; for that way lies ruin, as Mr. Papillon has assured us."

THERE WERE FOUR CELLS NO BIGGER THAN A clutch of loose horse-boxes in the Alton gaol—for indeed the building had once been a stable, and the constable yard an accommodation for grooms, until the passion for local justice caused an alteration. I had visited gaols before—alone, when the occasion required it, and with Edward at Canterbury, in his capacity as magistrate; they held no terrors for me.

"Mr. Austen to see ye, sir," his gaoler called as he opened the oak door of the box with a heavy iron key. "No tricks, now, as we're prepared for anything you might offer."

John-Knight Hinton was lying in the straw of his prison, in clear disregard for the state of his clothes; the Hoby boots were dulled with dust, and he had not shaved since his arrival two days before. The physical dereliction of the gentleman was a sign of his oppression of spirits; and I confess my heart sank as I observed him.

He was master enough of himself to rise to his feet and reach for the coat he had discarded on the wooden bench that served as both seat and bed; he donned this article before deigning to notice us, as tho' we were servants that must await his pleasure. Then, having adjusted his cravat and shirtsleeves with careful dignity, he met my brother's impervious gaze, and bowed.

"Mr. Austen. To what do I owe this signal attention?"

"To a sincere desire to be of what help I may in your present trouble."

Hinton's lip curled. "I should be grateful, I suppose; but I fear I must decline your offer. I cannot believe any help of yours should *improve* my circumstances."

"I am uninterested in gratitude," my brother replied quickly. "Understand, Hinton, I neither expect nor wish for it."

"Are you come, then, to triumph over me?"

Neddie deliberately removed his hat and gloves. "I am come to learn the truth."

"Your sister"—Hinton inclined his head with sneering civility in my direction—"professes to know it already."

"My sister is well aware there may be various constructions placed upon a person's behaviour. It is to her insistence you owe our visit today."

"Really?" He stared at us with mock incredulity. "Miss Austen no longer has confidence in the power of a footprint?"

Pup, Edward had called him; and he was certainly a graceless one. I struggled to maintain at least the appearance of civility.

"Mr. Hinton, do you apprehend the gravity of your circumstances?" I enquired.

"—That I might hang for a murder I did not commit? Yes, Miss Austen, I think I understand that much."

"And have you heard that another person has lately died by violence—and the man believed responsible has fled the country?"

Jack Hinton's expression changed. The sneer—which I now recognised to have been born of a desperate defiance—drained from his face, to be replaced by a look of surprise and dawning hope. "I hear nothing in this beastly place. Not even my sister has come near me. What has occurred?"

"Lady Imogen Vansittart was killed while riding horseback yesterday morning. The horse was tampered with. Her acquaintance, Mr. Thrace, rode off in panic when the worst was discovered—and has not yet been found."

"Thrace!" he muttered in a goaded tone. "It *would* be he, of course. Life was quite different in this village before that gentleman came into Hampshire, Miss Austen."

"I can well believe that your own prospects changed as a result of his appearance."

Hinton glanced at me searchingly. "You know that Catherine Prowting betrayed me to her father?"

"Yes."

"There was a time when she did not treat me with such coldness."

"Are you suggesting," my brother broke in, "that

Miss Prowting lied about what she saw last Saturday night?"

"No." Hinton shook his head deliberately. "I will only say that she was too ready to believe me Shafto French's enemy, in part because of the talk circulated by *that person*. Thrace is rather freer in his conversation to young ladies than I should be."

"He told Catherine that you had pursued French's wife?"

Hinton laughed. "As indeed I had. Years ago— before she was married. It was a common enough flirtation in a country town: the idle gentleman just down from Oxford, with little to do of a summer's morn, and the pretty young maid all too often underfoot. Jemima cannot have been more than sixteen at the time, and I was but six-and-twenty. We had practically been reared together, recollect."

"And you were in a position of power over her," I added smoothly. "Being dependant upon your household for her wages, Jemima could hardly refuse to accept your attentions. Until your sister dismissed her for impropriety."

A hot flush rose in his cheeks. "I did not ruin the girl then or later. Nor did I get her with child under French's very nose. But Thrace would say anything to cut out a rival—and so he styled himself in Miss Prowting's eyes. The silly little fool believes herself in love with him—a man who will never honour her affections as he ought! Thrace is to be an earl one day—he told me so himself. He will never ally himself with the daughter of a provincial nobody, however many times he consents to take dinner at Prowting's table."

"I am sure you are right. But Mr. Thrace's actions suggest an intimacy with Shafto French's history. Was he at all acquainted with the man?"

"He had met him in the course of the repairs undertaken at the Earl of Holbrook's estate—Stonings, at Sherborne St. John. He affected to enjoy French's rough humour and easy ways. I do not think Thrace has lived all his life in the most select society, whatever his present affectations may suggest. I think he was rather more intimate with his labourers than you or I should be. Certainly he undertook to drink with Shafto French of an evening, at the Alton publick houses. I more than once observed him there."

Blood money, Jemima French had said; and *it was the heir as would pay. . . .* Shafto French had spoken more freely than he ought of his wife's adventures in the Hinton household; had Julian Thrace disclosed his private affairs under the influence of drink, and ruthlessly silenced his confidant when the man turned blackmailer?

"Will you not tell us what really occurred on Saturday the first of July, Mr. Hinton?" Edward asked quietly. "For however disappointed in Miss Prowting's affections, you cannot wish to throw your life away on her rival's account. I am sure you cannot."

Hinton glanced at my brother, weighing the odds of silence and disclosure. Speech won out.

"I cannot tell you how French died. I can say only what happened after."

"Very well."

He began to pace restlessly about the cell, his boots kicking up a cloud of dust and straw, his hands shoved into his breeches' pockets. "I had gone out to the prize-fight at Box Hill—"

"Are they still held there?" Neddie interrupted. "I once recall taking in a mill on my return from Winchester, having left the boys at school. Belcher won his match. Who did you see?"

"It was said the Game Chicken would show, but in the end he did not, and we were forced to observe a Basingstoke lad by the name of Crabbe," Hinton returned dispiritedly. "I had travelled a considerable distance in the hope of seeing Pearce, and was disappointed.[2] I went out to join my friends on Friday, the day before—"

"Your friends?"

"The Wilsons, of Hay House, Great Bookham. Hay Wilson and I were at Oxford together."

"Of course. And you were staying at Hay House itself? Pray continue."

"As I said, I went out on the Friday and the mill was to be held at noon Saturday. We were at the Box Hill ground near seven hours—"

"How many rounds did the boy Crabbe go?"

Hinton's expressionless eyes suddenly lit up. "Nearly nineteen, if you'll credit it, but in the end he could not be brought up to scratch."

[2] Henry Pearce, a prizefighter known as the Game Chicken, was named champion of England in 1805.—*Editor's note.*

"Who was his opponent?"

"John Gully."

Neddie whistled in deep appreciation; I felt myself to be increasingly beyond my depth.

"And so, the fight done," my brother said, "you retired to Great Bookham for high revel—and only after several hours' eating, drinking, and conversing of the fight to your mutual satisfaction sought your road home. You must have left Surrey rather late, Hinton. I wonder you did not remain the night with your friend Mr. Wilson."

"I had promised my sister I would not travel on the Sunday," he replied in a sulky tone. "She is most attentive to such things; it is the influence of our late father, who was once—"

"—the incumbent of the Chawton living," Edward agreed with remarkable ease. This reminder of his status—of the fact that it should be Edward who must dispose of the living when next St. Nicholas's came vacant, at Mr. Papillon's demise—restored Mr. Hinton to all his former dislike. No amount of shared enthusiasm for the sport of boxing could do away with his resentment of the Squire.

"You made your way back to Chawton," Edward suggested helpfully, "arriving just barely after midnight, and thus travelling on Sunday, but it is to be hoped in a manner your sister should not discover, being sound asleep in her bed."

Hinton swallowed with difficulty. "As you say. I rode into Chawton from the south, and found the Street entirely deserted. I was very sleepy, and little disposed to notice much—but the moon was high, and my horse shied at something in the road as I approached the pond. I glanced down, and supposed it to be a man. Naturally, I dismounted."

"And saw that it was Shafto French?" I enquired.

There was a pause. Hinton did not quite meet my gaze. "It was French. He was dead."

"You are sure of that?" Edward asked.

He nodded. "His body was wet from his waist to his head, and his eyes were open and staring. There was no response when I slapped his cheeks, no pulse in his throat."

"You did not think to give a shout? To summon help?"

"Mr. Austen—" The spiritless eyes came up to my brother's own. "I have said that I was sleepy. In truth, I was a bit foxed."

"I can easily imagine," Edward said drily. "What would be a boxing match, without Blue Ruin?"[3]

"Exactly so. I was not thinking entirely clearly. I had stumbled on a dead man, and one whom I had everywhere heard was intending to challenge me. —A man I was believed to have wronged. *He lay dead at my feet.* For an instant, the wildest imaginings coursed through my head. I saw myself accused—disbelieved—thrown into gaol . . ."

". . . for a murder you did not commit," I finished. He was rather prescient, our Mr. Hinton; for it had all occurred exactly as he had foreseen.

---

[3] Gin.—*Editor's note.*

"I would have sprung upon my horse and galloped for home as tho' all the imps of Hell were at my back," Hinton said in a low voice, "but for that wretched gin. I was pretty well top-heavy at that point, I may as well own, and was gripped of a sudden with the most extraordinary idea."

"You thought to make a fool of one enemy," Neddie suggested grimly, "by making away with another. You determined to place the body of Shafto French in the house intended for the Squire's family, and thus bring discomfiture upon us all."

Hinton nodded with painful difficulty. "It sounds mad when you put it that way—"

"On the contrary. It makes perfect sense, to a man disguised by spirits. You might have thrown a charge of murder on the Austen household."

"I believe I thought only of embarrassing the Squire. I dragged French by the heels towards the cottage—"

"Had you already provided yourself with a key for the purpose, knowing beforehand that you should stumble over the body on your way from Box Hill?" I asked.

"The door was not locked on the Saturday," he returned simply. "One of Dyer's men—French himself, perhaps—must have neglected to secure it when work was called that afternoon."

"But it was locked when I arrived the following Tuesday!"

"—Then young Bill Dyer performed the office

when he completed his job that Monday, and chose to say nothing about the neglect to his father."

"When all the talk of murder arose," my brother interjected, "the builder saw a further virtue in silence. Mr. Dyer and his son are fortunate that the coroner did not chuse to interrogate them harshly about the keys."

"Be that as it may," Mr. Hinton continued, "I found the door to the cottage unlocked. I placed French's body in the cellar and congratulated myself on my wicked genius. It should be quite the welcome, I thought, for a party of ladies too high in the instep for Chawton. And in the event—I was proved right."

I could not felicitate him on his triumph.

"When I awoke the next day, with an aching head, and recalled what I had done—I must confess to considerable trepidation. I was prevented from returning to the cottage immediately, due to my sister's Sabbath conventions—but stole out as soon as it was dark on Monday, and attempted to right the wrong. I found the door, as I have described, locked."

"And decided that silence should be your best policy," my brother concluded grimly. "I perfectly understand, Mr. Hinton, tho' I cannot approve what you did."

Edward rose and reached for his hat.

"I must offer you my apology, Miss Austen," Hinton said in a correct but exceedingly cold voice; and bowed.

I curtseyed in return, recognising his haughtiness for what it was—the discomfort of a man who knew himself to be in the wrong, and must disguise it at all cost, or die of mortification.

"I hope, Mr. Hinton, that you will consider yourself revenged upon me," Edward said with all the candour he might have reserved for one of his sons, "—and that in future we may endeavour to be better friends. For my part, I intend to intercede on your behalf with Mr. Prowting. He has merely to consult with Mr. Hay Wilson regarding the hour of your departure from Great Bookham, in order to ascertain the probable length of your journey on the road—and place you happily beyond suspicion. I cannot think it wise to keep you here in the Alton gaol."

"What of Thrace?"

Edward drew on his gloves. "I no more know than you, Hinton. He may be even now in the act of crossing the Channel to freedom—or caught in the snare of Mr. Prowting's Law. But I think we can safely assume it was *he* who forced French's head beneath the waters of Chawton Pond. The only question remaining to answer is—"

"—*Why?*" I concluded.

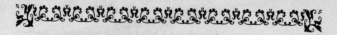

Chapter 21

The Faithful Wife

9 July 1809, cont.

~

"AND WHAT DO YOU THINK OF YOUR NEIGHBOUR now, Edward?" I demanded as we made our way up the Alton High Street in the direction of the George. "A nice, savoury fellow by way of a clergyman's son. And *he* wishes to be Squire of Chawton!"

"As I said: an ill-conditioned pup, for all he is five-and-thirty. But there is no real harm in him, Jane."

"And no real good either."

Edward laughed. "I have an idea of the Hinton household as it must once have been: a collection of over-fond sisters and half-sisters; a young boy sent away to school and disliking it as much as any boy could; indulged at his term leave, and petted by the women of the family long after such attention should be necessary; intended, like his father, for the Church. Only young Mr. Hinton has no taste for Holy Orders: He wishes to cut a dash, to be *top of the trees* as the young bloods would put it; *up to snuff, awake upon every suit;* a cock of the game. In short: a sporting man of the first stare. Instead, he is a shabby-genteel country gentleman with too little blunt and no opportunity for display—no means to set up his stable or hunt in style; no independent estate other than the Lodge his father left him; and to add insult to injury, the daughter of the most established gentleman in the village spurns his suit for a Bond Street Beau of no family and dubious character. I cannot wonder Hinton took to playing pranks better suited to a boy half his age."

"Or aspiring to a fortune not rightly his own," I added thoughtfully.

"It is in the worst order of fretful childishness," Neddie agreed easily. "Recollect that I have sons of my own, and all of them sighing for the airs of a Corinthian. But in a fellow of Hinton's years—!"

"Your sons, I hope, will know better how they should get on."

"My sons were not spoilt from infancy!" Neddie retorted impatiently. "There was never time enough between them to tell one from the other, if you must know! And I thank God for it. They have not lacked for masters or instruction; if they wish for mounts or the means to pursue any peculiar passion, I generally grant their wishes. But my boys earn their rights, by Jove! And not by whining."

"Well, Squire Austen—and what do you intend to do for the odious Mr. Hinton?"

"Find William Prowting as soon as may be—and suggest the sneering lout be returned to his sister's leading strings. I have an idea of her contempt for all matters of sport; and think her brother deserves to suffer a little beneath Jane Hinton's management."

"For my part, I should not wish such a purgatory on any man." I could not forestall a shudder, tho' the morning was warm. "You are a hardened case, Edward. Hinton's revenge is as nothing to *yours*."

I LEFT MY DEAR BROTHER HAPPY IN ORDERING HIS dinner at the George, and reflected that there was nothing like a little useful activity to dispel a fit of the megrims. Edward loves Godmersham and the society of Kent—but the perfect serenity of that great estate may throw too profound a veil between my brother and the world. He has endured a winter of isolation, and a summer of slow awakening; the Jack Hintons of life should bring him only good, in the folly of their ways and the absurdity of their cares.

The pleasant summer's day was drawing in as I walked south towards Chawton, the air grown oppressive and a weight of cloud hovering to the west. We should have thunderstorms by nightfall, and the dusty lanes turned to quagmire; the good turnpike stretches, however, were well maintained between this part of Hampshire and the principal towns of the coast. Henry must long since have reached the Earl's household at Brighton. How had the former Freddy Vansittart—with his rakehell dark looks, his charm, his easy conversation—taken the news of his daughter's death?

"Miss Austen!"

I lifted my head at the salutation, my mind recalled from distant wandering—and observed a slight woman with her hair neatly bound beneath a kerchief, and a look of unease around her eyes. Her face must be familiar, tho' she no longer held a babe to her breast. Rosie Philmore, the laundry maid, and wife of the man who had stolen Lord Harold's papers.

She stood near the verge of the Alton road, her back to Chawton, and curtseyed.

"Good day, Mrs. Philmore. How are your children?"

"Well enough, thank you. I left them in the charge of their grandmother, ma'am, while I walked to Chawton." She hesitated, and then said in a rush, "I've been and gone to visit Old Philmore—but he still is not returned, and no one in the village can say where he is gone, or when he is likely to come back. He has not stopped in Alton in near a week, and my Bert is that put out! Afeared, he is, that summat has occurred to harm the old man."

"I am sorry to hear it."

"It's not like Old Philmore to leave Bertie in the lurch. Clutch-fisted he may be, and nip-cheese into the bargain, but blood is blood when all's said and done."

"I understand. Did you enquire of Miss Benn, at

Thatch Cottages? For she is one of Old Philmore's tenants."

"And right glad to be shut of him. Miss Benn hardly opened her door to me, lest I had come to collect the rents in the old man's stead."

"Have you seen your husband at Alton gaol?"

"I spoke with Bert last night, when I took him a bit of supper."

"He must be familiar with his uncle's habits. Can he offer no hint of where Old Philmore might be gone to ground?"

Her work-hardened fingers fretted at the edge of her apron, and her eyes fell. In an instant I understood the poor woman's dilemma—she did not wish to see her husband imprisoned for years, or even transported to Botany Bay, for an offence that had brought no good to the household; and yet, Bertie Philmore had probably bound her to secrecy when he sent her in search of his uncle. How much did Rosie Philmore truly know of the two men's adventures?

The thought of Lord Harold's chest, broken and discarded with all its contents, flamed within me. *I must have it back.*

"Mrs. Philmore," I said gently, "I dislike to see you in such trouble. I fear for the well-being of your little ones. If there is any way in which I may help you, be assured that I will attempt it."

"That is kind in you. But a woman did ought to stand by her husband, ma'am. You're not to know, being a spinster lady—"

"You cannot make your husband's case worse

than it is already, by speaking; for his silence has already placed him in Alton gaol. Do you wish to find Old Philmore?"

"It's Bert as is hankering after the old man!" she cried. "He's that worried—thinks his uncle was taken ill on his road, or been killt—or something worse."

—*Something worse* being, no doubt, Old Philmore's delighted release from all his Hampshire cares, through the spoils of burglary of which Bertie Philmore now had no share. The nephew, I saw, was torn between a very real anxiety for the man who had long served him as parent, and the jealous regard for his own interest, which the uncle might long since have betrayed. Sitting alone in his cell, hour after hour, his thoughts could not be happy ones. He must suffer the delusions of the forgotten: seeing first in his mind's eye the image of his uncle's corpse, trampled and abandoned in some woodland hole; and then again, the picture of his uncle in a far distant land—the West Indies perhaps—and surrounded by every luxury.

"Mrs. Philmore, you know that your husband and Old Philmore stole a valuable chest from my cottage. I must assure you most earnestly that the papers within, which you have already described, cannot save your husband's life or contribute to the well-being of his family. The person who wished them stolen—the person I believe hired your husband and Old Philmore—is lately dead."

She emitted a shriek, and pressed her hand in

horror to her lips. *"Dead?* —The gentleman from Stonings is dead?"

"Gentleman?" I returned, my thoughts swiftly revolving. "Did your husband say that he was hired by a *gentleman?"*

Too late, she saw her error. She stepped backwards, as tho' in retreat. "He might have said something. I don't know what. Not really."

"A gentleman from Stonings wished the papers stolen?" It was not impossible, after all. We now knew that Julian Thrace had a taste for low company, and was much given to drinking with Dyer's builders; I had found in this a ready explanation for Shafto French's murder. But why not for the theft of the chest, as well? Thrace would have learned of Lord Harold's bequest in much the way Lady Imogen knew of it, and was quick enough to apprehend the danger its contents might pose. He had ample knowledge of our invitation to dinner at the Great House, for he had been present at the very moment of Mr. Middleton's issuance of it. He might all too easily have secured the services of Bertie Philmore on the night in question, and delayed our arrival home by his elaborate telling of fantastic anecdotes, and his prolonged losses at cards.

And yet—I had thought Lady Imogen so happy yesterday morning, as tho' she possessed the key to her entire future. If Julian Thrace had been the one to seize the papers, how had she come by her certainty? He should have destroyed the evidence of his birth, and attempted to hide the truth from the Earl and all his household. The very last person Thrace should tell was surely Lady Imogen.

"If it is Mr. Thrace you would mean," I said to Rosie Philmore, "I fear for Old Philmore's life. Thrace has two murders already to his account, and is believed to have fled the country."

The woman frowned. "I know of no Thrace, ma'am. 'Twas not of him my Bertie spoke. My man was hired by the master of Stonings—that Major Spence, what walks with a limp—to rob ye of your chest."

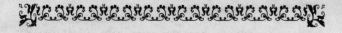

Chapter 22

The Figure in the Night

9 July 1809, cont.

~

I RELATED NOTHING OF ALL I HAD LEARNED AMONG
the cottage circle tonight, but allowed my sister to talk
of the beauties of the surrounding country—in which
she had walked a little with the dog Link, so that he
might become acquainted with his neighbourhood. "It
is full of dells and hills, Jane—a rolling, varied country
quite unlike the flat monotony of Steventon in which
we were raised—" I listened to a letter from Fanny,
which had followed Cassandra on her journey from
Kent, the post having no concern for the delays imposed by broken axle-trees and the ostlers at Brompton's
Bell. And I was made privy to all the minute concerns
of Edward's household, which Neddie should never
bother relating and which Cassandra has not yet

learned to give up: how the four youngest children—
Charles, Louisa, Cassandra-Jane, and Brook-John—are
as yet in the charge of Susannah Sackree, the beloved
Caky of the nursery-wing, while the elder girls—Lizzy
and Marianne—are *not* to be sent away again to school,
Marianne having most bitterly despised her exile from
the rest of the family. The two eldest boys, Edward and
George, are to return to Winchester in the autumn
term, and then Fanny may well obtain some peace and
quiet—a governess being to be hired for Lizzy and
Marianne, a tutor for young Henry and William. Of the
tutor in particular Cassandra had great hopes: he was a
nephew of the Duke of Dorset, only lately having quitted Cambridge, and intended for the Church. She only
hoped he should *not* fall in love with Fanny, as she is
barely *out*—as such things may be determined in
Kentish society. There could be no question of a real
London Season for Fanny; Edward's spirits were not up
to the hiring of a house in Town.

"Good God," I murmured. "And to think that
poor Fanny is expected to manage all this! I wonder
she could consent to part with you, Cass—despite the
allurements of our six bedchambers and numerous
outbuildings. Shall you miss Kent exceedingly?"

She flushed pink, and returned some small nothing
regarding the insignificance of her own contribution,
and the worth of Fanny's talents. I recalled to mind a
picture of Godmersham as I had myself left it only a
short while ago—the elegance of its apartments, the
plasterwork above the mantel in the entry hall, the marble floors, the pleasing aspect of the high downs behind

the house. In the environs of Canterbury one meets with only the most liberal-minded and cultivated of friends; no Ann Prowtings or Miss Benns for Cassandra's edification. Kent is the only place for happiness, after all; everybody is rich there, and my brother's household not excepted. I must endeavour to remember that Cassandra's spirits might be a trifle low in coming months, until she has grown accustomed once more to the simplicity of our arrangements.

My mother announced over our Sunday meal of buttered prawns and cold beef that she had quite given up her scheme of retrieving the Rubies of Chandernagar. Mr. Thrace's guilt she had taken to heart, and regarded it as a sure sign of duplicity in everything the man had said; for how else must she account for the failure of her searches? Mr. Papillon's sermon on the evils of avarice had proved no less salutary. She should not like the Companion of My Future Life—for so she persisted in regarding poor Mr. Papillon—to believe his prospective mother-in-law a hardened sinner. Then, too, she had happened to catch Sally Mitchell laughing with the baker's boy about the eccentric habits of her mistress, and was *most* discomfited to find that she had broken three fingernails in digging.

We left her after dinner to all the pleasures of a hot bath in the washroom, and sat down to compose a few letters: Cassandra to Fanny, and I recounting what I could of Chawton events to my friend Martha Lloyd.

Thoughts of Charles Spence, however, could not help but intrude. I might sit by the Pembroke table, in the soft air of evening, and attempt to write in compact lines of the people we had met, and the alterations we had effected in the cottage; but the Major's dark eyes *must* sketch themselves on the sheet of paper. His serious, earnest gaze—the dreadful pallor of his looks at Lady Imogen's death—the fury of the man, as Thrace escaped—all must clamour for my attention. I had wondered before if Spence's honour might be suborned by a woman of Lady Imogen's power—if her bewitching charm and his desire for her affection might compel him to all manner of actions he should never undertake alone. I was now certain that they had. Charles Spence could find no peculiar interest in Lord Harold Trowbridge's papers, absent the interest of the woman he loved. Lady Imogen had bent him to her purpose—cajoled him, as a steward well-acquainted with the labouring class—to secure a pair of ruffians who might force their way into my house.

Had they also, I wondered, forced their way into Henry's bank nearly a week ago?

Had the plan to find Lord Harold's bequest been in train long before my arrival in Chawton? It was certain that Lady Imogen possessed an understanding of the chest's contents for some months; she should have learned of their true nature from Desdemona, Countess Swithin, during the last London Season.[1] Locating the chest itself, however, had demanded some time and exertion; no doubt Lady Imogen had

---

[1] The Season, a period of intense social activity among the Upper Ten Thousand of London society, ran generally for twelve weeks—from Easter through June, when the wealthy of Austen's period departed for their country houses or Brighton.—*Editor's note.*

recruited others besides Spence to the task. Who might her accomplices be?

I concluded my letter to Martha with a request that she bring some peony cuttings from her sister's garden at Kintbury—and rose to take a restless turn about the room.

"What is it, Jane?" Cassandra asked.

"I hardly know."

"You are thinking of our acquaintance in Sherborne St. John. Has there been no word yet of Mr. Thrace's capture?"

"None that Edward or I have heard. The renegade appears to have vanished into thin air."

"Then he will soon be desperate. With all the country alive against him, how can he hope to obtain so much as a cup of water?"

"—Unless he has found friends who will help him."

"How can such a man—a stranger to Hampshire—recruit friends?"

"He might buy them, I suppose, among those who have no concern for murder."

She set down her pen. "And what of Henry?"

"He must have reached Brighton some hours ago—but has not seen fit to despatch the news to his sisters Express. I suppose all such activity must be reserved for the Earl, and all such letters for Charles Spence."

Charles Spence.

I had written to him myself only this morning; he might even now be reading my letter—the post between Chawton and Sherborne St. John being no very

great distance.[2] What should be his feelings upon pe-
rusing my words?

> . . . *pray accept my very deepest condolences on*
> *the sad loss you have recently suffered. Lady*
> *Imogen was all that was lovely and amiable, and*
> *to witness her sudden taking off—at such an*
> *interesting period of life, when youth, high spirits,*
> *beauty, and the privilege of birth must conspire to*
> *make her existence a blessed one—is a dreadful*
> *reminder of the end we must all someday face, and*
> *our daily proximity to our Maker.*
>
> *It is regrettable at such a moment to allow the*
> *personal to intrude. Circumstances, however,*
> *require that I be perfectly frank. I have reason to*
> *think that her ladyship's natural exuberance—her*
> *desire to best Mr. Thrace at every turn—and her*
> *very commendable wish to prevent her respected*
> *father from committing an error his friends must*
> *all deplore—may have led her to engage in an*
> *activity injurious to her reputation, and beneath*
> *her better sense. In point of fact, I believe the chest*
> *taken from my home—a bequest of my friend Lord*
> *Harold Trowbridge—might even now be found*
> *among Lady Imogen's effects.*
>
> *If what I have related causes you pain, I am*
> *heartily sorry for it. I am aware, however, that*

---

[2] The rapidity and frequency of mail delivery during Austen's era, despite the relatively bad quality of the roads, is astonishing compared to
the infrequent but predictable service of the present day. Sunday mail
service, such as Austen describes here, was expected. —*Editor's note.*

*Stonings may soon be shut up and yourself gone
from the premises, as must only be natural; and I
should wish the chest returned before all your party
has quitted Hampshire. Do I ask too much, Major
Spence, or may I be allowed to wait upon you at
Stonings as soon as may be convenient?*

I had taken a good deal of trouble over the letter,
as being a most awkward composition to a man in
Spence's state of mourning. Indeed, I had winced at
the brutal force of it—the necessity of putting so delicate a matter into the bluntest prose. But I had done
my work, and seen it into the hands of the post some
hours before; and could not call it back again. The
knowledge that Spence himself was encompassed in
Lady Imogen's crimes, however, made the communication a bitter one.

It was possible he should read in my letter a veiled
threat to his own security. If I professed to know that
Lady Imogen had taken the Bengal chest, how could I
be ignorant of the methods by which it was obtained?
Did Charles Spence think to find me at Stonings'
door with Mr. Prowting the magistrate at my back?

I feared that I had blundered in writing as I did.
Spence was no fool; and despite the misery of his present circumstances, must be alive to the implication of
my charge. He was as likely to sink Lord Harold's
chest in the bottom of the Stonings' lake, as return its
contents to me; and I had only my own impatience to
thank.

I placed my letter to Martha near Cassandra's

own, for posting on the morrow; made trial of a novel in three volumes that my sister had brought especially from Canterbury; picked up and set down a bit of mending the light no longer permitted me to see; and at the last, went up rather earlier than was my habit, to bed.

IT WAS THE DOG, LINK, THAT WOKE ME: STARTING up from a sound sleep and barking furiously into the night. His small, sinewy body trembled with indignation; his attention was fixed on a disturbance below; his outrage filled our ears.

"Link!" Cassandra hissed. "Lie down, boy! There's a good fellow! *Link!*"

I threw back the bed linen and reached for my dressing gown. The terrier dashed to the window, his forepaws on the sill.

"What is it, lad?" I whispered. "What do you see? Another burglar, perhaps, come to steal into the household?"

A low growl escaped his quivering throat; I hushed him with a hand to his head.

The full moon of the previous week—which had allowed Julian Thrace to ride out at midnight, Shafto French to be murdered, and Jack Hinton to make his way from Surrey despite the befuddlement of his senses—was nearly gone. The night was dull as a blown candle, and heavy shadow lay about the fields surrounding the house. Chawton Pond was barely a gleam on the edge of my vision; no figures swayed in desperate combat beside it tonight. I strained to pierce the darkness of our yard, and could make out nothing; no furtive movement of man or beast could be detected near the henhouse or the privy. It might be any hour between the tolling of St. Nicholas's curfew bell and dawn; I could not undertake to say.

"What is it, Jane?" Cassandra demanded in a hushed voice; there was anxiety in her accent.

I lifted my hand for silence, and Link growled again.

Perhaps he had seen what I had: a faint wisp of light bobbing down the sweep from Prowtings.

It was, I guessed, the pale glow of a candle encased in a lanthorn—the kind that might be shielded from prying eyes by the fall of a cloak or wrap. Someone was setting out through the darkness on an errand that did not admit of scrutiny; and as the fugitive achieved the Gosport road, I thought I understood why. In the form and height of the figure—the hesitant, half-furtive movement—I recognised a woman.

Catherine Prowting.

I have found it difficult to sleep of nights for some weeks past.

Where was she going, alone and at such an hour?

Her errand was not an open one. She did not intend her family to know of it.

With all the country alive against him, how can he hope to obtain so much as a cup of water?

I had been wrong. One friend at least in the neighbourhood Julian Thrace had no need to buy.

I might follow Catherine, I thought, as Link strained against me.

I might rouse the neighbourhood and her father, bring a man to justice, and ruin forever the reputation of a young woman rather like myself—restless for life, bounded by country lane and glebe, her prospects lowering with each passing year. A starling beating against the bars of its cage.

Lady Imogen. Shafto French.

Justice.

"Jane?" Cassandra repeated. "Is anything amiss?"

I shut the window.

"Nothing at all, Cass. Your dog must have scented a hare on the wind."

I lay sleepless long into the night, listening for Catherine Prowting's return.

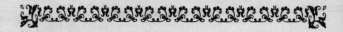

Chapter 23

An Unexpected Visitor

Monday, 10 July 1809

~

"MAJOR SPENCE?" I CALLED, PEERING HESITANTLY
from behind a marble column; and then I observed
him, motionless and upright at the far end of the room.

It was Rangle who conducted me to the library, a
handsome apartment in the very heart of the great
pile that was Stonings. I had not glimpsed it during
my previous visit, and once led through a series of passages by the chapfallen butler, could hardly have
found my way out again. But the space in which I now
stood was in better repair than any other part of the
ramshackle estate; indeed, it was a delightful room,
and perfectly suited to study. The chamber's ceiling
was painted indigo blue, and an array of stars and
planets swam across its firmament; the walls were full

two storeys in height, lined with bookshelves and myriad volumes; at the far end was a bank of tall windows, undraped at present, through which flowed the dull green light of a rainy summer's morning.

Charles Spence was posed with his back to me, his gaze fixed on the landscape. The prospect here gave out onto high woody hills, rather than the lake that sat to the south; he could not have noticed the arrival of the gig, but I was certainly expected. Rangle had instructions to convey me to the steward the moment I arrived.

Of Lady Imogen's remains there was no sign. I had half-expected a bier in the hall, surrounded by candles and bouquets of summer flowers; a few domestics bent in prayer by her ladyship's side. Certainly I had thought to find Charles Spence in an attitude of suffering—on his knees, perhaps, on the stone floor, while the hours passed unnoticed around him. But one cannot cry without ceasing, I must suppose; and there were all the duties of the estate still to be attended to. Not to mention the inconvenient supplications of chance acquaintance.

I had received the gentleman's reply to my letter at breakfast.

> *Miss Austen—*
>   *It seems we have much to discuss. Pray wait upon me at your convenience today, as I expect to quit Stonings on the morrow.*
>   *Your most obedient servant,*
>   *Spence*

A brief note, imparting little of the man's mood or intentions. I determined to go to him immediately, however, and walked into Alton in search of my brother.

It was no very great matter to prevail upon Edward to drive me to the Earl of Holbrook's estate. Being as yet in black clothes for his wife, he had no desire to break in upon Charles Spence's mourning; however, I impressed upon him the idea that a call of condolence was unexceptionable at such a time, and indeed a most necessary form of notice from the Chawton Squire.

"It will be those papers you are after," Neddie retorted, "and no call of condolence, I'll be bound, Jane. All the same—I should like to see a place of which I have heard so much; and who knows whether the Earl will ever come there in future? We might take in the Vyne on our way home; Chute is sure to be in residence during the summer months, and I have not seen the man this age."

I told my brother nothing of Rosie Philmore's tale, or the conjectures I had formed regarding the Major's integrity. I had determined, in the magnanimity of last night's sleepless reflections, that I should not press Spence for particulars. They should better be sealed in Lady Imogen's tomb—provided Lord Harold's chest was returned to me. And so I preserved a notable silence on our road to Sherborne St. John, and allowed Edward to talk of the improvements he intended for the Chawton estate.

The storm had broken at dawn, and thus a closed

carriage was preferred; we hired one from Barlow at the George. The going was very heavy, and I blessed Heaven for the forbearance native to my brother, and his sportsman's indifference to any kind of wet. It had been some days since Neddie had been privileged to drive alone; and simply having the ribbons in his hands, a light curricle and a tolerable pair of horses at his command, seemed to have raised his spirits remarkably. A bit more than two hours was required to cover the fifteen miles between Chawton and Sherborne St. John; but my brother remained cheerful despite the quagmire of the country lanes and the ruts to which the carriage was subjected. He was even now seeing to the horses' stabling with Robley the groom.

At the sound of my voice, Major Spence turned away from the storm-swept prospect. His tall figure suited the proportions of the room, and I had an idea of the kind of comfort he must have found here during the long winter months after Vimeiro. There would have been his wounded leg to attend to—all the repairs to the various wings, and the architect's designs; the plans for the grounds; the management of Lady Imogen's affairs. Frequent meetings with the lady herself, perhaps, and a growing intimacy with her ways. And then Thrace had appeared to destroy his peace.

"Miss Austen." Spence moved around the great desk that fronted the rain-swept windows and bowed.

I curtseyed in return.

I was struck by the alteration two days' time had made in his appearance. The great dark eyes I had so frequently remarked were sunken in their sockets; his brow was careworn and lined. He must hardly have slept in the interval since Saturday morning, and his expression suggested the chronic invalid—a man's whose war wound was likely never to entirely heal, and never to be forgot. I knew from bitter experience the ravages grief may do; and deeply pitied him.

"You are well, I hope?" he enquired.

"Very well, I thank you. I was grateful to receive your letter this morning, and came as soon as may be. I hope I do not intrude," I added, as he preserved a distracted silence.

He motioned towards a chair that sat near the great desk, and I sank down into it. He remained standing, however, his gaze fixed upon me; the persistent staccato of storm upon windowpane was all the sound in the room.

"You are a curious woman, Miss Austen," he observed. "You write to importune me for a meeting—you cast the grossest aspersions on the character of a most beloved lady, as that lady lies in death elsewhere in this house; and yet you apologise for *intruding*. Is this intended as a pleasantry? A sad kind of joke?"

"Major Spence—"

He turned from me abruptly and limped painfully towards the door through which I had lately passed, some thirty feet behind; and for an instant, I thought he intended to show me out—that he had summoned me all this distance for no other purpose than to deliver his crushing rebuke, and be done. But as I watched, he secured the lock with a key, and tried the knob to be certain the door was immovable.

An unaccustomed thrill of fear ran through me, and I rose from my seat. Two additional doors stood at either hand, on opposite sides of the great desk; these, too, were closed.

"You need not eye the passages so hungrily," Spence told me. "I am not so ill-prepared. When I wish to be private with a woman, and have ample notice of the fact, I undertake certain precautions. No one will come except at my express summons, and no one will hear you, Miss Austen, should you cry out. Pray do me the honour, therefore, of answering my questions—and do not be wasting your time on a fit of hysterics."

"You clearly do not know me, sir," I informed him coldly.

Of Edward, even now walking up from the stables—of which Major Spence could have no view—I chose to say nothing. I merely preserved my position before the desk, and faced him.

"In your letter of yesterday you mentioned a certain article stolen from your cottage in Chawton, Miss Austen."

"A Bengal chest of curious workmanship, filled with a quantity of papers. Yes, I did mention it—and still believe it to be in your possession."

"*My* possession?" he repeated, in an incredulous accent. "From Lady Imogen you have passed to *me* as your thief? I shall take care in future to guard my acquaintance most carefully, if the result of every dinner among friends is to be a criminal accusation."

"A man who had nothing to hide should have no need of locking doors."

He laughed bitterly, and leaned against the massive desk. "Did you think to malign the Dead, Miss Austen—and be paid off for your silence? Was that your object in petitioning the lady's steward in such frank terms? What is the price to be put upon scandal? How much, to preserve my poor darling's frail name, in the hours remaining before her interment?"

"You misunderstand me, sir."

"Do I?"

"I wish only for the return of my property."

"And if it cannot be found?" He thrust himself away from the desk and approached me menacingly. Despite my best intentions, I shrank back before his advance. "Tell me about this chest. Describe it. For I have looked in her ladyship's apartment—have set her maid to searching high and low—and nothing can I find but what accompanied the Earl's daughter from London."

"It was quite large and heavy," I replied, "and should certainly be obvious. Perhaps two feet wide by three feet long—with a curved lid and massive hinges. There was a lock set into the front, which could only be opened by a key in my possession—unless force were used against it. The contents were a quantity of papers."

"And why should Lady Imogen care for this thing?"

"Because she thought to find the truth in it."

His brows came down in a heavy frown. "The truth? What truth?"

"The details of Julian Thrace's parentage."

"Why should the slightest clue to that renegade's origins be held in a chest of your keeping, Miss Austen?" he demanded contemptuously.

"The papers it contains were penned by one who may have witnessed Mr. Thrace's minority—a friend of the Earl's, Lord Harold Trowbridge." I offered my replies as the commonplaces they were. I did not doubt that Spence already knew the answers to his questions. Why, then, did he pose them? —To suggest, in my mind, an ignorance I could not believe he harboured?

"You have read these papers, then?" he demanded. "You interest me greatly. I have long wondered where Thrace sprang from. Tell me, Miss Austen, if you know."

"But surely, sir, Lady Imogen shared the fruit of her researches? From her easy manner on Saturday, I had assumed that she learned from the documents that Thrace was a fraud—and had informed him of as much. That seemed the only possible compulsion under which the man should act to murder her ladyship: so as to suppress her proofs, before they should be communicated to the Earl."

Spence threw up his hands in an attitude of bitterness. "I was not her ladyship's confidant. And I will tell you, Miss Austen—there is no chest here—and there never was! The existence of such a chest, I put it to you, is entirely a fabrication of your own—devised for some mischievous purpose!"

•

"And yet," I returned quietly, "the man who stole it from my cottage is sitting even now in Alton gaol—and names *you*, sir, as his employer."

For an instant, gazing at Spence's grim features, I quailed. But then his figure lost its air of tension, and he appeared once more in command of his usual calm.

"Impossible," he said. "I know that for a lie."

What certainty had he grasped? What knowledge could so reassure him in the midst of self-righteous rage?

Old Philmore, I thought. *Spence believes me to refer to Old Philmore. And he knows the man is missing.*

A deliberate knock resounded on the door at the far end of the room. Charles Spence called savagely, "I asked not to be disturbed!"

"I beg your pardon, sir." Rangle's reply was muffled by the heavy mahogany. "I thought the present circumstance an exception. The Earl of Holbrook is only now arrived from Brighton—and is most anxious to speak with you."

I WAS SAVED A MOST UNCOMFORTABLE PERIOD by the descent of Freddy Vansittart on the scene.

Charles Spence, after standing frozen for several seconds, advanced hurriedly to the library door and threw it open.

"Major!" barked a massive figure looming in the doorway. "What the *deuce* do you mean by closeting yourself with a female when Imogen's but two days dead? Where's my poor girl to be found? Must see her, when all's said and done. Dreadful business. Thrown from her horse—and Immy a neck-or-nothing gal from the time she could walk! Don't make sense. Mark my words, I told that banking chap as brought the news—mark my words, they'll find the Devil was in the business. And so it proved! Poor Julian! A wolf in sheep's clothing—or a wolf in a coat cut by Stultz, come to that! Poor boy. I should not have thought him capable of such an offence. So where've you put her, Spence? Must be a rum thing, this time of year, what with the heat. We'd better see the rites observed, and no delay."

The speaker was a bluff, florid-faced man in his early fifties, clearly a martyr to gout and the claims of a voracious appetite. The brim of his beaver glistened with the wet, and, as I watched, he handed it carelessly to Rangle along with his many-caped driving coat of kerseymere. The Earl's frame must once have been powerful, but was now sadly gone to fat. The charm so marked by Lord Harold in his youth, could be only a memory preserved in the barking impetuosity of his speech. I thought I detected in Lord Holbrook's lively eye, however, a ghost of the rake he had once been; and tho' he betrayed no excessive sensibility at the loss of his only child, I noted a quality of strain in his countenance, as might suggest a sleepless night, and the hard travel born of necessity.

"My lord," Charles Spence stammered. "This is most unexpected. I had understood you to be posting to London."

"What—and have the remains sent up to Town, and August almost upon us? No, no, my dear chap; Imogen must be interred here in the family tomb. I am persuaded it is what the girl would herself have wished. We can ask the Steventon clergyman to say the Holy Office—I believe he also serves at William Chute's pleasure. What's his name? You know, the thin, reedy, prosy fellow who fancies himself such a punishing rider to hounds."

"Mr. James Austen."

"That's the ticket!" the Earl replied, brightening. "But no, dash it all, Spence—Austen was the name of the banker chap. One who came to Brighton."

"We are a numerous family, my lord." I curtseyed to the Earl.

"Miss Jane Austen, sir," Spence supplied in a colourless tone. "She and her brother were present when Lady Imogen was thrown. Mr. Henry Austen then rode with despatch to Brighton. We are all in the Austens' debt."

"Holbrook," the Earl said with a bow, "tho' my friends call me Freddy."

"I believe we have an acquaintance in common, my lord—the late Lord Harold Trowbridge."

"Harry!" Holbrook cried. "Best friend in a tight spot a man ever had! Pity he had to be killed in that way, by his manservant. Foreign fella—snake in the bosom. Rather like young Julian—dashed odd, my opinion, that he should murder Immy like that. I'd only just carried him into Carlton House, you know.

Put him up for the best clubs. Good *ton*. Whole world before him."

"Pray accept my deepest sympathies, sir, on the untimely loss of your daughter," I returned, deliberately avoiding Charles Spence's eye. The steward, I thought, would have seen me out the door before I had exchanged two words with the Earl. "She was all that was charming and lovely—and her passing must be deeply felt."

"By her creditors, above all," Holbrook observed wisely. "Immy owed a fortune among the tradesmen in Town; they have been offering odds on her expectations, and the likely purchase of my life, a twelvemonth or more. Detestable creatures—I shall have to settle with them, I suppose. Or perhaps Spence may do it when I am gone."

I did not immediately apprehend the meaning of his chance remark, but I observed the Major's pallor to heighten.

"Indeed, my lord?" a cool voice enquired. "And why should Spence have the settling of an earldom's debts?"

I turned, and espied Rangle waiting in the hall with my brother Edward behind him. Neddie's dark hair was damp with rain, but neither he nor the butler had eyes for anyone but the Earl. They had certainly overlistened the whole of our conversation.

"Why, dash it," Holbrook replied with an air of impatience, "Spence is my cousin twice removed on the distaff side. With Immy dead and Julian bound for the gallows—the Major is now my heir."

Chapter 24

History of an Heir

10 July 1809, cont.

~

THERE WAS AN INSTANT'S HEAVY SILENCE, AS SEVeral of the party assembled in the library passage contemplated Holbrook's communication.

"I would give an earldom entire," Charles Spence said with difficulty, "to see Lady Imogen returned to us in health and beauty! And now I believe, my lord, that you must long have been wishing me to conduct you to your daughter. The office may no longer be delayed. If you will excuse me, Miss Austen—and Mr. Edward Austen, with whom the Earl is as yet unacquainted . . ."

"I must beg leave to present yet another of my brothers, Lord Holbrook," I supplied. "Mr. Edward Austen, of Chawton Great House and Godmersham Park, Kent."

Neddie bowed correctly to the Earl, but his eyes were for the Major alone. "*An earldom entire.* Is that what you would give, Spence, to restore Lord Holbrook's daughter? Or was it an earldom you thought to gain, by running a thorn deep into the lady's saddle some hours before she undertook to ride?"

"That is a lie." Spence drew himself up to his full height. He appeared every inch the cavalry officer; every inch the heir to a noble house. "Rangle, show this gentleman out. He and his sister have trespassed on our patience already too long."

"Now, Spence," said the Earl unexpectedly, "that is decidedly unhandsome. The Austens would pay their respects to Immy before they go. And you have not offered them the least refreshment! I should like a glass of strong ale myself after that journey—pray go and fetch it, Rangle. Twelve hours I have been on the road from Brighton, if you will credit it!—and hard going, too, what with all the mud. Thrice we were forced to change horses. Come into the library, Mr. Austen, if you will—and explain what you mean about thorns and saddles."

"Thank you, my lord—I will."

Charles Spence remained fixed, however, by the library door, and appeared disinclined to open it. The Major's looks now were dreadful. "Nothing can be served by canvassing the manner of Lady Imogen's death," he said coldly. "It is enough to know that she was brutally cut down in the prime of her youth—and all for gain. Thrace will hang for it, once he is found; I pledge my life on it."

"I rather think you *do* pledge your life on it," my brother agreed. "The Earl has commanded us to sit down, Spence. Will you move away from the door?"

The steward hesitated, then complied. With a smile, Neddie indicated I must precede him into the room, and waited in deference for Lord Holbrook.

"Pray accept my sincere condolences on the death of your daughter, my lord," he said with a correct bow. "Her murder cries out for justice."

"Where is that ale?" the peer demanded irritably. "Mr. Austen is soaked to the skin, and this demmed house is so vast and draughty, it requires a legion to staff it. Still they cannot make their way from kitchen to parlour in under a quarter-hour. I should not live in this wreck for worlds. It ought to be pulled down— and so it shall be, now Immy can no longer live in it."

"My lord," Spence interposed abruptly, and then halted in mid-speech, with an eye for my brother. "I do not think you perfectly understand the beauties of this place."

"Don't preach fustian," the Earl retorted. "I was raised in this barracks, boy and man. Beauties! It is stifling in summer and freezing in winter; and the bill for coal is extortionate. Do not be prating to me of *beauties*. Now then, Austen—what is this you would say of Charles and the thorn? Speak, man!"

"I think it is rather my sister who should answer you," Neddie replied, "as she is more fully acquainted with the particulars."

Being as a stranger to the Earl, I might have hesitated to lay before him so hideous a charge as had

formed itself in my brain, for indeed I had no proof—
merely a subtle association of ideas, that had wanted
only the truth of Major Spence's relation to Lord
Holbrook to harden into conviction. For an instant I
nearly demurred. But some thought of that lovely
young life so brutally destroyed—and of the man even
now being hunted the length and breadth of
England—quelled my last doubt. With my eyes fixed
on the Earl's countenance, I began.

"It was Lady Imogen who observed on the day of
her death, *I believe Charles loves this place better than all of
us.* I did not know then that her steward could be
tempted with the prospect of inheriting the place he
had lately seen restored to its former beauty; but I
may own that I understand the immensity of that
temptation. I, too, have been rootless most of my life,
and shifted from lodging to lodging. I have seen my
relations established in a security that must appear
paradisiacal in comparison with my own. I have
known envy, Major Spence, as well as want—but have
never been offered the opportunity to amend my condition. I perceive, now, that this has been your down-
fall."

"My lord," Spence said without the slightest suggestion of having heard me, "if you wish to see Lady
Imogen interred at Stonings, there is much to do. I
cannot like this delay. There will be time to philoso-
phize on life and death once the funeral rites are observed, and Thrace is in the hands of the constabulary."

"I have an idea," I persisted, "that you first conceived of your plan during the winter months, as you

grew in intimacy with Lady Imogen's ways. She was charming, and profligate, and on any trip up to Town you might observe her dalliance with a host of suitors intent upon securing her fortune before she should gamble it away. The title and the earldom were entailed upon yourself, a fact you knew; but there was always the danger that the funds to support Lord Holbrook's estates should be spent before you obtained them, if Lady Imogen was allowed to pursue her ruinous course. Why not marry the chit, and command her purse strings in a tidier fashion? You offered her marriage; she deliberated on her answer. Lady Imogen, perhaps, had doubts as to your character. *Major Spence should never be parted from his treasure so easily,* she said once; and *I know you for a blackguard of old.*

"And then, around February when your flirtation with her ladyship had reached a desperate point, Thrace arrived to take the *ton* by storm. Did you apprehend immediately, Major, that you should be left with only the lady and her debts, did Thrace's claim to paternity prevail?"

Charles Spence walked deliberately to a table near the window where a decanter of brandy was placed. He poured himself a drink, then turned with courtesy to the Earl, whose affable countenance had acquired an expression of fixed attentiveness. "My lord?" the Major enquired.

"I should like to wait for the ale," he returned with a dismissive wave. "Pray continue, Miss Austen. I am devilish fond of stories, particularly when they concern people I know. I should like to hear how this one turns out."

I inclined my head. "Mr. Thrace was poised to deprive Major Spence of all expectations. Poised, as well, to strip Lady Imogen of property vital to her survival—the jointure of Stonings. Rather than commanding the full power of an earldom and the lady's income upon your marriage, Major, you were now forced to fight for the right to remain the Earl's steward—until such time as Thrace should appoint his own. Outright hostility to the prospective heir could only harm your chances. And so you played a deep game—preserving the appearance of dedication to Lady Imogen; establishing the right to call Thrace your friend, and consort with him on terms of easy intimacy; and fomenting, whenever possible, the discord and rivalry between the half-brother and sister."

Spence tossed off his brandy and grimaced as it coursed down his throat. "Like all ladies' stories, I fear this one is a horrid romance," he observed calmly. "We shall presently be treated to a skeleton in a tower and a tomb behind a veil. Cannot I lead you to your beloved daughter, my lord, and continue this entertainment at a moment better suited for the Gothick?"

"It was from Lady Imogen, I collect, that you first learned of Lord Harold's papers," I said.

"Harry's papers?" The Earl glanced at me in a startled fashion. "Thought he left them to some light o' love by way of payment for services rendered. Heard it from Wilborough myself. Poor old fellow expects to be petitioned with blackmail at every mo-

ment. Dashed odd of Harry, my opinion! Must have
been devilish smitten with the gel."

"Lord Harold left all his papers to me," I replied
with what I thought was commendable command of
countenance. The Earl's expression of shock was so
blatant as to border on the insulting. "Lady Imogen
had learned so much from the gossip of the *ton* in the
months following Lord Harold's death. She knew that
his lordship had long been intimate with you, my
lord—that the two of you had endured several years'
exile on the Subcontinent together, at about the time
Julian Thrace was born. I imagine that is when your
daughter conceived of her plan to steal the documents, with the hope that she might find in them the
truth of Thrace's parentage. And she recruited you,
Major Spence, as her champion."

"I would that she had," he returned evenly. "I
might have spared her a brutal and senseless death."

"Nothing Lady Imogen could say or do would
spare her *that*," I observed, "for you had already concluded it to be necessary. When she came to you here
at Stonings, and proposed a dangerous gamble—the
theft of the papers on the very day of their arrival in
Chawton—she came to a man she had long known for
a renegade. The sort who should *never be parted from
his treasure without a fight*. And you agreed to help her.
You had already determined to use the papers to
throw guilt upon Julian Thrace—and thus be rid of all
your enemies at a single blow."

Spence threw back his head and laughed. It was
not a pleasant sound; and from the corner of my eye,

I observed Edward to move quietly between myself and the steward, his gaze watchful.

I continued. "I imagine it was while you conversed with Lady Imogen—perhaps in this very room—that you were overheard in your plans by Shafto French. He was at work in some part of the building that afforded an opportunity to eavesdrop, perhaps; the gallery that runs along the front part of this room, or one of the neighbouring apartments. French must have taxed you with his knowledge, and was satisfied with promise of payment; he told his wife that he expected to come into blood money, and that it was *the heir as would pay*. I thought, quite naturally, that it was Thrace he implied; and that mistake could only strengthen your case against the gentleman, once you had covered him in guilt for Lady Imogen's murder. But I run ahead of myself—I beg your pardon, my lord."

Holbrook waved his hand distractedly; a soft knock on the door announced Rangle's appearance with the desired tankard of ale. He waited while the Earl drank the entire draught in a single gulp, bowed as tho' unconscious of any strain in the atmosphere, and retired once more.

"Ah!" Holbrook said brightly. "That's better! All the mud of England might have been caught in my throat! And so Charles arranged to pay off the man who would have split on him, I collect, and proceeded to murder my Immy?"

"Exactly so. You are admirably succinct, my lord. I perceive now why such a depth of friendship obtained between yourself and Lord Harold. The Major arranged to meet Shafto French near Chawton Pond on the very evening Julian Thrace was expected to dine at Chawton Great House. I recollect that Spence was said, by Thrace's own admission, to have been otherwise engaged that evening. Having ridden on horseback from Sherborne St. John to Chawton alone, and back again, Thrace could bring no witness as to his actions along the route. He might protest his innocence when charged with French's murder all he liked; he could offer no evidence that he had *not* killed the man."

At this point, my brother interrupted. "You must have been greatly discomfited when French's body was not found, Spence."

"I am sure I should have been," the steward replied acidly, "had I killed him."

"What motive did you intend to offer for Thrace's violence? Were Lord Harold's documents—which you thought to secure in my brother's banking branch in Alton on the Monday—to be found among Thrace's things? In the event, you had neither a body nor a wooden chest to show for all your efforts; and so we proceed to the second chapter of our story."

"Good God!" Spence cried. "I pray it does not run to a third! Is this not tedium enough, my lord, for one morning? You have had your refreshment; pray let me carry you to your daughter's chamber."

"I collect that French's body was found, however," the Earl said testily, "or you should not have known to suspect Spence in his murder."

"I discovered his corpse myself; but that is another story. For the nonce, it is enough to know that the poor man was drowned while Thrace was in Chawton. The Thursday following, one of French's mates forced an entry to my cottage, and stole Lord Harold's papers—which have still not been recovered. We believe the man to have had a confederate: one Old Philmore, who has also disappeared."

"A confederate?" Spence objected. "But—"

"—You believed Old Philmore to have acted alone," I replied, "and are astonished to learn that in silencing the old man, you failed to end his tale entirely. I am sorry to disappoint you, Major Spence; but so it is. Philmore's nephew is even now in Alton gaol, and weakening in his loyalties."

For the first time, Spence betrayed his fear. He turned restlessly about the room, his gaze abstracted, as tho' debating what best he should do. He came to a halt behind the great desk, staring out the windows at the driving rain.

"I was very stupid, when all is said and done," I admitted. "I thought from Lady Imogen's looks on the Saturday that she was privileged in the knowledge of her own triumph. I thought Thrace was vanquished by Lord Harold's proofs—that he knew himself exposed as an imposter. I actually believed he might have arranged her ladyship's race and subsequent fall, in the faint hope of suppressing all knowledge before the Earl should learn of it. In short, I behaved in exactly the fashion *you* might have hoped from all our party,

Major Spence. You were a consummate plotter—and I was your dupe."

He did not move, did not reveal that he had heard me.

"You may have already perused the contents of my chest. I cannot say what you found there. But the sequel must give a partial knowledge. By Saturday, Lady Imogen was dead; and Julian Thrace accused of her murder. I collect, then, that the unfortunate Mr. Thrace *is* undeniably Lord Holbrook's heir—and that only a noose could prevent him from inheriting your earldom, Major Spence."

"Lord," the Earl of Holbrook murmured, "it is as good as a play! Dolly Jordan is as nothing to you, Miss Austen. But you need not have gone to such trouble, Spence. I could have shown you the proofs myself, had you only asked. They are not to be found among Lord Harold's papers, you know. They are among *mine*."

We turned as with one will and stared at Freddy Vansittart.

"Wrote to me direct from France," the Earl explained, "when he recovered the boy. Wrote the particulars and enclosed Hélène's dying words. Didn't need Harry's fist to convince me of the gel's constancy. Never had any doubt regarding Julian's blood. I've maintained him in school all these years, haven't I, and made sure he was raised an English gentleman?"

The Earl withdrew a wallet from his coat with thick and fumbling fingers. They trembled slightly as he extracted a thin sheet of foolscap, fragile and transparent with age and much folding. Even at a distance of ten paces, I could discern the familiar sloping hand.

Lord Harold's writing.

"There," the Earl commanded. "You may read it for yourselves. I've never parted with Harry's letter. It's all I have left of Hélène."

We all of us stood paralysed, uncertain to whom this charge was directed. And at that moment, Spence made his move.

HE THREW HIMSELF NOT AT THE EARL OR THE PRE-cious relic held in his hand; nor did he grapple with Edward in a desperate surge for the door. He did not knock me down, or hurl himself through a window as Thrace had done; he dived for the great desk's drawer.

I believe that Edward understood before I did what the Major intended. But by the time my brother had reached him the cavalry pistol was already levelled against Spence's own temple.

"No!" Edward cried. "I beg of you, Spence—"

But the report of gunpowder and ball must serve as his only answer.

Letter from Lord Harold Trowbridge to Frederick, Earl of Holbrook, dated 8 January 1792; two leaves quarto, laid; watermark fragmentary ELGAR; signature under black wax seal bearing arms of Wilborough House; *Personelle, Par Chasseur Exprès,* **in red ink.** *(British Museum, Wilborough Papers, Austen bequest)*

Dearest Freddy:

I achieved Paris three days since, and have spent the interval in searching for the Citizeness Hélène. I will not tax your patience with a report of the state of affairs in this miserable place; I will say only that I have found her, but she is in no condition to be restored to you. To be brief: she is to meet the guillotine on the morrow. Nothing I can contrive among her gaolers— neither payments of what gold I still possess, nor the promise of safe conduct to my country—has succeeded in winning her freedom. It appears Hélène committed the fatal errors of remaining in the city when all was lost, and of championing the cause of a childhood friend similarly consigned to execution. Someone—I know not whom—has informed upon her as the paramour of a conspiring Englishman, and you know well that such trahison shall never go unpunished.

I shall endeavour to do what I can to disrupt the Committee's plans, but will say no more here lest this missive go astray.

Of your son I have better intelligence—he is placed with a cottager near Versailles and knows nothing of his unfortunate mother's fate. I have seen him, and when all is concluded—for good or ill—I shall get him to you in Marseille, or die in the attempt.

You may expect us within a fortnight.

You would find your poor lady much changed. She remains, despite the grossest of indignities and a cause for despair beyond imagining, the sweetest-tempered female I have ever met with. She begs to be remembered to you and her father, and asks on her dying eve that you guard well the life of your son. Some token he bears with him which you will recognise; I know not what. Pray God that we arrive safe.

Yours ever,
Harry

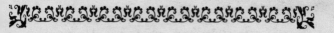

Chapter 25

The Earl's Story

10 July 1809, cont.

~

IT WAS EDWARD WHO RODE OUT TO FETCH THE
surgeon, Mr. Althorp, from Sherborne St. John, in order that he might pronounce another sudden death
to have been achieved at the great estate of Stonings.
I remained with the Earl of Holbrook while Charles
Spence's valet took his master's body in charge, and
saw it washed and laid out for burial with his own
hands. I had not encountered the Major's manservant before, but was much struck by the expression of
suffering that was writ on his countenance; clearly
Charles Spence had been beloved of somebody.

The Earl escorted me from the scene of gore and
misery that had become the library, and deposited me
with a decanter of sherry and Lord Harold's precious

missive in the white and gold saloon. He disappeared for an interval, in which I assume he paid his respects to his daughter's bier, and issued orders regarding the Major's remains. I walked about the room in some disorder of mind, debating every moment of the past week and my own tragic miscalculations regarding the persons I had lately met. The Earl returned after twenty minutes, in apparel freshly exchanged for his garments of the morning, and looking the better for his respite.

"My dear Miss Austen," he cried, "I could wish us to have met under more cheerful circumstances. It is shocking indeed to consider the scenes to which you have been subjected. But I am grateful to you for the perspicacity you have brought to Stonings; I should not have suspected Charles Spence in an hundred years. Altho'—given his ruthless determination to acquire my property—I doubt my life would have lasted so long."

"I must agree with you, my lord."

He threw himself onto the settee at my side and patted my hand encouragingly. "I apprehend, now, why Harry left you his papers, m'dear. You're as shrewd as you can hold together, aren't you? I wish Immy had possessed a little of your understanding; the gel might yet be spending my money hand over fist."

He looked so troubled that I felt an unwarranted desire to protect and support him; the sort of desire that must often have attended Freddy Vansittart's adventures, and ensured him the love and good will of those around him.

I offered the Earl Lord Harold's letter. "I collect from this communication that the boy his lordship speaks of was Julian Thrace?"

"Indeed. Delivered like a package to my inn at Marseille not ten days after the date of that note. There was never anything like Harry for dependability; when Trowbridge gave his word, he backed it."

"Had you known the boy before?"

"But naturally! I fell head over ears in love with Julian's mother when I was a young man out in India, and by the hour of her death was almost Hélène's sole support. I should have gone to her myself, at the last, but for the price the Committee had placed upon my head."

I had an idea of the story, but forbore to interrupt him.

"She was the daughter of a French count, and the daintiest piece of work you should ever have seen, m'dear." He sighed reminiscently. "No sapskull, neither. When we met Hélène was betrothed to another—a peer of the British realm—and her sense of what was due to her father, who had arranged the match, dictated the most scrupulous fidelity to his wishes. Her heart, however, was another affair altogether. Wonderful how these French women can reconcile the very Devil!"

I murmured assent.

"I cannot recall a happier time than those few short weeks aboard the *Punjab*, Miss Austen. When we achieved Plymouth, however, I gave her up for lost. No sooner did I find myself back in London, than I was riveted meself—it was only expected, as I had come into my brother's title, and must stand the business. Amelia was well-born, well-looking, and without a penny to her name; that meant little to me, as I had made my fortune already in the East. I fear, however, that I was unable to accord my wife the sort of affection and fidelity a young woman might expect from her husband. My heart was already commanded by another, you see. Amelia left me when our child was but three years old, and I was forced to raise Immy myself. Not that I minded; it was preferable to living with my lady wife's highjinks. All the same—I never undertook to marry again. Hadn't the desire for it, if you see what I mean."

"I do understand. But the French lady . . . ?"

"Couldn't stick the Viscount," he answered bluntly, "and naturally, she must have appeared in his lordship's eyes as rather tainted goods. I will not deny that Hélène achieved her wedding day already two months gone with my child. I suppose she thought to brave it out—to deceive the gentleman if necessary, and endure a loveless marriage, provided he could be kind to her—but the truth is, St. Eustace was the Devil's own cub, and there was no living with him for any woman. Hélène sought my protection within six months of her marriage, and I saw the poor gel safely home to Paris with all possible speed. Set her up in a lovely little house in the Rue de Sèvres, and prepared for both of us to be happy. That would have been

1786, I suppose—the year of Julian's birth. But what with one thing and another, I only saw my French family perhaps four times in a twelvemonth. And then the Revolution began, and it was hard to know where an Englishman's duty lay."

"Particularly an Englishman of the Whiggish persuasion," I observed.

"That's the rub," he agreed. "We were all for liberty, at first—for the reign of Reason, and the power of a Constitution, and the curbing of royal prerogatives; it was like mother's milk to us, don't y'know. Even Harry was wild for French republicanism. But then he saw at first hand the excesses of the populists bent on murdering all those they could not persuade. He wrote back to his friends at home that measures would have to be contrived, once the blood began to flow. And so we all agreed to serve as the rescue party for our French brothers. Charles Grey conceived of the details, and Harry and I volunteered to carry them out."

"With Lord Holland as your second," I mused.

"Exactly so! Are you acquainted with Henry?"

"Not at all."

"Must introduce you. Old friend of Harry's from schoolboy days."

"And so the boy—Julian Thrace—was rescued and given over to you in Marseille," I persisted, "in the winter of 1792."

"He was then but six years of age. I could not leave the lad in France, of course, but I did not think it right to bring him home to the Holbrook nursery—there were Immy's feelings to consider, and the awkwardness of questions. Henry—Lord Holland—suggested that Julian might be sent to school with the Swiss, where Holland might observe him from time to time, and send reports as to his progress. It served very well. Holland and his lady had made a habit of living abroad—first in France and then in Spain—and it was as nothing to them to pay a flying visit to Julian several times a year. They have even had the boy to stay in their household. Yes, it answered very well."

So well that the boy's father had never been put to the slightest trouble beyond paying his son's bills. That should answer a man of Freddy Vansittart's indolence very well indeed.

"What were your feelings, sir, upon hearing that Julian Thrace was believed responsible for your daughter's murder?"

"I thought it the grossest misunderstanding, and could only lament that Julian had bolted—not from want of courage, to be sure, but a lamentable ignorance of the British system of justice. I never believed him capable of killing Imogen. Why should he, after all? There was no claim he was required to prove in order to inherit the title. I should always have known him for my son; his nose is my father's, after all, and his eyes are entirely Hélène's. Besides, there were the rubies to think of. The little chap arrived in Marseille with them tied in a leather pouch under his shirt, like one of Ali Baba's thieves."

"The rubies?" I repeated blankly. "Not the Rubies of Chandernagar?"

"He has told you of them, then!" Holbrook exclaimed with delight. "An heirloom of Hélène's house, and owned at one time by Madame de Pompadour, if the old stories may be believed. I think Hélène expected me to sell the stones, in order to support our son's education; but that is nonsense, of course. The stones are his inheritance from his mother, and must remain in his possession until he determines to place them about the neck of another."

Poor Mamma, I thought ruefully, *and her blistered palms.*

The Earl rose from the settee and wandered restlessly towards the window, where the prospect of lake and parapet could dimly be seen through the rain. "A black coach, and an outrider; that will be your excellent brother, Miss Austen. I do so dread a publick recital of Charles Spence's affairs. He is, after all, *family.* Cannot we agree to bury the truth with the poor fellow's body? Publicity cannot return Imogen to life, after all."

"That is true," I assented, "but the truth could do much to clear your son's name. That must seem essential, as Mr. Thrace is all that remains to you."

"Julian?" The Earl glanced at me ruefully. "He shall be well on his way to Switzerland by now, and such friends as he still possesses. I suspect it will be months before I am able to locate him; and many months more before he will consent to receive me."

"I do not think he is fled to the Continent," I replied, with a swift recollection of Catherine Prowting's nocturnal wanderings, "and you will be happy to learn, sir, that not all your son's friends are so far from home. An application in the right place should secure his return before nightfall, if you will consent to place the matter in my hands."

"I cannot conceive of a better course," Holbrook said simply. "Pray tell me in what manner I may serve you in return, Miss Austen."

"You might order Major Spence's valet to search his effects," I suggested, "for a Bengal chest that was once in Lord Harold's possession. It contains all that remains of the gentleman—and I have sorely missed the whole since Charles Spence made off with it."

"It shall be done," the Earl replied, and bowed low over my hand. "Now tell me, Miss Austen—how came we never to meet when Harry was alive? Do you never get up to Town for the Season?"

He is a stout fellow, and clearly given over entirely to dissipation—but Freddy Vansittart *does* possess an infinite abundance of charm, as Lord Harold once noted. In this quality alone, we may certainly recognise Julian Thrace's father.

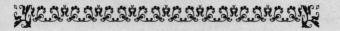

Chapter 26

New Beginnings

Wednesday, 26 July 1809

~

My dearest Frank, I wish you Joy
Of Mary's safety with a boy,
Whose birth has given little pain,
Compared with that of Mary Jane.—

SO FAR I HAD MANAGED TO COMPOSE, IN MY LET-
ter to my brother Captain Frank Austen, when the
Muse failed me. Lord Harold might love to instruct
that writing is *all we have*—but in my experience, on
too many occasions we may not command even so
much as a word. I sighed, and set aside my pen, and
determined to take a turn in the garden to refresh my
jaded senses.

Cassandra and my mother were gone out to Alton,

and the cottage was mine to possess alone. In the past few weeks since our descent upon Chawton, turmoil had given way to peace, and the rightful enjoyment of the summer months in all their lazy plentitude. We had the imminent arrival of Martha Lloyd from Kintbury to look forward to; and increasing intimacy with the Great House family to leaven the simple bread of our usual days; restorative walks through the surrounding country; and the promise of an occasional visit from some one of our brothers. Not to mention the delights of the hopeful family in Lenton Street, and the babe so newly born.

For my part, the past few weeks had been one of discovery and acceptance. The salvation of Julian Thrace from a murderer's gibbet, and the determination of his father to present the young man as his son and heir without further delay, had sent the most interesting part of our local acquaintance flying from the country. The Heir to the House of Holbrook had been discovered sheltering in a shepherd's cot long since abandoned on Robin Hood Butts. By Julian's side, in terror of his life, was Old Philmore—who had been brutally served with a club by Charles Spence after delivering the Bengal chest into the Major's hands. This cowardly act had been achieved in darkness, on the very night of the cottage burglary; and it having been a night of waning moon, Old Philmore succeeded at escaping from Stonings with his life, and a great wound to the head. Knowledge of his own guilt in the matter of the chest, and a terror of what the steward might further do, had convinced the old man to lie low until such time as Justice had been served. A chance meeting with Julian Thrace, who had his own story of persecution to tell, had sealed the matter, and made of the two fugitives friends in need.

My application to Catherine Prowting—without the necessity of informing her father or betraying the folly into which his daughter had plunged—had wrested the young man's location from her terrified lips. The Earl himself rode out to find Julian, and no one else was privileged to witness their reconciliation, or to know what was then said. My brother Edward, however, was able to satisfy Mr. Prowting that Charles Spence was entirely responsible for the murders of Shafto French and Lady Imogen; and in the conversation of the two magistrates, Justice was allowed to have been served.

Catherine Prowting received a very pretty round of thanks from Mr. Thrace for her care of him in distress, but no offer of marriage; and as that gentleman is now gone a fortnight from Hampshire, and no one knows whether he is ever likely to return, the unfortunate Catherine appears certain to fall into a decline.

To supplement the loss of such compelling society, however, I have had my Bengal chest: returned with a forced lock and a splintered face, but with the contents mostly intact. Great disorder reigned among Lord Harold's papers, as Charles Spence had obviously gone through them in immense haste, and failed to discover the proofs he so desperately sought; but there is a satisfaction in bringing order from chaos, against which even I am no proof. I have spent many consuming mornings closeted in my bedchamber, with packets of letters and journals spread out all around me, and am in a mood to welcome any shower of rain, as discouraging all other activity but that of reading.

Cassandra, observing me, sniffed with disdain that I was as much Lord Harold's inamorata in death as in life—and I did not trouble to argue the point. Entire worlds of experience have been opened to me through his lordship's letters; and I feel now as tho' I hardly knew him, when he stood in my parlour with one booted foot on the fender, and his hooded grey eyes fixed on my countenance. There is much to trouble, and much to shock, among these papers; much also to admire and love. But what a burden he has placed in my safekeeping! I no longer trust to the security of a cottage.

I have written to Mr. Bartholomew Chizzlewit of Lincoln's Inn, and desired him to despatch a special courier to Chawton, so that Lord Harold's bequest might be returned to the solicitor's offices. There, from time to time, I might visit his lordship's ghost— and determine how best to fulfill the heavy charge he has placed upon me. The writing up and publication of the Rogue's memoirs will prove no easy task—but if it is to be a lifework, it is one I feel myself equal to undertake. The effect of the *Memoirs of a Gentleman Rogue* should be as a bombshell bursting upon the Polite World; and nothing would deprive me of the privilege of unleashing so cataclysmic a force.

I have not yet learned to ignore Lord Harold's loss. Here, in the simple beauty of this country garden, with the prospect of my family's society always around me, I must know myself even still for a woman set apart. Great love denied has been my burden; and its bastards are silence and loneliness. It is my very singularity I must struggle with now—as perhaps I have always done. It was Lord Harold alone who understood this; and honoured me with his esteem despite the ways in which I shall never be quite like other women.

Or perhaps—as he told me once—*because* of them.

Letter from Lord Harold Trowbridge to Miss Jane Austen, dated 3 November 1808; one leaf quarto, laid; watermark Fitzhugh and Gilroy; sealed with black wax over signature.

(British Museum, Wilborough Papers, Austen bequest)

My dearest Jane——

If I survive the morning's work—as no doubt I shall—this letter will never reach you; but if I am fated by some mischance to fall under Ord's hand, I cannot go in silence upon one subject, at least.

I am no sentimentalist. I will tell you that you are hardly the most beautiful woman I have ever known, Jane, nor the most enchanting. Your witchery is of a different order than others'—and springs, I believe, from the extraordinary self-possession you command. It is unique in my experience of women. You have my unqualified esteem and respect; you have my trust and my heart; and if I love you, my dear, it is as one loves the familiar room to which one returns after desperate wandering. In this room I might draw the shades upon the world and live in comfort forever.

Do not cry for me, Jane—but carry me always in your heart, as one who loved you for that courage to be yourself, and not what convention would have you be.

Your Rogue

Editor's Afterword

THERE ARE MANY WHO MAKE IT THEIR LIFEWORK
to study Jane Austen and her novels, and to them I
owe a considerable debt. There are others, however,
who are content to simply enjoy her words and live for
a while in the world she created; and to many of these
devoted readers, the town of Chawton—and the cottage in which Austen lived the final eight years of her
life—have become a shrine to a lost time and place.
They will probably object to my portrait of the village
as hostile to the Austens' arrival in 1809, but there is a
good deal of evidence to suggest that the four women
who took up residence in Widow Seward's cottage
were not immediately beloved. The claims of the
Hinton family, and their relations the Baverstocks and
Dusautoys, against Edward Austen are well docu-
mented, and resulted in a lawsuit in 1814 demanding
the reversion of the Chawton estates to the direct
heirs of the Knights of Chawton. Edward was forced to
settle the claim with a payment of fifteen thousand
pounds to Jack Hinton, which he raised by the sale of
timber from the Chawton woods. In that same year,
Edward also prosecuted one of the Baigent boys for

assault; but history does not tell us whether it was Toby or in what manner he attacked the Squire.

Ann Prowting submitted to fate and married Benjamin Clement of the Royal Navy. After the end of the Napoleonic wars turned him on shore, the young couple took up residence in Chawton and remained there until their deaths. Catherine Prowting never married.

Edward Austen and his children took the surname of Knight in 1812, when his patroness Catherine Knight died. He stayed briefly in the Great House in 1813 and again in 1814, but remained until his death a resident of Kent. The Middleton family gave up the lease of the Chawton estate in 1812, and in the years before Edward's eldest son, Edward (1794–1879), moved into the Great House in 1826, the place was at the disposal of Jane's naval brothers, Frank and Charles. Frank's fourth son, Herbert, was born there in 1815.

For those who wish to know more of Jane Austen's neighborhood in Hampshire, I must recommend Rupert Willoughby's slim volume, *Chawton: Jane Austen's Village,* The Old Rectory, Sherborne St. John, 1998; *Jane Austen and Alton,* by Jane Hurst, copyright Jane Hurst, 2001; Nigel Nicolson's *The World of Jane Austen,* Weidenfeld & Nicolson, London, 1991; *Jane Austen, A Family Record,* by W. Austen-Leigh, R. A. Austen-Leigh, and Deirdre Le Faye, The British Library, 1989; and *Jane Austen's Letters,* edited by Deirdre Le Faye, Oxford University Press, 1995.

Chawton Great House was sold in 1993 to Ms.

Sandy Lerner, an American, who has completely refurbished the house and grounds as a Center for the
Study of Early English Women's Writing—a use Jane
Austen might have approved, although she would certainly have lamented its inevitable passage from family hands. Chawton Cottage is in the care of the Jane
Austen Memorial Trust, and can be toured most days
of the year.

Stephanie Barron
Golden, Colorado
January 2004

About the Author

Stephanie Barron is the author of eight Jane Austen mysteries. She lives in Colorado, where she is at work on the next Jane Austen mystery, *Jane and the Barque of Frailty.*

If you enjoyed **Jane and His Lordship's Legacy,**
you won't want to miss any of her superbly tantalizing
mysteries featuring Jane Austen.
Look for them at your favorite bookseller's

And read on for a special early look at the next
Jane Austen mystery,

Jane and the Barque of Frailty

Coming soon in hardcover
from Bantam Books

Jane and the Barque of Frailty
COMING SOON

Chapter 1

A Night Among the Great

No. 64 Sloane Street, London
Monday, 22 April 1811

~

CONCEIVE, IF YOU WILL, OF THE THEATRE ROYAL, Covent Garden, on an evening such as this: the celebrated Mrs. Siddons being rumored to appear, after too many months' absence from the stage; the play *Macbeth*, with all the hideous power of Shakespeare's verse and Maria Siddons's art; and the Polite World of London brawling in the midst of Bow Street, in an effort to reach its place in the box before the curtain should rise.

Such a welter of chairmen, link boys, fashionable carriages, street sweeps, porters and coachmen! Such oaths, blasted into the ears of delicately-nurtured females, carried hurriedly to the paving lest their satin slippers should be soiled in the horses' dung! Such an array of silks and muslins, turbans and feathers, embroidered shawls and jeweled flounces! The scent of a thousand flowers on the air, the odor of tobacco and ripe oranges and fish from the markets in Covent Garden, the great theatre's windows thrown open against the warmth of the spring night and the heat of too many bodies filling the vast hall! The flickering of wax candles, a fortune's worth thrown up into the gleaming chandeliers; the rising pitch of conversation, the screech of a woman's laughter, the impropriety of a chance remark, the hand of a gentleman resting where it should not, on the person of his lady—all this, like a prodigal feast spread out for my delectation.

The vague shadow, too, of a Bow Street Runner lounging in the doorway of the magistrate's offices opposite—which I chanced to glimpse as brother Henry swept me to the theatre door; lounging like an accusation as he surveyed the Fashionable Great, whose sins and peccadilloes only he may be privileged to know.

It is a scene hardly out of the ordinary way for the majority of the *ton,* that select company of wealthy and wellborn who rule what is commonly called Society; but for a lady in the midst of her thirty-fifth year, denied a proper come-out or a breathless schoolgirl's first Season, a shabby-genteel lady long since on the shelf and at her last prayers—it must be deemed a high treat. Add that I am a hardened enthusiast of the great Maria Siddons, and have been disappointed before in my hopes of seeing that thespian tread the boards—and you will apprehend with what pleasurable anticipation I met the curtain's rise.

"Jane," Eliza murmured behind her fan as the Theatre Royal fell silent, "there is Lord Moira, Henry's particular friend and an intimate of the Prince Regent. Next his box you will recognize Lord Castlereagh, I am sure—was there ever anything so elegant as his lady's dress? It is as nothing, however, to the costume of the creature seated to our left—the extraordinarily handsome woman with the flashing dark eyes and the black curls. *That* is the great Harriette Wilson, my dear—the most celebrated Impure in London, with her sisters and intimate friends; do not observe her openly, I beg! Such gentlemen as have had her in keeping! I am sure our Harriette might bring down the Government, were she merely to speak too freely among her intimates. They do say that even *Wellington*—"

The pressure of Henry's hand upon his wife's arm silenced Eliza, and I was allowed to disregard the late Minister of War equally with the demimondaine in her rubies and paint, and sit in breathless apprehension as a cabal of witches plotted their ageless doom.

I am come to London in the spring of this year 1811—the year of Regency and the poor old king's decline into madness, the year of Bonaparte's expected rout in the Peninsula, of straitened circumstances and immense want among the poor—to watch like an anxious parent over the printing of my first novel. Yes, my *novel*; or say rather the child of my heart, an infant, which is to be sent into the Great World without even the acknowledgement of its mother, to be published by Mr. Henry Egerton only as *By a Lady*.

And what is the title and purport of this improving work, so ideally suited to the fancy of ladies both young and old?

I have been used to call it *Elinor & Marianne*, after the fashion of the great Madame D'Arblay, whose exemplary tales *Camilla, Evelina, Cecilia*, etc., have set the fashion in literature for ladies. Mr. Egerton, however, is of the opinion that such a title is no longer the mode, the style being for qualities akin to Miss Edgeworth's *Self-Control*. I have debated the merits of *Worthiness and Self-Worth*, or *An Excellent Understanding*. Eliza, on the other hand, would hew to the sensational.

"How do you like *The Bodice Rip'd from Side to Side*, Jane? Or perhaps—I think now only of Marianne—*The Maid Forsworn and All Forlorn?*"

"But what of Willoughby?" brother Henry objected. "Should he not be given pride of place? Call it then *The Seducer*, and have done."

"It shall be *Sense & Sensibility*," I replied firmly, "for I am partial to sibilants; and besides, Cassandra approves the division: Elinor a creature of Reason, and Marianne entirely of Feeling. You must know I am in the habit of being guided by my sister. —Insofar as my inclination allies with *hers*, of course."

Henry and his wife cried out against this, abusing Cassandra for the excessive starch of her notions, and the quiet propriety which must always characterise her views. I ought possibly to have paid more heed to their opinions—it is Henry, after all, who has franked me in the publishing world, having paid Mr. Egerton to print my little book—but I am tired of toying with titles. All my anxiety is for the pace of the printing, which is excessively slow. I am resident in London a full month, and yet we have arrived only at Chapter Nine, and Willoughby's first appearance. At this rate, the year will have turned before the novel is bound, tho' it was faithfully promised for May—a set of three volumes in blue boards, with gilt letters.

"Jane," Eliza prompted as the curtain fell on Act I of *Macbeth*, "You are hardly attending. Here is the Comtesse d'Entraigues come to pay us a call. How delightful!"

I roused myself quick enough to observe the lady's entrance into our box, with a headdress of feathers nearly sweeping the ceiling–a quizzing glass held to her eye—an expanse of bony shoulder and excess of décolleté—and schooled my countenance to amiability. There are many words I might chuse to apostrophize the French countess—one of Eliza's acquaintances from her previous marriage to a nobleman of Louis's reign—but *delightful* is not one of them. The Comtesse d'Entraigues was used to be known as Anne de St.-Huberti, when she set up as opera singer in the days of the Revolution; but by either name she is repugnant to me, being full of acid and spite. Eliza hints that her friend was the Comte's mistress before he was constrained to marry her— and at full five-and-fifty, Anne de St.-Huberti must be grateful for the protection of his name. She paints her pitted cheeks in the mode of thirty years since; is given to the excessive use of scent; affects a blond wig;

and should undoubtedly be termed a *Fright* by the ruthless bucks of Town.

"Eliza, *mignon*," she crooned as she presented one powdered cheek in all the appearance of affection; "how hagged you look this evening, to be sure! The years, they have never sat lightly upon you, *bien sûr*! You have been fatigued, *sans dout*, by your visit to Surrey last evening—it was a great deal *too* good of you to solace my exile!"

We had indeed ventured into Surrey last night, despite all my doubts regarding Sunday travel, to enjoy an evening of music at the D'Entraigues' abode. The old count spoke nothing but French, and I understood but a fraction of the communication, tho' Henry admirably held up his end, and declared the gentleman to be a man of parts and considerable information. The son, young Count Julien, who appears everything an Exquisite of the Ton should be, with his excellent tailoring, his disordered locks, his shining boots and his quantity of fobs and seals, delighted us with his superior performance upon the pianoforte.

The Comtesse deigned to sing.

Taken all together, I should rather endure a full two hours of her ladyship's airs in the Italian than a few moments of her conversation; and as she and Eliza put their heads together, I considered instead how the Theatre Royal might serve in a novel: the comings and goings of great personages, a lady's chance encounter with an Unknown; or the appearance of a Rogue, for example, who might interpret the slight nothings and subtle displays of the *ton* with an understanding far more penetrating than my own . . .

It was impossible to be in London at the height of the Season without reverting in thought to Lord Harold Trowbridge. That late denizen of Brooks' Club, that consummate sportsman and intimate of princes, should certainly have graced one of these lofty boxes, and been in close converse even now with Lord Castlereagh, perhaps, however little he liked that Tory gentleman's conduct of war. Lord Harold should have profited by the play's interval in dallying with a lady, or shown himself one of Harriette Wilson's favorites, his sleek frame displayed to advantage against the marble columns of the tier. But would he, in truth, have noticed *Jane*?

The question arose with a pang. At five-and-thirty I cannot pretend to any beauty now. My evening dress of blue, the beaded band encircling my forehead, the flower tucked into my hair—arranged with all the genius Eliza's French maid could command—is yet nothing to draw the eye. One must be possessed of extraordinary looks or a great deal of money to figure in London. Had his lordship lived, he might have *called* at No. 64 Sloane Street, as he condescended to do in Bath and Southampton—and left his card as Willoughby did for Marianne—but in the Greater World, Lord Harold's notice must have been denied to me.

I like to think, however, that he would have approved of my book. It was always an object with Lord Harold that I should write.

"Blue-deviled, Jane?" my brother Henry enquired gently as he reappeared in the box. "We have been leading you quite the dance these past few weeks. I daresay you're wishing yourself back in Hampshire!"

"Not at all," I replied, banishing my ghost with effort. "You know me too well for a frivolous character, Henry, to imagine me ungrateful when such divine absurdities are laid at my feet! What writer worth the name should prefer the confined and unvarying circle of the country to this? But tell me—who is that woman with the aquiline nose and jeweled tiara, quite alone in the box opposite? She cannot tear her regard from Lord Castlereagh. I should consider her excessively rude, did I not imagine her to be a princess of the blood royal, and thus beyond all censure."

"A princess indeed," my brother replied with a careless gesture of his quizzing glass, "but not of English blood. You have detected a Russian noblewoman, my dear—the Princess Evgenia Tscholikova. She is resident in London nearly a year, and may be ascribed one of our neighbors—for she has taken a house in Hans Place, hard by Sloane Street."

"A princess, rusticating in the oblivion of Hans Place!" I declared. "I should rather have expected Grosvenor Square, or Brook Street at the very least."

"Her means, no doubt, are unequal to her station."

"But why does she gaze at Lord Castlereagh so earnestly? His lady certainly does not notice the princess; and the gentleman is deep in conversation with another."

"That is like Evgenia," broke in the Comtesse d'Entraigues, with a disparaging glance at me over her bare shoulder. "She will always be playing the tragic actress, *non*? A man has only to spurn her, to become the most ardent object of her soul."

Eliza rapped her friend's hand with her furled fan. "You will *shock* my sister, Anne. Do not be letting your tongue run away with you, I beg."

"But surely you have seen the papers, Eliza?" The Comtesse's voice was immoderately loud; several heads turned. "It is everywhere in the *Morning Gazette*, if one has eyes to see and the mind to understand. The Princess's letters to Castlereagh—most importunate and disgusting, the very abasement of a woman in the throes of love—were sold to the *Gazette* but a few days ago. The editors would disguise the principals in the affair, of course—as 'Lord C——,' and 'the Princess T——,' but the truth is everywhere known among the *ton*. Evgenia has disgraced herself *and* his lordship. He has only to conduct himself as usual, and the impertinent will be silenced. But I wonder that *she* dares to show her face."

The malice behind the words was pitiless; a worse enemy than the Comtesse d'Entraigues I should not like to encounter, and of a sudden my sympathy went out to the Russian noblewoman, who alone among the great at the Theatre Royal was lapped in a chilly solitude, no friend to support her.

"But how vile!" I cried. "Who should undertake to traffick in a lady's intimate correspondence?"

"Her maid, perhaps—if she was turned off without a character," suggested Eliza.

"But the letters were to Castlereagh," Henry objected, "which must point to a culprit in his lordship's household."

"Unless he returned the letters to the Princess," I offered.

"I will lay odds on it that she sold them herself," the Comtesse d'Entraigues pronounced viciously. "She would enjoy the fame, however black."

"You are acquainted with the lady, I apprehend."

"Twenty years, at least. She has the habit of inserting herself in my affairs; I will not deny that I abhor the very sight of her." The Comtesse rose abruptly, smoothed out her silk gown, and said, "Eliza, I will wait upon you in Sloane Street tomorrow. Do not fail me."

Eliza bowed her head in acknowledgement, and the Comtesse swept away—the curtain being about to rise on the second act, and all further conversation being impossible, in the presence of Maria Siddons, and the blood that stained her hands.

BY THE MORNING I HAD ENTIRELY FORGOT RUSSIAN princesses and French countesses, their affairs of the heart or their implacable hatreds—for it was *Tuesday*, the twenty-second of April, and thus the very date determined by Eliza nearly two weeks before, for an evening of musical entertainment, the professional performers to include a player upon the harp, one upon the pianoforte, and a succession of glees, to be sung by Miss Davis and her accompanists. The evening was intended as a sort of tribute to Mr. Henry Egerton, the publisher of my book, and I was thus expected to serve in some small way as hostess. There was a great deal to be done—the final orders to the cook, the shifting of a quantity of furniture from the passage and the drawing room, the disposition of candle lights—but at ten o'clock in the morning Eliza and I paused to draw breath, and to drink a cup of tea. Eliza has suffered the slight indisposition of a cold, resulting no doubt from the necessity of quitting the coach briefly on our journey into Surrey Sunday night—it being a chilly evening, and the horses gibbing at some rough paving on the hill prior to the descent into the village, and all of us forced to stand about in the cold air while the coachman went to the leaders' heads and led them over the broken ground. Eliza's nose is streaming, and she will not be in looks this evening for her party—a vexation she is happily able to disregard, in all the bustle of preparing for her guests.

"Here is Henry," she said impatiently as my brother stepped into the breakfast room, the morning paper under his arm, "come to eat up all the toast! I dare swear you smelled the bread baking halfway down Sloane Street, and hurried your feet to be in time."

I held out my plate, but my brother was not attending to Eliza's teasing words. His face was very white, and his countenance unwontedly sober.

"What is it?" his wife demanded with sudden perspicacity. "You look entirely overset, my dearest. Surely it is not—not one of your *brothers*?"

Henry shook his head, and set the newspaper on the table. "Nothing so near, thank God. But terrible, for all that. I suppose it is because we saw her only last evening. I cannot get over how *alive* she was, at the Theatre Royal . . ."

As one, Eliza and I bent over the *Morning Gazette.* And read, in implacable print, the news: the Princess Tscholikova was dead—her throat slit and her body thrown carelessly on the marble steps of Lord Castlereagh's house.